THE STARWOVEN SONG

BRIT BRYNDELL

ONYX & INK PRESS

Published by Onyx & Ink Press

First Edition: September 2025

ISBN (paperback): 979-8-9992999-0-1

Cover Design & Chapter Header Art: Brit Bryndell

Copy Editing: Hannah G. Scheffer-Wentz, English Proper Editing Services

Proofreading: Maia Morgan and Micheala Stahl, Stahl Literary Lodge

Map Design: Melissa Nash

To all of those who felt like they didn't belong and longed to live within the pages of a fantasy novel—this one is for you.

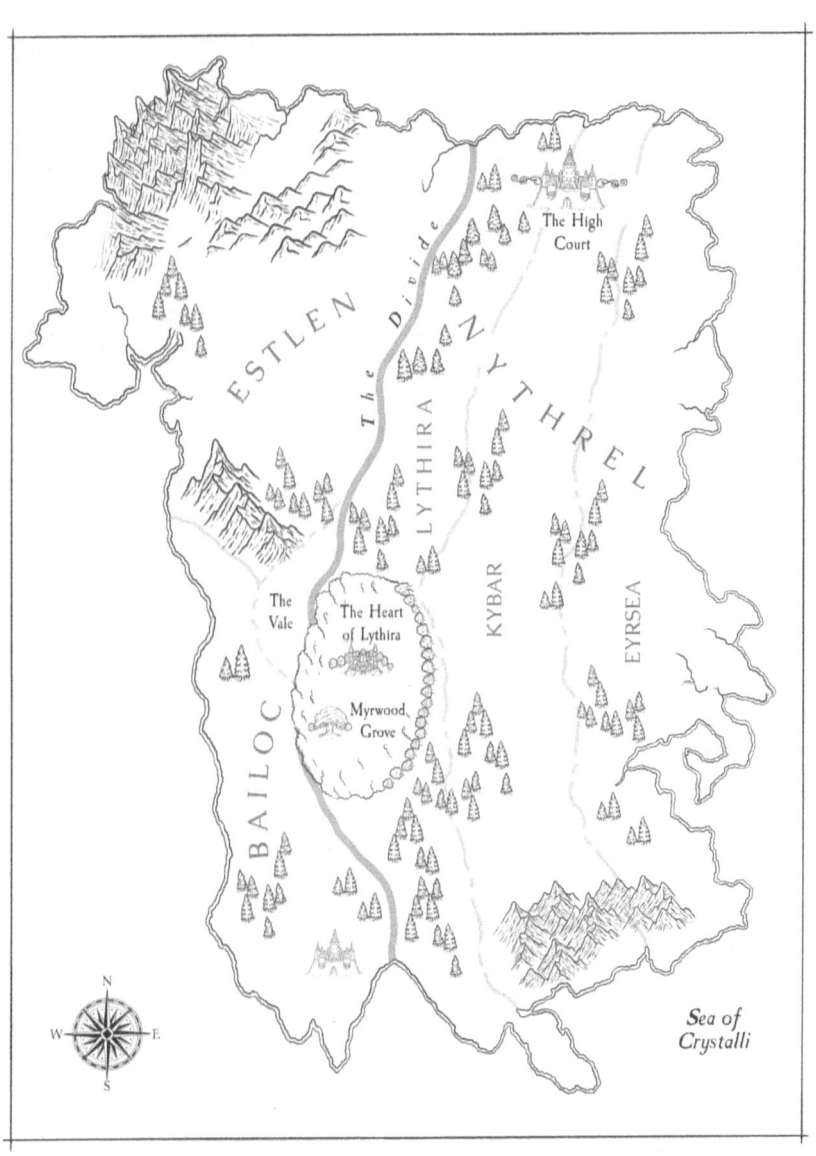

ESTLEN

The Divide

LYTHIRA

ZYTHREL

The High
Court

The
Vale

The Heart
of Lythira

Myrwood
Grove

KYBAR

EYRSEA

BAILOC

N
W   E
S

Sea of
Crystalli

*The Starwoven Song contains themes that may
not be suitable for all readers.*

*This book explores the following: anxiety, grief, loss, emotional
trauma, threat of abduction, manipulation, non-explicit bodily
injury, and non-explicit sexual content.*

Reader discretion is advised.

CHAPTER 1

I had stolen them. In the middle of the night—when not even the palace guards noticed. I crept to the Western Tower and took what was kept from me—a gemstone necklace and a little leather book. They were all that I could stash in my satchel.

I hadn't planned to steal them, but in my dreams a melody laced in sorrow called me there. The song felt real. For a moment I thought I heard it even after I awoke from restless sleep, but that would be impossible.

Songs don't play without instruments.

They don't call people to forbidden spaces.

Real or not, it was my only chance to slip in unseen. Someday I'd go back for the rest. Piece by piece I would take all the things my father kept from me.

My fingers still clutched the silk pouch when dawn broke. My mother's black gemstone necklace lay safely inside.

I brought it to her garden. A memorial hidden in plain sight. At least it was for me. I would never forget my mother, Queen Selene of Bailoc.

The point of the stone protruded, causing the fabric to bulge. I tucked my fingers inside and traced the curved edge, still concealed from the eyes that always assessed me.

"Time is no longer on our side. If it is uncovered—" Lord Joran's voice carried into the garden from an open window in my father's study.

"It won't be," My father's voice was a low rumble as he spoke with his advisor.

"So, you've arranged it?" my brother, Agan, asked. I caught sight of his golden braid as he passed in front of the window.

I quickly stepped closer to the palace wall. If they saw me the conversation would end instantly. Milana, my lady's maid's, gaze hardened on me. An unspoken warning, before she returned to her book.

"The King has yet to give his approval." Joran's usual confidence wavered as he spoke. "Lord Thalen is the best option. He has the resources and has inquired about Princess Aelira directly."

I didn't want to hear the rest, but I couldn't bring myself to step away.

"The Lord of the Vale?" Agan asked. "Do you really think he's our best choice?"

"We don't have time to find another. The supplies he can offer Bailoc will be enough to keep the threat at bay," Lord Joran began.

"The blight will not cease, father" Agan said. "The people are only growing more desperate. It is only a matter of time before they—"

"Enough. You do not need to lecture me," My father's voice suddenly boomed. A stark bang echoed throughout the study. "The Vale is secluded?"

"Entirely," Lord Joran replied. "He is equipped to handle her."

They couldn't have known I went to the tower. That I stole her things.

I always hid the parts of me that didn't please others until I was breaking from the inside out. Every word carefully said, even when I was barely holding it together.

It didn't matter what I did. My father, King Ardyn, was always disappointed. Now he assumed I needed to be handled —to be controlled.

"Why would he want to marry her?" Agan asked as if he couldn't believe anyone ever would.

"It would ensure he's in Bailoc's good graces when the war begins again," Lord Joran said. "King Ardyn, even if you do not wish to ally yourself with him, you must consider what is at stake."

No one had mentioned a war starting. I tried to read between the lines, to uncover the truth none of them wished to say. Whatever they were hiding—it couldn't have just been the blight. The lack of resources had been a problem for years. Yet we still thrived. Maybe it had grown worse. If it had, they never spoke of it to me.

"It doesn't matter what his intentions are. We will move forward with the plan," my father said.

The chill of the castle wall traveled through my palms. Each breath I drew became shorter than the last.

"He will arrive in a few days to discuss the pact," Lord Joran said.

"Ensure it happens. Whatever you need to do—do it," my father replied.

I wouldn't have a say. I didn't expect to. It was a miracle that he had waited so long to marry me off. I always wanted to imagine it was because some part of him wanted to arrange a pact with a man who was worthy of me. But with each word he spoke, I knew. It was something else entirely.

They would use me as a bargaining tool to ease the pain our kingdom felt.

I wouldn't even get to smell my mother's roses before they bloomed.

My fingers traced the rim of my gilded teacup—the sun glinted off its raised embellishments. Rose petals floated to the top of the pale liquid.

"It's too hot for tea." I exhaled.

"Drink. It'll do you a world of good." Milana's expression softened.

The liquid jostled around the cup as I trembled. "They said he could *handle* me." I couldn't stop thinking about their words.

"Princess." Milana's hand slid over my shoulder. "You know how your father is."

"Cruel...fueled by his hatred for his eldest daughter?"

She straightened her features, fighting a smirk. "Your spirit is too much like your mother's."

"She never challenged him. And even when I try not to, he still sees me as a threat."

"You were too young to notice, but your mother..." Pain flashed in her eyes. Her death still haunted us both.

"Was never someone he could love."

"I'm afraid there's more to it than that." Her words dropped to a whisper.

Whatever it was—nothing would explain the way he spoke to her. The way he spoke to me. My father would never call me his favorite. Every attempt I made to maintain the peace failed.

Now he would pass me off to another. Someone he didn't want to ally himself with at all.

Tea seared my throat as the door creaked, but I only stared into the cup.

"Lady Reina is here to see you, Your Highness," Milana said.

Reina's blonde curls trailed over her delicate, pink gown.

"You sent for me?" Reina curtsied as she entered my chambers.

I gestured to the velvet sofa beside me.

"You look displeased," she said as she sat down.

I wished my mother was there to handle the news alongside me.

"Are you going to tell me what's bothering you?" Reina asked.

"A marriage is being arranged for me." The words clawed at my throat.

Her blue eyes glistened. "That's wonderful news. When did King Ardyn inform you?" She slid her teacup onto the table with practiced precision.

"I overheard it." Milana's brow raised as she organized the dresses in my wardrobe.

"Don't tell me these things—it's unseemly," Reina scolded.

I was about to be bartered for supplies, and yet Reina knowing what she shouldn't was her biggest concern.

A shrill cry echoed from my balcony. I rose to meet it.

A hawk perched on the railing. Its head rotated.

Glittering russet eyes landed on mine.

"How unusual..." I uttered, unable to look away.

She groaned. "The falconer should keep a better watch on his birds. They'll be dropping dead mice on your balcony next."

Its broad wings unfurled as it launched into the sky.

A single feather lay on the balcony. Even as the wind blew, it remained.

"It's a political trade." My gaze still fixated on the single feather, until she placed her hand on my arm.

"Aren't all royal marriages? He may be exactly what you've wished for."

All I longed for was to be accepted, to be loved—to live a life far away from the palace. He would at least take me away from here. "Perhaps."

"Well, you must ready yourself." Her eyes narrowed as she assessed me. "You can't meet him looking like that."

"Like what?" I asked.

"With the look of utter disdain. It doesn't become a princess."

I scoffed. Her lack of compassion didn't become her either.

The midday sun blazed down on the field. Reina provided little comfort, as she seldom did. I had come to expect it—maybe even tolerate it—but after the news I needed more.

The thin branches of the willow tree freely danced on the wind.

My mother and I would lie under the willow, gazing at the stars. She told stories of a world beyond ours—of the fae kingdom, Nythrel, and its three territories. I knew about the mystical forests of Lythira, the bustling marketplaces of Kybar, and the crystal sea that surrounded most of Eyrsea. Each detail I forced myself to remember until I could picture each place in my mind.

After she died, I scoured our library for the tales, wanting to relive them, but none remained. All tales of the fae and their magic were burned after the war. Speaking of them was forbidden. I hadn't known it was when my mother whispered their stories in secret, but once I learned it, I never repeated it to another. Not even my younger sister, Ashlyn.

My fingers grasped a winding willow branch as the wind blew.

"Your Highness." Sir Cael held out the bow to me. I rolled my quivering fingers firmly around it. "Aelira..." Hearing him utter my name, without my title, broke my trance. "I hear preparations are underway for a special visitor to arrive."

I gripped the bow harder, digging my fingernails into it. "Has he announced it? He hadn't even told me."

"But you knew?" He squinted as the sun's rays shifted. I nodded. "I didn't realize. I'm sorry." His voice lowered, meant for only me—a rare moment between friends bound by expectation and duty. "And how are you feeling about this news you do not yet know?" He pivoted toward me.

"If you had to guess?" The strings caught on my fingers as I launched the arrow. It plummeted straight into the soil.

He glanced around us, watching for those who would oppose him moving any closer. "I'm going to guess by that aim you are not happy with it."

"You always make excellent observations." Sarcasm laced my words as I dragged my teeth over my lip. Cael's fingers brushed mine as he placed another arrow in my palm. The shaft rolled down my hand before I caught hold of it again.

"You usually find my observations useful," he reminded me.

"Well, maybe you should keep your observations on the state of the kingdom and less on my terrible aim," I scoffed.

"This Lord of the Vale..." He lowered his voice. "I hope he comes prepared."

A sharp inhale caught in my chest, recalling everything I overheard. "Prepared for what?" My hands inched along the bow, gripping it harder.

"To handle you..." His voice was a whisper on the wind.

What had I done that made everyone think I needed to be handled?

"What dangerous words for a knight," I said.

"You may look like a beaming princess..." His voice barely carried over the sound of the wind. "But I know somewhere hidden underneath it all, something different stirs in your veins."

His words landed, and my arrow launched. I winced as the fletching tore into my flesh—blood trickled down my fingers. He pulled a linen cloth from his pocket and dabbed the blood. A bitter sting remained even as it clotted.

"I don't know if I can do this." I slammed the limb of the bow into the grass.

"For as long as I've known you..." Cael lifted it and thrust it back in my hands. "You've never truly let anyone dim your light."

He didn't know the tears I cried. The nights I spent wondering why I wasn't enough. I never spoke to anyone about it at all.

I grabbed another arrow from my quiver, setting it against the nocking point. It flew freely until the head pierced the center of the target.

Cael smirked. "Good luck to the Lord of the Vale."

My stomach dropped.

CHAPTER 2

My father sneered at me from the great hall's arched doors. He looked down at my dirt-laced hem—trace remnants of my archery session.

"You will finally serve your people well," he growled.

My sour stomach curdled, but my chin raised.

"Don't you wish to ask how?"

"I have no doubt you will instruct me as to how I will do so." The words slipped out before I could stop them. My body stiffened, waiting for the repercussions.

"Your marriage is being arranged. Lord Thalen of the Vale will be here soon to discuss the proposed pact." He stroked his silver-streaked beard. "I expect you will play your part. Keep your thoughts to yourself. He won't want to hear them."

The edge of my sleeves concealed my fingernails biting into the flesh of my palms. No tears would fall—that would be too enjoyable for him.

"Lord Thalen's alliance will ease Bailoc's affliction. That is all that matters." He waited for my retort, but there were no words I could muster. My father left me with a single scoff.

To save my home—I would leave it.

He came as swiftly as they promised. I longed to bask in the sunshine, to smell the sweet blooms in my mother's garden—instead, I would prepare to greet my future husband.

"Silver or blue?" Milana held up two gowns.

I didn't know what he looked like, what he liked, or what he hated.

All I knew was his name—Thalen. I mouthed it and my throat constricted.

"Which one would my mother wear?" A mirthless smile spread across my lips.

She raised an eyebrow as her head angled. Milana loosened the ties at the back of the light blue gown. With an uneven beat, my heart lodged further into my chest.

He could be cruel. He could be kind. Maybe the Vale would grant me freedom. Maybe I would like him after all.

My mother's pearls felt like ice as Milana fastened them around my neck. A single set of pearl adornments was one of the few things of hers he left for me to keep. The rest was sealed in the tower. We were forbidden from entering.

"Could you style my hair like you used to style hers?" I handed my mother's pearl hair pins to her to slide into place in my braid.

She lowered a pearl circlet on my head.

"Milana, you were my mother's lady's maid. You knew her better than anyone. I need to ask you something."

She nodded.

"The rest of my mother's things…that were transferred to

the western tower." The dress slipped in place over my straight figure. "Do you think—"

"You know it's forbidden." Milana pulled the corset ribbons tight to make curves I didn't have. My dark, long waves fell on the embroidered swirls of the blue fabric.

Milana tugged again at the corset ribbons. "Don't try his patience. Whatever you're planning—"

"I've already been."

"Now that you've gotten that notion out of your mind. You'll do your best to stay away." Milana tugged the corset ribbons tighter—the weight of the boning pressing into my chest. "Tell no one that you went."

"I didn't just go there..." I wedged my fingers into the narrow gap.

She removed my hand and tied the bow in place. I should have loosened it more.

I grasped the glass drawer pull and yanked it open. Milana peered inside at the leather book. With trembling hands, she combed her fingers through her hair as I pulled the necklace free.

She shook her head and then froze. "The king locked the tower. How did you enter? How did you find them?"

I couldn't tell her what I thought I heard. What made me go. "It wasn't locked. These were the smallest things I could find to take." The gemstone shone brightly as it hung from the chain. "I don't remember seeing her wear this—or keeping this book."

Her brow rose. "You wouldn't. They're not hers."

I had stolen things that didn't belong to her. Risked my father's wrath to take something that wasn't even hers. I almost dropped the chain, before she spoke again.

"They are yours, Your Highness. She planned to give them to you when you grew up."

There were so few things I owned of my mother's. So few memories I got to keep. Yet these things were mine. A gift from her I could always keep.

"Why would he lock them away? He kept them from me." I felt the heat growing steady, rising through my chest with each word I spoke. He had to have known they weren't hers. Maybe he even knew what she intended—and he kept it all from me.

"I don't know." Her lip quivered.

She knew—and wouldn't tell me.

"We can discuss it another time. Your father will not tolerate you showing up late." Milana shut the drawer.

As I headed for the door, she placed her hand on my back. "Your Highness. Wait." Her hand hovered over the drawer pull as if she debated opening it again. "Your mother always believed that if you look to the stars, they will share their wisdom with you. Later tonight may be the perfect time to reflect. Take the book with you."

I had peeked at it already. It was a blank book, but there wasn't time to argue.

"Now don't delay. Your future husband awaits." Her lips curved into a tender smile.

I wanted to keep them all waiting. I needed answers no one would give me—about what I overheard, about the gifts he held from me. It was clear no one would give that to me.

I peered at my reflection in the mirror, and for a moment, I felt my mother's presence with me still. It wasn't enough, but for now it would have to be.

Silence settled as my slippers hit the marble floor of the throne room. I lifted my chin as my shoulders rolled back.

My father sat on his gilded throne—his gaze lingered on my mother's pearls. My younger sister, Ashlyn, wore a braided blonde crown upon her head—a sweet smile formed on her face the moment she saw me.

Agan stood beside her, his golden braid taut, his head high. I willed my hands to still at my sides. My legs resisted every step that moved me closer to the throne. When my body pivoted toward the court, the room stilled.

"Presenting Lord Thalen of the Vale, your majesty," the herald announced.

Three men lined the entrance to the throne room, each dressed in inky black tunics. A golden emblem hovered over their shoulders where cloaks met leather.

Only one stepped forward.

His white-blonde hair hung well below his shoulders, braided back away from his face. The candlelight flickered in his cerulean eyes.

Heat rose to my cheeks. Even if I wanted to look away, I couldn't.

Lord Thalen dipped into a deep, practiced bow before my father.

"Your majesty, it is an honor to stand before you." Thalen sounded regal as he spoke with an unfamiliar, melodic accent. My fingers twitched as I finally diverted my eyes from his.

I had been staring far too long.

"Welcome to Bailoc, Lord Thalen." My father's words commanded the attention of the court. "We have much to discuss."

"I look forward to our discussion." Lord Thalen's eyes settled on mine again. "I have brought a gift for the princess."

My father nodded.

A velvet pouch hung from Thalen's belt. He reached into it and carefully uncovered a pale pink rose dipped in gold—

stilled for all time. The once velvety petals were cold against my palm. Lord Thalen's fingers trailed over mine as he released it. Its unnatural beauty glimmered.

The rose slipped from my grasp, but Lord Thalen caught it. He pressed my trembling fingers around the rough petals. A thin smile spread over his lips. My father smirked.

"Thank you, my lord, it is...extraordinary." I forced a smile.

His stare lingered, taking in every detail.

"It is true—you rival the rose," Lord Thalen said.

My father's eyes softened.

"We will celebrate your arrival with a feast tonight. Come, we have much to discuss before we dine." My father's crown beamed in light as he rose. They walked side by side.

The room spun. I gasped for air, stumbling backwards.

"Aelira?" I wasn't sure how long Ashlyn had been standing there.

"Let's take a walk." My eyes searched for Milana in the crowded room, desperate for her to loosen the corset—it dug into me further with every breath I drew. As we slipped past joyful smiles and greetings, a sharp pain ran through my lungs.

"I just...need a minute." I gripped Ashlyn's arm tighter; the embroidered fabric of her sleeve left an impression in my skin. She flinched. "And someone...to rip this corset...off of me." Panic surged through me. I couldn't breathe.

"My lady, you are extremely pale." Milana stepped behind me, her words quaking with concern. I knew she couldn't have wandered far from me.

"The corset...it's too...tight." My words tethered to my throat as I gasped for air.

"Oh, my goodness." Reina slid to block me from the crowd as Milana began loosening the corset. My chest constricted. Each breath was a struggle as I tugged desperately at my bodice. Even as the ribbons loosened, it wasn't enough.

"Let's go somewhere else. The court is starting to take notice." Ashlyn pulled me toward the arched doors that led back to the palace corridors.

I nodded.

"We have time before the feast if you wish to take a break, Your Highness." Milana trailed behind us.

Ashlyn firmed her grip on my back, steadying me as we ascended the stairs toward my chambers. I backed myself into the stone wall, clutching my chest.

"I've got you," she whispered.

"Perhaps you should send for a physician." A flicker of concern danced across Reina's face.

"I'll be fine." I didn't know what to think, how to feel—I was raw.

"You can't let him see you like this. It won't bode well." Reina shook her head. Her perfectly coifed hair didn't move.

My breath steadied, but my chest squeezed with each breath I took. "I'm just overwhelmed. I didn't expect—"

"How extraordinary he would be?" Reina straightened her gown—the fabric billowed out around her.

He was handsome and kind, but I didn't know him at all.

"It must be overwhelming." Ashlyn sank beside me on the sofa, her hand cradling mine. Her eyes reminded me of our mother, her face was just like hers.

"I can't get past the feeling that if my father approves of him...there's something I'm not aware of yet."

"Princess Aelira," Reina scolded.

"You know he despises me, so if he's arranging this marriage..." I pulled my hand back from my sister's.

"It will benefit the entire kingdom." Reina's words were sharp and unforgiving. "Imagine what your life might be like as a lady of your own house. It may suit you nicely."

What would that be like? A life without my father's condescension, without upholding every court expectation. Milana held a glass out to me—the cool water cooled the fire rising inside me.

"The way Lord Thalen looked at you..." Reina continued. "It was so romantic."

Maybe they were right. "I'd like to take a moment to myself. Milana, can you stay to help me freshen up?" I dusted my dress off as I stood.

"You haven't much time. The feast will begin shortly," Reina said.

"Take what time you can. He needs to see how incredible you are." Ashlyn tugged at my hands once more before the two left my chambers.

"What do you think of him?" I raised an eyebrow. Milana tucked my loose tendril back into the braid.

"It doesn't matter what I think of him. What do you think, Your Highness?"

"When he touched my hand briefly...it made me feel..."

She smirked at my words. "Are you having feelings for him already?"

I twirled my mother's pearl ring, winding it around my finger. "How would I even know?"

"When you do, you'll know it."

I bit my lip. "That's entirely unhelpful."

"It's too soon to know anything—you just met him. Let him show you who he is." Milana retied the loose corset strings. "All you know is he's handsome."

"It doesn't matter what my feelings are." My voice trailed off.

"How does it not?"

"It's not my decision to make. My father will decide."

"He will decide the marriage, but you will decide the rest. If you have feelings for him. That changes everything." She slid the clasp of my necklace back into its proper place. "You deserve happiness, Your Highness. Let yourself have a little for once."

"And if I don't? I'll be married to a man I'll never love." A fate like my mother's.

"Give it time...May I offer advice?"

I nodded.

Milana steadied the pearl hair pins in my wavy tendrils. "You're giving them both too much power. Take some of it back for yourself. Make Lord Thalen earn your respect."

I was so worried about being controlled by my father that I hadn't given myself time to assess any of it—to think about what I truly wanted for myself.

A future with Thalen was full of uncertainty, but maybe, just maybe...I would discover something good behind it all.

Milana's words steadied me as I moved through the palace corridors. By the time I reached the grand hall, I was ready to face Lord Thalen again. The candlelight flickered against the golden damask curtains in the great hall.

My head held high.

"You're late..." My father scowled as I sat beside him.

"I'm making an entrance," I retorted. He drove his fork into the fish on his plate. "I thought you wanted him to notice me."

My eyes caught on Thalen's again.

My father smirked with a hint of approval—he had never looked at me that way before.

I prodded the food already on my plate, unable to take a bite, as a server poured wine into our goblets.

"A toast to our visitors from the Vale." My father raised his glass. "I hope you find your stay in Bailoc most welcoming."

I raised my glass—my forced smile lingered. Lord Thalen raised his as well. "I am most honored, your majesty."

He commanded attention from every corner of the room the way my father did. At my father's gesture, the musicians played the first note of the evening, and the dance floor filled.

Lord Thalen appeared in front of me, his hand extended. "It would be an honor to have this dance with you, Princess." Thalen's confidence was unwavering. "You are a vision."

My hand slid into his. "Thank you, my lord."

"Please, speak freely with me." His palm pressed into mine as we moved in unison. "You are to be my wife."

A dull ache settled in my chest. "Have you both settled on a decision already?"

"Negotiations are underway. In the meantime, I would like to get to know you."

"I would like to get to know you as well, my lord."

"Something tells me we're more alike than you think."

"What makes you think that?"

"Oh, I've had my suspicions ever since I laid eyes on you." He twirled me around him. "I'm rarely ever wrong about these things."

My jaw clenched. We had spent mere moments together, but he spoke as if he knew me.

As the final chord was struck, Lord Thalen took my hand and lifted it to his lips.

The king raised his glass at us both and gulped down his wine.

"Come with me." He led me through the crowd out onto the balcony. The palace guards silently took their place. "You're nervous." His eyes locked on mine. "My father used to always remind me to look to the stars whenever my nerves overwhelmed me."

The stars glittered behind him. I marveled at them. My mother always said the stars watched over us.

"What makes you think I'm nervous?"

"You're trembling." He clasped my hand in his. "The thought of marrying someone you barely know. It must be overwhelming, but it doesn't have to be."

His hand lingered on mine. There was something about him I couldn't place, a feeling that was new, but strangely familiar.

I needed to remove intimacy from the conversation. "Can you tell me about the Vale?"

"It's very secluded. It's nestled between the corners of Bailoc, Estlen, and Nythrel." He paused, his voice growing cautiously quiet. "Do not let that alarm you, Princess. There are no threats from the fae there. My land remains protected by the divide." My heart drummed louder as he spoke.

The idea of a far-off land was enticing. I had only lived my life within the palace walls.

"It sounds lovely."

"What would you do without the weight of the court on you?" Lord Thalen asked as he tucked a loose curl behind my ear.

I didn't know how to answer. No one had ever asked me what I wanted before.

"I'm not sure if I would know what to do with myself."

"Well, we can figure it out together," Thalen whispered.

I closed my eyes, daydreaming of life away from here—a home I could make my own. When my eyes opened, Thalen was closer—a warm smile spread across his face.

"Why do you want to figure it out with me?"

"The feeling I got when I met you..." He trailed his finger

down my arm and my breath caught in my chest. "It's different than I've ever felt before. And from the look in your eyes right now, I think it's something more to you, too."

"I'm not easy to figure out." I didn't know why I said it.

"Oh, you're a challenge, then?" He grinned. "That's even better."

An unspoken calm settled between us as the stars glittered above. His eyes locked onto mine. "Let's return to the celebration." He extended his hand back to me.

My father bowed his head to him as he watched from the grand hall.

CHAPTER 3

Milana tugged the corset ties, freeing me from their hold. The gown dropped, and Milana laid a silk robe over my shoulders. I never wanted to trade it for another corset.

"The stars are shining brightly tonight." Milana gestured to the book, set out on my nightstand, before she slipped out of my chambers.

My thumb caught one of the rough edges of the paper as I stepped out on the balcony. The night sky glittered as if the stars had assembled only for me.

A gust of wind blew the pages before they settled—blank parchment lay unmarked.

Inky swirls danced across the pages.

My breath stilled until words formed.

It is time you knew who you truly are, Aelira.

The message vanished the moment I read it.

A lump settled in my throat, rigid and heavy. My name appeared on the page as if by magic, but that wasn't possible. The human realm held no magic.

Magic was forbidden.

It belonged to the fae.

I should have hidden the book away and pretended I never found it, but I couldn't look away. New ink settled deeper into the parchment.

Your story is written in the stars.

Ice ran through my veins. The leather book bent beneath my grip.

Time will reveal all.

Why would my mother want to give me this book?

A loud thud echoed as I slammed the book shut.

I stashed it at the back of the drawer, but its words were etched into my memory, impossible to ignore.

Sleep took me swiftly. When the morning sun crept over the horizon, Milana dressed me in silence.

Afterwards I took to the corridors, wanting to escape.

Cael appeared as I rounded the corner. "I hear he's arrived."

"You're back! Have you heard any news of the trade agreement with Estlen?" I waited, hopeful that my father's emissary made progress. If they reached an agreement, maybe I would have more time. Maybe the marriage wouldn't be solidified.

"From what I hear, it didn't happen." Cael wiped the grime from his brow.

An exasperated breath escaped me. "Why?"

"The blight is expanding. Whispers of rebellion are at their border. Trade with Bailoc is no longer desired." Cael motioned me forward. "The resources the Vale can provide are our only hope."

Beads of sweat formed along my spine. "I will have to marry him."

"I hear many are fond of Lord Thalen. That he is charming

and handsome." He shifted his weight, his hand resting on the hilt of his sword. "I also hear that he is very fond of you."

"They haven't reached an agreement yet." I scanned the halls as knights walked past. My father's guards observed us from down the hall.

"Your father will push for this marriage now more than ever," Cael said. "The things I've seen, even on patrol the past couple of days..."

"Tell me." My hand hovered over his arm, but I quickly pulled back. "Please, Cael. You're the only one who will tell me anything beyond these walls." My voice was a soft whisper, so delicate I wasn't even sure if he heard my words.

"The land continues to decay—it's only getting worse." Cael scanned the corridor. "Unable to sustain new growth of any kind. On the journey back, a child stopped in front of our order, begging for food."

The blight had only intensified since the war between the fae and human realms—a curse from their kind that only seemed to grow with each passing year. They separated our worlds with a magical barrier of golden light.

"People are begging?"

"Yes. We had very little to give on our return journey. One of our knights tossed the boy an apple—food from his own rations for the day. The people rallied around the boy, demanding more from our kingdom. A woman, maybe the boy's mother, began throwing stones at us."

"What happened?" I didn't want to know. To assault a palace knight...I didn't want to imagine it. Yet my thoughts remained on the boy desperate for food, his mother even more desperate that she would bait a knight of the king's guard—with no chance of winning.

"I won't repeat how it ended," Cael said.

"Don't let him startle you, sister. We have a handle on it

all." Agan snuck up on me, his hand pressed into my shoulder. "Sir Cael, you're dismissed."

"I was only…" Cael's eyes met with my brother's.

"Standing too close to the Princess of Bailoc…without a chaperone. The king would be most alarmed to hear of it," Agan scolded. "As would her future husband."

"Agan." I would not let him treat Cael this way.

"Don't start with me." Agan's voice was a low rumble. "Sir Cael, you're dismissed."

Cael lowered into a silent and obedient bow to us both. My fingers trembled as they rolled inward.

"How could the Vale have enough to offset the rapid decline of supplies in Bailoc?" I asked.

"Damn it, Aelira…" Agan scolded, his voice a low, seething roar. "It is not your place to question the solution. Your only role here is to make sure Thalen remains interested."

"He will make his own decision."

"We can't afford him to lose interest," he scoffed. "Appease Thalen, tempt him. You do whatever you can to make sure this marriage happens." Agan towered over me.

"Tempt him?" An icy chill ran through me. My stomach turned. It was one thing to suspect that was all I was worth to the crown, but it's another to hear it from my own brother.

"You heard what I said. Make this happen," he growled.

The sun was stifling. There was no relief from the wind. I wandered to the willow, wanting a moment to myself— needing a distraction from my conversation with Agan. The grass crunched beneath my slippers.

Thalen stood before me—a falcon rested on his gloved hand. His gaze was calculating.

"Hup." He loosened his grip on the falcon's jesses, and it soared off into a nearby tree. His eyes never left the bird, his stoic expression intact. Leaves rustled as he slid the grotesque remnants of a rodent onto his glove—the fleshy pink meat poked through the gaps in the leather.

A shrill cry of the bird repeated as it flew directly overhead and perched again on his glove. He revealed the pink, lifeless creature to it, causing my stomach to churn.

"Would you like to see her?" His gaze never lifted from the bird. Thalen sensed me as well as the falcon sensed its prey. He slid the thin leather straps beneath his gloved thumb. The falcon ripped apart the fleshy meat.

"You command her well," I said.

The falcon's eyes followed mine.

He held his arm still while she perched on it. "These creatures possess an untamed spirit that I find enthralling." Thalen's eyes slowly shifted to mine. "She requires constant handling to remember her purpose."

Many men felt the same about me.

Thalen and the falcon were completely in tune with each other.

"She's fascinating," I said.

"I thought you might enjoy her."

The falcon finished devouring its reward. Thalen commanded a nearby falconer, then transferred the falcon to the falconer's glove.

"Walk with me." He undid his glove, thrusting it into the other man's open hand. Thalen extended his arm to me, just as he had the falcon.

"I'm surprised to see you out here."

"I needed fresh air." My hand rested on his arm, his muscles tense with my touch.

"I don't think you should wander alone," he murmured. My stomach twisted at his words, completely aware that Milana wasn't with me.

"The guards are my constant shadows."

"It would be safer if you walked beside one." He tucked his braid behind his shoulder. "At least I am with you now."

I didn't know what he could be worried about. No one let me go anywhere alone.

He brought his arm in closer, pulling me toward him. The scent of leather lingered on his skin. My cheeks burned.

"I hope I'm not making you uncomfortable," he said.

"Not at all, my lord," I lied—Agan's words echoed in my mind and my body stiffened.

"I can't stop thinking about you." His words trailed over me, lingering longer than I wished. Heat rose from within me as he gestured to a bench in my mother's garden.

"My lord..." A slow tingle ran down my spine as his gaze locked onto mine. I grew aware of every line that settled around his eyes; the way his white, blond hair framed his face.

"You may soon be my wife. Please address me without my title." He lifted my hand to his lips. The kiss lingered even after he removed his lips. His warmth radiated through me.

"Thalen..." His name felt forbidden. "Why did you choose me?"

"I came here to form a political alliance." His fingers dragged down his jaw.

My heart dropped deep in my chest—my gaze diverted from his.

"But when I saw you...I couldn't take my eyes off you. There was something calling to me—something familiar." His shoulders set back. "I know you feel it, too."

26

My legs trembled beneath me.

"I didn't expect any of this." He leaned in. "Being near you is undoing me. I'm agreeing to trade far more than I planned to call you mine."

I leaned into his lingering touch, but my blood ran cold.

Marriage to me was a part of a trade—a transaction between two powerful men.

His eyes narrowed. "This pact doesn't just benefit me. You will have power over your life in the Vale."

It was like he knew I longed for that.

Thalen slid his hand firmly over mine. His lips hovered above mine. With a quickening breath, he pulled away from me.

He traced the gemstone that hung around my neck. The inky black stone cooled at my chest despite the sweltering sun. A smirk spread across his face and his jaw released.

I was crumbling with his touch.

"Lord Thalen," Lord Joran called as he approached. "King Ardyn requires an audience with you in his study." He folded his arms as he turned toward me. "Princess, it is good to see you looking so lovely today."

"Hopefully we will have much to celebrate later, Your Highness." Thalen towered over me, his head tilted into a subtle bow, before he fell in step with Lord Joran.

The force of Thalen's words, the feeling of his touch, lingered even after he left. It all felt real, but what if it wasn't? What if the excitement faded after his trade was complete?

My hands met the chill of shaded concrete. I clenched the flower box behind me until my fingers turned purple. A cascade of vibrant flowers surrounded me. My mother's roses were still tightly furled.

I gripped the stem, careful to avoid the thorns. The gemstone warmed against my skin as unease tightened within me. My palm trailed the velvety buds as I breathed in their scent.

If only I could see my mother's roses bloom before I had to leave, then I could enjoy them one last time. I blinked back the tears, the lump in my throat solidified.

Then the petals slowly unfurled until each one bloomed after the next. I had never seen anything like it.

Heaviness settled in my muscles. I yanked a rose from the flower bed.

A thorn pierced my flesh and blood trickled over my hand.

CHAPTER 4

My father rose to stand, his hands pressing into the mahogany desk. The rich scent of scotch and leather lingered in the air in my father's study.

Thalen's boots scuffed across the floor as he gripped the back of my father's armchair. His eyes glittered in the darkness, even though the candlelight hadn't reached them.

My heart thundered, racing on without my permission.

He was handsome.

He spoke the words I longed to hear.

But still my heart drummed within me, and it felt like a warning.

Thalen hadn't done anything wrong, but long after his words were spoken, after a moment of excitement faded, I couldn't get past the feeling there was something I was missing.

"We have reached an agreement—the two of you shall be married tomorrow. The Vale and Bailoc will prosper from such a partnership." My father squared his shoulders, drawing in a deep breath.

The decision was final.

The stagnant air held thick around me. I clutched the edge of the desk as my vision blurred.

Thalen reached for my arm, attempting to brace me, but I recoiled.

My father furrowed his brow.

"Princess Aelira..." Thalen's voice softened.

The wooden doors of my father's study collided with the stone walls. "Your majesty, there has been a disturbance...at the divide." Lord Joran stepped between us. "I must speak with you privately."

My father's eyes were wide with horror, yet he didn't flinch.

Thalen's eyes narrowed at Joran's words, his head tilted, but his calm didn't fade. He nodded to my father and Joran before he left the study.

My father yanked me back. His fingers pressed deep into my flesh until I winced. "It is your duty to uphold—so our people don't starve." As he released me his voice lowered. "Do not defy your future husband. Soon you will be his, and then he may do with you what he likes."

Tears threatened to spill down my cheeks, but I blinked them back.

I would be his.

He could handle me however he chose.

"Are you all right, Your Highness?" Thalen reached for me again when I stepped outside my father's study. His hand brushed my arm.

"You reached an agreement so quickly."

"It is the way of these arrangements." Thalen studied me. His composure held.

"You are not concerned over the news of the divide?" I asked.

His eyes narrowed once more. "The divide is made of fae magic. It is unpredictable, but it's held for over twenty years. You will be safe in the Vale."

My father wasn't unfazed—neither was Joran.

His blue eyes settled on mine—no longer glittering in the fragmented sun that shone into the corridor.

Thalen took my hand in his, leading me sit on a corridor bench. "The thought of leaving your home weighs on you, but you may learn to love the Vale."

I trembled in his grasp. "I appreciate the aid you bring Bailoc."

He braced my cheek with his palm, and a shiver ran down my spine. "You do not need to play politics with me. Speak to me as you wish." Thalen slid closer to me on the bench until I could feel the heat of his body next to mine.

Tomorrow I would be his wife.

A slow, steady smile spread across his face, almost as if he could hear how fast my heart was racing.

"Thalen..." My voice cracked. He leaned in toward me, his lips hovered over mine for only a heatbeat, before he kissed me. His warmth greeted me, but it felt wrong.

I pulled back, wanting to be free of him. His lips clamped down on mine as he pulled me closer, locking me into place.

The fabric of my gown caught on my fingernails as I dug them into my thighs.

I couldn't move.

I couldn't breathe.

He lifted his lips from mine. "Who you ally yourself with will be extremely important." A tilted smirk spread across his face. "We will be everything together, Aelira."

I knew once he kissed me—when he wouldn't let me go.

The only thing I'd be with him was broken.

My heart hardened and I blinked back the tears before they could fall.

The words of protest were left unspoken.

Even in the solitude of my chambers, I still felt his presence.

Loud. Threatening. Domineering.

The leather book's embroidery protruded into my fingertips. Its blank pages taunted me. Who knew what answers it held, but if it held anything at all—I was desperate to hear it.

Lines etched into the parchment quicker than before.

It is no longer safe for you to remain in Bailoc.

I won't be here much longer. Soon I'll call the Vale home.

You mustn't go.

Where else could I go?

Lythira.

The fae territory—a kingdom that hates humans. They attacked us, then cursed us with the blight. They stripped our people of everything.

Things are not as you have been told.

The fae did not cause the blight.

They do not seek to destroy your kind.

Then who did?

It began once the war ended. Once the land had enough.

An impassable divide lay between us, held in place by their magic. Why did they want to keep the humans out? Why did they fear us? I hadn't stopped to ever consider everything I was told.

The fae didn't start the blight. And they couldn't reverse it.

Cross into Lythira.

It is your destiny.

Humans can't cross the divide.

You can, Aelira.

Lythira is waiting for you.

Why would Lythira be waiting for me?

It has begun.

Do not wait.

Exhaustion crept in. It squeezed every muscle.

Freedom can be yours.

Freedom was nothing but a dream that fate stole from me.

A knock interrupted my thoughts—even my daydreams were not mine to keep.

I slid the book under my bed and tried to sit upright.

Reina peeked her head around the door. "I know you haven't sent for me, but I heard the news. I thought maybe you'd want to talk to someone about it—or maybe even celebrate." She waited for me to say anything at all, but still I only stared back at her. "You look pale."

"I just need some water," I finally said.

The glass trembled as I brought it to my lips. I took a sip but could barely swallow.

"Your wedding is tomorrow." She was beaming as she sat beside me, like the news was her own. "You should be excited. Not sitting on the floor." Her nose crinkled.

"It is." The cool liquid trickled down my throat again. "It's a lot to take in. A big change." My thoughts were lost on the book. Its words left my heart racing.

"He may not go through with it if you look like you're terrified," she scoffed. When I said nothing, she spoke again, her words a little softer than before. "He's extremely handsome. He has land far from here. Land that you both would own. This is not a death sentence."

How simple it would be for her, but it wasn't for me. I studied the disgust that clung to her face. Reina doted on my brother, curtsied deeply to my father, and only tolerated my sweet sister. She never once stopped to listen when she asked how I was feeling. We had been friends since childhood. I was leaving. I may never return, but she didn't seem to care at all.

A deep twinge of sadness burrowed in my chest.

I knew the truth. There were few who cared that I would leave.

"I wish to be alone." My words were firm.

"You know what I mean." She coyly slid her curls over her shoulder.

"I do know what you mean. You may leave now." I pointed to the door.

She didn't protest.

I reached under the bed for the book. The words greeted me the moment I opened it again.

Be careful of the company you keep.

I stared at the door. Her perfume still held stagnant in the air.

Your world is taught to fear the fae, taught to hate our kind.

But you already know the truth.

It is as your mother told you.

The tales my mother told of the fae—nothing ever stopped her from whispering them in the darkness. Why are you concerned about Reina?

She is not of our world and only has hatred for our kind.

The words vanished. My heart raced louder, as if soon the entire palace would hear it. It echoed in my ears until my head throbbed.

She is not of the fae world, but neither am I.

The clarity you seek can be found.

Look for a letter your mother kept.

34

Go to where you found this book.

The leather cord wrapped easily around the book—concealing its secrets once more. I would search for the letter. I wouldn't rest until I found it.

I gripped the stone wall. A chill rippled down my spine as the door creaked a warning.

My time was limited.

For a moment I swore I felt my mother's presence still.

Her golden eyes looked back at me in the mirror. My cheeks reddened as tears fell from my eyes. Our people were starving. Marriage to Thalen was the only solution.

I would have to endure him for them even if I broke.

The book had to be wrong about where I was meant to be.

Footsteps echoed from the chambers beneath the tower floor. I tore through each crate. The contents scattered across the floor. Each was stuffed to the brim with gowns. He kept them all, but we weren't allowed to speak of her. He forbade us from entering this space.

I tugged at a lid. A stray splinter pricked my finger as I ripped it free. Inside lay her books. A heavy book bound in green leather caught my eye, it bulged at the binding. I traced the pages, pressing through to where it bulged and a single piece of parchment fell free.

The lines were deeply set in the folded parchment with ink smudged in a round ring—like water droplets.

Selene, my love,

    It's growing harder to keep my distance from you both, but now the divide separates us, I fear we will not be together again. My thoughts are with you both always as I grieve the life we will never live.

My dreams are full of visions of our daughter with my dark locks and your golden eyes. From the moment I held her, I knew she would always be the best of both of us.

Conceal and protect her for as long as you are able. The stars have determined her fate—she will mend what's broken.

Grant her strength to stand. They will only wish her to fall.

This gemstone will awaken it all. You will know when she is ready.

Until we meet again in the next life.

I will love you always,

Z

A single tear struck the letter, smearing the ink further.

A letter to my mother, about her child with dark locks and golden eyes.

Agan and Ashlyn looked just like my mother and father—blonde and golden.

I didn't. I was the only one that fit that description.

The letter was here just as the book said, written by a man who wasn't my father—claiming to be. Someone who lived on the other side of the divide—a fae. All this time, my father looked at me as if I disappointed him, as if he hated me.

He knew.

I needed answers. I needed more than this.

Sunlight crept through the window, reflecting off the mirror. It illuminated the stone. Heat spreading through me from it. Each rage-filled breath left me quivering. King Ardyn would trade his problem to give the people of Bailoc a future.

The problem was me.

The book didn't trust Reina, because she wasn't fae. Yet it spoke to me—trusted me, because I was.

I pried the window latch free, letting the wind gush into the tower.

Even if it were only for a moment, I could breathe again.

CHAPTER 5

I raced down the corridors back to my chambers—back to the book. Without hesitation, I pressed it open.

"Who is my real father?" I whispered to it.

You already know.

"The letter doesn't tell me who he is."

Someday you will know his name.

But it must wait for another day.

You're running out of time.

"Why am I running out of time?" I seethed through gritted teeth.

The marriage pact will bind you.

"What can I do to be free?"

You must cross over into Lythira. Now.

Do not delay any longer.

"Why should I believe you? How do I know you're telling the truth?"

This book is a gift from your parents.

It is meant to protect you.

Milana recognized the book. She instructed me on how to

communicate with it. The book knew the king wasn't my father. It knew about the letter.

You are dealing with something far greater than yourself.

Your future lies with the fae.

"Why?"

It is your destiny.

"My destiny is to be human in a fae world?"

Half-human.

Half-fae.

You belong to both realms.

The tears flowed freely. My mother told me the stories of the fae. She wanted me to know.

If King Ardyn knew I wasn't his daughter, then he knew I was fae. What would Thalen do if he found out? I shuddered at the thought.

"How will I know the way?"

Ride through the woods to the lavender.

The divide resides there.

I pressed the pages closed and slid the book back into the drawer.

An impossible decision lay before me. I would have to sacrifice my freedom for a kingdom that never wanted me, or escape into a mystical world that could destroy me.

"Tonight, we celebrate an alliance between Bailoc and the Vale. Tomorrow, Lord Thalen and Princess Aelira will marry." My father raised his wine goblet above the crowd, before he slowly lifted the glass to his lips.

I braced my back against my chair. No one could see me quake.

Thalen raised his glass. His ivory tunic shimmered in the candlelight. I raised my glass to my lips, pretending to take a sip, but my stomach couldn't handle the wine. I had to remain the glowing bride, dressed in ivory to match my future husband.

A forced smile settled on my face.

Thalen stood. "To a most prosperous future."

The king's secret would soon be locked away.

Hunger ravaged me, but I couldn't bring a single morsel of food to my lips. I rose to my feet and pulled Ashlyn with me. "I need to speak with you. Somewhere we can be alone," I whispered.

She nodded and rose slowly from her chair. We stepped out onto the terrace.

"You're looking pale again."

"It's my nerves." The words raced from my mouth.

Ashlyn played with the frayed end of her braid. She reached for me. "What did you want to tell me?"

"Ashlyn...things aren't always what they seem." I exhaled sharply. "When I'm no longer with you, promise me that you will take every opportunity to learn about life beyond these walls. That you will make decisions on your own. That you respect your instincts always."

There were no words to convey what I needed to. Time was running out.

My sister watched me as I spoke. She lifted her brow. "What aren't you telling me?"

"Someday you may learn truths you may not wish to face," I whispered.

"There is nothing you could tell me that would change how deeply I love you, sister." Her soft smile settled. "It is okay to say you don't want this. I know it changes nothing about the plan, but maybe your heart needs the truth right now. You can tell me."

I wanted to tell her the truth. I needed her to know who I truly was, but I barely knew who I was myself. It was my secret to keep alone. I wouldn't endanger her by telling her what I debated.

"I love you, always." I blotted the tears away from her cheeks. And then I blotted mine.

Starlight flickered in her eyes. Joyful naivety lingered behind them. She saw the world only as it was told to her, but I couldn't blame her for it. Our mother's death robbed us both. Ashlyn didn't get the chance to know her at all.

All that remained was the memories I shared with her. The stories of the woman she was before she died. She lived only days after my sister was born. Gone far too soon.

Tomorrow, I would make my choice in silence. There may not be a last goodbye. My sister deserved so much more than me disappearing, but now that I knew the truth, I couldn't pretend I didn't.

"And what are my sisters up to this evening?" Agan crept between us.

"Just saying our goodbyes," I murmured.

"Goodbyes? There will be plenty of time for that after the ceremony tomorrow, Aelira," he scoffed. "Ashlyn, I need to speak with Aelira. Alone." The lines set around his eyes. When she didn't budge, he firmly grasped her arm. "Now."

Ashlyn didn't look up at Agan as she left us both.

"That look in your eyes tonight...it reminds me of the history books."

"What are you talking about Agan?"

"When you hid them from the tutor. None of us knew where they were, but there you were...sitting in the library with a certain gleam in your eyes."

"You know I hate history. All the good details are always missing." My throat tightened thinking of all the stories that were burned, but my forced smile didn't falter.

"Now I see it again. And that's concerning me. Don't tell me you're planning something that would disappoint us all." He approached me slowly.

My sweat drenched palms caught in the folds of my dress.

"We need Thalen. The fate of this kingdom requires this marriage to go *exactly* as planned." He leaned over me until I cowered.

I had to think quickly. His suspicion couldn't linger.

"You misunderstood the look."

His jaw tightened.

"It's triumph. You don't see my hatred, brother." With my words, he eased his stance. "You see my joy."

"It looks nothing like happiness."

"Don't steal my moment from me." I turned from him. My face would give everything away before I even decided which fate would be mine.

"Your Highnesses, I'm sorry to interrupt, but I promised Lord Thalen I would find Princess Aelira." Reina's curls blew softly in the wind.

Agan's gaze softened.

"There you are." Thalen trailed behind her. "I've been looking all over for you."

"Perhaps you will share a dance with me so we can give them a moment." Agan held his hand to Reina.

"I would love to." Reina beamed as he led her out onto the dance floor.

"Finally," he said, "a moment alone in the moonlight with you." Thalen extended his hand to me.

I reluctantly placed mine in his. With each step we took, I reminded myself of how tonight needed to look—how calm and strong I needed to be. He swept a wavy tendril away from my eyes and traced my face.

"Tomorrow you will be my wife." His fingers trailed down my arm.

I didn't want to be—I wasn't given a choice at all. He didn't even notice me shaking.

The starlight glimmered down on the terrace, down on me. I wished they could guide me, was desperate for answers the fae found in them, but only silence hung between Thalen and me. Thalen's eyes closed, his lips hovering over mine.

"It would be more romantic if we save it for tomorrow." His heart raced beneath my palm as I gently separated us.

"Very well, but tomorrow, you will be mine. I won't wait any longer."

My chest constricted under the weight of my gown, but instead I held a smile that couldn't have fooled anyone.

"There is much to prepare for tomorrow. Perhaps I should retire for the night." My words flowed so smoothly, even I almost believed them.

"Until tomorrow, my bride." His lips grazed my hand.

The ivory gown dragged over the stone walkway until I walked safely around the corner. My back slid against the cold stone wall. An exhale finally escaped me.

He wouldn't kiss me again...at least not tonight.

CHAPTER 6

I t was my wedding day, but there wouldn't be a celebration—because I wouldn't marry Thalen.

The stars held my fate. I knew so little of their power, but in their twilight, a quiet certainty settled. My destiny was on the other side of the divide—in Nythrel—with the fae.

The scent of my lavender tea washed over me. Milana looked at the riding dress I laid out on my bed. I tucked my satchel near my feet as she clutched my riding boots.

"A ride may do your nerves some good, Your Highness. I had hoped you wanted to take in fresh air this morning." She placed the boots near the door.

"My nerves have gotten the best of me." I gripped my teacup harder.

"I will pack some food in your satchel, in case you get hungry on your ride," she said.

She knew my ride in the meadow would be brief. The wedding would be here soon. Milana never packed food for a short ride.

"Milana." Her name lingered on my lips until it faded. "Thank you, for everything."

She doted on me ever since my mother passed—guided me in times my mother couldn't. I wanted to tell her, but I couldn't put her in danger. The plan would remain mine alone. If she knew, she pretended she didn't.

A moment of tranquility hovered between us as her smile grew broader.

My robe rolled effortlessly off my shoulders as she slipped my forest green riding dress over my head. Milana braided back my long, dark waves. I hugged her tightly, knowing it might be the very last time.

I needed to devise a plan to escape past the guards. No one would expect me to run—as far as they knew, there was nowhere a human princess could go. The sea lay to the south of the palace and a magical impassable barrier to the east.

If I requested time to myself, time to reflect, and they granted it, I could escape.

Milana tidied my night gown. She paused for a fleeting moment, pivoting to look at me once more, before she left me alone in my chambers.

My eyes caught sight of the stars that dazzled the ceiling— a design my mother requested just for me. This was the only home I ever knew.

Time wasn't on my side. The wedding was hours away.

I gently opened the little leather book. The words appeared quickly.

Find the lavender.

Cross the divide.

"I am risking everything." My pulse raced, thundering through my body.

All these years, you felt alone, like you didn't belong.

Now you know why.

Now you know where you were meant to be.

The ruffled edges of the journal caught on my satchel as I hurriedly stuffed it inside.

What if only horrors met me on the other side of the wall? My fate there could be worse than here.

I thought of Thalen's hand on my waist, his lips on mine.

His presence smothered me still.

If I stayed, he would help our people, but would it be enough to save them?

It was a risk with the greatest cost—my freedom.

I slid a sheathed dagger into my boot, even though I had little skill for using it. I wouldn't cross into Nythrel's outer territory, Lythira, unarmed.

It was a tradition in Bailoc for the bride to give a dagger to her new husband—a demonstration of her trust in his protection.

The dagger was forged for me to gift to Thalen, but instead, I gifted it to myself.

"We must make the ride quick," the taller knight said to the other.

Cael approached us. "Where are you headed, Your Highness?"

"To the meadow. I need to calm my nerves." I was unable to look at him.

I felt briefly for the satchel that I had passed off to Milana and found it secured discreetly on my horse.

Cael surveyed me. "Don't go too far." His jaw tensed as he

eyed my satchel. "Preparations are already well under way. You will be expected to dress for the ceremony shortly."

"I must be on my way then." The reins grated against my palms. "Keep your distance. I will need space to reflect." My voice held firm.

"We are under Prince Agan's orders to not let you out of our sight," the taller knight said.

I buried my fingers in Briar's mane to hide them as they shook. "If I can't calm my nerves, I will not be ready."

"Let her ride ahead," Cael interjected. "I will trail behind her."

I froze at his words.

This wasn't what I planned. He would keep me from crossing the divide.

"You will watch her by yourself?" The taller knight raised an eyebrow at Cael.

"From a distance," Cael confirmed. "The meadow is visible from the palace walls. There is nowhere else for her to go."

A lump rose in my throat. I tried to swallow past it. "I will be back quickly."

Riding ahead may not give me enough time to escape, but I had to try.

"Keep your ride brief, Your Highness." The knights climbed up on their horses, reins in hand.

A thinly veiled smile spread across my lips.

"Go ahead and start your ride, Your Highness. I will get my mare and follow you shortly," Cael said with a nod.

I blinked back the tears. Ashlyn wasn't in her chamber this morning before I left—there wasn't enough time to wait for her to return. And now I would betray my friend who only ever sought to protect me, too.

The first half of the journey I knew, but the rest would take me farther than I had ever traveled. The main path was fenced in by gigantic oaks—the perfect place to slip out of sight, but only if I could get to them first.

Briar raced onward. Doubt encompassed me. The only world I knew faded fast behind me. The wind trailed us, as if it were guiding me along the path. The trees loomed over us, the blazing sun fading from view. Briar's reins slipped in my palms.

To flee was one thing.

If I was caught, everything would be taken from me.

A verdant haze blurred past as Briar sped onward. Lavender perfume wafted toward me. Purple buds rippled through the rolling hills. Briar came to a halt at my command. The satchel slid over my shoulder. The leather stuck against my skin with the early morning heat.

It wouldn't be long before Cael realized what I had done. He wouldn't let me escape.

Golden, glittering light that rivaled the sun shimmered—the divide. It pulsed and swayed with the wind. I could not tell where it began or ended. The stories didn't do it justice.

It sang—the sound radiated through me. Something was calling me, guiding me here.

I froze as the sound of hooves echoed in the distance.

Tell us who you are.

A whisper rippled in my mind as I shuddered. The energy radiated off the divide, rippling through my body with every word.

"I am Aelira."

Why do you wish to cross?

It hissed in reply as the pulse of the divide quickened.

"To be safe. To be free." The necklace heated around my neck—a grounding warmth that stilled me as I spoke.

Only fae may cross into this realm.

"I am both human and fae."

Humans seek only to harm.

"I mean Nythrel no harm. Please, I don't have much time. It is not safe for me to remain in Bailoc." The thundering in my chest drowned out each word I spoke.

The rumble of hooves amplified.

We sense the blood of the fae in your veins.

You are fearful of the other side of the divide and all you do not know.

Yet it doesn't stop you.

We will let you cross, but you must make a choice.

To cross means you enter our world and forsake your own.

Could I go across and never come back?

The distant hooves grew louder.

Someone is coming.

A human.

He will take you from us.

"Aelira! Don't!" Cael's voice called from the hill as he dismounted and ran after me.

I unsheathed the dagger and pointed it at him.

"Don't touch me!" I wailed. The blade quivered.

He drew back. "Put the dagger away. I'm not here to harm you." He reached again with heavy steps—my back almost touched the divide. "Stop!" he snapped. "Don't touch the divide!"

I tightened my grip on the metal hilt. "I can't stay." I held my breath.

Panic flickered in his eyes. "Please. They're going to realize you're gone. We can say your horse was spooked. No one has to know."

"I can't marry him." I could barely breathe through the words. The hilt of the dagger was like ice in my hands.

"Drop the dagger." His words quaked. "Come to me."

Another step brought me closer to the golden glow. Energy vibrated through the ground—it spiraled through me.

He darted at me.

"You don't know the truth. I'm not who you think I am."

"You're Aelira. I have always seen you for who you are even if they don't. This is not your story. I will not let you die today."

I froze. The dagger shook.

My teeth clamped down on my lip. A bitter metal taste rushed my tongue. "King Ardyn isn't my father. I'm not just human. I'm fae."

"No. That's not possible." His hand wrapped around mine.

"Please. You need to let me go. Don't take this from me."

The way he looked at me shifted. Either he couldn't believe it, or he couldn't accept it.

I would never forget that look.

His hand slipped from mine. He backed up without another word.

"Pretend you never found me." Tears trickled down to my lips.

With the dagger at my side, I stepped back. The golden light washed over me.

Welcome home.

Lythira has been waiting for you.

The voice acknowledged me one final time. Then the divide fell silent.

Lavender rolled through the vibrant glade; the scent more alive than before. The divide's hum trailed off. He was on his knees. Agony etched into every laugh line.

I reached for him. My hand collided with the divide. Its energy pushed back on me—firm but gentle.

"I'm so sorry." My words echoed off the divide. "Thank you

for always being my friend." I didn't know if he heard me, but his eyes softened.

Cael never feared the truth, but something shifted within him the moment he knew. Maybe he'd never understand the decision I made.

A white haze settled.

Everything I ever knew vanished.

CHAPTER 7

With each step I took, the land pulsed beneath me as if it were a breathing being. The dagger slid easily back into its sheath.

My mother always returned from her visits to the meadow with bundles of lavender for me. She called me her *princess of the flowers*. I never knew why, but always wondered if it was because I enjoyed every bloom as much as she did.

I felt her in the wind. It brushed against my cheek. Salt-tinged tears slipped onto my lips.

I grabbed a lavender bunch by its stems and ripped it free. When I looked down again, only a sea of lavender remained. It was just as lush as before, as if I had never tampered with it at all. It didn't seem possible. I shouldn't have been holding them at all, yet I watched the flowers drop from my hands back into the meadow.

Shimmering water rippled across the pond as I knelt beside it. Water trickled from my cupped hands as I splashed my face.

My golden eyes were glowing back at me. I traced the edge of my ears. They were slightly pointed.

The fabric of my riding gown caught the water dripping from my hands, before I pulled the book free from my satchel.

"Did traveling through the divide change me?"

The words appeared quickly.

You see who you truly are now.

Grass crunched behind me—I froze beside the book. The horizon revealed no one. Weathered pages caught on my satchel as I tried to cram it back inside.

Her tales were all the knowledge I had of this strange world. Now I would have to navigate it alone.

A low but mighty growl reverberated through the land—the ground trembled in its quake. Thrashing wind struck my cheeks. The mighty branches of the trees tossed about.

Another feral growl sounded. It was louder than before. The metal sang as I slid the dagger from its sheath. Fragments of sunlight caught on the blade temporarily blinding me.

When it passed, a pair of jade, lucent eyes glared across a rock-laden path. Terror seized my body.

The creature was wolf-like, but it towered over any creature I ever saw. Ragged pewter fur outlined its clenched stance and crimson stained the edge of its lips. Fragmented sunlight slid through the canopy of leaves overhead, illuminating the beast. A mouth full of grotesque fangs gleamed as its jaw opened—a cascading growl released.

Dewy sweat coated my palms.

The dagger tilted in my grip.

It crept forward—stalking me.

I screamed as I ran further into the woods.

Pain seared through my leg as a thorny bush tore through

my riding pants beneath my dress and straight into my flesh. I crumpled onto the forest floor, gripping my leg.

The fabric resisted as I tugged—it ripped free. I aimed my dagger at the beast. Its calculating stare measured me. Tears streaked my vision as my pulse quickened.

A man ran toward me.

"Enough!" His guttural voice boomed—the land rumbled with it. Unreadable chrome eyes studied me and the beast, both of us frozen at his command. His hand extended over the creature and golden light flowed from his fingertips, swirling in the space between them. "Stand down!"

The wind stilled.

His gaze fixated on mine despite the crouching beast before him. The golden light shifted and settled. His eyes widened.

"Please!" I cried.

His head turned, tilting slightly in its direction. Then I saw his pointed ears—more drastic than mine. This was their world, I was privy only to mercy if he granted it.

The fae and the creature paced—their dance steady. Each step he took was a calm beat. He raised his hand again, and beautiful, golden light flowed only for a heartbeat longer.

My unconditioned muscles betrayed me—useless and frozen. The world spun as I slumped back into a tree. The man slowed his dance, until he stood between us both.

He exhaled, resting his hand on the hilt of his sword. Then stepped aside.

The creature pivoted closer to me, snarling.

"Please," I cried again. "I need your help."

His lips parted, but he said nothing.

Its dripping fangs were inches from my face. Clammy breath grazed my skin. I lunged to escape, and the creature's claws reached me first, scraping through my flesh.

Cascading crimson painted my arm—pain seared through me, threatening to never release.

I pressed my palm into the gash, desperate to make the bleeding cease.

I closed my eyes—too exhausted to flee or defend.

My blood-drenched hand slid into the dirt, as I silently pleaded for anything, anyone, to help. Its breath thickened. The eerie sound crashed into me.

The creature bowed its head, its jade eyes peered into mine.

It stepped forward ready to conquer its prey. Then it stopped.

The creature quietly turned from me and fled back into the woods.

It retreated, but the fae remained. He crouched beside me. The metal hilt of the dagger fell from my grip, it clanged against the rocks.

I braced myself against the tree and rose with my feet planted firmly on the ground.

My eyes sharpened on the fae's.

"Who are you?" He scanned me.

"Aelira," I uttered my name without the title.

He braced my injured arm. I flinched, pulling away from him. The blood spiraled down my arm as I stumbled.

A strip of shredded fabric dangled from my dress. I tore it free. A groan escaped my lips as the fabric flopped about, resisting me as I tried to cover my wound.

"It has to be cleaned, or it'll get infected," he said.

He pulled the wrap off and rinsed my arm with water from his flask. I fought to stay silent as my teeth caught on my lip. He laid his hands on my shoulders, easing me back into the tree. "You should thank the stars. It could have chosen to kill you."

I saw his golden light. Remembered how he stepped aside to give it a clearer path.

"You were going to let it?" I tucked the loose hair that fell from my braid behind my ears. His eyes fixated on them for a moment.

"I couldn't stop it. If I had tried harder, it may have chosen differently."

"You were letting it choose my fate?"

"The sylkren have an innate sense of good and evil. Fae stand on their own if they are worthy." He tied the clean side of my dress bandage around my arm. He pressed firmly around the bandage. "It seems Lythira hadn't decided on you yet."

"Because I'm human?"

"You're not just human. Only fae can cross the divide." He sneered. "Tell me who you really are and why you are here."

He knew I had crossed, but I hadn't seen him anywhere once I had. My legs buckled and I collapsed. With a ragged inhale, I pulled myself up to sit.

"Tell me now," he commanded.

I flinched. A decision had to be made. I could continue being only Aelira, or I could speak the truth. His glare cut through me as if he already knew.

"I am Princess Aelira of Bailoc."

His head shook. "No..." He assessed the divide. It pulsed just as it had on the other side, swaying with the wind. "That's impossible. You can't be." He ran his hands through his dark curls, causing them to fall from the leather strand that tied them back.

I took a sip from my water flask. "I assure you, that is exactly who I am."

"Who sent you?" His nostrils flared and his brow furrowed.

"No one." I stood, this time not faltering.

"The King of Bailoc doesn't know you're here?" His eyes widened.

It was a dangerous game.

I told him who I was and implied no one was coming for me.

"I'm sure he knows...by now." Every muscle clenched as pain radiated through me.

A smirk crept across his face. It made my stomach churn.

"They weren't expecting you to go missing today?"

"It was certainly a day that it would have been very notice-able I was missing." I pressed the bandage against my arm, watching the blood pool against the fabric. "Who are you? I told you. It's only fair you tell me."

He shifted in his spot beside me on the ground. "Lioran."

Tattoos adorned his sun-kissed skin. Three black bands. Each one held my gaze for a moment too long. If he noticed, he pretended not to.

He could have left me to bleed to death, or die of infection, but he stayed with me. Lioran scanned the land around us, as if he was waiting—or watching for something.

Dizziness crept back in faster than before.

"You need to rest," he said.

He placed his hand out, his eyes closed. The leaves on the trees rustled as the winds picked up. Dust flew as a beautiful, black stallion glided over the hill, floating like a shadow. His mane glittered in the sunlight, and his metallic eyes reminded me of Lioran's. The horse nuzzled its head into his hand.

"Veylar will take us to the village of Evyn. You can rest there," he said.

How could I trust him? What if going with him was worse than staying?

"I will walk."

"You can barely stand," he grumbled as I stumbled past

him. I fell back into him. He stumbled with me, his hands braced my waist for a moment, before he pulled back.

Veylar was massive. He would have towered over Briar. I couldn't slide my foot into the stirrups. My arm burned with each movement. I winced, fighting back tears.

His arm hovered near me. "I can help you," he said softer than he spoke before.

I nodded.

Lioran effortlessly lifted me onto Veylar. As he climbed up onto the powerful stallion, I felt his warmth behind me. I pulled myself upright.

The land bowed to Veylar. Branches swayed from the path.

My eyelids grew heavier. Veylar's steady rhythm lulled me. As I slipped, Lioran held me tighter. My body slumped back into his—I leaned into the darkness.

"We're here." He spoke softly. Beams of sunlight collided with my blurry vision. As I rubbed my eyes, a magnificent village built into the trees came into focus. Nothing in Bailoc looked like this. Nothing I ever saw, at least.

Stairs ascended toward wooden homes that wrapped around colossal trees. Their dense trunks supporting the weight of an entire village. He jumped down from the stallion. A fae taller than Lioran approached, his skin glowed with a golden tan I had never seen before.

I slumped in the saddle, too weak to dismount Veylar. The fae lowered his head—his body lowered, too. Lioran flexed his hand in front of him, before he gestured toward me. The other fae rose, squinting in my direction.

I tried desperately to focus—to take my new surrounding in, but the burning pain made it impossible.

Lioran lifted me out of the saddle. "Neena, we need herbal tinctures for an open wound," he told a woman as she sped toward us.

She nodded before disappearing into one of the low-lying buildings.

"Fyn, this is..." Lioran started.

"Aelira," I said.

"She had a run in with a sylkren," Lioran said.

The fae took a step toward me. His olive eyes widened as I leaned back into the stallion. Veylar was a gentle, swaying wall behind me. With each movement exhaustion claimed me more.

Fyn tugged Lioran away from me. Their words floated away on the breeze. Lioran wiped his brow, rolling his eyes at Fyn.

"You can't just bring her here." Fyn's voice grew louder.

Lioran looked over his shoulder, and I glanced away.

With each unsteady breath, my strength drained further. My hands collided with dirt as I braced my fall. Lioran ran toward me, scooping me up into his arms.

"You just left her standing here?" The fae woman scolded him. Her silver streaked, golden hair fell forward in her eyes. Glass bottles clanked within a wooden crate. She placed it at Lioran's feet. "It's good you came when you did. Let's get her inside. I'll take a look at her." She nodded toward the stairs that braced the massive tree.

The spinning haze of brown and green wouldn't stop. My eyelids snapped shut. He ascended each step, bracing me against his chest. An icy chill rolled through me. My only warmth from him.

Light caught through scattered leaves when my eyes opened again.

Fyn pressed his forearm against a curved wooden door. It moaned as it swung open. I quaked. Lioran brought me closer to his chest as he hurried through the little cabin.

"In here," Neena urged.

He gently lowered me onto the bed. It cradled me.

Lioran leaned against the wall in the corner of the room. He sat there, staring at me.

Neena unwound the strip tied around my wound. "She's feverish. All of this is from this wound?" Neena fumbled through her wooden crate. "There's something else you're not telling me."

She brushed the hair from my face. A muffled gasp slipped from her lips as her eyes settled on my ears.

"Considering her state, we can discuss it later." Lioran grunted.

"As you wish, your—" she began, but Lioran raised his brow.

"Please don't start with that," Lioran interjected.

"This will sting, but if I do not treat it, you will succumb to infection," Neena said as she ran a wet rag along the wound. It burned fiercely.

I wailed. The fragments of sunshine blurred.

"You could have at least sent word of what you were doing." Fyn grumbled from the other room.

Lioran didn't respond.

I exhaled as exhaustion threatened to take me once more. When my eyes opened again, Lioran was watching me still. I longed for home. Wished I hadn't crossed the divide, but I knew I was lucky. He saved me.

The dense aroma of herbs and spices trailed into my nostrils, followed by lingering stench of blood. Neena slathered paste onto my wound. I squeezed the bedding between my fingers. Lioran remained planted where he sat. Monitoring me from the distance.

"I've known these two a long time. You're safe with them." she said in an even voice. "I'm sorry I didn't catch your name."

"It's Aelira," I whispered.

She squeezed my hand in hers. "What a unique name. I am Neena. I will return to check on you later." Neena placed her hand on my shoulder before she rose.

"Let her rest," she said.

Lioran stood. He bowed his head to me without another word, before he gripped the handle and pulled it closed.

The crackling fire drowned out their hushed voices.

I made it through the divide. Somehow, I survived the sylkren. I would have to trust the fae to survive.

He protected me and didn't ask for anything in return.

At least not yet.

My eyelids grew heavy, and I succumbed to the darkness.

CHAPTER 8

"She's the Princess of Bailoc. Have you lost your mind?" Fyn's voice cracked.

I awoke to their muffled voices. The moon's glow drifted in through the window.

"The divide let her cross. She's part-fae," Lioran said.

"She may be part-fae, but she is still very much part-human," Fyn growled. "Even if he isn't her father, he will still come for her. Bailoc isn't going to let their princess cross into enemy territory and stay."

"They can't cross the divide to get her."

"No, but there are those who may cross it for him," Fyn warned.

I didn't know of any who would. King Ardyn would never make a deal with the fae.

The fireplace cracked as the sound of shifting longs stirred.

"And when your father finds out? What will you do?" Fyn asked. "Your position won't protect you both."

Whatever his position was, he hadn't disclosed it. Fyn mentioned it like it was important, but maybe it wasn't signifi-

cant enough. He introduced himself only as I had first introduced myself.

I waited in the quaint room, too nervous to come out and
face them. My stomach had other plans—it resounded with a
loud growl.

The floorboards creaked with each unsteady step. A navy,
silk nightgown clung to my curves, more revealing than I was
used to. Had someone changed me? I had no memory of it, but
sincerely hoped it was Neena.

The cool metal doorknob twisted in my hand. I hoped it
would creak and alert them before I stepped foot into the main
room.

Lioran and Fyn sat up in their chairs as I slid my arm
across the nightgown. Fyn lifted a woolen blanket from the
chair and draped it over my shoulders. Lioran fixated on the
fireplace.

I adjusted the rough fabric and slid into a seat next to the
fire. The scent of herbs still wafted through the air.

Lioran ladled soup into the bowl. "It's all I have to offer
right now, but if you're hungry, eat." He handed me a small
clay bowl.

I hesitated, clutching the bowl with shaking fingers.

"Eat, Aelira." His melodic voice drew out my name—*Ay-
leer-uh*. "You'll need to regain your strength," Lioran
commanded.

"That's not how you say my name." I had never heard it
said that way. "It's *Uh-leer-uh*," I replied firmly.

"I said it how the fae do. If you insist, I say it the human
way, I will," Lioran responded.

I stared at him. My name had a place in their world—they
knew how to say it in a way that made it beautiful.

"No." I liked the way it sounded when he said it. "You knew
the King of Bailoc is not my father." I lifted the bowl to my lips,

sipping the steaming broth. Warmth ran through me. My stomach whined, calling for more.

Lioran nodded as I sipped the soup again.

"Did you know there was a half-fae princess in Bailoc before you met me?" Fyn and Lioran exchanged a telling glance.

"Yes." Lioran's voice softened. His fingertips tapped an uneven rhythm on the arm of the chair.

"How did you know?" The broth splashed on my lips.

Lioran leaned forward in his chair. "The reason you're part-fae has caused a great deal of animosity on both sides of the divide."

"She doesn't know." Fyn's eyes grew wide. The firelight glimmered off the golden streaks in his hair.

Sprigs of herbs floated on the hazy surface of my soup. "Why?"

"Your father...your true father is one of our people." Lioran shifted in his chair. His voice was softer than before. "When King Ardyn found out, he was outraged."

"She betrayed him." I read the truth, but hearing it was different.

Fyn shook his head. "It's what started the whole war."

My bowl landed with a thud on the table. I gripped the wooden arms of the chair even harder.

"Everything I was taught...everything I was told..." I shook my head. "The fae didn't start the war?" My leg muscle clenched, spasming. "How is that possible?"

"It's easier to alter the story rather than face the consequences of the truth." Lioran pressed the palms of his hands together. "It is well known he tells his own version." Lines set around his eyes as he squinted at me.

"So, he just lied...about all of it?" I traced the edge of my bowl. "No." I shook my head. "It can't be."

Lioran's gaze softened.

Silence hung between us.

"You've been through a lot. We will discuss this another time." Lioran leaned back in his chair.

"No. You will tell me now." I slammed my palms into the arms of the chair. "This is why you took me with you, isn't it? You're going to use me to get back at him."

My legs struggled to bear my weight with the next frantic step. I crashed down into the chair again.

Fyn let out an exasperated sigh.

"You crossed the divide and nearly got yourself killed. I took care of you. Yet you're going to command me?" Lioran scolded. "You are insufferable."

Fyn's hand curved around his mouth.

We sat in the silence until my body grew heavier.

Lioran didn't look up at me as I finally mustered the strength to pull myself upright again. I gripped the wall, guiding each stumbling step back into my room. Sleep greeted me the minute my head hit the pillow.

The blank walls of the cabin room startled me when I woke again—I had forgotten I wasn't in Bailoc anymore. Sunlight filtered through the sheer curtains. A new riding tunic lay on the bed.

Each muscle resisted as I yanked the stiff, olive tunic over my head, and again when I freed my hair from the braid. My dark waves cascaded down and covered my ears—the lingering proof of my heritage.

The hinge creaked as I opened the door and peeked into the cabin. Rustling leaves shimmered in sunlight outside the cabin. The view transcended any I had seen before. Bird song rang through a slender crack at the base of the window.

Steam rose from Lioran's drink, it encircled his face. Dark shadows settled beneath his eyes.

Lioran was dressed in a fresh tunic, the same shade as mine.

"Did you stay here all night?" I didn't know why I asked it.

"Yes." Lioran gripped ruffled papers. His eyes skimmed words etched into parchment.

"There isn't another bed. Where did you sleep?"

Lioran peered over his papers. "I slept in the chair."

"Why?" I asked.

"The bed wasn't big enough for both of us." A flicker of amusement gleamed in his eyes.

My cheeks seared.

"I was only joking," he said.

"Oh." I sat down in the chair. "Of course." I cursed myself for the words I uttered—for my expressions that gave away my every thought.

Lioran said nothing.

"I'm sorry," I spoke again. "You've been nothing but kind to me. I shouldn't have demanded anything."

"Yesterday...was a lot for us all." He didn't look up again.

"Thank you for helping me." I wanted to ask why he did— wanted to know why he risked bringing me here. Fyn had been so opposed to me at the mention of my name.

Lioran nodded. "You look like you're feeling better."

"I am," I replied.

"You should eat something. You'll need your strength before the rest of our journey." Lioran set his papers down. He pointed to a plate full of vibrant red fruits, eggs, and the most vivid greens. I sat in the chair beside it, bringing the first morsel to my mouth. The sweet juice squirted into my mouth as I took my first bite. I hadn't had anything so fresh, so ripe, in years.

"Where are we headed?" The nerves that settled while I slept stirred again. My life had been so monotonous, but now I did not know what the next hour held. He still had not told me what he planned to do with me.

"The Heart of Lythira."

"And what will become of me there?" I asked. The sharp pain in my arm nagged at me as he spoke.

"As long as you are in my care, I will provide everything you need. We will devise a plan from there." He sipped his drink.

An ache gnawed deep inside me, rivaling the pain in my arm.

"You will decide my fate?" Silence rested between us for a moment. "If you intend to turn me over to Bailoc or keep me locked away...then take me back to the woods so the sylkren can finish what it started."

"I'm not sure that would be safe for the sylkren." His eyes softened, and for a minute a faint shadow of a smirk formed. "It is not in my nature to use anyone for political gain."

Lioran's calm unsettled me.

No matter how much I prodded, he held his ground.

"Where will you go after you take me to the Heart of Lythira?"

"The Heart is my home. It is the capital of our territory." His words were stark as they left his lips. Tension melted from his shoulders.

Lioran walked toward me, towering over me. His fingers gently brushed my arm as he released the bandage. "This will heal nicely with some rest." He held my arm as he tightened the dressing again. I exhaled the moment he released me.

"The food tastes incredible."

He raised an eyebrow at me. "Your fae senses have developed nicely then."

"My fae senses?" I shook my head in confusion.

"Fae smell, hear, and taste better than most humans."

The fruit juices slid around on my tongue. I savored each bold flavor.

"When I crossed the divide, something about me changed. Could it have altered me?" The book ensured me it hadn't, but I wasn't sure if I believed it.

"I don't believe the divide holds the power to alter."

"My ears..." They were still foreign to me.

"They didn't look like this in Bailoc?" he asked.

I shook my head.

"There are many types of magic. If there was a concern for your safety in Bailoc, someone may have used protection magic to conceal your fae side," he said.

My father told my mother to conceal me in his letter. They were protecting me from the human realm. I slumped back into my chair.

"Magic..." I repeated, thinking of his glittering light. "Does your magic protect others too?"

He exhaled. "I can't conceal the way you look, if that's what you're asking."

"No...I...." I didn't know what to say.

"I have business to attend to in the village. Stay here and rest. I'll be back to check on you later." Lioran exited the cabin quickly.

Had I offended him? Maybe, you're not supposed to ask about someone's magic. There was so much I had to learn.

The view from the cabin window taunted me. I couldn't bear to remain inside any longer. Each angle revealed more cabins as I descended the steps. Every home relied on the strength of the tree.

Fruits, vegetables, and vibrant herbs were all on display in a marketplace at the base of the tree—I had never seen so many in one place. Rows of farmlands were arranged on uneven ground—food grew freely here.

Cael told me there were still small patches of land used for the same in Bailoc, but it wasn't enough to feed our people.

Lythira had everything it needed.

My life existed only within the palace. I had walked the village that shared our protection walls a handful of times, but I had never seen anything like this. Laughter and chatter sounded from the marketplace.

Guilt seized me—I condemned Bailoc the moment I stepped foot over the divide. Thalen would never supply resources to Bailoc when I left him on our wedding day.

"My lady, you should be resting. Are you okay? You look as if you might faint." Neena braced me, her voice bringing me back to the present.

"I'm fine. Just needed some fresh air." I shook my head and exhaled.

"If you're looking for his highness, I just saw him in the stables."

I froze. "His highness?"

"You're looking for Prince Lioran, right dear?" She released her grip on me.

Prince Lioran—he was a prince of a kingdom that warred with mine.

We were raised to be enemies. He hadn't told me. He stopped Fyn from even hinting at it.

"Yes, I am."

He demanded the truth from me, but kept who he was a secret. Anger rippled through me. Did he hide it because of who we are—who we should be to each other? I kept my face still. Neena didn't know what she just revealed.

"I'm not sure he will be happy to see you up. You should be resting."

"I've never been one to sit and rest." My meek voice quivered.

Neena bowed her head before slipping away into the market ahead.

Fyn nearly bowed to him. He mentioned Lioran's father— the King of Nythrel. It's why he said Lioran risked everything when he brought me here.

I froze on the steps, clutching the wood railing that wound around the massive oak.

My boots grazed the hay when I entered the stables moments later. Lioran was in the corner, brushing Veylar. With each step I took, the horses all turned to me, their eyes set on my every movement.

"You're supposed to be resting," he grumbled as he slid a brush through Veylar's mane, bracing the stallion's massive head in his hands.

"Neena told me where I could find you...Your Highness." My chest constricted. Lioran's back went rigid, his glare engulfed me.

Lioran inhaled.

"You could have told me."

"I wasn't ready to." His voice lowered.

"I was finally starting to trust you." I crossed my arms.

"You never trusted me. You still don't." Veylar's brush clanged into the metal bucket as it dropped from his hands. "Having you here with me...it's dangerous for both of us."

"Do your parents know I am here?" I asked.

"No." His eyes narrowed. "If they knew you were here..." Lioran's fingers gripped my uninjured arm and he pulled me back beside him. His eyes darted around the stable as another fae male entered.

"Go back to the cabin, stay hidden. We will discuss this later." He towered over me.

I hurried back to the steps. Lioran watched me as I began to climb the stairs. The instant he turned the corner, I stepped back down.

A dense thicket of trees lay beyond the massive trees that housed the village. The winding breeze blew, and a melodic hum sounded with it—calling me into the woods. I followed it, not wanting to be there any longer.

Lioran was waiting to decide my fate, waiting to decide if I was worthy of being here. If he decided I wasn't—then my life wasn't my own. The ability to choose my fate wasn't a luxury I'd have on either side of the divide.

The wind rallied as the first tear fell. Grey clouds overtook the white before the droplets fell from the sky. The more I cried, the more the water cascaded, until the sky opened and a downpour began.

Cool rain slammed into me. I wailed—it vibrated through me into the ground.

Freedom was a fleeting dream.

There would always be more powerful men to decide my future.

Bits of emerald grass and mud embraced my boots. A canopy of leaves barely covered me as the rain pelted me harder. A force swelled within me, reverberated through me, something grander than my anger.

The ground beneath my feet quaked.

I stood alone in a world that would never be my own.

Grass shriveled and decay overtook the ground with each

step I took. It all crumpled beneath my feet. An intoxicating surge stirred within me—commanding something I couldn't control.

Succumbing to the vibrations, quivering uncontrollably, my body was no longer my own. I sank into the middle of the destruction, fear gripped my throat. I gasped for air.

The war began, because I was born.

The gemstone was like ice on my chest. An unknown weight seized me. My fingers etched channels in the soil. Mud settled in the crevices between them.

"Aelira!" Fyn darted toward me, Lioran raced behind him. "You need to stop!"

Lioran's chest heaved. Horror dulled his silver gaze—his eyes scanning everything I touched.

He knelt, glaring at me.

Waves of golden light rolled around his fingertips. He pressed his fingers deeper in the soil. The shimmering light rolled over the land between us. A hovering layer of magic that couldn't touch the soil, it dissipated.

Lioran's eyes were wild. "It won't...I can't do anything."

"How?" Fyn's single word hung between them as he backed away from me.

"Fix it! Now!" Lioran yelled.

"I...don't know how," I cried.

A desperate hum rose from the land, growing louder until I covered my ears, but it didn't keep the call at bay.

My hands settled back on the ground; the destruction rough against my palms.

There was no coming back from this.

I closed my eyes, desperate to be somewhere else.

Thoughts of my mother's lavender field drifted into my mind—a place where my hands tore the lavender free, but it only regrew. I thought of the roses that unfolded beneath my fingertips. The memory of their smell still lingered in my nose as if I was still there breathing it in.

Fire stirred in my veins, hot and unrelenting. My fingers met something new and stiff.

My eyes opened revealing the source of the perfume as it wafted toward me. It was stronger than my memory could have ever recalled. Lavender stems shot up from the soil. New life bloomed—the decay restored to emerald. The enchanting tune became soft and calm.

The gemstone ran warm on my skin.

Lioran ran his hands over the restored blades of grass.

Fyn kept his distance, his eyes widening.

Lioran's dark curls flew over his eyes as he shook his head. He braced himself on the nearest tree.

"You..." Lioran swallowed hard. His fingers still trailed the lavender—checking to see if it was real.

I couldn't have done it.

My feet squelched in the mud as I shifted.

Lioran's glare bore through me as if he suddenly saw something in me that terrified him. He ran his hand along his clenched jaw.

"You have magic..." Lioran exhaled, uncertainty flickered in his silver eyes. He took a step closer to me and stopped.

"I don't."

I couldn't. There was nothing magical about me.

I was only Aelira—a mostly human princess.

"We both saw it." Fyn's head tilted.

No. It wasn't possible. Nothing like this had ever happened before. Or had it?

The lavender field—I ripped it free, but it regrew. The roses bloomed.

It wasn't just happening—it was me. I looked down at the

tips of my fingertips. They were still tingling. Each inhale wouldn't fully take, my body weakened.

What if I couldn't control it? What if I destroyed the land more? I pressed my palms together, drawing them in toward my chest, too afraid to touch anything else.

Fyn exhaled forcefully; the sound startled me. "It's not just any magic, Lioran..."

Lioran glared at him, commanding him into silence. Was my magic something horrible?

"I destroyed it all."

"You have not yet learned how to control it." He slowly approached me. "But when you do—it won't be like this." He extended his hand, but I didn't take it.

Lioran lied to me about who he was.

"Lioran..." Fyn's voice was slow and hesitant. "Her magic is like—"

"I will find someone to mentor you." Lioran reached again for a flower. He pulled it free from the soil and he brought it to his nose.

"Why would you?" My fingers rolled inwards as I stepped back.

Lioran ran his hand through his hair. I thought he couldn't waver from his unnatural calm, but here he was, completely undone.

Lioran exhaled. "I planned to tell you. I wanted to."

"Lioran," Fyn warned.

"She knows," Lioran replied.

He watched me destroy the land.

He could have left me there. I half expected him to.

"I'll give you two a moment." Fyn nodded to me before he walked off.

"You didn't, because you didn't trust me." I crossed my

arms over my chest. He shouldn't have. Even I knew that, but it didn't stop my frustration from boiling over.

"I think you know what's it's like to keep secrets you wish you didn't have to keep." Lioran stepped forward again. "This spiral didn't just happen. It's been brewing within you." His eyes met mine.

"How would you know?" I asked.

"Your magic existed within you long before you knew it. You walked amongst those who hated your kind—some who maybe even knew what you possessed."

"You know nothing about me, or my magic," I protested. "You couldn't stop it."

"Your magic is like mine." Lioran's eyes narrowed. "We're connected to the land."

I shook my head in quiet protest. It didn't feel like I was connected to anything at all.

"Are there a lot of fae like us?"

"No, before today, I thought it was only me." His throat bobbed. "I meant what I said. If you come to the Heart with me, I will help you find someone to guide you. It doesn't have to be like this."

I didn't know if I could ever trust him, but I knew I couldn't risk my magic spiraling again. There were no words I could have spoken. I only nodded.

CHAPTER 9

"Those few days of rest were exactly what you needed." Neena bowed her head, placing salve in my bag. "Have patience with him. He's stubborn, but when he finally lets someone in, he cares completely."

"Thank you." I smiled softly.

Lioran tugged his black leather vest taut. His hand gripped Veylar's saddle. "Thank you again for everything, Neena."

His hand wrapped around my waist, steadying me as I pulled myself up onto his stallion. Veylar's rhythm was one with the land as he carried us through the lush forest of Lythira. Lioran commanded his horse without words down the winding path.

A familiar screech cut through the rustling trees—a falcon soared overhead. Muscles seized in my back as it slid into a nearby tree.

Lioran and Fyn exchanged glances.

The falcon circled us.

Memories of Thalen flashed in my mind—the way he

commanded the falcon as if it were an extension of him. My fists clenched tight until my palms throbbed.

Only fae could cross the divide. Could his bird?

"Keep an eye out, Fyn." Lioran shifted in the saddle, gripping Veylar's reins tighter.

The falcon circled us for an hour and then finally disappeared before sunset. Thunder cracked, dividing the sky. Tiny orange embers descended into the darkness as Fyn prodded the fire. Lioran unrolled mats not far beside it.

A chill had descended. I longed for the cabin's warmth, for anything that felt like the home I once knew. It was all gone and now only this world remained. Everyone I knew was gone with it.

Lioran and Fyn spoke so softly that I could barely hear their words. Lioran's gaze softened on me as he caught me watching.

He didn't have to be kind to me.

He could have left me where he found me.

Golden glittering flecks cast a glow in the inky sky. Looking to the stars would always remind me of her.

"The stars hold our stories. They design our fate." Lioran sat beside me. My palms caught the heat from the fire.

"My mother used to always tell me that." I wiped a stray tear that escaped. "Where I'm from, no one else believes it."

"They don't need to understand it. Bailoc hasn't experienced their call." He offered a tender smile. "But you have."

A breathy gasp escaped my lips. The tower. The book. It was the start of it all.

"They chose the wrong princess." I nervously laughed, but Lioran's gentle expression didn't falter.

"They don't make mistakes." His voice lowered. "Only those who are worthy of their favor are chosen."

My heart stilled. No one had ever spoken that way to me before. Something settled within me—a calm that pulsed through me until my shoulders loosened. I had never felt it before.

"Few will agree with you. I am the princess of a kingdom that destroyed yours."

"No one will challenge you in Lythira." He looked around to the horses, to Fyn. "I'm Guardian of Lythira. This territory and the fae that live here are my responsibility." He wrapped his hands around his knees. "As long as you reside in my lands, you are my responsibility, too."

He brought me to safety. He even offered to find someone to train me. Despite everything he was taught about me, about my people, he was kind to me. Maybe he truly meant to protect me.

Lioran watched the fire flicker. His eyes avoided mine.

"It's his fifth year in the role, and already he's making lavish promises," Fyn interrupted.

"Fifth year as prince?" I asked.

"No, fifth year as Guardian. My father waited until my brothers, and I reached thirty to assign our territories. Lythira is mine. Calyth oversees Eyrsea and Pyrran is responsible for Kybar. Each a living, breathing part of the Kingdom of Nythrel."

"You're thirty-five? I assumed you were much older," I said.

"Do we look it?" Fyn warmed his hands by the fire.

I shook my head.

"We all know how old you are." Fyn tilted his head toward Lioran.

"You must have just turned twenty-five," Lioran said.

"How did you know?" The hairs rose all over my body.

"The war started just after you were born." Lioran exhaled slowly. "It's not a year I can forget."

Pain radiated deep within my chest—I would always be a reminder of the war. My lips parted, but as I opened my mouth to speak no words came.

"Do you all really think we live for thousands of years?" Fyn asked. A snort escaped my mouth.

"I thought I remembered it from my mother's stories, but honestly it's been so long since I've heard any tales of the fae to know whether I remembered correctly," I said.

Lioran raised his brow. "I imagine they're not shared frequently."

"No." My smile faded remembering all that was lost from our library. "Any book that once contained your stories was..." I exhaled. "Burned."

Silence held like an unnatural divide between us as I watched the embers shift.

"My mother made sure I knew as much as I could."

"So, you would know the truth," Lioran spoke as if he knew.

My smile faltered as my eyes filled with water again. "So I would know the truth," I repeated, digesting his words. "I think I'd like to rest now."

As I rose, my muscles resisted. Each step toward the sleeping mats brought me closer to the book—to the answers I needed. I waited for Fyn and Lioran to speak again before I pulled it from my satchel. With an exhale, I pressed it open, breathing in its scent. Something about it felt like home.

I wondered still if they were telling the truth. About the war. About me. About my magic.

Each letter formed quickly.

The fae prince speaks the truth.

It is how your story began.

The war started from hatred and jealousy.

You did not make the decision—it is not your burden to carry.

A chill trailed my spine. So many truths had been hidden from me, and now I was uncovering them all. All my life there was something within me that felt unnatural. It was a pain that hovered in my chest even long after I walked through grief.

King Ardyn and Lord Joran were so quick to act on the marriage pact. Maybe they knew that in time who I was would be revealed and then they couldn't hide it anymore.

I still saw glimmers of the destruction I caused in Evyn. They danced through my mind. I didn't know what my magic was, or what it would do if left untamed. The ink dashed across the page, catching my eye.

Your magic is a gift from the stars.

You were chosen to be one with the land—it is a rare and special gift.

It was a gift I couldn't control.

I slid the book into my satchel. There would be a time I'd open it again, but for now, I needed only the starlight. The stars twinkled in an uneven cadence as I lay back on a mat. Maybe they knew I questioned them.

An unfamiliar, melodic laugh echoed. I turned on the mat to see a wide smile spread on Lioran's face as Fyn spoke. The wind drowned out their words, but still I watched their joy with envy.

The day had been warm, but the night brought a crisp chill. The wind bit at my cheeks until I trembled, yet a gust of warmth trailed through me. A calm and quiet energy that left me feeling as if everything would be okay.

"You're shivering," Lioran said. I hadn't heard him

approach. He knelt beside me with a wool blanket in his hands. I was already draped in my own. The lines around his eyes softened as he looked at me. "Take my blanket."

"I'll be fine." My hand met his as I shook my head. His warmth flooded me and I pulled back.

"Maybe, but I won't be able to sleep knowing you're awake shivering." The scratchy wool sifted over my skin as he lay the blanket on top of me.

"I would hate for that to happen." My smirk quickly shifted. I spoke that freely with Cael before, but never another. "Thank you," I quickly whispered.

"You're welcome, Your Highness," Lioran said as he lay down on the mat beside me.

I froze—I hadn't thought to shift the mats, to give myself space, and now I would have none. Lioran rolled over on his mat, until only his back greeted me.

My body relaxed. I trusted him. I trusted them both. Maybe I would regret it, but for now, I felt safe.

Fyn pulled his mat off to the side, shaking his head.

Then only the stars held my attention until my eyelids grew too heavy.

Veylar raced down the path after the first glimmer of light danced over the horizon. Lioran shifted in the saddle behind, his thigh pressed firmly against mine.

The shrill screech amplified. Lioran held one hand tight on the stallion's reins, and another firm at my waist. I would have pulled away, but Fyn's joyful demeanor shifted. He pulled his fist back and Lioran pressed Veylar harder.

He leaned into me in the saddle. "Whatever happens, hold

your ground," Lioran hissed in my ear. "By any means necessary."

A bitter taste settled on my tongue.

Hooves pounded the land in the distance. A stallion and a rider gaining speed on us—and then another. Veylar sped down the winding path.

Brush scraped over my legs, over Veylar, but still he continued onward. Lioran tightened his grip on me. His breath quickened against my skin. I counted the riders—four, five, and then the sixth came into view. The dagger bounced at my riding belt. It called to me.

The unsteady terrain jolted my hand as I attempted to free it.

"I've got you. Go. Now!" Fyn yelled as he fell back behind us.

They were closing in on us. In moments, they would be beside us.

Finally, I wrangled the dagger free. The chill met my palm. My stomach lurched.

"We've come for the princess." The rider gripped the hilt of his sword as he raced beside us. "Give her to us and we'll let you leave."

They knew who I was.

Lioran didn't stop Veylar, but I heard his breathing quicken.

A hand clamped around my leg. Without thought, I lifted the dagger and drove it into the attacker's hand. He released me as the dagger struck—his low, guttural growl left me quaking. The dagger tumbled from my grasp as the terrain shifted. An impassable, dense thicket of trees lay ahead of us. Veylar reared back. Lioran braced me as my body slammed into his.

With a final thud of his hooves, Veylar spun. We were surrounded. Each breath was heavier than the last.

"Who has come to claim her?" Lioran jumped down from the saddle. As he lifted me off the saddle, his eyes locked on mine. His biceps tightened under my grip.

Fyn ran to our side. He snarled at them as he firmly held his blade.

"She will be returned to where she belongs," another rider spoke. Beneath the hoods, their eyes glowed in the sun. These riders promised to return me, but they couldn't be working for the human realm—they were fae. I waited for Lioran's instruction. His warmth greeted me as he gripped my waist with one hand. The other hovered at the hilt of his sword.

The hum of the blade sang as he pulled it from the hilt and swung it around in front of us. It didn't stop at our attackers. He stopped it in front of my chest. I pushed back at him but couldn't free myself from his hold without the blade scraping my skin.

He held it still. There was barely even room to breathe.

"Enough! Let's settle this now." Lioran's tone fell flat.

"Please. Don't do this." My throat constricted until my words were barely comprehendible.

I was a hunted fool—one who trusted a prince who held his sword to my chest.

He could kill me. He could hand me off to them.

There was nothing I could do about it.

The men stood with swords drawn, glimmers of glowing eyes assessed him. Lioran's breath was hot on my cheek. I winced as the blade moved with each breath I took.

"What do you want for her?" the rider asked.

"What is she worth?" Lioran growled.

He had saved me. He took care of me. I believed him.

I looked to Fyn, desperate for him to intervene, but his stoic gaze was set on the riders.

Lioran's grip on my waist softened. "Run," he whispered in my ear as he pushed me back away from him.

I sprinted as metal clanged behind me. Brush ripped my pants, scraping my flesh. It didn't stop me. I couldn't look back. I wouldn't stop running.

A cloaked rider growled in my ear as he tackled me to the ground. Dirt pelted up into my eyes. I scratched at him. I kicked. I screamed, but I couldn't get free.

The stench of the rider's foul breath overtook me. White-hot pain ripped through my arm as my attacker pinned my arm down with his knee. Blood slid into the soil from my arm.

"Aelira!" Fyn yelled. Lioran lifted his sword and darted toward me, but the four attackers closed in on them.

Boots crunched beside me. A cloaked rider knelt beside us. His hood fell back revealing long, straight, black hair, deep brown eyes, and pointed ears. "I wouldn't defy him. Do you know what he will do to you when he sees blood on her?" The sun illuminated a metal fastener on his cloak with an insignia etched into it.

My attacker didn't flinch. He didn't let me go free. Instead, he pulled me onto my knees and pinned my wrists together with one hand. His other gripped rope that hung at his belt. He wrapped it around my wrists and laughed. The rope gnawed at my flesh. "He could have at least warned us how difficult she would be," he told the other rider.

"Who sent you?" I demanded. King Ardyn wouldn't work with the fae.

The dark-haired fae held my dagger. Blood dripped from the blade. "What a pretty little dagger. It's fit for royalty," he scoffed. The other fae shoved me forward. I screamed again.

Lioran slashed his sword down another attacker's leg, and then the hilt of his sword came down on the crown of the other fae's head. He didn't move again. My eyes scanned the ground beside him. Another attacker laid in a pool of blood.

Fyn nodded to Lioran as his sword clashed between the other two. Lioran darted toward me. His sword raised toward the attackers, but he looked only at me. Tears ran down my face.

"Was she worth it?" the dark-haired fae asked as he slid my dagger across Lioran's abdomen. He dropped it and unsheathed his sword.

"No!" I cried as I tried to pull myself free.

Lioran roared, but still he crashed his blade down into the dark-haired fae. The land glowed beneath his feet. A brilliant golden glittering light pooled.

Hands clenched around my bound wrists. The other rider pulled me back.

A fierce growl reverberated through the ground, and then another, and through the trees a dozen sets of jade eyes peered through the dark crevices of the forest.

The largest sylkren raced ahead of the others. It slid in the dirt, stopping inches from me. I braced myself, but it only crouched before me.

With its jaw clenched shut, it roared.

My captor dragged me back again, his body cowering behind mine.

As the beast lunged, I braced myself for impact that never came.

My captor wailed.

The sylkren clenched his jaw around his leg, dragging him back over stony ground. The dagger tumbled from his grasp. I collapsed as screams flooded the forest. I closed my eyes, unable to watch as the sylkren attacked them all.

Lioran placed his hand on my shoulder.

"You...you called them?" I shuddered.

He gritted his teeth. "Yes. Are you hurt?"

A gasp escaped my lips, but no words formed. My whole body trembled. "I'll be fine." Nothing about me felt fine. I wasn't sure if I would ever be again.

He staggered as he stepped forward and pulled my blood-soaked dagger from the grass. He wiped it clean and then slid it through the rope that bound my wrists. Then he handed it back to me. The dagger shook in my unsteady grip. I slid it back in its sheath.

Scarlet droplets dripped from Fyn's brow. "We need to leave. Now," he commanded.

All traces of radiant silver drained from Lioran's eyes. His chest heaved with ragged breathing as Veylar darted to his side.

He tried to lift me up on the horse, but stumbled back, crumpling into Veylar's side. Pain rippled through me as I clutched the saddle with my remaining strength and swung my leg over. He struggled to mount behind me.

The howls of the sylkren faded as we raced ahead.

Crimson caught my eye as I glanced over my shoulder—Lioran's tunic pooled with blood. His face grew paler with each beat of the land beneath us.

I ripped hanging fabric from my tunic and pressed it to his side. He flinched with my touch. Veylar carried us further into the forest. My heart thundered, rising higher in my chest.

Lioran's blood coated my hands.

CHAPTER 10

"Fyn! We need to stop!" I yelled.

A ring of blood seeped past my hand.

"I'll...be... fine." Lioran's words caught. "We can't stop here...it's not...safe."

"I'm not going to let you bleed out." I grabbed Veylar's reins and yanked hard. Lioran's stallion was loyal to a fault— he refused to stop.

Fyn rode closer. His eyes scanned Lioran.

"We're stopping now. You can be stubborn all you want later." His tone was sharp.

"We will stop...when...it's...safe." Lioran grunted with each word. His body slumped into mine.

"Stop now, Veylar. Unless you're not opposed to Lioran dying." I yanked the reins harder.

The stallion halted.

Fyn raced to secure Lioran as he slid out of the saddle. My hands shook as they gripped the satchel.

Fyn desperately ripped Lioran's tunic, tearing it free. Crimson gushed freely.

89

I couldn't help.

I didn't know what to do.

A vial trembled in my hand—remnants of Neena's supplies.

"Bring me anything—I need everything!" Fyn yelled.

His satchel caught on the saddle, but I ripped it free. Fyn braced Lioran at the base of a tree as I darted back to them. He removed a thin strip of light brown bark from his bag and shoved it into Lioran's mouth. Lioran groaned as his teeth clenched around it.

Brown liquid trickled over the wound from Fyn's quaking hand.

Lioran roared. Every muscle in his body tensed.

I quickly pried the lid off an herbal salve Neena gave me before we left. Fyn slathered it on the wound.

Lioran grunted—sweat dripped from his brow.

I was his enemy's daughter, but he protected me anyway.

"They were fae." I said.

My thigh muscles spasmed. I could still feel the hand on my thigh, but no one held me. Tears crashed down my face.

"Bailoc is full of surprises," Fyn huffed.

Lioran's groans reverberated through the ground. His fingers dug into the dirt. Fyn frantically pulled the dressing tight around his wound.

"He looks awful."

"I...can...hear...you," Lioran wailed, spitting out the bark.

"I'm so sorry." I sank into the dirt beside Lioran.

His chest barely rose and fell—his breath too shallow to grip air.

"I shouldn't have crossed the divide." I reached for his hand and held it mine. He didn't pull away.

"We...can't...st...ay..." He tried to lift himself up, but Fyn pressed his palm against his shoulder.

"You are not going anywhere right now." Fyn steadied him. "Red isn't your color."

Lioran tried to laugh, but a ragged inhale echoed.

My abdomen burned at the sight of all the blood.

Lioran was bleeding out, because they were hunting me. My shoulder twinged with the pain of my own reopened wound. My hands gripped his still. The same hands that sliced a dagger through flesh.

I clenched my eyes shut, but it didn't stop the memory.

The fae's eyes in the woods haunted me. I could still smell the stench of the sylkren. What if they didn't come? I shuddered.

No, I couldn't think about it.

I dropped Lioran's hand and turned from them both. As I stepped away, I vomited.

"Ae...lira." Lioran's hoarse voice called to me.

"First time in battle, huh?" Fyn handed me the flask of water with his free hand. I nodded as I let the drink flow through me, cooling the heat in my cheeks. "You did good." He nodded.

Lioran's eyes closed.

"Fyn!" I screamed, before I saw his chest rise with another shallow breath.

"He's breathing." Fyn stilled my quaking hands in his, blood tinged us. "Lioran cares more about others than he does himself. One of his biggest faults."

Lioran's blood pooled through the dressing. Fyn applied another one on top, gripping it firm. What if it didn't stop?

"Fyn...will he?" I couldn't even get my words out.

"We will get him to help, but we can't move him yet," Fyn said. Suddenly, I found myself desperate to hear he would survive, but Fyn didn't say it.

Fyn tilted his flask over my hands. The water ran red

beneath them. My thoughts retraced every detail of the attack. King Ardyn wouldn't have called the fae. He would never ally with them to get me back. He probably didn't want me back.

The dark-haired fae wore an insignia on the metal clasp of his cloak. I tried to hold the image in my mind, to commit every line to memory, but Lioran bellowed again.

"Thank you for protecting me." My voice was a low whisper. His fingers twitched. I clutched them in my hands again.

Please let him live.

The stars weren't visible, but maybe they could still hear my plea.

The midday heat settled on us. We spent the last hour monitoring him as he went in and out of consciousness. "We need to get moving." Fyn hovered over Lioran. "It's still early. We can pass through Othryl to gather supplies for Lioran before heading to the Heart."

"Do they have a healer in Othryl?"

"They may. The village isn't what it used to be." Fyn began packing the few supplies we had left. "If we can keep him on a horse today, we may get there before nightfall."

"Lioran." Fyn lifted him slowly. "Drink." Fyn lifted the flask to his lips.

He was awake. He was alive.

"Tell me what I can do." I felt his forehead for fever. He didn't have one.

Veylar didn't hesitate as Fyn led him closer to us.

"I'm going to help him stand. Help brace his back." Lioran leaned into Fyn, his arm swung around Fyn's neck. My hands gently rested on Lioran's back. I was too afraid to hurt him further.

Lioran groaned with each step.

"Try to pull yourself up a bit. I'll help with the rest." Fyn's voice softened.

Lioran clenched his muscles as he tried to grab onto Veylar's saddle. He moaned as his boots slid in the dirt. Fyn braced him again, helping him into the saddle.

"She can't manage you by herself. It won't be comfortable... but I have to tie you to Veylar." Fyn's hands steadied a rope around Lioran's waist—he tied it to the saddle.

"Aelira, you'll ride behind Lioran. I need you to hold him up best you can." Fyn extended his hand to help me into the saddle, but his hand wrapped around my arm instead. "You're bleeding. We need to wrap it again."

"No." I pulled free. "We don't have enough supplies left. He needs it more than I do. I'll be fine."

"You two..." Fyn slid his dagger through the bottom of his shirt, ripping a strand of fabric free. I winced as he tightened the fabric around my wound. "You're both just bleeding all over the place like it's no big deal." He smirked.

He lifted me up behind Lioran. My hands rested lightly on Lioran's back.

"He won't bite." Fyn slid my arms around Lioran's chest. "He's lost too much blood." Even as he joked, his voice caught.

Lioran let out a low scoff. I pulled my hands back.

"This will only work if you actually hold on to him!" Fyn yelled as he mounted his horse.

Lioran howled as Veylar's hooves pelted the rocky ground.

"I need you to hold on, Lioran." If he heard me, he didn't respond.

Wind thrashed at my cheeks, a moment of relief from the

midday sun. Lioran swayed in the saddle, but I gripped him harder, desperate to keep him upright.

Fyn rode alongside us until the path narrowed. Even then, he monitored us. My muscles seared with pain with every effort to keep Lioran from slumping in the saddle. Despite how fast he was fading, he attempted to hold himself up.

"I've got you. We're going to make it to Othryl soon." I didn't know how long it would take, but I needed him to stay conscious. My hands pressed firmly against his chest until I could feel each shallow slow breath.

Rustling sounded from the trees.

"Fyn, did you hear that?"

Fyn commanded his horse to halt. I pulled on Veylar's reins. Lioran wailed as he shifted too abruptly in the saddle.

"There's nothing out there, but if we keep stopping, we may stumble into something."

He was right. I couldn't let my fear get the best of me. My arms trembled, Lioran suddenly felt heavier.

"Stay with me," I pleaded as tears pooled in my eyes. My heart clenched firm in my chest.

"We need to get to Othryl," Fyn warned.

When I was sad or hurt, my mother used to always hum a soft tune to me. I remembered it still and hummed it to him. He may not have heard it all, but the familiar song kept me steady.

Two wings crossed with a vertical sword—their insignia was seared into my memory. It felt so familiar.

As Veylar's hooves pounded the rocky ground, I remembered it. The day the marriage pact was announced. Thalen kissed me and when he pulled back, the sunlight illuminated something on his tunic—a golden emblem.

It couldn't be the same.

Maybe it was just similar.

"Are you okay?" Fyn yelled to me.

The path finally widened enough for Fyn to bring his horse beside Veylar. My hands shifted on Lioran's chest.

I remembered it clearly. My throat tightened. The insignia was identical. They said *he* wanted me back safely—it hadn't been King Ardyn.

It was Thalen.

He had fae riders in his command. They knew how to track me.

The divide couldn't stop him. More would come.

"The attackers in the woods...one wore an insignia."

Fyn's eyebrows knitted.

A low, dull groan rumbled through Lioran and collided with me like he was listening and waiting for my answer.

"King Ardyn has an ally, Lord Thalen of the Vale." I exhaled louder than I intended. "He wears the same insignia."

"The King of Bailoc and Lord Thalen of the Vale are allies?" His words echoed in my ears. How did he know him? I nodded.

Fyn shifted in his saddle. "Why would a king who hates the fae ally himself with one?"

He couldn't have said what I thought he had.

Thalen wasn't just the Lord of the Vale.

He was fae.

His eyes glowed in my father's study, but I dismissed it. When he touched me, something stirred within me. I thought I was having feelings for him, but what if it was something else entirely?

My head throbbed as I recalled their first conversation about the marriage pact. Each pointed question asked after the next. My father...Lord Joran...Agan...they all knew. They chose him not just for the supplies, but because he could handle the parts of me that were like him.

"You...know him?" I asked.

"He has a bit of a reputation in our kingdom. Thalen's highly tolerated by those in powerful positions in the High Court, but many of us see him for who he truly is."

"And what is that?"

"A self-serving opportunist." Fyn's words rang in my ears.

What opportunity did he see in marrying me?

A chill ran from the gemstone through my body.

"How well do you know him?" Fyn wiped the sweat that was dripping from his brow.

They'd never look at me the same again, if they knew he could claim me. "Minimally." The word caught in my throat.

I steadied my hands on Lioran's chest, hoping he couldn't feel them trembling.

Veylar hit a divot in the ground, jolting us. My hand slipped from Lioran's chest. He bolted upright in the saddle, growling. Lioran slumped forward again. I desperately pulled him back into my chest.

"Aelira, what happened?" Fyn brought his horse in line with Veylar. "Come on, Lioran. Stay with us."

"I didn't mean to..." I struggled to breathe through my words.

"You can do this." Fyn's eyes widened. "We're almost there."

My focus settled on the leaves swaying in the wind—a welcome distraction to forget the pain that gripped my muscles.

The once green horizon turned brown, and the splendor of the woods vanished. Rotting decay sifted up into my nostrils as we passed piles of soot and ash. Orange mushrooms grew on the tree trunks, the only sign of life, or color.

Veylar veered around fallen tree trunks and his ears flickered.

A hollow cry rose from the land. It was desperate. The wind howled with it. For a moment, it sounded as if it whispered my name.

But that was impossible.

Fyn pushed forward without response.

"What caused this?" I gripped Lioran closer to me.

"The blight," Fyn said. "You've never seen it before..."

Barren fields lined the edge of the village. Broken down equipment lay behind. Discarded and forgotten.

"No..." I never saw it with my own eyes. Only heard the stories that were told. "Bailoc believes it's a curse from the fae."

"Why would we curse our own lands?" Fyn snapped.

"You wouldn't," I murmured. "How does the village find food to eat?"

"Lioran sends resources in from the Heart and other communities contribute what they can, too. It will never be enough to sustain."

"They will have to leave."

"It's the only home they've ever known. Different villages can take them in, but we can't guarantee they'll stay together." Fyn's voice grew quieter. "There isn't enough room anywhere."

We stopped at the entrance of the village. Homes had crumbled. Their remains were held up by beams of rotten wood. "So you bide the time with resources."

A mother and her two children, all too thin and pallid, walked quietly in the village. There was no laughter between them.

Fyn reached for Lioran, bracing him. "Aelira, try to climb

down." My aching legs trembled as I jumped down from Veylar, his body swayed with the force of mine as I fell back into him. "This is going to hurt, but we need to get you out of the saddle." Fyn lowered Lioran out of the saddle.

Lioran roared.

"The prince is injured?" A fae man ran to greet us, his body was emaciated.

"Yes, we seek your healer and whatever resources you have to give," Fyn pleaded.

"You know we have very little, but we will do what we can for our prince." He sprinted across the barren village. Fyn lowered Lioran to sit beside me. His body crashed into mine. I pulled him upright even as my muscles screamed in protest.

A slender fae woman approached, deep circles set under her eyes. "I am Neva, the healer of Othryl."

Her hands hovered over Lioran as she shook her head.

She pried my fingers from him without another word and then lifted his dressing.

My eyes squeezed shut as she assessed it.

"Shipments from Evyn were delayed. Nothing I have is strong enough." She inspected the fresh blood that colored my skin.

"His situation is dire." She opened her satchel and pressed coarse, ragged dressings into my hands. "Keep it covered and make haste."

"If we race forward, it may rip his wound open further." Fyn yanked at the stray hairs that fell around his face.

"It will." She sighed. "But if you don't, he will not make it through the night."

Her words left me empty. My hope had been frail—what little remained was ripped away.

Fyn's eyes set upon mine—a silent pact passed between us. We would do whatever we could to get him there. I nodded.

"Thank you. We will send supplies your way as soon as we are able. The prince will not forget your kindness," Fyn said.

The healer placed her hand over Lioran. A flicker of white light flowed from her fingertips over the wound. The bleeding slowed. She fell back.

"I'm too weak to do anything further."

Lioran fell as Fyn tried to bring him to his feet again. He swung Lioran's arm around his neck.

"I don't know how much longer I can hold him on the horse." I instantly regretted my words. It seemed so selfish to even think on my pain considering his.

"You've done more than enough. I'll take him on my horse," Fyn replied. "You'll ride Veylar back to the Heart."

I didn't know how to command Veylar. With gritted teeth, I used the last of my strength to hoist myself up onto the saddle. "Guess it's just you and me," I whispered to the stallion. "Let's get him home."

He resisted me when Lioran was wounded and bleeding. He could have resisted me still, but he gently swayed with my touch.

Lioran's eyes half opened. His focus sharpened as he looked at me. I wasn't even sure if he saw me, or if he heard our words at all.

"Fy...Fyn." Lioran's words were low and broken.

"Save your energy," Fyn warned as he pulled Lioran up into the saddle of his horse.

"Take...care...of... Ae...Aelira," Lioran groaned.

My heart caught in my throat.

"I know the plan. It will be done. Now please stop talking," Fyn scolded as his muscles clenched.

Lioran's gaze met mine for a fleeting moment before his eyes closed again.

Time wasn't on our side.

If we weren't fast enough, we'd lose him.

CHAPTER 11

Gold and pink hues skimmed the horizon. Lush green filled the path once more, like we had exited one room and entered another. The warm wind thrashed against my body, keeping me alert.

Veylar darted forward. Our pace was dangerous. Lioran's body slumped against Fyn. For hours he moaned and shifted in the saddle, but in the last hour, it all stopped.

The once even beat of Veylar's hooves floundered. His ears drooped, but he pressed on as if the bond between them were deeper than my command.

"Follow the river to the right!" Fyn hollered. "We're almost there."

As we rounded the corner, racing alongside the river, an enormous stone castle glimmered in the last flicker of sunlight. Massive trees arched over the castle and entwined themselves through a city built upon the forest.

Fyn let out a startled groan, tugging me back into the moment.

"Veylar will take you the rest of the way!" Fyn yelled.

His horse challenged fate as it raced over the path, until they faded from view. We were so close, but Fyn raced ahead. It could only mean one thing.

We were losing him.

I couldn't breathe. "Veylar, we need to get to him," I cried.

Despite Veylar's exhaustion, despite mine, we raced on. I held onto the sliver of hope that he could be saved.

Shifting winds propelled us forward. With each jolt, we grew closer.

The castle grew larger, the trees more massive as we stopped before it.

I jumped down from Veylar onto the pebbled path. Fyn's horse stood still. Several fae lifted Lioran from Fyn's horse. His body was lifeless, his hands dangled.

Lioran's chest heaved as they lay him out on a cloth draped frame. I cradled Lioran's clammy hands in mine.

Breathless sobs escaped me.

Fyn's arms wrapped around me. He pulled me back from Lioran.

"We've done what we can. The healer has him now."

A woman in a plain brown gown ran her hands over him. Tears pooled in her eyes as she nodded to the fae around her.

"It's...my fault." My chest tightened. "He can't..."

Fyn spun me to face him. "Lioran chose to do what he did."

A woman ran down the stone stairs of the castle, her copper hair glowing in the emerging moonlight. She darted to his side, cupping his hand in hers. Her body crumpled over him as she wailed—her cries so deep they echoed through the Heart.

Fyn didn't pull her back—not the way he did with me.

"I need to..." I murmured, then collapsed into Fyn.

"There's nothing you can do." His voice cracked.

"Take him inside, to the infirmary." The healer turned

toward us, her head bowed to Fyn before she followed behind him.

They lifted the carrying frame and darted inside. The red-headed woman spun toward us. "How?"

"We were intercepted this morning before we got to Othryl. Lioran did his best to protect—" His voice trailed off.

"You should have—" she said.

"Stopped him?" Fyn's eyes narrowed. "You know him better than that, Cora. When he has his mind made up on something..."

Only then did her eyes meet mine—fury boiled behind her emerald glare.

Cora ran back into the castle. I stayed at Fyn's side. It wasn't my place to follow Lioran, but maybe it was hers.

I looked to the stars; they glimmered in the darkness as if they didn't know what would be lost if he didn't make it. Could they even hear me?

"There's nothing we can do out here," Fyn said quietly.

Fyn parted with me only for a moment. "Juniper will guide you to your room, my lady." He returned with a slender younger fae woman.

"Here?" Our voices carried through the entrance of Lioran's castle.

"I promised I would look after you." Streaks of red ran through Fyn's eyes. He exhaled. "He wanted you here."

Lioran used his remaining strength to tell him—to ensure I was safe.

"Please send for me if anything changes."

"I will." His hands trembled around mine.

We ascended a grand staircase in the entry and followed the corridor to the very back. My muscles throbbed with every step I took down the dimly lit stone halls.

"Your room is here, my lady. I will help you with whatever you need."

"Thank you." I pressed my hand against the wall. "I don't know what I need."

Juniper pried open the door. "Let's get you bathed and changed."

"We've readied her chambers," another fae woman whispered to Juniper as she slipped out of the space behind us.

Candles lined the open windowsills, a soothing glow cast light on the grand room. Stone ceilings pitched high above.

"My lady, you're covered in blood. Do you need a healer? Lord Fyn didn't tell me." She hesitated before peeling back the bloodstained tunic.

"They should all be with the prince now." I loosened the bandage on my arm, the tear still visible, but the bleeding stopped. "I will be fine."

My wound would heal, but if we lost him a part of me would never recover.

"If you change your mind, let me know." She gestured to a large wooden soaking tub. Steam rose from it. My heart dropped as my clothes fell to the floor—the satchel wasn't with me. I left the book inside of it.

"I had a satchel. I think I left it on Prince Lioran's horse." My palms were drenched in sweat. "I need it." I reached for my neck and relaxed as I realized I was still wearing the gemstone.

"I will send someone to fetch it for you, my lady." She slipped out of the room.

I plunged my head under the surface, letting the heat wash over me. My breath held for only a moment. The grime slipped away as I came up for air. Hot water wouldn't ease the chill that flooded my body.

Silence tore through me. The storm strengthened within me. I scrubbed at my skin until the last of Lioran's blood ran into the water.

My thoughts drifted to the red-headed woman. She was probably with him now. Maybe she already knew whether he would live or die.

Juniper's voice was soft as she opened the chamber door. "I will bring the satchel in when they find it, along with food. You must be starving from the journey."

"I'm not hungry," I said.

Water pooled at my feet as they hit the stone floor. Juniper dropped a blanket around my trembling shoulders and gestured to the nightgown on the bed. "Would you like help?"

"No, thank you." She nodded before departing. Wet hair clung to my back. The chill of the stone floor was unforgiving as I made my way to the bed.

I traced the delicate leaf carving of the headboard. The tears hadn't stopped falling, but for a moment I forgot I was crying. Juniper quietly slipped back into the room with the satchel. She placed it on the chair in the corner and crept back out without another word. As soon as the door closed, I darted for it.

The book was still inside. I should have been relieved, but all I could think of was Lioran. His lifeless face flashed through my mind. His hand hanging off the carrying frame.

How could he go from calling me insufferable to just laying there?

"He almost died because of her." Cora's voice carried through the corridor.

I held myself in the corner of the corridor, steps from them, but still out of view.

"They were hunting her, Cora..." A long pause held between them. "You know how he is."

"He's so stubborn. He insisted on all of this."

"She held him up for hours on the back of Veylar." Fyn's boots scuffed against the stone floor. "In less than a week, she's learned she's half-fae, crossed the divide, escaped a sylkren, and battled for her life. She did whatever she could to take care of him. I can't even comprehend how she did it. Have you looked at the girl? She's tiny."

I stepped out from the corner and into view. "Are there any updates?"

"It was a long night. He's stable, but depleted," Fyn said.

My hand slid to my mouth as I caught my breath. Fyn's eyes were bloodshot, and his hair was disheveled. Had he been there with him all night?

The red-headed woman looked the same. A pang of guilt ran through me for sleeping while they waited with him.

"We made it...in time." I steadied my hands at my sides.

"Lady Cora, Lord Fyn, his highness has asked to see you both." A slender fae man approached. "Keep your visit brief. He requires rest more than he needs visitors right now."

He was awake.

My lips parted, but what I wanted remained unsaid.

I couldn't bring myself to ask to go with them. Would he even want me there? I leaned against the wall, watching them as they left for the infirmary. Fyn didn't look back at me.

My body slid down the wall.

"Aelira, Lioran would like to see you." Fyn crouched down to get eye level with me.

Our footsteps echoed down the quiet corridor. I grasped my gemstone, embracing its gentle warmth. My breath held as we entered the infirmary wing.

Cora tucked her hair behind her ears. She hovered over Lioran from a nearby chair. His hand was in hers.

A hint of pink brushed across Lioran's cheeks. "I need a... moment...with Aelira," he said.

He struggled as he attempted to sit. The healer pressed against his shoulder, her eyes narrowing on him. Cora hadn't released his hand. Fyn tugged on her arm. She finally let him go.

"You...do not let him sit up. If he doesn't listen, you come get me," the healer warned me as she pointed to the door. I nodded. "Your Highness, do not overexert yourself."

"Rowena has a point. Maybe I should stay to help." Cora hesitated at the door.

"Cora." He groaned. "I'm not...asking."

She watched him until she slipped through the door.

He was so large, yet so frail in the infirmary bed. "Aelira..." He strained to lift his hand. "You're...okay."

I sat beside him. "Yes, I'm fine. How could you possibly worry about me?"

His laughter was fleeting—a moan soon followed.

"I'm so incredibly sorry. I would have never put you and Fyn in that position had I known." Tears rolled down my cheeks.

He wiggled his fingers, lifting them ever so slightly.

"Don't...be sorry." He gasped as he tried to adjust himself in the bed.

"You need rest." I instinctively grabbed his hand but pulled back. If he and Cora were something more. If they were together, this was overstepping.

"I wanted you...here." He reached his hand toward mine, straining. "Thank...you." He was reaching for me, the way I reached for him.

"Why are you thanking me?" I rested my hand next to his until our fingers brushed. Warmth flooded me.

"Fyn told me...how you..." He tried to shift in the bed, then clamped his jaw tightly, groaning through his teeth. I laid a hand on his shoulder, gently steadying him. "Took care... of me."

"It was the least I could do. You saved me."

His dull gaze caught mine, but a hint of a smile lingered. "And you saved me...so now we're even."

It was so good to see him smile.

"Do you want me to send Cora back in?"

He winced and his eyebrow raised. "No...she'll just...chastise...me some...more."

I stifled my laughter. "She despises me."

"No...she's just...overprotective. There's no way...she can... hate you. Not if...she gets to...know you like...I do." His breath grew heavier.

"Please rest. You can tell me I'm insufferable when you're better."

He smirked and his eyes closed.

CHAPTER 12

Time slipped away quickly until I lost all sense of it. The Heart was vast, but my fears kept me close to the castle. Lioran asked for me daily. He slept through most of my visits. I sat with him still, watching his chest rise and fall.

Gratitude overwhelmed me. The healer's magic gave him a second chance. Without it, he could have died.

Magic hummed in my veins—it called to me, but I couldn't respond. The book remained tucked away. I couldn't bear its answers.

I admired the dazzling sunlight that reflected off the stream as it wound through the Heart. A small waterfall trickled into the stream at the backside of the castle. Its song lulled me into a rare moment of calm.

"Lioran wants me to train you." Cora's sharp tone cut through the silence. "To help you channel your magic."

Apparently, he hadn't been awake long enough to see how much she loathed me.

"I have no interest in tapping into my magic again," I said. "I've destroyed enough already."

She watched me carefully.

"What do you want from me, Cora? Do you want me to stay away from him? To leave?" We both knew there was nowhere I could go.

"You wouldn't be here unless he trusted you." Cora's shoulders settled as her breath escaped her lips. "I don't want you to go. Seeing him there...like that, it broke me."

"And you blame me?"

"No." Her voice softened.

"I would never have crossed the divide knowing that it would lead to all of this. Every day I see him lying there—"

"Every day?" she repeated, as if she didn't know.

Had I said too much? My shoulders rounded as I looked back at the waterfall.

"I will train you, because your magic is a gift. It may be essential to the balance of the lands." She tucked loose, red waves behind her ears.

"I can't control it—I caused so much destruction in Evyn." My eyes flooded. I steadied my breath, wishing the tears wouldn't fall.

"Until you learn to control it, it will test you in ways you can't imagine. Ways none of us can stop." The lull of the waterfall crept back into my head. The sound steadied me.

Deep down, I knew she was right. I wouldn't be able to ignore my magic forever, but the thought of facing it again was too much to bear.

"We will start tomorrow." Her voice softened.

I hadn't even accepted, but it didn't matter. She had already decided. My chest tightened as I reluctantly nodded.

I pressed open the door to Lioran's infirmary room.

"Aelira." The corners of his mouth curved slowly into a gentle smile as he sat upright in bed. He quickly straightened his lips, trying to hide his discomfort.

"You're sitting." For a moment, he seemed whole again.

A chuckle escaped his lips and then he winced. "It's good to see you."

Sunlight crept in through the window, illuminating Lioran's eyes. Shimmering silver sparkled within them again. I slid into place next to him in a chair already pulled by the bed.

He reached for my unbandaged arm and traced the newly formed pink scar. "It's healing nicely." The hairs on my arms rose and the gemstone radiated warmth. I slid the stone over on the cold silver chain. "Your necklace is beautiful. A family heirloom?"

"A gift from my father...my fae father." I clutched the stone. I held my breath for a moment. "I don't really know much about it."

"May I see it?" he asked.

For a moment, I hesitated before I unclasped the necklace. I wound up the silver chain before setting it in the palm of his hand.

"It's an onyx—an earth grounding stone." The light caught on the facets of the stone, illuminating the black stone. "A fitting gift for someone with your magic."

"Do you think he knew what my magic would be?" He held the necklace back out to me.

"It's possible. Some fae can see the future through visions like Cora." His voice trailed off as he yawned loudly. He was struggling to keep himself upright.

"She knows the future?"

"Only what the stars show her—fragments of moments that have yet to pass." He shifted himself and his fists clenched as he stifled a moan.

"Can I help you?" I extended my arms to him.

"I'm fine." With an exasperated exhale, he leaned back into the pillows behind him. "I keep asking to get out of here, but no one will let me."

"Maybe it's because you can't sit still." I adjusted a pillow that shifted behind his back. My hand caught the side of his arm, lingering over his tattoos for a moment too long. "Is there anything I can do? I have plenty of free time today."

"Sit with me a while longer." His dark curls hung over his eyes. I wanted to brush them aside but resisted as I nestled into the chair beside him. "Maybe in a few more days I'll get out of here. Then we can walk around the Heart."

"When you're ready, I'd love to see it. Fyn said I should stay close to the castle for now."

"My men haven't returned from ensuring the borders of the Heart are secure yet. I'll feel better once we know the threat hasn't extended here."

"Me too." I flinched at the thought of the attackers, at the thought of Thalen. My finger trembled against the side of the bed.

He slid his hand over mine, the warmth of his touch grounding me.

"You're safe here," he said. For a heartbeat, I sat with his tender touch.

"Lioran..." I looked out the window as I spoke.

Silence met me.

When I turned around, he was asleep.

The next morning, Fyn led me down a stone path further into the Heart of Lythira. Wildflowers sprawled in the dirt. Winding stairs led from the edge of the path up the trunk of a tree where homes stood. They reminded me of the cabins in Evyn, but these were grander.

"Cora is waiting for us." Fyn barely glanced back.

My boots fell heavy on the stone steps as we ascended the spiral stairs. My navy gown dragged on the stonework. The dagger swayed in its sheath, beating against my body with each step. After the attack in the woods, I went nowhere without it. I lost track of the number of stairs we climbed until Fyn stopped outside an entrance to one of the homes.

Fyn pressed the wooden door open. Cora lounged on cushions in the corner. The sun illuminated her red hair as she sipped her tea.

"I'll be back for you later. Cora, Lioran has specifically requested you do not exhaust her." He smirked.

Cora let out a little snort but didn't promise not to. Fyn slid out the door, leaving the two of us alone together.

"What if I can't control it?" I blurted. My nerves were ripping through me.

"You will figure it out—you've only just discovered it." She set the teacup down on a small table. "Would you like some?"

"No, thank you."

"Lioran said you made flowers sprout and bloom in Evyn. Can you try to use magic on this flower?" Cora removed a tightly furled bloom from the vase on the table. "Ask it to open up."

I recalled the blooms in my mother's garden, the flowers in Evyn and wished the bud would open—nothing happened. I tilted the stem of the yellow rose, my fingers gliding over the severed edge. Everything that responded to me—the flowers, the land, were all still connected.

"This flower is no longer a part of the land. It was cut to fill your vase," I said.

"Let's go outside then." Cora led me through the trails further into the Heart of Lythira.

I didn't know if I would be able to make anything happen at all.

"Try again." She gestured to another yellow rose; its roots still embedded in the soil at the bottom of the stairs. I knelt beside the bloom, and with my hands cupped around it, I asked it to bloom. Silence greeted me.

Cora's face was guarded.

She pointed to a different bloom and grazed her hand across it. "Magic doesn't always work the first time we ask."

The ground rumbled, fire pulsed through my veins into my fingertips—then it all disappeared. My thoughts returned to Evyn and the small patch of land I almost destroyed.

Cora tilted her head as she monitored me.

"Give yourself grace." She crouched beside me, and her voice grew softer. "The journey is not always direct. There may be times when you can't feel it at all."

"Do you even know what it's like? To be thrust into a different world and not know what any of it means?" I shook my head, sending my waves tumbling around my face.

"I used to have glances of visions of the future—fragmented bits that left out major parts of the story. I would tell my father to be helpful, but I would miss the details that mattered most." Cora clasped her hands together. "I worried no one would ever believe me. My father gave me grace when I didn't give it to myself. And now, I will give you grace when you wont give it to yourself, Aelira."

My shoulders bobbed. "I don't know how to show myself grace. The King of Bailoc..." As I spoke, I remembered glimmers of his gentle spirit when he spoke to Ashlyn. He beamed with pride whenever he looked at Agan. He never granted me those moments. "Never wanted me there."

"Let's take a break." Cora's hand wrapped around mine. She tugged, lifting me to stand beside her. "Maybe we can go get a cup of tea."

In silence, we strode down the crooked stones that lined the path along the water's edge. Across a thin bridge there was a sliver of land, and on it stood a willow tree. Without hesitation, I split from her and followed the bridge to the tree—it reminded me so much of my mother. It reminded me of home.

The willow's branches danced on the wind. I lifted my hand to catch a branch as it grazed my shoulder. The onyx grew warmer.

My fingers trailed the willow's leaves until golden light trailed the veins. The branches extended, shifting my hand with them. I knelt beside the tree, the cool soil settled beneath my fingertips.

A hum radiated from it, cascading through my body in gentle vibrations. Green stems sprouted from the soil, raising my hands from the ground—shimmering light trailed with it. The light glimmered in the sunlight a haze of gold shifting to shimmering white as the sun's beams shone on it.

Perfume wafted toward me. Petals unfurled, tickling my palms as the vibrations of the land rolled through me. A rainbow of color bloomed. My nose wrinkled as the smell of each combined. It was overpowering and messy.

The display felt like me.

"Lioran was right." Cora ran her palm over the tips of the new blooms.

I grew tired and leaned back into the tree.

"My magic is like his." I spoke the words, not even sure what they meant.

"He told you then—I wasn't sure if he would." She hesitated, still trailing the flowers beneath her fingertips. "Magic is a blessing from the stars—it's a rare thing for the stars to gift such a gift twice. Before we met you, it was assumed Lioran was the only one with the power to restore. Time will show how yours manifests. You both have grounding magic, but you are not the same."

A pale pink peony sprouted near the roses; I broke it free. Sunlight cascaded over it, detailing every vein in the petals—so fresh and new. The stem slid easily into my hair, behind my ears.

Fyn eyed the blooms at the base of the willow as he stepped closer, his gaze then shifted to Cora's. She silently nodded toward him.

"Get some rest. You're bound to be tired after today." Her palm rested on my shoulder. That moment was so small to her, but it meant everything to me. To be seen for who I am. To not just be the Princess of Bailoc.

"Lioran would like to see you, if you're not too exhausted... and if you are, that's probably fine, too, because he sleeps most of the time anyways." Fyn gestured ahead. His green eyes caught mine, assessing me. Cora proceeded down the path in the opposite direction.

"I would like to see him," I said.

His boots scraped over the stone path that led back to the castle. "You two...have been seeing a lot of each other."

Heat rose in my cheeks. I studied the uneven stone path. The blades of grass as they moved in the wind.

"He has nothing to do in the infirmary. He's bored." I pulled at the neckline of my tunic as it slipped past my shoulder. "It helps him pass the time."

"You're there every day. Even I don't go there every day and we work together."

"Where else would I be?"

"Oh, I see. So, you're bored, too."

I stopped in the path in front him. "What exactly is it you do around here? Just hover and make sure I stay out of trouble?" His smirk faded.

"I oversee trade and logistics. It's my duty to keep Lythira running." He paused as we approached the thick oak castle doors. "But lately, being your personal guard also seems to be my responsibility."

I hadn't thought to ask, but now that I had, I knew why he was opposed to bringing me here. There were so many moments we fought together to keep Lioran alive, to bring him home. Somewhere along the way, he grew to respect me.

"Thank you," I said.

"For what?"

There were so many thoughts swirling through my mind, but I only said one. "For protecting me." He silently nodded, and for a moment, there were no jabs, only a quiet understanding.

He motioned forward. "We shouldn't keep him bored and waiting."

"You're going to stay and visit with him?" I bit my tongue. As the twinge of pain settled, I realized I didn't want him to.

He pushed the door open, but no guard greeted us on the other side. Guards were very rarely seen roaming the castle halls. "No, Your Highness," he whispered. "My presence would only be a disappointment."

I ignored his words. I knew he reveled in moments when I looked annoyed.

"It's most amusing really," he said.

"What is?"

"How you don't notice the way you are around him."

I stopped, frozen with his words. He was only just being Fyn. He was only testing me.

Fyn paused outside the infirmary. "Or maybe you do."

"I don't know what you're talking about." I squared my shoulders back.

He pushed the infirmary door open. I forced a laugh as my chest tightened. It was the only thing I could do to keep from breaking in front of Lioran. His eyes avoided mine as I entered. When he looked up, he only looked at Fyn.

Lioran pushed scrolls aside in his lap.

"You're supposed to be resting, not working." Fyn lifted the scrolls from Lioran's bed.

"I need something to occupy me, and the work won't wait."

"I already told you; we're handling everything just fine. I brought your favorite half-fae to occupy you." I tapped my elbow into Fyn's rib cage harder than I intended. He grunted.

Lioran's eyes narrowed. "I hope you're not taunting her, Fyn."

"I would never," Fyn said as he slid back out the door.

"Sorry he..." Lioran finally looked at me again, but it was different than he had before.

"Can't help himself," I cut him off, assessing his glow that had slowly returned overnight. "You look much better."

"You mean I don't look awful anymore?" He winced as he laughed, but my smile faded. Visions of crimson on my hands, all over him etched further into my mind. "Aelira? I was joking."

"I..." My words caught in my throat. "I thought I was going to lose you."

He gestured at the chair beside his bed, now in its permanent spot for me to visit. "I'm right here...with you."

The chair embraced me, as exhaustion took over.

"How was training?" He traced the flower tucked behind my ear. I freed it from my hair and held it out to him.

His hand curled around the stem. "You made this flower bloom?"

"And several others."

"I've never made a flower bloom." He rotated the stem, watching the petals carefully. "What is it?"

"A peony." Each petal was so fragile. "And I've never summoned a sylkren...not that I'd want to."

"I don't exactly call them." He placed the flower back in my palm. "When you arrived, I couldn't even command it. You were so afraid. I wanted to stop it, but I couldn't."

"So, you really didn't want it to destroy me then?"

"You know I didn't. If I didn't care, I wouldn't have interfered at all. When the riders came for you, when I was injured... I called to the creatures of the land to come to our aide, because I knew I could no longer fight them off myself."

"And the sylkren responded...like Veylar."

"Veylar trusts me. The creatures in our world are not always as easily persuaded."

"When you're better...can you show me how to try and call an animal?"

He pointed to the window. "Open it."

"You need your rest."

He studied me as if he was considering whether he'd listen. Lioran settled back against the pillow and extended his hand. "Open the window."

My fingers caught on the latch, and I pried it free. The window released from its frame with a loud click. His hand twitched as his eyes closed. A cool breeze jostled his hair.

He winced as sparkling light collected at his fingertips. A dull groan escaped his lips. Her song sounded before she came. A pale-yellow bird, plump and tiny, landed on the windowsill.

"Put your hand out for her," he whispered.

With his command, I extended my hand toward the window. She stepped into my palm. Her little feet pinched as she nestled into my hand.

"She's beautiful," I whispered.

"Almost as beautiful..." he started to speak but groaned as he adjusted himself in the bed. I waited, wanting to hear the words he would have said, but silence hung between us.

I reached for him, and the little bird flew off, back out the window. "You're too drained. You could have waited."

"Maybe...but the look on your face was worth it."

"Someday you can show me more, but until then, please rest." I slid my hand over his without thought. My heart fluttered faster—warning me to move, but I couldn't.

The silver in his eyes flickered again, filling me with warmth in a way I had never felt before.

I blinked the feeling away, too drained to think on it any further.

When he fell asleep, I crept out of the room to my chambers. The elegance of the room rivaled mine back in Bailoc. Open windows gave views of the streams and the lanterns illuminating the water.

The onyx shimmered in the moon's glow. I traced the book's uneven pages. It vibrated beneath my fingertips.

I nestled myself into the thick bed covers and unbound the amber strap. Silence fell, and I didn't know what to ask it.

I sense your magic.

Lythira needs you—you will serve it well.

A lump formed in my throat as I pressed the pages closed. It said *I sense your magic.* The book wasn't just a magical force, its words were being written by someone. I did not know who, or what, I was communicating with. What if everything it made me do was wrong?

Tears spilled faster than I could stop them. I concentrated my thoughts back on the book, opening it again.

"Who am I speaking with?" It remained blank for a heartbeat.

In time, you will come to know what inspired the words on these pages.

It's time you focus on who you are, Aelira.

The book slipped from my fingertips as I sank further back into the covers. The onyx poked into my palm as I gripped it too tightly. Its unknown magic haunted me long after the words disappeared from the page.

I may never know the source of its magic, but I now felt mine steadily flowing through my veins—it had awoken.

There was no hiding from it.

CHAPTER 13

My palm pressed into the wooden infirmary door.

"Aelira," Lioran called from behind me.

"What are you doing out of the infirmary?" I spun to face him.

His body towered over mine again. Warmth surged through me as his gaze met mine.

"Oh...He's simply defying what's recommended as always." Fyn stood beside him. "He's just been standing here waiting for..." Fyn smirked. "Who were you waiting for?"

Lioran wouldn't even look at Fyn. "I didn't expect to see you."

"You should be resting," I said.

"Fae heal faster than humans." Lioran crossed his arms over his chest, wincing.

"Rowena's healing magic may have had something to do with it. Or maybe the fact that we dragged your lifeless body back here. But sure...go with the fae heal fast explanation."

"I owe the three of you my gratitude." Lioran's tone softened.

"True." Fyn leaned back into the stone wall. "Rowena did say you're supposed to rest, though. So maybe you should go do that now."

"I said I would." Lioran winced as he shifted his body weight.

"What you told her you'd do and what you're planning to do are two different things." Fyn rolled his eyes. "I've known you too long."

Their banter brought warmth back to the chilled corridor.

"I was just going to check on you before training with Cora," I said.

"Oh? Let me walk you." Lioran stood tall, but his breathing was uneven.

"You will not walk her." Fyn slid in between us. "I will walk her. You will go sit somewhere and read some boring prince paperwork, or whatever it is you do around here."

Lioran laughed through gritted teeth. "Fine. You walk her." He leaned back into the wall. "I will see you both later." He braced his body against the wall, his face growing paler.

"Are you okay?" I reached for his arm to brace him but drew my hand back to my side.

"Your Highness, it's good to see you up." A fae male as tall as Lioran with silver-streaked hair approached him before he could answer me.

"What news do you have of the borders, Lord Elric?" Lioran's tone shifted.

"Borders are all secure," Lord Elric responded.

"No signs of the riders crossing into the Heart?" Lioran's eyes narrowed.

"No. My men and I rode out on your return and have not spotted them anywhere." Lord Elric shifted slightly until he faced me. "You must be Lady Aelira." Lord Elric raised an eyebrow.

He took my hand and planted a kiss on it as his gaze lingered. I shuddered with his touch. Thalen was the only one to ever kiss my hand like that.

"Who knew a disturbance would be so beautiful?" His tone grew so soft I struggled to make out his words.

He knew I crossed the divide. Lioran must have trusted him —he sent him searching for our attackers in the woods. Had he told him who I was?

Lioran's jaw clenched. "Thank you, Lord Elric. We will discuss the plan in greater detail later."

"Until then, Your Highness." Lord Elric nodded, bowing to Lioran before he left us.

My gaze trailed him until we turned the corner.

"Is he always this stubborn?" I asked Fyn.

"Always." He smirked. "It's surprising he stayed in bed as long as he did, or maybe it isn't, since you've been visiting him every single day."

I stopped in front of him, my voice lowered. "You're not going to give this up, are you?"

"Give up what?"

"Whatever you think is happening—it's not," I scolded him.

"If you insist." He raised his hands up.

My breath caught as I inhaled, a hollow pain responded in my chest. He couldn't. He didn't feel that way. I didn't feel that way.

"You're wrong, Fyn. About all of it."

"Aelira..."

"I'll go the rest of the way on my own." I stepped ahead of him.

"Lioran wouldn't forgive me if I just left you out there to navigate the Heart on your own."

I shot him a cutting glare.

"I meant that in a completely non-romantic kind-of-way... just in a *he cares for your safety* kind-of-way."

My thoughts returned to Lioran, the way he towered over me again. The way his silver eyes met mine.

I breathed deeply. Fyn's words were getting to me, but I wouldn't let them.

The branches of the willow waved in the wind as we approached. Cora rested beneath it.

"Lioran is on the move," he warned her.

"And you needed to warn me why?" She laughed.

"Something tells me he won't be able to stay away." His eyes shifted from her to me. I glared in response.

"Ah, well, I won't hesitate to send him back to bed." Cora's hands wrapped around the branches, lifting them out of the way as they swung about. "Let's get to work."

Fyn disappeared over the tree trunk bridge.

Cora stumbled back. She collided with the willow quaking —a blurry haze formed over her eyes. I gripped her shoulder— steadying her.

"Cora?" I called to her, but she didn't respond. I pulled the blade of my dagger from my belt aiming it in front of us. "Cora?" My voice cracked.

My hand trembled, the sweat from my palms loosening my grip on the dagger.

Cora gasped loudly, struggling to inhale.

Fear laced her eyes as she examined my dagger.

"Put...that away," she scolded me.

The metal scraped against the leather, chewing it raw, as I slid it back into the sheath. "What happened?"

"I had a vision." Her voice quaked with each word she spoke.

I pressed my water flask into her hands. "You looked as if you saw something horrific."

She chugged the water. The flask violently shook in her grip. "Thank you."

"Do you want to talk about it?"

"No..." Her voice trailed off. "Let's get back to training." She dusted herself off as she stood. Her legs betrayed her, and she stumbled again.

"Maybe you should rest."

"We need to keep training until you can control it." She took a deep breath and rose again.

"Because of the vision?" I asked.

She gulped and pulled her hair back from her face. Silence greeted me as I awaited her answer—a chill rippled through me. She was breathless, shaken by a reality that she didn't want me to know.

"Forget the vision. Just focus on what I tell you." Her fingers twitched at her sides.

We spent the next hour listening to the ground, touching tree bark, and trailing plants with my magic glow. The ground remained still under my touch, but I felt it: the steady, familiar hum. The land was calling to me still.

The whisper of the wind, the roots of the tree—I could feel their energy moving through me. The steady heartbeat beneath the dirt reverberated through me, racing in time with my own. I traced the roots of the willow before I pressed them deeper into the soil.

A distinct vibration interrupted the melody, grounding me where I stood. Its calm washed over me—familiar and safe. My eyes remained shut. I feared breaking whatever bond I'd established.

Its pulse strengthened, trailing through my veins, winding around my heart, steady and sure.

I was eager to see what I had created, but when I opened my eyes, the land was still—it hadn't changed at all. But someone was standing in front of me—Lioran.

He studied my expression and held out a cautious hand. "I'm sorry. I didn't mean to startle you."

The vibration, the feeling—it wasn't the land at all.

I felt his presence like it was my own.

Cora's lips pursed.

"Aelira?" Lioran waited.

My throat grew dry, the words faltered as they trailed over my lips. "Sorry, I...I felt..."

"You felt what?"

"You." I knew the moment I said it that I shouldn't have.

Lioran's lips parted. "You felt me?"

My skin simmered with a rising heat. "I think so..." I didn't even know what it meant.

"Aelira..." He reached for me, but I stepped back.

"No. I'm just tired. Maybe I need to take a break." Sweat glistened over my palms. I tucked them inside the pockets of my tunic, to conceal everything I felt.

Cora nodded.

Their voices trailed further behind as I stepped onto the stone bridge until only the sound of the rippling stream greeted me.

Cora had moved around the tree, but I didn't feel her movement at all.

Only his.

Fyn's words replayed in my mind.

"I'm surprised to see you alone." The fae lord with the silver hair was standing inches from me. I hadn't even noticed him approach.

"I was enjoying a moment to myself. I'm sorry, my lord, I don't recall your name," I said.

"It's Lord Elric." He stepped closer. "It must be a little unnerving to be amongst the fae after growing up in the human realm. I hear Bailoc differs greatly from Nythrel."

Lioran must trust him. We had discussed how important it was to conceal my identity here, but he knew everything. "Yes, very different."

"If you ever need someone to show you around the Heart, I am happy to do so." Lord Elric watched me carefully as he spoke.

I crept backward until I collided with someone—warmth greeted me. Lioran let out a low groan. He folded his arms across his chest as his body pulled from mine.

"I will show her around." Lioran's tone was sharp.

"You should rest." Elric's gaze flickered with something unspoken. "My offer stands, my lady. If you find yourself in need of company."

"I will walk you back." Lioran pressed his hand lightly against my back as he stepped forward. His palm lingered as we stepped away.

I couldn't look at him.

The water trickled steadily down the stream alongside the path we followed back to the castle. The same energy whirled around me—his energy.

"He's right. You should rest," I said.

"Maybe, but I'm glad I was here to spare you. Elric always—"

"I can handle myself."

"I know you can." He grew quiet for a moment as his breathing labored. "What happened at the willow tree?"

My heart raced on—wild and untamed. "I'm not sure.

Everything is so new to me." I turned from him toward the stream.

"Whatever you're feeling...you can tell me." His voice grew softer.

"It was nothing."

It wasn't nothing. I felt something deep and unrelenting settle within me.

"It sounded like... something." He steadied his hands on his hips, his arms tensing with each breath.

"Please. Just forget what I said." I needed him to forget it— *I* needed to forget it.

"Forget that you felt me? I can't just forget that."

"I told you. I don't know what it was." I wanted to turn from him, to sever the hold he had on me.

Yet I stood there, staring back.

"You're right. You're probably exhausted." The sparkle in his eyes dulled. "Would you rather Fyn walks you back?"

I didn't know what it meant, but I knew I needed him to stop questioning me. "Yes."

He didn't look at me like that again.

The days passed in a haze of mist covered mornings full of training sessions with Cora. My identity remained concealed in the Heart.

Here I was known as Lady Aelira, a traveling visitor from Eyrsea—his brother Calyth's territory that lay to the west of the sea. For once, I was just like everyone else. All I had to do was hide my ears beneath my hair—to conceal the human part of me.

Lioran and I had barely spoken since the moment at the

willow tree. I found myself thinking only of him—the curve of his smile, the melodic sound of his laughter, the way he clenched his jaw whenever words were left unspoken.

"Would you like me to do your hair this morning?" Juniper asked as she peeked into my chambers. I had already dressed without her.

"No, I'll do it myself," I replied.

My messy strands resisted as my fingers combed them into a quick braid. They poked out unevenly, an unsightly mess that Reina would no doubt scoff at, but it didn't matter.

Here I was, just Aelira.

"His highness asked that I give you this." Juniper dug into her apron pocket and removed a slender piece of parchment for me. As I unfolded it, I read the unfamiliar uneven writing.

Meet me at the clearing near the stables. - Lioran

"Did he say when?" I asked.

"The prince is there now I believe, but he asked that you not be rushed." She looked me over, waiting for my response.

"I will make my way there," I replied.

"Do you need anything else my lady?" she asked after straightening the blanket that lay across my bed. I shook my head, and she slipped out the door just before I did.

Intricate stonework decorated the corridors—leaves etched in a random pattern down the hall. I traced the delicate pattern on the walls while breathing in the air that swept in through the open windows. The sweet smell lingered as my boots collided with each stone step.

The sun kissed my skin as I stepped out into the courtyard. It illuminated the stone path that severed unruly patches of grass. I followed it toward the stables, listening to the bird song that greeted me.

"Good morning, Aelira." Lioran leaned against the stable

wall. His melodic voice sang my name. He never stopped pronouncing it as the fae did, and I never asked him to.

Sunlight danced over the thatched roof, spilling over him.

"I have someone for you to meet. Wait here." He held his hand up in front of me before slipping into the stables.

A brown mare walked at his side when he emerged from the stables again. Flecks of gold shimmered in her eyes and off her dark mane. A slender white patch grazed her forehead.

He guided her slowly with the same gesture he used with Veylar.

The mare stared at me, as if she knew me—as if she had been waiting for me. My heart settled. I let my shoulders fall back as our gazes intertwined.

"Do you like her?" he asked.

"She's incredible." Guilt ran through as I thought of Briar. Cael would have seen her back safely, but I abandoned her. My fingers uncurled toward the mare, and she shifted away from me. Lioran held his steady stance, his gaze shifting between us. He didn't reach for her, or for me.

"Her name is Gaia."

I reached for her again, running my fingers down the bridge of her nose. "Hello, Gaia." She inched closer, and as her eyes connected with mine, she felt like home. I had never once shared a moment with Briar like this.

"She likes you," he whispered.

"Could I ride her sometime?" My eyes hadn't left Gaia's, but it wasn't just my bond with her that kept me from diverting my gaze. I didn't want to hold his.

"Well, that will be up to her, but it seems as if she's taking to you already, so I don't think she'll mind it."

"She must choose to?"

"The fae do not force a bond between horse and rider. We believe that when a proper match is made, both will feel it." He ran his fingers through her mane. "If the horse resists it, it isn't forced."

"You are lucky to have both her and Veylar." Jealousy tinged my words. This was his world. It wasn't mine. I was lucky to have the rooms he gave me, the clothes I wore. I stopped petting Gaia, and she nodded her head closer to my hand.

"Something about her reminds me of you." His lips curled upwards, and his gaze softened on me. "She is at ease with you. The two of you will get along nicely. She is yours to ride whenever you both wish."

He crossed his arms in front of me, his gaze didn't shift as my eyes focused on his.

"She's mine?"

"I want you to feel at home here—like you belong here." His words grew hushed until I almost didn't hear the rest.

The gemstone's heat surged through me. Gaia nuzzled my shoulder. When I touched her, there was a familiar rush, almost like when I made the flowers bloom, or the willow expand. Like she and I were one and the same.

"Thank you." A single tear slid down my cheek.

He placed her reins into my palm.

"Let's try to take her for a ride." His melodic voice was a low whisper in my ear.

With a silent command, Veylar left the stables and came straight to his side.

"You're still recovering. It might be too much for you," I said.

He smirked. "We'll soon find out."

"Please." I shook my head. "I can't stand the thought of you in pain again." I recoiled at my own words.

He only exhaled. "I'll be fine. I promise."

As I climbed up on the saddle, I caught sight of Lioran

holding his breath as he climbed onto Veylar. "See...I'm fine," he said as he finally exhaled.

He wasn't fine.

Gaia shifted beneath me as I settled in place. "I don't mind taking her out on my own."

She snorted as if she agreed with me.

"You already have her concerned about me, too." He chuckled.

"It seems she's a very sensible horse, but I'm guessing neither of us will talk you out of this."

"You have tried and failed." He smirked.

My brow furrowed.

"The way you look at me sometimes..." He smoothed his tunic as he let out another laugh. "You don't look at others like that."

I tried to relax the muscles in my face. "You haven't seen me around Fyn then," I retorted.

If anyone else enjoyed prodding at me, it was Fyn. There were so many faces I made at him too.

His smile faded, and without so much as a nod he took off. Gaia followed obediently without my command.

Even and rhythmic, her hooves struck the land beneath me. The wind blew against my cheeks—I was free. She raced alongside Veylar, their strides falling into a perfect rhythm.

Veylar came to a stop a while later and Gaia did, too. Sweat beaded at his brow as he climbed down from Veylar. His breathing was uneven as he placed his hand out for me. He winced as I took it.

"You're in pain. I shouldn't have—"

"You must think so little of me that you think I can't help a lady off her horse." He quickly unclenched the muscles in his face as if nothing happened.

"I am fully capable of climbing out of a saddle on my own." I was, but it wouldn't be graceful. I almost always had help.

I looked away the moment I noticed I had been staring for too long. So many words were left unspoken after I sensed him at the willow. I hadn't wanted to say anything about it at all.

"Lioran..."

"Yes?" He patted Veylar as he leaned against the tree. "You can let her go," he nodded toward Gaia, "she will stay close by." I ran my hand through her mane, before she walked off with Veylar.

"Thank you. Truly." My voice was soft. "It felt so freeing. To ride by myself again."

"She's yours. You may take her out when you like. I would be happy to ride with you."

I wanted that, but I was too afraid to say it.

"Or Fyn if you would prefer his company. You two are together often."

My laughter echoed across the meadow.

He only tilted his head.

"You're different around him." His words slowed.

"There are few bold enough to joke with me."

He folded his arms across his chest. "Where you come from...others don't joke with you?"

"No, but most are more reserved around me." Like he was. I felt his unease, watched the way he slowly tilted his head again as if he was carefully listening to each word I spoke.

"And you enjoy Fyn's humor?"

"It's a refreshing change."

"One that has enhanced your feelings for him?" He peered around me back at Veylar and Gaia. Both horses grazed freely. He didn't need to check their whereabouts. I had no doubt that Lioran could sense them even without looking at them.

"You think I have feelings for Fyn?" My lips parted, ready to say I didn't.

He was asking as if he cared if I did...as if it meant something if I did. I didn't know if it meant something to him, or if he was just curious. I wanted to ask why it mattered, but I stopped myself.

"Sometimes he leaves me feeling annoyed," I said.

A hint of the slightest smirk settled on his face.

"He is usually laughing at my expense or making jokes at the worst possible moment. In fact, when you were bleeding out, he only continued his commentary. You probably don't remember."

He mostly kept his stoic expression, but his lips tugged upward into a slow grin. "I won't tell him that you said that... yet."

"I have no doubt he already knows it."

"I remember his commentary...I also remember you. You were holding my hand." His gaze landed on me and I couldn't look away. "You kept me holding on. When I wasn't sure if I could any longer."

My cheeks flushed, burning with a fire I couldn't calm. "I was so scared..." I would never see him again.

He reached toward me, his fingers stopped inches from mine. "I hope neither of us face that again."

Something in me shifted—strange and new. Suddenly I was disappointed his hand fell from mine.

It wasn't possible.

It shouldn't be.

But when I looked up into his silver eyes, and he looked back into mine, my heart only raced faster.

He pushed up his sleeves, revealing the three band tattoos around his arm.

"What do they represent?" Without thinking, I traced the design.

"My three titles—Guardian of Lythira, Prince of Nythrel, and Heir to the Throne."

My fingers curled slowly into my palm.

"You're the future King of Nythrel?"

"Yes." He lowered his head for a moment before he continued.

I hadn't even considered he might be.

"What does the future King of Nythrel plan to do with the daughter of his enemy?" His expression hardened as I spoke. "You can tell me." There were so many things I wanted to say, but none of it mattered until I knew.

"I have offered you safe haven in my lands. The life you choose to make here is yours for as long as you wish to stay. I will protect you however I can."

His words were a whisper on the wind.

My heart thundered in my chest, but for a moment, I reveled in the peace his words brought. We both knew the truth that remained unspoken. My time here in Lythira, with him, would be fleeting.

CHAPTER 14

S ummoning my magic was impossible the next
morning. Lioran's gaze lingered on me, long after we
parted. My heart thundered—my chest tightened
with it.

"Focus. Open yourself up to your magic." Cora glared
at me.

A surge pulsed through me, but stilled before it ever met
my fingertips.

"I am," I snapped back at her.

"Don't lie to me." Cora's crossed her arms over her chest.
"You're distracted. You could at least tell me why."

Heat rose in my cheeks before spiraling into my chest. "You
chastising me isn't helping anything." I sprang to my feet,
stepping toward Cora.

"Fine then. We're done for today." Cora pulled her amber
hair from her face and tied it back with a thin leather strip.

"Can you two at least wait until I'm not present to argue?"
Fyn's humming faded as he walked closer to us.

"I would be happy to, but it seems she has other plans," Cora murmured under her breath.

"You and Lioran...you don't just share magic? You're in the same mood, too." Fyn rubbed his temples.

"What are you talking about, Fyn?" Cora raised an eyebrow at him.

"His glares rival hers. Had to leave the castle to get a break from him. He's just snapping over every little comment I make." His shoulders shrugged. "Normally everyone likes my commentary."

"Do they, Fyn?" I cast an icy glare at him.

"Well...most do." He leaned back into a nearby tree, rolling a twig between his fingers. "Thought you two would be up for a little humor and fun, but seems I'm wrong as usual."

"Everything is a joke to you, isn't it?" My tone was sharper than I intended.

Fyn dropped the twig.

"I'm sorry. There's a lot on my mind," I said.

"Thinking about your new horse?" He smirked.

My glare held as his lips pursed.

"He gave you a horse?" Cora looked intrigued.

"A pretty lavish gift if you ask me...but no one asked me," Fyn said.

I reached past Fyn, my hand running over the trunk of the tree he leaned against. The jagged bark snagged at my skin. The usual hum wasn't there. I couldn't feel its energy at all. Beneath his feet, brown tinged blades of grass encircled its twisted roots.

"Again?" Fyn placed his hands on the trunk. "Just fix it like the last time."

"I didn't cause it." My inhale caught in my chest. "I need to tell Lioran."

Fyn crouched beside me, his fingers trailing the lifeless

grass. "This is not really an ideal time to bring it up. I wasn't joking about the state he's in. Did something happen yesterday?"

"I was gifted a horse...but you already know that," I retorted.

"He needs to know," Cora said.

"Don't say I didn't warn you," Fyn groaned as he combed his hair back.

"Consider me warned. I will tell you all about it later." My fingers caught on the end of my braid.

"I wouldn't miss this. I'm coming with." Fyn chuckled. "It's bound to be amusing."

An amber candlelit glow illuminated the halls. Cora and Fyn led the way to Lioran's study. As we turned the corner, I heard a regal voice, deeper than Lioran's.

"You're late again. Your shipments were due weeks ago. We had a deal." The voice growled.

"The land is decaying faster than I can control. I have an entire territory that I need to feed." Lioran's voice boomed.

"Figure something out. Your people are farmers by trade. Kybar has deals riding on your missing crops, our market shelves are barren—fae won't just be hungry here. Soon it'll be everywhere. Will the future king let the other territories suffer while he only cares for his own?"

"Your territory makes the deals. Figure out how to leverage what I give you. Manage Kybar and I will manage Lythira. I have other more pressing matters to attend to," Lioran responded.

Tension rolled through me, locking my muscles.

"Maybe if you weren't so distracted with your special guest, you could focus on solving the problem."

"What are you talking about?" Lioran's voice faltered as he spoke, each word slower than the next.

"The Princess of Bailoc," the voice said. "The one that crossed into your territory recently."

"We should go." Fyn leaned in close, whispering in my ear, but I couldn't stop listening to their conversation—especially when it was about me.

"What makes you think she's here?" Lioran's voice fell flat.

"I don't think she's here—I know."

The voice trailed off for a moment. Fyn tugged on the flowing sleeve of my lilac gown.

"We're going..." Cora's hushed warning trailed to me. "Aelira..." I shook my head. "Fine, I'm going then." She began walking down the hall.

"Who are you dealing with, Pyrran?" Lioran's voice was a guttural growl.

Pyrran scoffed. "Judging by the look on your face—you already know. I hear she's extremely beautiful. Must be hard for you to resist her, brother." I tried to turn, but my muscles refused—and still, their voices echoed. "Have you told them yet, or were you just waiting for me to tell them?"

"She may help Lythira—help this entire realm." His words were cold and calculating.

My heart pumped frantically.

Was that all I was to him?

All this time I wondered what he felt for me—hoped to be something greater to him.

I wasn't.

I was just a solution.

A tear rolled down my cheek. I wiped it away, my sleeve tugging at my skin. Fury swelled within me as his words repeated in my mind. I exhaled, desperate to calm the storm, before I couldn't any longer.

Fyn's fingers curled around my wrist, pressing deeply. As I turned to leave, footsteps echoed behind us.

"Looks like you have company, brother." The voice echoed through the corridor and the hairs stood on my arms. Cora stopped at the end of hall. Fyn and I slowly pivoted towards them. "Aren't you going to introduce me?"

I recoiled under Lioran's glare—the air escaped my lungs. His brother pushed his longer, flowing raven locks over his shoulder, as his brow furrowed.

"I am Princess Aelira of Bailoc. It is a pleasure to meet you, Your Highness." The words tumbled off my lips effortlessly, as if I was standing in the grand hall at Bailoc.

"You're just as beautiful as I was told." Pyrran took my hand in his. His lips pressed against my knuckles—I inhaled, unable to exhale.

Lioran's jaw locked.

"Thank you, Your Highness." My formality vanished the moment I crossed the divide into Lythira, but I hadn't forgotten how to act like a princess.

"Lady Cora, it is a pleasure to see you again. I'm surprised to see them both here." A controlled smirk spread across Pyrran's lips.

My eyebrow raised.

"It's so hard to keep track of all of Lioran's love interests. The two of you are still together, right?" Pyrran asked Cora.

Silence fell in the corridor. I clutched the flowing fabric of my gown and twisted it.

They were together—no one told me. I glanced at Fyn. His lips were pressed firmly together. Fyn was never silent, until now.

"Oh...I hope I didn't say too much. It seems I've made the princess uncomfortable." Pyrran chuckled.

I smoothed my expression—my face would betray my every thought.

"Prince Pyrran, will you be staying with us?" Cora held her head elegantly high.

Anger flooded me. He averted his gaze from mine.

"I believe my visit will be brief this time. Lioran and I have business to attend to before I head to the High Court." Pyrran leaned in, towering over me.

"Prince Lioran. There is a matter I wish to speak with you about when you have a moment." My voice quaked.

"Certainly, let's discuss it." He nodded at me, before returning his attention to his brother. "I've had a room arranged for you. We will feast tonight and continue our conversation then. Lady Cora can show you the way."

Cora flinched at the mention of her name.

"I imagine you know your way around here well, Cora." Pyrran placed his hand out for Cora. She looked back at me as she placed her hand in his, before they disappeared from view.

"Fyn, keep an eye on them," Lioran commanded.

"Yes, Your Highness," Fyn murmured as he started after them.

The smell of oak and moss hovered inside his study. Candles flickered in the windowsills where ivy sprawled. Bookshelves curved with the edges of the room and rose all the way to the ceiling. Lioran gestured for me to sit. His nostrils were still flaring.

"I didn't know your brother was here." I gripped the back of the leather armchair, still seething at their words.

"It was an unwelcome surprise for us all." He braced his hand on the edge of a bookshelf. "What did you want to tell me?"

My fingers dug further into the stiff leather.

"I think the blight has reached the Heart. When we were in Othryl, the trees were lifeless." I traced my hands on the leather-bound books, inspecting them. Some written in another language and some in ours. "I usually sense something from trees when I touch them, almost like a hum, but when I touched one earlier, I felt nothing from it. I think the blight is here, too."

He drummed his fingers on his biceps as his chest heaved. The candlelight flickered highlighting the deep circles beneath his eyes.

"You're not surprised," I said.

"No." He lifted a glass of deep brown liquid from his desk and took a single sip. "I've felt it for some time. It's slowly shifting through the lands."

"You feel it, too?"

"I sense every bit of change in these lands that happens... like it's a part of me."

I had to touch something to fully sense it. But he just felt it.

"Why didn't you tell me?"

"The blight is *my* problem to deal with."

"You brought me here to fix it?"

"What could possibly make you think that?" he snapped as he set the glass back on his desk.

My breath caught. "I heard you tell Pyrran it's why I'm here."

"Eavesdropping?"

"It concerned me."

He scoffed. My heart stilled for a moment as the room fell silent.

"Politics and roles of royals here are not like yours. My brothers and I were assigned our territories—they are ours to manage. Lythira's responsible for agriculture—we provide food for the kingdom. Each year, the blight worsens, and I have less to give." He reached over for his drink again and took a sip, thrusting it harshly back down on the table. "If my territory fails... if I fail...then entire kingdom of Nythrel fails."

"Once you saw my magic you knew. You brought me here to save Lythira?" My voice strained.

Air held in my chest—I hoped he would tell me what I heard was wrong.

I thought he brought me here because he cared about me, but it was only for political convenience—for his kingdom's survival.

It was foolish to ever hope I'd mean more.

"Aelira..." Something in his eyes was pleading. "You and I both have magic that can restore the land. Maybe together we can save it." My eyes watered as he spoke the words I didn't want to hear.

He ran his fingers over a rolled-up map.

I wanted him to tell me he cared about me beyond my magic.

His silence was answer enough. I couldn't let it go.

My boots echoed in the circular study until I was standing before him. "I've been a political pawn long enough. I refuse to be yours. Take me back to the divide."

His head tilted as his breath grew hot on my skin as he stepped closer to me. My hand slid to his chest, pushing him back. I couldn't let him get closer.

His hand slid over mine, holding it in place on his chest "If you wish it, Your Highness." He gripped my hand tighter. "I will take you there. You were never my pawn to wield."

"We both know I will never belong here." My voice was so low it barely carried over the crackling fire.

He released my hand, but his touch still lingered.

"Why didn't you tell me that you and Cora were together?" I still couldn't believe I didn't know.

"We're not. Cora and I were once together, a long time ago. Pyrran mentions it every chance he gets." He sighed loudly. "Why do you even care?" His hand slid over his lips.

It should have made me feel better hearing they weren't together, but it didn't.

"I don't need an explanation," I said.

"You don't need an explanation...but you pry until you get one. When I ask you about it, you don't even answer me. How am I supposed to know what you're thinking?" Lioran inched closer again, removing the lingering space between us. "What do you want, Aelira?"

He wouldn't give me what I wanted.

"I want nothing...from you," I said through gritted teeth.

He shook his head. "Then leave."

He lingered beside me a moment longer, before returning to his desk.

"All of this was only ever about my magic. I thought you brought me here because you cared about me." I choked on my words. They were barely a whisper. I wasn't even sure he heard me.

It didn't matter anymore. I needed it not to matter.

If I stopped to think about it, I wasn't sure I would ever be able to come back from the pain that settled deep within me.

The chill of the metal handle grazed my palm as I opened the door.

He remained standing at his desk flipping through his papers. He wouldn't look up at me at all.

I welcomed the stir of noise that came through the hall.

CHAPTER 15

J uniper shimmied a celadon gown over my hips. A delicate leaf embroidery brushed against my skin as the bodice shifted into place. Sheer sleeves fell from my shoulders—my fingers wrapped around the bedpost.

I inhaled sharply as she pulled the corset tight. "You look beautiful, my lady." She offered a sweet smile as she finished my braid.

"Thank you," I whispered through ragged breath. The corset pinched my skin as I shifted.

I didn't want to go—wasn't sure if I could handle seeing him after our conversation earlier. With a sharp inhale, my eyes welled with tears.

"My lady? Are you alright?" she asked.

"I'm fine," I whispered, but a single tear escaped. It rolled down my cheek. Juniper pulled a cloth from her skirt pocket and handed it to me.

"Do you want to talk about it?" She fumbled with the clasp on my onyx. With one more click, it finally snapped back into place. I shook my head, talking about how I felt would only make it worse.

"You will be expected shortly in the great hall—but if you need time, you can take it. He won't send for you if you're a little late." She grabbed her cloak and left quietly out my chamber door.

He wouldn't send for me.

Not until he needed me.

Everything he did—giving me Gaia, pressing me about how I felt him at the willow. I thought maybe his feelings matched mine.

They didn't.

I thumbed the onyx, admiring its glimmer in the mirror, until finally the tears stopped. My gown caught on a loose wooden floorboard; I pried it free. Unraveled threads poked out of the hem. I exhaled.

I smoothed the hair at my part that led into my braid. Tonight, I would be exactly what they expected. Everything was riding on it. At any time Lioran, or Pyrran, could decide my fate in a way that couldn't be undone. I couldn't go back to Bailoc, not after I fled into Nythrel.

An enchanted tune lured me out of my chambers and toward the great hall. A grand staircase gave way to the ballroom below. Elric stood at the bottom. His silver hair glimmered as he smoothed his pristine sky-blue tunic. For a moment I relaxed in his gaze—grateful for a familiar face before I faced the ladies and lords of Lythira.

"My lady, you look like a dream." He extended his hand out to me. "May I walk you in?"

I hesitated for a moment. Facing the crowd alone felt impossible. Lioran would be in the center of it all. I didn't want to see him. My hand slid into Elric's, and he nodded, as if he didn't even notice my hesitation.

Massive, broad tree trunks braced the walls of the grand room—tree limbs and vines wrapped the walls framing an opening where the ceiling should have been. Cora stood to the side in a simple golden gown. The fabric hugged her curves—no corset held her in place.

Fyn surveyed the crowd beside her until he came across Elric and me.

My hand trembled in Elric's, but he held it steady. "Breathe," he whispered. I hadn't realized that for a second, I wasn't. My next inhale left my lungs throbbing.

No formal announcements were made, only whispers in a grand ballroom aglow from candlelight and the glittering sky.

"You have nothing but my admiration, Aelira." I stiffened at his words. What would make him admire me at all?

The crowd parted. Lioran and Pyrran were standing side by side. Their silk tunics gleamed, perfectly pressed—Lioran in emerald and Pyrran in scarlet red. Lioran looked at my hand, still in Elric's grasp.

My breath hitched. "Thank you."

"It is an honor, my lady." The chill of his lips pressed my knuckles. Elric's attention shifted to Lioran, and I dropped my hand from his.

"Lord Elric, it is good to see you." A fae lord approached, and I slipped away back toward Fyn and Cora.

"Well, I must say I'm surprised." Fyn fumbled over the silk fabric as he attempted to cuff his sleeves. Cora grabbed him by the arm, she rolled the fabric without thought—until his cuffs were both even. "I am almost never incorrect about these things, but here you are...trying to prove me wrong."

"Fyn..." Cora's gaze held on my tear-stained cheeks too long. "Aelira can make her own choices."

"I didn't want to enter by myself," I said.

Fyn grinned. "Oh, so I wasn't wrong."

"I need you to stop." I recoiled from them both.

"I don't know what the two of you are going on about," Cora's hand rested on my shoulder. "But surely Fyn, you can give her a moment of peace."

He only nodded.

My gaze met with Lioran's from across the room. He held it for only a moment, before turning to speak with his brother.

Starlight and the moon's glow cast light onto the intricate stone floor through the opening in the ceiling. As the musicians lifted their instruments, fae ladies and lords collected in the center of the room.

"A dance, my lady?" Elric returned to my side, his hand extended. I tensed at his request. "It may calm your nerves."

"Aelira." Lioran's jaw hardened as he stepped in front of us. "You look stunning."

"Thank you, Your Highness." I curtsied toward him as Elric's voice eased the silence.

"Please excuse us, Your Highness. Lady Aelira and I were just about to dance," Elric said sharply.

"You were?" Lioran gripped his biceps as his gaze hardened on mine. He didn't interject. He said nothing at all.

"We were." I slipped my hand into Elric's. Lioran nodded without another word.

The fae felt the music—there was no formality in their dance, only the freedom. I tried my best to move in unison with the music, to bring myself back to the moment.

My thoughts remained with Lioran as I waited to see who he would dance with. He lifted his wine goblet to his lips, his eyes peering over it at me.

"We are much alike." Elric's grating voice brought me back. His blue eyes fixated on mine and the hairs on my arms rose.

"How are we alike, my lord?"

"Lythira isn't my home, either. I was sent here by the High

Court to help the Prince as he attempts to restore his lands."
With the next beat he stepped closer, his hand slid down to my
waist.

I wanted to pull away—to free myself from him, but it
wouldn't be worth the scene it would cause.

"Do you work for the high court, or for Prince Lioran?" I
searched for Lioran as the crowd turned around me, but he had
vanished.

"I serve the greater good of our people and the kingdom of
Nythrel. My assignment in Lythira is only temporary." His
hand held steady on my waist, pressing the corset into me
further. "May I offer a piece of advice?" I nodded.

He cast a glance in Cora and Fyn's direction. "Who you ally
yourself with will be extremely important." A knowing smirk
crept across his face.

His words were so familiar—my stomach curdled as they
echoed.

Thalen said something similar to me.

Elric bowed to me as the final note was strummed. I
lowered into a shallow curtsy as everyone parted from the
dance floor. He couldn't have known. They were only words. It
was only a phrase.

Cora reached for me as I pushed past her. I didn't turn
back.

My feet trailed the steps, pushing me out into the open.
The crisp night air swirled around me, but my ragged inhale
caught.

"Aelira." Lioran chased behind me. "You left abruptly. Are
you okay?" He motioned to a stone bench for me to take a seat.

Suddenly he cared—suddenly, he wanted to say
something.

"I needed...air." Elric's gaze felt like it still had a hold on me
even as I slipped away.

"Did Lord Elric say something to upset you?"

"No," I lied.

He sat beside me on the bench. My breathing slowed to match his, and his hand slid over mine.

"I'm sorry about earlier," he said, his shoulders rounded. "Pyrran has a way of unraveling me. And the blight...it's haunting me in every waking hour of the day. The pulse of Lythira is slowing." My lungs caught a sharp inhale. "It's dying. And I can't save it."

I had to touch the trees, where it existed, to feel it. But here he was telling me he felt it always.

"You feel it? All the time?"

"Every breath I take, every waking moment—I feel it."

I saw the pain behind his eyes and wanted to reach for him —to take his hand in mine, but I couldn't.

"Why didn't you tell me?"

"You don't carry it like I do."

"How do you know what I carry? You're not the only one that carries this burden." I pulled back from him. "It doesn't hover over me, like it does you, but I hear when the land cries, when it falls silent."

"That's not what I meant." He shook his head.

"Earlier, you were trying to deal with all this weighing on you? When I walked into your study...I thought—"

"I don't just care about your magic." A loose strand of hair hung over my eyes, but I couldn't break the hold his gaze had on me. He brushed it away. "I care about you...immensely."

My breath stilled in his grasp. "Lioran..." I almost told him everything, but instead I swallowed hard, tucking the truth deep inside of me. It would linger under the surface, unspoken.

He leaned in closer to me. "There's something I need to tell you. Something I should have told you earlier."

"You won't mind if I steal my brother, Princess." Pyrran

interrupted Lioran—I needed to know what he needed to say. "It seems my visit was appropriately timed," Pyrran continued.

Lioran sprung up, he hovered in front of me—like a shield between me and Pyrran.

"It is amusing, really. She's even dressed like she's yours—the green, the regal gown," Pyrran scoffed as his hands settled on his hips.

Juniper said he requested I wear it. It wasn't like what Cora wore. Did he think this was what I wanted?

Pyrran took a step forward and a menacing smirk crept across his face as he assessed me. My thoughts had betrayed me, again—the truth written all over my face. Delight flickered in Pyrran's eyes as if he were savoring this moment.

I rose to stand beside Lioran.

"That's enough, Pyrran." He growled as he spoke. "Don't drag her into this. Your qualms are with me."

"You and the Princess of Bailoc..." His laughter boomed. "It's too good to keep to myself."

"I can assure you, none of this is what you think." My voice held steady. I didn't know if there was truth in my words.

"How intriguing." He glanced down, towering over me. "Lioran, a word alone."

My nails bit at my palm. He would use whatever he thought this was against him—against me.

"Oh, Aelira...Save a dance for me later. My brother can't be the one having fun with you tonight." Pyrran's voice trailed behind me, and I froze for a moment.

"Touch her, Pyrran, and I will—"

"I think whatever you're implying is best left unsaid," Pyrran scoffed.

Lioran's hand curled into a fist. "Don't test me, Pyrran. If you lay a single finger on her, I will break it."

I didn't stay to hear the rest. Pyrran wouldn't have another moment near me.

Stepping back into the great hall reminded me I was an outsider in their world. Heads turned; whispers mixed with the lulling violin. I couldn't hear their words, but the concerned stares gave me enough to imagine the rest.

My gown dragged across the stone floor.

"Aelira?" Cora reached for my hand as I passed her and Fyn. "Please tell me what's wrong." Her hand squeezed mine.

There was nothing I could say. Each moment with Elric, Pyrran, and Lioran left me feeling haunted. No one here could understand the pain I felt.

If Ashlyn was here, we'd escape to my chambers. I'd cry, she'd make me laugh, and the sun would rise before we ever made it to bed. My chest ached. I had traded that world for this. Ashlyn was too far to reach, and if I ever saw her again, she wouldn't want me there. I wasn't her sister anymore—I was fae, or half of one.

My hopes were bound tightly by the words Lioran could have said, but he hadn't said them at all. "I..."

Fyn slid between me and the rest of the room, shielding me as the tears pooled.

I gripped at the fabric of the gown, a desperate yank at the fabric as it suffocated me. Too many thoughts flooded my mind. I had to get free. "I'm going to my chambers. Goodnight."

"I can walk you back," Fyn said.

I shook my head. "Thank you, but I just want to be alone."

The bustling noise from the feast faded with every step I took.

The door slammed behind me as I tore at the corset laces free. The gown fell to the floor. I was free—the weight of it was gone.

Silky, white fabric slipped over my head. It fell around me. I laid down on the bed, but my thoughts remained with Lioran. The door remained still. No one knocked. The handle didn't turn.

He almost said something that felt real. Pyrran made sure he didn't.

Their world was so different. Maybe the fae were freer with how they interacted. Touch might not mean what it did in Bailoc. The way we were together would have never existed in my kingdom.

Maybe it meant nothing to him. Tears pooled on the fabric of my night gown.

It meant everything to me.

Lanterns flickered on the river, their golden light lulling me into stillness. My hands hid my tear-streaked cheeks. I sat with the silence for a moment, letting every feeling wash over me.

Then I reached for the little leather book—it had been too long since I read its pages. There were times I felt I didn't need to be guided, but tonight, I needed its wisdom. The weathered parchment pressed open easily.

Trust yourself.

I growled, thrusting it down on the bed—the words faded.

"I can't go after something that may hurt me. I don't belong with..." I couldn't say his name. Just thinking of him caused another surge of pain to shift through my chest.

Ink raced across the page again, curving as it formed each letter.

This isn't about him.

It's your story.

Your path.

You worry you can't belong amongst the fae.

"What if it breaks me? What if staying here...trying to fit into this place is a mistake?"

157

All the strength and magic to stand on your own is there within you.

No one can take that from you.

"Everyone has always seen me as less than what I am. King Ardyn couldn't love me, Agan couldn't bring himself to understand me...Because maybe they both knew what I was."

It is their loss to never know your strength.

Do not carry that with you here—release it.

My fae heritage revealed a side of me too raw for me to accept. Everyday felt like I was pretending to be something I wasn't—pretending I fit in when I didn't. Pretending Lioran could have feelings for me, when maybe the truth was, he didn't.

Fear hovered over me; it controlled my thoughts—controlled every word I said. A part of me was still the hurt little girl, looking up at her father, begging for love he could never give.

I was her still—always looking for someone to approve of me.

That life, that hurt, lingered even after I left it. Maybe it always would. I never sat with it, never truly felt it until now.

If I continued to live in that story, it would break me.

It was time to change it all—to rewrite it.

To breathe, to run—to embrace everything that made me, me.

If Lioran couldn't see it, or Fyn, or Cora...then I would accept it.

At least I would see me.

CHAPTER 16

A golden sliver of sunlight gleamed on the horizon. Gaia whinnied as I gripped her saddle. My hand settled in her silky mane. He wouldn't want me out here alone, but this morning I slipped out unnoticed.

Gaia's hooves pelted the ground as I commanded her—we darted down the path toward the forest edge.

Pyrran enjoyed taunting Lioran too much. If their parents didn't know I was here already, Pyrran would be sure to tell them.

Gaia slowed to a stop—her ears bent backward.

A chill rushed through my veins. The land was quiet, but I felt its ache course through me.

My eyes scanned the edge of the forest, until I saw it. Cracks etched into the bark of an old oak tree. Pigment drained from its limbs. Its leaves had fallen. Not from a change in the weather, but something more desperate.

I dismounted.

As I gripped the bark a solemn hum crescendoed, slicing

through the silence. Moisture leached from my palm into the tree.

Magic slipped from my fingertips. Its light circled the tree. As I gave, my body grew weaker—my grip slipping with it.

Then I felt it—the same steady energy I felt at the willow. I couldn't see Lioran, but his magic called to mine. It strengthened mine.

He ran up behind me and placed his hands around the oak, around my hands. Our golden light wove together—it encompassed the tree.

The cracks shifted beneath our touch until no trace of them remained. A simmer of heat flickered through the onyx.

He struggled to catch his breath. "You shouldn't be here alone."

"How did you know where to find me?"

"I felt you—I felt your magic and knew you needed me." His eyes darted around the perimeter of the clearing.

"How is that possible?" I clutched onto the tree still.

"You sensed me at the willow tree, like I've been sensing you." His dark curls tumbled down as he leaned toward me—his chest heaved, still breathless.

A steady pulse wrapped around me, his calm grounding me.

"Before you crossed the divide...it felt like you were calling me. I went there. I searched for you."

Air struck my lungs too quickly. Lord Joran mentioned a disturbance at the divide before I crossed it. Was it him?

"When you finally did. Something shifted in me."

"That's why you were there? How you found me?" I asked.

He only nodded.

I never stopped to wonder how he got to me so quickly. But now I knew. He chose to be there—to wait for me.

Lioran winced as he leaned closer. I thought he had healed,

but now I saw it—his composure was cracking. Even as he unraveled, he fought to keep himself together. "Ever since I've laid eyes on you...you've driven me absolutely mad—"

"You came here to tell me you can't stand me?" I pushed past him, but he grabbed my wrist. As he pulled me closer, his silver gaze searched for everything I wouldn't say.

"I came here to tell you what I should have told you sooner. Ever since I found you...I can barely sleep, barely think...the need to be near you is consuming me."

"Lioran...I..."

"You are my rose blooming among the decay. I lost hope, but you gave me a glimmer of light."

A single tear grazed my cheek.

"I tried to keep it to myself, but I can't any longer."

I shoved down every feeling I had for him. Denied it all even as Fyn prodded me. It terrified me that I could want someone as much as I wanted him. That I could give my heart and trust it wouldn't break. I was so afraid it would that I couldn't see how he felt.

He released his hold on me. "Aelira..." His hands brushed my cheek, wiping my tears away. "If you don't feel the way that I do, I will give you whatever space you require and never speak of it again."

The tears fell faster. Every word I could have uttered remained unsaid.

He saw me—he truly saw me.

"I need to know. Not knowing is destroying me." Desperation etched into every line of his face. "Tell me anything—tell me you don't feel the same." His jaw hardened.

"I can't tell you that...because it would be a lie. I was so broken in Bailoc, but here with you, I feel like me again."

"I love you, Aelira. Entirely."

He looked at me—as if I meant everything. I couldn't

speak. His lips collided with mine, and everything inside me strengthened. I gripped his arms and sank into his kiss, into him.

"And you said none of this was what I think it is." Pyrran clutched the trunk of a nearby tree. "Making a human believe you love her, that you could ever love her. It's pathetic, even for you."

Anger swelled within me. I looked to Lioran. His eyes pleaded with mine before he turned toward Pyrran.

"Enough," Lioran growled as he stepped in front of me.

A chill nipped at my neck through the gemstone. I felt my magic tumble—I breathed through it. My eyes welled, but I wouldn't let the tears fall.

"I will send regards from both of you to our parents when I make it to the High Court." Pyrran paced as he spoke, yet his words were calm and collected. "They'll be most shocked to hear that the future king has forgotten his duty already."

All the remaining air was knocked from my lungs. My fate hung in his hands.

Pyrran shook his head and then glared at me. "Lord Thalen sends his regards, Princess Aelira. He's most eager to see you again. He hasn't forgotten what he's owed. I'm sure you'll oblige him."

My stomach lurched. He knew I was here before he arrived. Thalen made sure of it. He wouldn't give up his claim to me— and now, Lioran would know it, too.

Pyrran smirked.

"Take your leave of Lythira. Now," Lioran commanded.

"Gladly. Things were getting a bit too predictable on this side of Nythrel, anyway. I'm sure I'll see you both again very soon. Enjoy your fun while it lasts." Pyrran shrugged, leaving us in an unsettling silence.

Orange embers sizzled in the fireplace as Lioran paced his study. Firelight flickered in his eyes.

After everything Pyrran said, I didn't know what to believe —or what to think. His brother didn't think I was worthy of Lioran's love, or that he would ever give it. I carefully studied Lioran as he clasped his hands behind his neck.

"What is Thalen owed?" He suddenly snapped.

I shriveled back, sinking deeper into the couch.

"What do you owe him, Aelira?" The lines around his eyes deepened.

I eyed the door—wanting to flee. "Me."

"You?" He shook his head. "How? You said you barely knew him. I heard you tell Fyn."

My voice cracked. "I left Bailoc on our wedding day."

"You're his?" His jaw locked tight.

I allowed myself to forget. The pact still stood. "I had only met him days before. King Ardyn and Lord Thalen made a pact. A trade."

"What kind of trade?" The lines softened around his eyes.

"Me... in exchange for the crops we couldn't grow." My eyes watered as I spoke.

His head lowered.

"Tell me you didn't marry him before you left. Tell me that you're not bonded with him."

"No, I left before the ceremony ever began."

"Thank the stars." A flicker of relief shone in his eyes as his jaw relaxed, but he glared at me still. "When were you going to tell me?"

"I don't know. I didn't want you to know." The air grew

thicker around me. "I knew I wouldn't be able to handle the way you're looking at me now."

"He sent those men after you, because he wants his bride back."

"I'm not his."

"The pact was made. You are his by law in your realm. Are you not?"

"I'm not *his*." I hissed as I ground my teeth together. "He hasn't even come for me."

"No. He did something much worse—he sent Pyrran after us instead."

"Why would he send Pyrran?" I was almost too afraid to ask.

He drummed his fingers on the chair. "He's a hunter."

I pictured the falcon on his glove, recalled his words. Remembered the way he watched his bird—how he watched me.

"He stalks, he waits...he assesses how to make someone break. It isn't strategic. It's his magic. He uses it to hunt humans and fae like..."

"Prey." I was his prize. He was waiting. A knot folded within me, tense and tight. I pulled my hair off my shoulders as my skin grew hotter. Thalen wouldn't give up. Not now. Maybe not ever.

"Thalen took the Vale, Aelira...He made himself Lord of it. He finds a way to get whatever he wants."

"Pyrran didn't do anything to help him get to me," I said.

"Didn't he?" Lioran's eyes widened. "He said that you were nothing to me."

"They're just words." I didn't want to hear anymore. Those words gnawed at me still.

"And if that wasn't enough, he made sure you knew that Thalen was waiting for you. He made sure that you'd tell me.

So if his words didn't threaten you enough, the pact would threaten me."

Thalen and Pyrran weren't the only threat.

"Your parents wouldn't want me to be with you, because we're supposed to be enemies." The words cracked in my throat.

"It's more than that." His eyes finally met mine and his shoulders slumped forward. "You're part-human."

"And human isn't good enough?"

"We could never be bonded. It wouldn't be accepted."

I had never heard the phrase *bonded* before, but the way he said it invoked so much power.

"What does it mean to be...bonded?" I asked.

"Bonding is a union of love and commitment that is sealed with magic—It's sacred for the fae. It can only be undone by death. In the human realm, you call it marriage."

I had only ever been kissed by Thalen—chosen by Thalen. I knew no other kind of intimacy. Bailoc only permitted it between promised, or married, couples.

Lioran kissed me without reservation, without needing to know I was his—without ever being able to promise I would be. It was freeing, it was beautiful, even if everything I was taught said it was wrong.

I wanted to say it didn't matter—that we could just exist without anything beyond what we were. Yet I didn't know if I could. The kind of future I had always envisioned for myself involved a promise he could never choose. There was no time to consider what we could be—what we even wanted. The choice would be made for us.

Tears brimmed to the surface, threatening to release. I was desperate to hear a different explanation.

He sat beside me, taking my hand in his. I didn't have to

say how I felt—he knew. "I still want a future with you. However, we can have one. For as long as we can have one."

"Why wouldn't it be accepted?" My hand rested in his. The warmth of his touch radiated through me.

A heavy sigh escaped his lips. "I am the heir to the throne. It is my duty to keep the royal fae bloodline alive."

I wasn't fully fae. I was only something in between—someone wrong for him. My heart slid down deeper in my chest; each aching beat echoed through me. He would have to marry someone else.

"Has your future queen been chosen?"

He fell silent for a moment too long, but he kept my hand in his. It broke me. Tears cascaded, and I didn't even wipe them away.

"Not yet."

"Yet..." I glared at him. "How could you get so angry with me about Thalen? You should have just let me go." How could I feel so upset with him now knowing that my future was spoken for, too?

"I planned to, but I can't. My heart feels like it's no longer mine...like it only responds to you."

Hearing his words, knowing his destiny—it shattered me.

He pulled me closer to him, his breath caressing my skin. It ignited something deep within me that I struggled to control.

"Aelira?"

"I just didn't expect..." I breathed through the uncertainty. "In Bailoc there are only arrangements and future promises. They were all made for me. No one ever asked me what I wanted."

"What do you want?"

A soft, but twitching, smile spread over his lips. When he asked me, I knew it still wasn't my choice.

Fate—the stars—whoever was responsible, led me here.

My heart was already his. Even if I wanted to take it back, I couldn't.

"You can tell me. I want to know what you want."

"To be with you," I said.

It was too late to choose anything else.

My heart would break now if I walked away or later when the king and queen decided I couldn't be with him any longer. I pressed my lips into his, to steal a moment I couldn't keep.

CHAPTER 17

"Is Pyrran gone?" Cora handed us crystal glasses filled with wine.

"He couldn't have left soon enough," Lioran muttered through a strained jaw.

"Thank the stars I don't have any brothers." Fyn chuckled before gulping down more of his wine.

"What happened?" Cora nestled into the cushions in the corner of her cabin. Her hand patted the cushion beside her.

Lioran massaged his temples. His eyes darted to mine, seeking my approval before he began. We had already discussed it, agreed to tell them both—I nodded, feeling the weight of our decision settle.

"Pyrran found us in the woods earlier...alone together." Lioran shifted his weight. I gripped the stem of the goblet.

"Finally." Fyn jolted his wineglass down on the table. The crimson liquid splashed to the brim. Cora shot him a glare that could have shattered the glass.

"Finally?" Lioran's laugh echoed.

"You both tried to deny it for far too long. I even tried to delicately bring it up, but neither of you wanted to admit it. Pyrran observing it is obviously most unfortunate."

"That was you delicately bringing it up?" I bit my lip.

"I thought you were only prodding me." Lioran glared at Fyn.

Fyn shrugged as he gave me a knowing look. "It turns out she's just as stubborn as you are."

"Pyrran won't just let this go," Cora interrupted.

Lioran shifted slightly in his seat. He slid his hand over mine. "He won't. We will have to face what's coming together."

The warmth of his touch ran through me. I thought he would tell them about Thalen, but Lioran only brought the cup to his lips.

"I'll get us more wine." Cora stood, clutching her glass.

I rose to follow her. Fyn and Lioran's words faded as we entered the kitchen.

"Are you upset?" I asked. She reached an unsteady hand for the wine bottle to refill her own glass and then hesitated before pouring more liquid into mine. "I know you and Lioran once..." My voice trailed off as I struggled to say more.

The concerned look on her face grew more exaggerated with my words. "Oh no, it's not that. I'm just worried about Pyrran. He's been searching for anything he could use against Lioran." Cora's low tone left me feeling unsettled as she glanced at Lioran then back to me.

And now he had what he wanted. "I know when there's something you want to say but won't...you can tell me." She pushed her frustrations down deep within her, bottling things up—I had seen it so many times during our training sessions. Now I saw it all clearly on her face. Something was terribly wrong.

"I'm so happy for both of you." She clasped her hands

together rigidly. "It's just...it's more than Pyrran. Bigger than all of us."

What could be bigger than Pyrran telling the king and queen I was in Nythrel? I forced a swallow, my throat constricting. Had she seen something?

"Your vision?" My words caught in my throat. It was the last time I saw her this unraveled. "Please. Whatever it is you can tell me."

"I don't know enough yet to reveal what I saw."

"It has to do with us...doesn't it? You're not going to tell me? You won't even tell Lioran?"

"I will share when I can, but now is not the time."

Lioran's laughter echoed through the quaint space. I pressed my lips closed, wanting him to have his moment of peace.

Cora clutched the bottle in her trembling hands. "Who needs more wine?"

Lioran and Fyn held their glasses up in unison. Once she filled his glass, Lioran came to find me in the kitchen. His lips slowly grazed mine, and I pulled back.

"Are you alright?" Lioran slid his hand onto the small of my back. I pulled away from him, my instincts flaring. "Am I making you uncomfortable?"

"This is new to me—you kissed me in front of Fyn and Cora. In my kingdom...no one could kiss me unless they were marrying me." His eyes narrowed. I wanted to be close to him —this world was so different. The rules of Bailoc didn't matter here.

"I didn't know." He hovered close, his hand almost resting on mine, but he pulled away. "I will try to be more reserved, so you will be comfortable."

"No..." I reached out, grabbing his hand. "This is just new to me."

His eyes gleamed as moonlight streaked through the open window.

"Are you two going to just stay in there chatting all night? Things are going to get dreadful boring around here." Fyn looked out the window and tapped his wineglass.

"Fyn." Cora smacked him in the stomach. She lifted the glass to her lips. "How will you contend with Pyrran?" Cora's cracking voice piped into the conversation.

"I don't know yet. He'll travel to the High Court soon," Lioran said.

Fyn and Cora both tensed at the mention of the *High Court*.

"Do you think they know already?" I asked.

"It's possible. My father has a way of finding things out." Lioran's eye twitched.

"Well, that's putting it mildly." Fyn coughed, choking on a sip of his wine.

"How?" I snapped.

Fyn's eyes widened.

"My father can compel the truth out of anyone." Lioran's eyes lingered on mine, waiting for me to say something, to react at all.

I sat frozen beside Lioran. The warmth of his palm settled against mine.

"But he hasn't sent for me." My words challenged me even I knew it didn't mean they wouldn't.

"Yet." A chill rippled down my spine at Fyn's words.

Either they didn't know I was here yet, or they were merely waiting.

The moon was my constant companion that night. Each time I drifted back to sleep, Pyrran's threats pulled me awake. The sun traded places with the moon. A dense fog crept in. Lioran's kiss still lingered on my lips—a reminder of the stolen moments I would keep.

My hand sifted over the raised edges of the leather book's embroidery. The tie slipped loose and dangled from the binding. As I opened the ruffled edge pages of the book, I told it everything.

Your mother would have been much better at this.

A tear trickled down my face almost unnoticed. It pooled on the page.

"You know my mother? I look to you for guidance and am met with cryptic answers. Who are you?"

I will share the truth when you are ready.

"I am ready now. Whoever you are—whatever you are—you can't care enough about me to continue to leave my questions unanswered." The pages remained blank for a moment, and then new words formed.

My breath caught as I looked away. I was terrified to see what it might reveal. Curiosity consumed me, and I read it anyway.

I am Lord Zayric of the High Court of Nythrel.

You are my daughter, Aelira.

This book was a gift, to guide you when I could not cross the wall.

I've thought of you every day since I laid eyes on you.

Your mother brought you to me after you were born.

It was our first and last meeting, before the war began.

The air thickened—my lungs rejected each inhale.

My *father* wrote every word.

A storm raged inside of me, blurring my vision until it was almost impossible to make out the new words that formed.

"Are you still at the High Court? Where can I find you?" A sharp, searing pain reverberated in my throat.

Where I am you cannot go—until we meet again these pages will guide you.

The book rattled against my chest with each heavy breath. The pages were still damp with tears. This whole time he kept the truth from me. He just let me tell him everything, about Lioran—about my fears.

You deserve the life you've dreamed of.

Do not settle for anything less.

He is not worthy of you.

Lioran protected me ever since I crossed the divide. He loved me in a way that I never thought possible, yet he called him unworthy.

I stopped directing my thoughts to the book. He knew I was here and did nothing about it.

My words can't be easy.

I feel your silence and sadness.

All that I share is to protect you.

Tears pooled on my silk nightgown, setting outlines in the fabric. My resentment rolled like thunder until I wailed.

I clutched my pillow.

The chamber door slammed open mere moments later, Lioran's disheveled hair hung free. His silk robe lay open, exposing his bare chest—a thick scar still trailed over him. His frantic breathing echoed in my chambers.

"Aelira?" He scanned the room for a sign of threat, scanned me. His hands trembled as he reached for me, his fingers ran through my hair. "Are you hurt?"

The squall sharpened inside of me. His brilliant silver eyes fixated on me. "I..." My voice caught between sobs. How could I explain that I was talking to a magical book?

"Are you okay?"

I nodded as I lifted the covers over my chest, pointing to my robe near my dressing station.

He placed the robe around my shoulders. "I can go. I just wanted to make sure you were safe."

"I know who my father is—my real father." With my words he sat beside me, clutching my hand in his.

"How?"

"King Ardyn hid this book and my necklace in a tower in the palace. I stole them." I held out the leather book, the cord that tied it shut dangling down.

"You *stole* them?" He quickly dropped the amused smirk from his face.

"He kept her things from me." I couldn't bring myself to tell him the dream that led me there. "My true father gave them to my mother to give to me. He's been communicating with me through it. It's how I knew to cross the wall."

Maybe King Ardyn knew what they were, or maybe he was hoping I would never find a single trace of the truth that may remain.

"He enchanted it somehow to speak to you...but he hasn't come to see you..." His eyes darted from the book to me.

"I didn't know I was speaking to *him* through it until now. I thought it was just magic."

"Do you know where he is?"

"No. Only his name, Lord Zayric. He says he's from the High Court. Had you ever met him?"

"I'm sorry, I don't think I have," he said. "At least not that I remember."

King Ardyn rejected me.

Lord Zayric wouldn't tell me where he was.

My fingernails traced the inside of my palms, pain settling as they scraped flesh. I desperately wanted to know who I was, where I came from. "Why wouldn't he tell me where he is? What if he doesn't want to see me at all?"

"He enchanted a book to guide you. Your father has been with you this entire time. If he won't say where he is there must be a reason."

"He said I can't go to where he is." I tucked the book beneath the covers.

"It's clear he wants to protect you. I spent most of my life at the High Court—I don't want you to be there either."

"It's that brutal?" I asked.

"The place itself is not...no, but my parents can be."

Lioran's eyes glimmered with a pain I knew too well.

He hummed something familiar as I wept—the same song I hummed to him when we tried to get him home to the Heart.

"That song..." The sound stilled my body. "You remembered it?"

"I've known it my whole life. It's a fae tune called the *Light of Night*—the song of the stars."

"My mother used to hum it to me."

Every detail had been carefully threaded. Their beliefs— their stories—were a part of my life for as long as I remembered. She planned it all, so I would know where I came from.

Lioran understood me, exactly as I was. He didn't need for me to be different. My father said Lioran was unworthy, but looking at him, seeing his devotion, it couldn't be true.

He ran his hands along my back. I stilled with his touch.

My heart burrowed further inside of me. I knew it fully then. I was in love with him, a hopeless love that tethered me to this moment—one that I would never forget.

"It's not fair." A long exhale escaped me.

"I know, I can imagine how heavily this is weighing on you."

"It isn't the only thing," I said softly.

He drew in a breath that held a moment too long. His body stiffened with it.

For a moment I couldn't speak. I was so afraid to tell him what I felt. If I said it, I couldn't pretend it didn't exist anymore. He sat there patiently waiting for me to speak.

He deserved to hear exactly how I felt. "My heart, it's yours. I never expected to fall in love with you."

"You... love me?" he asked as if he didn't believe it—as if he wasn't sure if he should have even asked it. It was the first time I had ever seen his confidence waver.

"Entirely. I love you, Lioran," I whispered.

He kissed me fiercely. When he drew back from the kiss, he replied, "I wasn't sure if that was even possible."

I was so lost in my thoughts that I didn't even stop to think how little time it took Lioran to arrive. "Lioran..."

"Yes, Aelira?"

"How did you get here so quickly?"

"I heard you." He took hold of my hand and brushed his lips against my palm. "My chambers are next to yours."

"Next to?"

"Your chambers are for the Lady of Lythira, the Guardian's bonded wife." I took in the room's opulence again, every carved detail etched into the furniture. The sprawling layout of the room—the windows overlooked the Heart—the ivy that crept in across the stone arches of the high ceilings.

My mouth opened, ready to protest, but I cleared my throat instead. "This is what you wanted Fyn to do? You were so concerned when you were barely holding on."

"I wanted to make sure you were safe and comfortable. Having you next to me ensured both."

The tears flowed faster as I took in his words—this space was never meant for me. "I can't stay here. It's for your wife. I am not your wife."

"It doesn't matter. I want you here."

His arm wrapped around my waist, and he lowered me onto the bed. My body settled under his as our lips grazed. The kiss traveled through me until I felt myself pulling him closer.

He pulled back. As he sat beside me his gaze swept over me, slowly taking me in. "If I don't stop now. I won't be able to resist you."

A gnawing ache stirred within me. I needed him next to me.

He lifted my palm to his lips and pressed a gentle kiss. I resisted pulling him closer.

CHAPTER 18

Lioran was called away to council. The castle halls twisted and turned, leading me to the garden. Perfumed air wafted on the midday breeze. I savored every sweet scent. Each time a flower grew from my magic, I remembered its fragrance like it was a part of me.

Dew drops decorated a row of pink roses. Their petals spread wide, revealing a perfect shape. My fingertips traced the edge of the bloom, craving its silky touch.

It shriveled.

I recoiled and another crumbled turning to dust from my hand's graze.

Something pulled within me, thrashing and whirling. Steeped in pain, my magic flowed chaotically. I clasped my hands together in my lap, terrified I would accidentally touch another.

"That's most curious..." Elric's voice startled me. "Are they questioning you?"

I wasn't sure when he arrived. He always seemed to find

me. "Aren't you needed in council?" My voice trembled. I slid in front of the blooms I ruined, wanting to hide them from view.

"Not yet. I thought I'd take in some fresh air." He gripped the stone flower box, peering around me. "It seems we are destined to keep running into each other. Some may say it's the stars' wish."

The hairs rose on my arms.

"It all comes with a price." He approached me slowly.

"What does?" I asked.

"Surely, Prince Lioran explained it to you." He brushed the stray silver hairs from his face. "Or maybe he didn't. I suppose he wouldn't."

"Tell me," I commanded.

"If you wish it. Only because I believe you deserve the truth." He ran his thumb over his fingernails. "We can all sense how fragile your magic is, Princess."

He knew. We had trained in the open, but always concealed what I was working on when others were around. Lioran thought it was safest to downplay what I could do to protect me, yet he shared it with Elric.

My magic shifted through me, threatening to release itself again, but I stilled my hands at my sides.

"When a fae isn't ready to channel magic, it will take just as much as it gives." His gaze locked onto mine, pinning me in place. I wanted to protest it, to question him further, but I thought of Evyn and didn't utter another word.

"When you use your magic, you probably feel yourself grow weaker."

It was true. Training sessions left me longing for my bed. Sometimes I was even unable to think clearly afterwards.

"The greater the magic, the greater the cost. They are training you to restore. Are they not?" He sat on the stone wall next to me, assessing the damaged rose with his fingers.

"Restoration of these blight-burdened lands would be most beneficial for all, but especially the prince."

"Everyone wants the blight reversed. Both realms would benefit."

"Yes...but one's very future hangs in the balance and a certain prince is about to be the king of a land that can't sustain itself."

I couldn't understand how Lioran could trust him. Elric showed little allegiance.

"They are training me because I asked them to. I needed to learn how to control my magic." I didn't know why I felt the need to explain, but once my mouth opened, I couldn't stop myself.

"It works even better when you think it's your idea." Elric took a step closer to me. "So, when the time comes and he asks you to make a sacrifice—you will. Without hesitation. Without thought."

Lioran would never do that. He loved me. He believed in me.

"You're lying." I leaned back into the flower box, but swiftly pulled myself away from it again.

"You offend me. I came to find you to tell you the truth. To save you. And here you are, calling me a liar. I could just leave you here and let you figure out the rest." He turned on his heels, but hesitated before taking a single step.

The words he spoke. He knew it all. It couldn't be as he said. I couldn't allow it to be. He finally stepped forward. "Wait!" I cried. If there was any truth in his words, I had to hear them.

Elric spun around to face me again. "Didn't you wonder how he knew you were the disturbance at the divide? How he was there waiting for you?" Elric's breath settled on my collarbone. "Lady Cora saw you coming and told him everything. You're the answer to all his problems."

"And they told you this?"

"Of course, he told me," Elric said. "He isn't keeping you a secret."

A hard knot formed in my throat, silencing me.

"He has a plan—and you, my dear, are a part of it. A very disposable part."

"What do you mean?"

"He will convince you that he loves you." He waited for my retort.

He kissed me like he meant it.

Lioran held me like he would never let me go.

If Elric was telling the truth—if it had all been a lie, then Lioran knew just how to fool me.

I couldn't accept that—I stood there, frozen and broken.

"Then you'll do anything for him. You'll hand him a fully healed Kingdom, but he won't care what it costs you. He'll continue his life without you. Marry, have children, rule the way he was always intended—until he forgets your name entirely."

I quaked under the weight of his words. Each thing he said was more painful than the last, until agony crushed me. Air withdrew from my lungs slowly until they ached.

"He wouldn't." I skirted myself over on the stone wall, putting distance between the two of us.

"It's too late, isn't it?" His eyebrow raised. "You've fallen for him already." He rubbed his hands together. "It can't be easy to hear this." He slid his hand on top of mine.

I pulled free from his grasp. "I don't believe you."

"You do. The truth is painful." His exhale collided with my cheeks. "The fae are cunning beings. This world isn't like yours." He pulled back for a moment and took a step away from me. "I must go, but I'm sure we'll find each other again soon. I'm here to help. All you need to do is ask."

He walked off and didn't look back. My hands dripped with sweat; my grip was slipping as I clung onto the stone.

Lioran wouldn't. He couldn't.

My presence here was supposed to be a secret, yet he knew everything. Lioran and I had only just confessed our love, but he somehow knew that, too.

I crumpled onto the stone path, afraid to touch the grass, or anything around me. A gush of wind tore through the garden and thrashed against me.

My father's words were etched into the book like he knew something I didn't. Lioran was unworthy.

Pyrran said he was using me—that Lioran couldn't love me. It angered him, but Lioran never denied it. Never challenged it. Not once did Lioran tell him he loved me.

He didn't even say it back when I told him I loved him.

My magic fizzled until all that remained was a bitter taste on my tongue. Smoky clouds rolled overhead. A chill stung my chest from the onyx.

I tried to recall moments with Lioran—his lips on mine, the way he looked at me, the way he told me he loved me before Pyrran interrupted us. It all felt real, but what if it wasn't?

I pulled myself up on the stone box, careful not to touch a single bloom. The rain pelted me. Drenched in agony, my gown clung to me. My body weakened with the chill that overtook me. I carefully followed the path back into the castle. My boots never left the stone.

"Usually, it's best to seek shelter before a storm." The light dimmed in Fyn's eyes as he assessed me. "Are you hurt?" He braced me as I stumbled. "I will get Lioran."

"No." The stone wall braced me. It was so cold, so lifeless.

I wanted Lioran to hold me, to tell me his love was real, but if he was lying to me—I would fall for it all again. If he admitted he lied it would break me.

"Please, let me walk you to your chambers. You need to change out of those clothes." Fyn reached for me, his hand hovering between us. "Lioran would want to be here for you."

Fyn's words left me aching, longing for a truth I couldn't grasp. Elric knew things he shouldn't have. Lioran promised to protect me. Yet he was there, waiting at the divide just as Elric said. Cora must have told him. She knew the truth behind it all.

"Where is Cora?"

"I'm not sure. Do you want me to find her for you?" He gripped my arm tighter as I stumbled forward.

"Yes."

Cora was hiding something.

She had a vision and wouldn't tell me about it.

I deserved the whole truth, and this time I wouldn't take no for an answer.

The fireplace blazed in my chambers as I buttoned the front of my silver riding tunic. Juniper hung the dripping gown in the window, shaking her head. "Have some tea, my lady. It'll warm you." Her tiny frame seemed childlike in the grand doorway to my chamber as she slipped through.

The leather book relaxed in my hands as I undid the wrap. I needed its guidance before Cora arrived. All of my energy went toward the book as I let the tea warm me.

"Why is Lioran unworthy?"

Lioran is the future King of Nythrel.

He can't offer you the future you deserve.

I am thankful for the protection he has granted you.

He must realize he can't keep you.

He couldn't. Maybe he didn't even want to. I replayed Elric's words in my mind directing them all to the book.

All magic comes with a price.

You must be balanced or it will take its toll.

The greater the magic, the greater the cost.

"And Lioran? Has he been lying to me this entire time?" I choked on the words as my chest constricted.

I can't read him.

I can only read you and what you choose to share with me.

Look inside yourself for the answers.

You have an excellent sense of who people truly are.

The clearing in Evyn and the rose petals—both times I destroyed the land with my magic because of my turmoil and uncertainty. Lioran told me that he hoped we both could save the land. He didn't deny what he said to Pyrran. If this was all a part of his plan, why would he tell me any of it?

"Aelira?" Cora knocked on the door. I slammed the book shut and set it aside.

"Come in," I called, sitting back in front of the fire. She peeked around the door, red hair glittering in the fire's warmth. Her green eyes were still, but skeptical.

"Fyn sent for me." Cora knelt beside me in front of the fire —her eyes searched mine. "He told me how he found you. What happened?"

I stared at her for a moment, too afraid to ask anything at all. The onyx's heat radiated through me a gentle reminder of my strength when everything around me felt so cold.

"Did you have a vision I crossed the divide?"

"Yes, I had a vision of someone crossing the divide. We knew you would come but didn't know who you were."

"You told him where to find me?"

"He sensed you before you crossed. He wasn't sent there to wait for you. In fact, I told him not to go."

My nose scrunched as my head pounded. "You didn't want him to find me?"

"Honestly..." She exhaled as she slid her hands through her fire red locks. "No. I didn't want him to go to you. We didn't know who you were, or what dangers would await when you crossed the divide." She shook her head. "Had I known it was you...I would have fought harder to keep him here."

"Because I'm the Princess of Bailoc...or did you have another reason?"

"You're the princess of our enemy. It's why you all were hunted in the woods. It was what almost got him killed." She squinted as the sun peeked into the dreary room.

I gulped. "Did he bring me here to restore the land?"

"Whatever reasons he brought you here are his. Why are you asking me this?"

"It's just all...convenient, isn't it?" I gripped the tea from the low table, chugging the hot liquid—letting it scald my throat.

"If you think he's being convenient, you don't deserve him. He's risked everything for you." She gripped her wrist tightly.

"You all say that, but what about what I've risked? What I will risk for him?"

Cora wouldn't look at me. "I can't speak to what you're willing to risk. You make those choices. I have known Lioran most of my life. He loves very deeply—his land, his people. He always puts everyone else first. I've watched him guard his feelings from everyone, including me, but he doesn't with you."

The lump solidified in my throat.

"What happened that suddenly made you question him?"

"I've been advised not to trust Lioran."

"Did Pyrran say that to you? He will stop at nothing to take the throne himself. He always undermines Lioran."

"No, Lord Elric." The scent of searing wood lingered in the air.

"Elric told you not to trust him?" Her nostrils flared and her eyes narrowed. "What did he say?"

"He wants me to believe he loves me so that I will save the land, because it grants him the best future." I struggled to repeat the words.

Her hand shook as she spoke. "Elric's words..."

"Unraveled me." I said.

"Why did you tell Elric about your magic?"

"I didn't. I thought Lioran told him."

"He wouldn't have." An uneven breath escaped Cora's lips before they tightened.

None of it made any sense. How could Elric have known any of it? Cora couldn't answer all of my questions. She didn't make me feel any better at all.

"I need to talk to him." I didn't want to. How could I ask him any of it?

She nodded as she rose. "You seem to have already decided what you believe. I'm not sure my words have any merit, but I know Lioran. He isn't deceiving you."

I paused at her words. "My heart is broken from the thought of it."

It didn't have to make sense to her.

Fyn and I waited for council to end. Lioran would emerge from the two slender wooden doors that stood before us and then just maybe I would know the truth. The wall cradled me as exhaustion crept in. The council room slowly emptied.

Elric was among the last to leave the hall. "My lady, good to see you again looking so...refreshed." He smirked.

Fyn's hand hovered over his sword hilt as he stepped in front of me.

"It must be tiring having no magic of your own, Fyn." He ran his fingers through his silver hair. "Always having to be at the prince's beck and call." Fyn's glare sharpened. He watched the door. Even when Elric left us, Fyn's stance didn't waver.

Lioran passed through the doorway. His eyes followed Fyn's hand to the hilt of the sword, and his body stiffened. "Fyn?" Lioran's eyes darted between us. "What happened?"

"Take her somewhere private," Fyn whispered.

Lioran's eyes narrowed. "Aelira?" His voice whispered my name, but I couldn't respond.

I bit my lip instead.

Dozens of celestial patterns danced upon the ceiling of Lioran's study—glowing from the flickering light of the hearth. An unexpected calm settled within me as I looked up above at them. For a moment, I was back in Bailoc, back in the silence of my chambers—where I used to look at an almost identical pattern of stars my mother had painted on my ceiling.

"What happened? Why was Fyn guarding you like that?" His voice quaked. I quietly stared at the ceiling. I didn't want to ask him.

He reached for my hand, but I pulled away from him the moment he touched me. "You didn't say anything the whole way here. You won't even look at me. What happened?"

My heart splintered with Elric's accusation. I hesitated a moment longer before I forced myself to ask him. The tears pooled as I struggled to ask what I needed to. "Do you love me?"

"Yes, I love you." His eyes narrowed. "You know that. What does this have to do with Fyn? Tell me now. If the two of you..."

I shook my head as I stepped back from him. My eyes searched his, desperate for the truth behind his words.

"This isn't about Fyn. It was never about Fyn," I blurted.

His stance eased. "Then please tell me why you're standing in my study looking at me like that...asking me if I love you."

"You came to the wall looking for me. You knew I was there. Once you knew what my magic was you brought me here."

"I told you. I sensed you."

"Cora told you I would be there."

"Yes. But why does that matter? I felt your presence—I found you."

I inhaled, holding tight on the air—too afraid that my words would tumble with it.

"Someone told me you wanted me to believe you love me so I would restore your kingdom. That it's all a lie." The words cut even deeper as I spoke them.

His gaze narrowed. "Who told you that?" The brilliant silver in his eyes faded.

"I..."

The air grew thick around us. His anger leached into it. "Who are you confiding in?"

He never looked at me like that before.

He was broken, too.

Seeing him that way told me a truth I shouldn't have attempted to uncover. He wasn't lying to me. Elric was.

"Lord Elric."

He grabbed a book off his desk and threw it at the wall. I flinched as the thud echoed. "Elric...and you believed him... you..." He shook with each word he spoke.

"You didn't tell Pyrran that you loved me," I snapped. "He said you couldn't... and you didn't tell him he was wrong."

"Do you know what would have happened if I challenged him then? We discussed what he was doing. But still you're standing in front of me accusing me of lying to you."

"I need to hear the truth—whatever it is." My heart crushed under the weight of the words I uttered.

"The truth is that I'm standing in front of the only woman I've ever loved and she's telling me that she doesn't believe it." His nostrils flared. "I don't know what to do to make you believe me."

He was telling the truth. I knew it then, but the damage had already been done. I sobbed. With a heavy exhale he paused. His glare faded as he wrapped his arms around me.

"I'm sorry," he said before I could utter the apology I owed him. "I never thought you would question my love for you—that anyone else could get to you." His breathing was rapid. "Why would you tell him about your magic? What else have you shared with him?"

"I thought you had. He knew so much about me from the day I met him." My fingers ran through my hair. "If you didn't tell him, who did?"

"I never thought anyone would love me for who I am. My father told me to hold my tongue. He condemned me for every pointed word I uttered. I spent all my years being the disappointment he tried to hide."

His eyes softened as they met mine.

"My father and brother both feared that I would be so unlikable that Thalen would refuse to marry me. My brother told me to..." I couldn't utter the words.

"To what?" His voice dropped.

I shook my head. "To tempt him...so he wouldn't refuse me." Agan's words caught in my mouth. The memory of it sickened me.

"What?" His chest heaved as he stepped back from me. "Why would he do that?"

"My worth has only ever been measured by what I could offer Bailoc. Because..." The realization hit me again. "Maybe King Ardyn felt like it was what he was owed for having to deal with me."

His lips opened and pressed closed again, as if he wanted to ask if I did. But he only shook his head.

"I would *never* use you for my own gain." The tenderness of his voice trailed over me. "I feel the storm trying to settle in you. I've felt it all day. It took everything for me not to walk out of council and check on you. When I saw Fyn there with his hand on the hilt of his sword, I nearly lost it." His piercing gaze met mine.

He leaned over me, his hand bracing himself against the door. My heart raced as his body towered over mine.

I sobbed as I pulled him closer until our lips met again. He reached for me; his hands settled on my waist—as if they were returning to where they belonged.

It felt familiar.

It felt safe.

"I am yours. Please. I need you to know that. To feel that."

"And I am yours," I whispered.

One storm settled, and another began.

I was falling deeper and faster than before.

CHAPTER 19

I rubbed my eyes, and the room sharpened into focus. Juniper tidied my chambers, setting a quiver down beside a bow in the corner of the room.

"Juniper?" I stretched my arms over my head. "Where did that come from?"

"A gift from his highness. He said you needed one."

I told him I loved archery when he was in a sleepy haze in the infirmary—I didn't even think he heard me.

The floorboards creaked with each step I took. The golden-hued longbow etched with leaves settled easily into my hands. He hadn't just heard me; he welcomed a side of me that few understood.

"It's beautiful." My fingertips trailed the leaves.

"Where did you learn to hunt, my lady?" Juniper poured tea into a glass mug. The hot liquid formed droplets on the outside.

"An old friend." I still remembered my lessons. Cael insisted that I learn to protect myself as things grew more hostile in the kingdom. King Ardyn never approved, but he didn't care enough to intervene, either. "I am not much of a hunter, but I enjoy target practice. It relaxes me. The prince is very thoughtful."

"Yes, indeed." She lifted a riding tunic from the dresser drawers, a perfect pale green, with a flowing split hem skirt, and matching pants. "It may be the perfect day to try it."

I dressed quickly and draped the bow over my shoulder, along with its matching quiver before I slipped out of my chambers.

"Going hunting?" Fyn passed me in the corridor. "I wasn't aware you were fond of the sport."

"There is much you aren't aware of, Fyn," I said.

"It does seem to be your mission to always keep us all on our toes." He chuckled.

"You mean my watchful companion wasn't aware of my new gift?"

"Believe it or not, Lioran and I do not discuss everything with each other. I'm not sure why he thinks giving you a weapon is a good choice, but he must have a reason."

A smirk settled on my face as I rolled my eyes.

"Join me?"

"As much as I'd love to see you beat me, as I'm sure you would, I have to attend to a shipment for Othryl." The light in his eyes dimmed.

"You were able to secure medical supplies?"

"Some. I should be going." Fyn nodded as he left.

I wished I could relieve the pain Othryl, and the other villages felt, but I didn't know how. My magic restored very little. New blooms wouldn't be enough to save anyone.

The sun greeted me the moment I set outside; its familiar hug embraced me. Lioran waited on a bench.

"You're up early this morning," he said as I approached. "The bow suits you."

"Thank you. I didn't think you heard me."

"I heard every word." He lifted the bow over my head and tucked it under his arm. "I had a target set up for you in the clearing."

We set off down the stone path together. "I've been longing to practice again. This bow is so much more beautiful than the one I left behind in Bailoc."

"It surprised me to hear you enjoyed the pastime."

My smile faded, remembering the look on Cael's face. "An old friend taught me."

"You miss this friend?" His head tilted.

"Yes. He protected me always." I clutched the quiver strap that lay across my chest.

His expression hardened. "This friend...was he more than a friend?"

"No," I quickly replied. "He was a knight who taught me so I could protect myself. He saw too much in his rounds in Bailoc. Everything I knew about the blight, about the unrest, was all because he told me. No one else would."

The ripples of the water followed us as we walked alongside the river. The memory raced through my mind. My dagger aimed at my friend. His desperation. Mine.

"What's wrong?"

"He tried to stop me at the divide." I wasn't sure if I should even speak of the rest. "I pointed my dagger at him."

Lioran stopped in front of me. "Whatever you had to do to escape—to get here. It doesn't matter. You're here. You're safe."

I tried to still my breath, but I couldn't stop picturing Cael's face.

"He didn't know why I was so desperate—until I told him. I still remember how he looked at me like I was someone he couldn't accept. He never looked at me like that before. Cael was one of the few people who never treated me like a burden."

"He let you go." Lioran's voice held steady.

"Because I had a dagger."

"A knight wouldn't have been afraid of you with a dagger." His lips curled upward. "I'm sure you were absolutely terrifying though."

I laughed, but soon that smile faded too.

"I left my sister, Ashlyn. She didn't deserve me abandoning her. I didn't even say good-bye the day I left."

"Does she know you're half-fae?"

"I'm sure she does now."

"If she loved you then, she loves you still," he spoke with such certainty.

"How could you possibly know that?" I asked.

"Anyone who truly knows you...understands you. They have to see what I do."

"And what's that?" I squinted as a glimmer of sunlight caught in my eyes.

"There is a strength inside you that can't be stifled—that couldn't be contained in Bailoc—or in the Vale," he whispered as he drew closer. "It's in your very name—*Ay-leer-uh.*"

"I like the way you say it—like it means something."

"It means everything," he whispered. "It means resilience."

I had never known my name meant anything at all. Never knew how beautiful it could sound until I stumbled into Lythira—until Lioran spoke it for the first time. He'd heard it before, but I hadn't thought about what that meant.

"King Ardyn wouldn't know it though...Because he didn't name you."

"What makes you say that?" I asked.

"A king who hates the fae wouldn't knowingly name his daughter a fae name." He chuckled.

"My mother..." I clutched the gemstone with my free hand.

"My father...they chose my name," I exhaled, releasing the stone.

My name was fae. I was fae. It was a piece of my story that had been silent. Now that I knew it—I felt a little more whole.

The quiver strap slipped off easily. My boots held it in place as it landed in the dirt. A lean arrow twisted effortlessly between my fingertips. Both the bow and arrow were longer than I was used to.

"Do you practice?" I asked as I gripped the bow firmly in my hand. My fingers settled on the string as I steadied the shaft of the arrow in place.

"No, I have no love for archery, but I am curious to see how you handle it."

"Well, do not judge me too harshly. It's been a while since I've practiced."

He chuckled as I focused on the target.

My fingers released the bowstring. The arrow lodged itself into the outer rim of the target. I wasn't sure if I would make it at all. His eyes narrowed as the sunlight washed over his face, embracing every angle of his face that I loved. His silver eyes dazzled even when he was squinting.

"I should have given you a bow much sooner," he whispered.

I set the bow down beside me. "And why is that?"

"You're glowing. You're doing something you love, and it brings you to life."

"I thought all fae glowed." I giggled.

"Not like you do."

I felt myself melting in his gaze. Craving him closer to me, but here in the open it couldn't be risked. Anyone could see if I so much as held his hand.

"Lioran..." I whispered.

He angled himself toward me as he whispered back, "Yes?"

"I wish we were alone together." The words felt dangerous as they left my lips. I had never said that to anyone, but with him it was different. I needed him closer. He brought me to life.

He inhaled deeply. His words releasing with an exhale. "When you are ready for it, we will be." My eyes met his for only a heartbeat. A slow but steady grin spread across his face. "For now, it's safer for us to remain here."

"You don't think I'm ready?"

"I want you to be sure of it." He thrust the bow back into my hands, but lingered at my side. "Focus on the target, Aelira."

The arrow settled on the bow as he exhaled sharply.

"I would be happy to, but you're standing too close to me."

His eyebrow rose as he stepped back.

"I didn't say I wanted you to move."

"I can't take you hinting at anything else. Just focus on the target."

"Oh I am." My shoulders relaxed as I held the stance, the string gnawing at my cheek as I released the arrow. The tip plunged into the center of the target.

"You're unbelievable."

"Well thank you." I leaned the bow leaned against the tree, sitting in the grass beneath it.

"Planning to grow some flowers?" He sat beside me.

"We haven't tried our magic together since we healed the tree."

"Would you like to?"

"Eager to make something bloom?" I chuckled. "It's all I really know how to do."

"That is not what Cora tells me. I hear you also make willow tree branches grow."

"Yes, most impressive."

"I'm just teasing you, you can do so much more."

"I want to call the little bird like you did. Will you show me?"

"Of all the things, I can do...that is what you wish me to show you? You know we could practice calling for magical creatures like the sylkren instead."

"No...I think I'll let you handle that one."

His melodic laughter boomed. "I'm sure the little bird would be delighted to see you again."

We slid behind the massive tree beside us. His fingers cradled mine, until my palm settled into his. For a moment, no one could see.

"Relax and imagine the little yellow bird." He braced my hand, and didn't move from my side.

Nothing happened.

He closed his eyes, his magic sifted over my hand like a gentle trace of his fingertips.

I scoffed. "Don't call it for me."

"This is why Cora trains you." His eyes softened.

"I thought it was because you didn't want to watch me destroy your territory again." I laughed.

He shook his head. "No. Cora remembers what it feels like to not be in control of her magic. I don't."

I closed my eyes and imagined the bird that greeted us in the infirmary, felt its little feet prodding at my palm. I opened my eyes, and two little black eyes were staring back at me. Smooth, glimmering, golden-streaked feathers nestled into my palm.

"There are times you're connecting with your magic, and you don't even know it." His melodic voice washed over me, grounding me. His hand hovered over my heart. "You carry such strength...not just in your magic, but in who you are. It's yours to claim. It was there even when I met you, but you weren't ready to see it."

"And you did?"

"The moment I did, my heart was no longer my own."

"When did you know?" I asked.

"It doesn't matter when."

The little bird lifted its wings and took flight from my hand. "It matters to me. When did you first start to feel that way?"

"When I held my blade to your chest. My heart clenched so tightly...and when they were dragging you...and you screamed. A part of me shattered."

They attacked him, because he was looking for me—fighting for me.

"You...didn't tell me."

"We were a little busy and then I was bleeding out." His laughter fell short. "I won't even ask you when you knew. You hated that you sensed me at the willow tree."

"I didn't hate it," I grew quieter. "Just didn't understand it. It terrified me."

"I terrified you?"

"Maybe at first." I folded my hands in front of me. "I had never felt like this before, and sensing someone... well that's something else entirely. You were so persistent, and I couldn't explain it to you."

"I wanted to hear you felt like I did."

I gasped. "And I told you it was nothing...said I wanted Fyn to walk me back."

"Not going to lie, that one hurt a little. I was so sure you only cared about him."

"It was only ever you. I'm sorry," I said.

"Don't be. It led us to this." He paused for a moment as he leaned back into the tree. "There's something I want to ask you about. There is a ritual coming up in a few days. I'd like for you to take part in it with me."

"What kind of ritual?"

"The Verdant Alignment. The night in which the stars align to bless the Earth with their powers. I use my grounding magic to perform a ritual that helps spread the celestial powers to the land."

"To ease the blight?" I asked.

"It strengthens the land, but can't ease the blight. I would love for you to partake in it with me. You are ready."

A chill crawled through me—flashes of the destroyed roses etched into my memory. "Maybe it's best if you just do it."

"If both of us partake in the ritual, it may enhance the celestial energy and help the land further." His stance eased. "I will show you exactly what to do."

"I'd like to help if I can." I looked back at the castle, the rose garden just out of view. "Will there be a cost?"

"The celestial energy gives more than it takes. I wouldn't put you in harm's way."

"If you're with me, I will do it." I spoke the words, for him —for the land, but I didn't know if I could do it. There were times my magic didn't respond at all.

CHAPTER 20

Golden embroidered flowers trailed the edges of my onyx gown—it hung off my shoulders. The fabric flowed behind me as I stepped closer to Lioran's chambers. My hand lingered above the handle of his chamber door. All this time, he was in this room. So many times I passed it and wondered what lay behind the door, carved with intricate detail that matched mine. He was right here, with me—the whole time.

I exhaled, my breath catching in my chest. Before I could move, the door creaked open. His chrome eyes glittered even in low light—they entranced me.

"I was starting to think you weren't coming," he said. "But then I felt you lingering here."

"What if I can't do it?"

"Then you just enjoy the stars' magic alongside me. It won't hurt you to try." He extended his hand to me, and as I slid my hand in his. The onyx's heat dissipated. A crisp chill lay beneath it.

"You look radiant." His voice lowered as he pulled me into

his chambers. His own inky black tunic shimmered in the candlelight's glow.

"I'm glad you like your dress choice." I didn't know where the dresses came from, but each one fit me exactly as it should —as if they were made for me. "Where did the dresses come from?"

"If I share all my secrets Aelira..." He rubbed his hands together. "Do you not like them?"

"They're stunning, but are they for her? For your future wife?" I asked, even when I knew I shouldn't. It didn't matter —it shouldn't matter, but every time I entered my chambers, and now his, I couldn't break free from the thought.

That everything belonged to her. Even him.

The glimmer of light that flickered behind his eyes faded as I stepped back. "They are yours. All of them were made for you. There's a fae in the Heart that uses her magic to craft clothing —yours and mine. She works very quickly."

"How could she do that without meeting me?" I asked.

"Juniper gave her the outfit I found you in."

I looked around his chambers, darker than my own, but just as ornate. Similar carvings, a similar hearth that glowed just as brightly as mine. Windows that overlooked the river just as mine did. I stepped back again, recoiling deep within myself.

"It's all yours, just like the room is yours. I want you to have everything. I want you to be here. I choose you—only you." He embraced me, pressing a gentle kiss on my forehead. "We get to have this, just us together right now. I am grateful for every moment."

"As am I." I was grateful for all of it. "Sometimes I just struggle with giving you my heart...knowing it will break. But I can't stay away from you. I don't want to even if I could."

My fingers trailed down his chest, I inhaled his scent—

warm and familiar. It settled something within me I couldn't name, until the knot in my chest slowly unraveled.

"This moment is just for us." He pressed a gentle kiss upon my lips. I pulled him in closer, kissing him again. "I'm starting to wish no one was expecting anything tonight...why do they have to be all down there waiting?" His voice was low, it rumbled through me with each word he spoke.

A flutter rose in my chest—and suddenly it ran deeper, intertwining with my veins, pulsing through me. I nodded, unable to say anything else. He lingered close to me, before tugging me toward his open balcony.

"What do we have to do?" I asked, desperate to pry my thoughts from him.

"The starlight doesn't just enhance the land—we must be conduits for its magic. Together, we can channel its power through the Verdant Alignment."

"I still don't know if I'm ready."

"I wouldn't bring you here if I didn't think you were. Your gift is from the stars—their power won't harm you." He lifted his hand to me, and I slid my palm on top of his. "Before we begin, there's something you must know. The celestial energy is powerful. It will awaken things in you...make you sense things with new depth."

"What is it like?" I asked.

"It's primal. If we partake in this together, it could heighten everything we feel for each other." His hand gripped mine tighter. "You must decide if you're willing to take the risk."

Something had already awoken in me the moment I walked into his chambers. It was hard to weigh my thoughts when my thundering heart threatened my focus.

"What if we...can't control it?"

"I know how to control it, but you may not." I settled into

his arms, and we looked up at the twinkling starlight overhead.

"I want to help." My throat constricted. I didn't know what the ritual would awaken in me, but I trusted him to keep me balanced.

The usual glow of candlelight was absent throughout the Heart. The lanterns on the water were extinguished—only the moon, and the stars, cast their glow tonight.

"Tonight is the one night a year when the stars assemble to bless the land with their light. We ask the stars for guidance—for restoration." His words grounded me. "I carry the weight of the stars with you, beside you."

He placed a massive, clear crystal in my palms. My hands gripped the uneven edges protruding from the stone.

"Speak with the stars like you do with the land, direct your energy toward them. They will cast their light into the crystal," he whispered to me. "I'll be with you the entire time."

Threads of light danced through the celestial heavens. Energy rampantly shot between the stars until a pool of light formed. A streak of silver light rained down on us, splitting only as it reached our crystals. A fierce vibration ran through my icy veins, shattering any calm that remained.

The crystals illuminated blazing white starlight. Once prevalent outlines of the world around us faded, casting a hazy glow until all I could see was him. An unsettling calm washed over me even as my heart raced on, thundering in my ears.

Then the crystal compelled me to be what it needed. The building energy released, and refracting light shot into the ground.

Even from a distance, I could see each blade of grass illuminated and thickened, plump with the stars' energy. The starlight rolled through a trickling path that poured into the stream. The water glowed, welcoming its power. It embraced the trees, willing them to stand taller, strengthening everything in its path.

Cascading light escaped the courtyard entirely until only its glittering traces remained. The overpowering scent of every blade of grass, flower, and tree filled me. Its lingering energy was a hum in my veins—pulsing, pulling something to the surface inside of me.

Twinkling light from the crystals danced on the balcony, a display only for us. Starlight glittered in his tantalizing gaze. A powerful heat that surged through me with his trailing touch —more intense than my magic.

He took me in, as if he was looking at me for the first time. "Aelira..." His hand gripped my jaw as he kissed me deeply. With a forced exhale, he pulled away. "We should get to the celebration."

"I want to stay—here with you." I spoke the words as if they weren't mine. A heavy exhale escaped my lips.

"There is nothing I would like more, but we need to go. Everyone's waiting."

I trailed quietly behind him, watching every step he made through the castle. There were no echoing boots, or trailing voices—only the sound of our steps, only the sound of his uneven breath. The scent of him wafted to me—stronger than before.

"We should enter the courtyard separately." He hovered over me, his eyes avoiding mine.

I reached for his hand before we parted. "Thank you for sharing that with me."

"I wish I could share how incredible you are with everyone." His voice wavered as he reached for my chin but pulled away. "I'll see you out there."

With his parting steps, an ache ran through me, as if something had pulled him from me permanently. The wall braced me as my fingers trailed my lips, savoring our last kiss. I held still, even though I *needed* to chase after him. When I couldn't sense him any longer, I stepped out into the courtyard.

The light still lingered everywhere it touched. I wished it would never fade. The stars illuminated the Heart so that no other light was needed. The crowd looked on with widening eyes.

Cora walked over to me; she placed her hand on mine.

"Where have you been? You missed it." Her eyes scanned the crowd. "At least you get to see it now. Just this once I wish I could see the ritual for myself, but Lioran always keeps it private." Cora's voice trailed off.

Lioran watched me from across the courtyard. He shimmered in the darkness, impossible to ignore, but only I took notice.

"The feeling of the starlight...it's indescribable." The words escaped me slow and uneven—my eyes couldn't part from Lioran's.

"Wait...You did it with him?" She slipped in front of me, blocking my view.

"It was magnificent."

Her glare shifted from me to him.

He moved ever so slightly, coming back into view. "It was... wonderful." I barely knew what I was saying.

Her fingernails dug into my wrist, pinching my skin. Cora tightened her grip on me. Her eyes peered into mine, studying me, but still I searched for him. "How could he possibly think that was a good idea?" She scoffed. "Let's go for a walk. I've been wanting to introduce you to a friend of mine."

As we shifted through the crowd, I noticed the fae lady she gestured to, elegantly dressed—a raven braid draped wrapped around her head. "Lady Aelira, this is my friend, Lady Aura." I tried to commit her name to memory.

With each word that was spoken, every attempt I made to speak, my thoughts returned to Lioran and the starlight in his eyes.

"It's a pleasure to meet you. Cora has said nothing but wonderful things about you. How is Lythira treating you? I imagine it's much different from Eyrsea...although I've never been." Lady Aura's eyes narrowed.

"Quite well." I tried to stifle the laughter that threatened to escape me. Lioran moved just an inch, and I sensed it.

"Good. From what I hear, it seems you have our prince's favor—which is no easy feat." Lady Aura surveyed me.

"He shows kindness to all of his guests," Cora interjected. Lady Aura scoffed.

"That is debatable, Lady Cora. Regardless...We are honored to have you here in the Heart." Lady Aura lowered her head. I heard her words, and deep down I knew the threat that lingered with them, but I couldn't respond. Lady Aura offered a faint smile before she left us.

Lioran's scent wafted to me on a gust of wind. His stare pinned me. Cora's jaw clenched, her grip pulsating around my wrist.

"Fyn." Cora pulled Fyn in with her free hand. "You need to watch Lioran. Now."

Fyn leaned in. "I see him—he's right there. Why exactly do I need to watch him?"

"Do you see her eyes? Have you seen his?" Cora gripped my chin, angling my face toward Fyn.

"Yes, they're brilliant tonight...very sparkly," Fyn said.

She groaned. "That is not what I'm talking about, Fyn." A deep breath escaped her lips. "They can't be alone together right now."

"I'm...fine." I stumbled for a second.

Fyn's voice was hushed. "Aelira, you can both do what you wish."

"Participating in the Verdant Alignment impairs his judgement. She completed the ritual with him." Cora's voice was a commanding warning. "You will stay with me tonight."

Fyn chugged a glass of wine. "Cora, stop worrying. She seems fine. He seems fine. Let's just have a little fun tonight." He grabbed another glass and handed it to her.

Cora pushed the glass away from her. "Pay attention, Fyn."

My stomach dropped. Cora told me she had never done the Verdant Alignment...only Lioran had. "How do you know it impairs judgment?"

"It doesn't matter. You just need to trust me. Neither of you will be yourself, and the way you are looking at each other right now..." Stray red hairs fell on her face, but she didn't release me to move them.

Every breath I took, I inhaled him.

"Cora, loosen your grip a little." Lioran snuck up behind us, his eyes wild.

"Fyn! What happened to watching?" Cora wouldn't release me as her piercing glare settled on Lioran. I slid my free hand over my mouth, stifling another giggle.

"I can't stop him from looking at her like that." Fyn choked on his wine a bit as he spoke.

My control was gone—I burst into a fit of giggles.

"You should know better," she groaned. "Just promise me you'll keep distance for a little while until the effects of the Alignment wear off a bit."

Lioran tilted his head. His eyes narrowed. She flinched.

"I am fine. She is fine," he snapped as he hovered over me.

"You have mere moments, before everyone notices the two of you." Cora dragged me to the other side of her body, away from Lioran. His eyes scanned the crowd before narrowing on her.

"Fine. Aelira, I'll see you in an hour." He sneered at her.

When he looked back at me, he was devouring me.

Something new stirred inside of me.

Alone. We were utterly alone.

When he showed up at my door later that night, I didn't turn him away. Firelight filled my chambers, the trickle of heat sifted down my back. Cora's last warning echoed. *Whatever you think you're feeling—it's not all real.*

I craved him, felt him without his touch—it felt real, very real. His chest swelled as he inhaled. I was losing control.

His hands grazed my corset—they trailed the laces at my back. Lioran's gaze shifted over me, lingering over my curves. His breath was hot on my neck.

He lifted my hand to his chest. His heart thundered beneath my palm. I wrapped my arms around his neck, I leaned into him, his warmth lulling me closer.

"I haven't stopped thinking about you all night," he said.

"Lioran..." His name hung on my lips.

"I haven't stopped needing you."

I closed my eyes and leaned into him. "I'm yours." The words barely escaped my lips.

He hesitated—his breathing sharp. "Aelira..." He growled my name.

His lips claimed mine, strengthening something inside me.

"You are mine." The words breathlessly left his lips—fire stirred in me.

He pressed his lips against my ear before caressing my neck. I caved with his touch.

He yanked at a ribbon, loosening the bodice of my gown. The cascading fabric caught on my arm. His hand pushed it further down. I slipped my arms out.

The fireplace cracked, echoing within my chamber walls as logs shifted. My breath stilled. A forceful pop sounded from the hearth.

I caught the bodice around my chest—the feeling too new, too exposing.

His lips entangled with mine, claiming me with each kiss. He gently slid my hands from my gown. He desperately gripped the fabric, until it sank lower.

An ember floated from the fireplace. As my dress dropped, I caught it again—my knuckles paled in the glowing firelight.

If I let him take me, I could never go back to who I was before.

With each touch—each kiss, I only craved him more.

He kissed my collarbone—warmth flooded me.

The embers cracked again, dancing in the air beyond the fireplace.

I pushed back from him.

This wasn't me. It wasn't him.

Pain gripped my chest with each frantic breath—a dull, aching warning.

"Lioran." His eyes glowed vividly, as if the starlight still had hold of him. "Wait."

"We can have this moment." His voice was low, but commanding.

My nails scraped over my gown. The fabric slipped from my fingertips, too ample to hold. I opened my lips to speak again, but my rib cage tightened as I clutched the gown hard against my chest.

I needed him to choose me, to love me without celestial influence. I wasn't ready. Silence filled a painful void that overtook me.

I didn't know what to say, couldn't figure out what to do.

"You...you need to leave."

I wanted to say something else, but I couldn't.

I stopped sensing him. Stopped tasting him.

Whatever magic had taken hold had vanished.

His teeth grazed his bottom lip, his shoulders slumped with a sharp exhale. "Aelira..." His fingers unfurled, reaching for me, but he swiftly lowered them to his side. Despair replaced his desperation.

He couldn't understand what I needed—not in this form.

"Please, just go. Now." If I didn't say it, didn't make him go, I would regret it.

"I'm leaving." His hand gripped the door; his gaze dropped from mine as he slipped out into the hall.

The gown pooled around me as my body collided with the cold wood plank floor. I stared at the door.

The handle would turn, he would come back to me. He would tell me how he loved me, regardless of my choice.

Moments passed, but the door remained as it was—still and shut. Sobs escaped my lips, filling my chambers with their echoes. The embers popped in the fireplace once more. My fingertips dug into my skin until the pain matched my agony. It shouldn't have been like this.

The stars glittered in the heavens—taunting me. "What do you want from me? Have I not given enough?" My seething reply was a whisper in the desolate space.

CHAPTER 21

My eyes burned as they opened, taking in the first morning light. The last tear was shed, but the pain lingered.

Cora knew. She tried to warn us.

They had been together, maybe even just like that. I tried to blink the thought of them together from my mind.

Maybe he could never control himself—not like he believed he could.

The bed still cradled me in my flowing gown. The ribbons were still loose enough for me to slide out of it, but I clung to it even as I slipped into the darkness.

I lay there as the sun steadied its place in the sky. Juniper came and went, leaving breakfast. It was left untouched. I'd never forget the way he looked at me when I told him to leave.

I left the book on my nightstand. There was no advice it could offer.

A rustling sound wove through the wind's whistle. Green ivy trickled in through the windows, glowing and growing into my chambers. I stiffened my grip on the jet-black fabric. It dragged behind me as I crept across the floor. Magic spiraled in my veins, buzzing through me.

The ivy crept inward again. My fingers cautiously trailed it. With my touch, it grew faster, creeping up the walls. I hadn't called it, but still it reached for me.

A leaf shifted over my hand and rested firmly in place.

With the leaf's embrace, I pulled my hand back slowly, but the ivy only crept further. It pulsated over me; each gentle vibration lulled me—the squall inside me diminishing with it until only tranquility embraced me.

The veins of the leaves illuminated as the sun peeked further past the clouds. The onyx fluttered against my chest in a way it never had before.

A knock sounded at the door, but I remained at the windowsill still clutching the leaf.

"Aelira... please." Lioran's voice was desperate on the other end as my silence greeted him. "I need to know you're okay. If you won't let me in, I'm sending Cora to check on you."

"Come in." I didn't look up at him when he entered.

The dancing ivy cascaded over the walls—the solemn stone walls transformed into a rippling sea of green.

"It just appeared." I was still clutching the leaf.

"You didn't call it with your magic?" He poked at a leaf beside me, and the vine recoiled. His finger trailed another, and it shriveled.

He shook his head.

"No. It just came to me. When I touch it, it calms the fire inside of me." I couldn't let the leaf go—its soothing movement grounded me. My other hand still clenched the black fabric of the gown, the weight tugged in the other direction.

"It's like it wanted to find me." It sounded absurd, even to me, but he remained beside me.

"I've never seen anything like it." He reached for the vine, but his hand wavered.

The dress ripped from my grip, but I caught it again. Tears brimmed to the surface of my eyes. I pressed the gown against me.

"You're still in your dress." He stumbled over his words.

"I didn't want to take it off."

Heavy rings hung under his eyes. "I know. I'm so sorry."

"Can you give me a moment? I want to change." For a moment, I fixated on the vines. Their energy lingered on my skin even as I pulled back, but I was desperate to feel it again.

"Of course. I'll be right here." He settled his back into the stone wall of the corridor as I shut the door. The black fabric fell to my hips as I finally released it. I reached for a simple navy dress to replace it.

Once I fastened the top, I called to him again. "You can come back in now." The door creaked and his boots echoed into the chamber.

"You haven't eaten anything." The plate clanged as he shifted it on the table.

"I'm not hungry." I never was when I was upset.

He stood in front of me, desperation etched in the wrinkles around his eyes. "I'm sorry."

"We should have listened to Cora." Her name caught in my throat. She only wanted to protect me—I knew that, but it didn't soften the sting of this morning's realization.

"Please...My heart is breaking." He extended a hand toward me, but I didn't accept.

"Last night..."

"I hurt you...could have truly hurt you."

"I wasn't ready. You weren't you." He flinched at my words. "I wasn't me."

"I knew that once the magic settled, but in the moment, I

didn't. I'm so sorry, I thought I had a handle on it. I always did until you came along."

"You never came back."

"I couldn't trust myself around you," he said.

My body sank into the armchair. I sobbed.

"I wanted you...I still do. When you are ready." He knelt beside me. His hand grazed my cheek. "The celestial energy awoke something within me, until I could barely control my own desires. I should never have put you in that position."

My throat squeezed tightly. "I wanted to be with you, but not like that. It couldn't be like that."

A breathy sound rose from my throat, but words didn't immediately follow.

He wiped my tears. "What can I do? I will do anything." His head hung heavy.

"Just hold me."

His hands slid around me, and as he pulled me in, his heart echoed. We were still for a moment—only birdsong sounded in my chambers.

"If you choose me, if we choose to be together in that way —it will only be when you are ready."

Something shifted within him, like a deeply rooted pain had taken hold. He meant every word he said. I knew how hard it was to fight the celestial magic. I would have caved myself if it weren't for the fire breaking my trance.

I reached for him. "Can you stay with me for a while?"

"There is nowhere else I'd rather be, my love." He lifted my hand to his lips.

He sat with me until he couldn't anymore—emergency council was summoned. His eyes darted from Fyn to me when Fyn arrived with news, almost as if duty couldn't pull him away.

"Everyone will meet shortly." Fyn studied us both. My hand trailed Lioran's. "Aelira, you should come, too." Fyn's solemn voice shook. "We have news from the other side of the divide."

My stomach sank further. "How? Where did the news come from?"

"Elric." Fyn hesitated. "He claims he has ties to someone across the divide."

"Thalen." I choked on his name. Lioran's fingers twitched beneath mine. "Everything he's said to me...What he put us through. Thalen was behind it all." My lungs clenched in my chest, the pain intensifying with each passing second.

"We don't have the proof of that yet. You're only assuming..." Fyn thumbed the buttons on his tunic.

"It's not a far-fetched assumption," Lioran grumbled.

"I changed my mind, Lioran. You can do what you want with him now," I said.

A hint of a smirk tugged at the corner of Lioran's lips.

"You know I'm normally up for whatever, but I don't think we need to attract that type of attention right now." Fyn gestured toward the door.

I wrapped a leather band around my hair, pulling my locks slightly loose to cover my ears. Council would have enough to discuss without discovering the half-human in their presence.

The three of us began walking down the lengthy corridor. Lioran rested his hand on my shoulder. "It's okay if you want to stay here. We can let you know what is shared after."

I wasn't sure if I'd be allowed in such a space—if I had earned the right to stand beside them. Bailoc was still my home, even despite everything that happened there—and I deserved to hear the news myself, if he allowed it.

"I want to come with, if I can," I said.

"You are welcome to be there. I just don't know what will

be shared. No matter what Elric says you need to remain composed. No one can know the truth about who you are there." Lioran's voice lowered as Fyn stopped ahead.

"What do you fear if they know the truth? Pyrran already does."

"Pyrran may. Elric may know it too, but we don't know who they've told yet. Once they know who you truly are—the strength of the magic you possess...the threat may become greater than Pyrran and Elric."

I had wondered how many prying eyes may have seen me practicing with Cora. In a single glance all they would know was that I made flowers bloom, or a tree branch grow. The depths of my magic, the way I felt the land's energy shift through my fingertips remained concealed.

Fyn walked back over toward us—his hand settled on my shoulder. "Maybe you two should not enter together. Everyone has been wondering where you've been all morning. Lioran, go ahead. I'll bring her with me."

"Don't let Elric near her," Lioran said to Fyn before he strode ahead.

"Oh, I most certainly will not." Fyn's smirk stilled. His hand hadn't lifted from my shoulder. "Are you okay?"

"I'm fine." I didn't even believe my own words.

"I know you see me as Lioran's friend, but I'm yours, too. And if anyone ever hurts you...I don't care who it is. I want to know." He towered over me.

"Thank you, Fyn. I am honored to have you as a friend." I hugged him and he stumbled back for a moment. "Sorry. Should I not have done that?"

"Humans are strange creatures, but I guess that's perfectly fine." He chuckled as we walked down the hall.

Sunlight beamed into the grand council room from windows high above. The gathering was unlike any I had seen in Bailoc —females were present. They stood intermixed in the space— not as if they were watching, but as if they were a part of it.

Ready to be heard.

Expecting to be seen.

They glowed with confidence.

It was a place where anyone could be heard—I could be heard.

Lady Aura stood with her arms linked with a fae lord. A soft smile spread on her lips as she caught me staring.

Cora stopped beside me. She placed her hand on mine.

"Who called this emergency council meeting?" Lioran stood at the center. There was no throne. No crown upon his head. He was dressed just as he had been in my chambers.

"I did, Your Highness," Elric said.

"What news do you bring?" Lioran asked.

"The blight is spreading. Our supplies are growing thinner." Elric paced the open space before Lioran.

"This is not news. Surely you did not call us all here for this," Fyn chimed in. "We have regular outgoing shipments of supplies to support Othryl, Symra, and Weston."

"It is as we've predicted. Despite the threat, we continue to look into where else we can seek resources." Lioran drummed his fingers on his arms.

"We are researching solutions. My team of scholars will share whatever they find," Lady Aura's husband spoke up as he left her side and stood beside Lioran. He settled his hands on his hips.

"Lord Orion, we are grateful for your leadership in these efforts." Lioran nodded to him.

"What about your grounding magic, Your Highness?" Lady Aura asked.

"What could his grounding magic do? If His Highness could reverse the blight, I'm sure he would," another fae lord spoke. I could barely see him over those who stood next to me.

"It's not enough to erase the blight," Elric said.

A fae lady stepped forward. "What hope is there then? We continue to research, to gather, to spread ourselves so thin we may never recover." Her golden hair was perfectly folded into three elegant braids.

"I will continue to see what progress can be made with grounding magic. As of now, it isn't enough. The blight is thriving still." Lioran's exhale cascaded through the space, echoing off the stone walls. "I can't promise an easy answer. We are all doing whatever we can."

"At what point will we stop sending aid?" A low voice spoke behind Lord Orion. "We can't carry the weight of these outlier villages indefinitely."

"Lord Mavik, you can't honestly suggest just cutting them off to fend for themselves," Lady Aura protested. "Where is your honor?"

"We will never leave any of our people to starve." Lioran's voice boomed. "I don't care what it costs us. We will stand by each other."

"For now, there is still enough to go around." Fyn clasped his hands together. "We will reassess as needed."

"Is it true the human realm suffers?" the woman with golden braid asked.

"Yes." Elric's sharp glare fixated on me. "The blight spreads through Bailoc at a rapid rate."

My fingernails scraped my palm at the mention of Bailoc.

"And what are they doing about it?" Lioran interjected.

"King Ardyn seeks resources from outside of his kingdom, still. There are murmurs of a rebellion as their blight intensifies —the kingdom won't sustain."

Whispers sifted through the room.

The sun's glow shifted until the room dimmed.

I knew I shouldn't say a word, but still my lips parted. Lioran shot a warning glance in my direction. I held his gaze only for a second before it returned to Elric. My family, my people, would suffer if a rebellion took hold.

"A rebellion?" My voice grew louder than I intended. Lioran took in a sharp inhale.

"Yes, whispers of overthrowing the monarchy. Nothing has come of it yet, but since Bailoc has rejected outside efforts, I imagine it's only a matter of time." Elric's eyebrows raised.

"Why would they reject outside efforts?" Lord Mavik asked.

"An opportunity arose for a most prosperous alliance through a marriage between the king's eldest daughter and an ally that could offer relief to Bailoc. It did not come to fruition."

"Why not?" A lady's voice piped in from the back of the room.

"Their princess refused to participate."

"And they allowed it?" Lady Aura asked.

"I can't speak for her. Surely only she could explain her logic," Elric scoffed.

Cora assessed me.

"How have you heard news from the human realm?" Lord Orion's voice boomed between us.

"The High Court is in communication with a fae lord that lives on the other side of the wall." Elric watched me, waiting for my response.

My knees began to buckle beneath me, but I held onto Cora.

"And how does this fae lord know? I wasn't aware there were fae who chose to live on the other side of the wall." Lord Orion folded his deeply sun-kissed arms over his chest. His eyes were midnight blue, almost as dark as the onyx I wore around my neck.

"He is in regular communication with Bailoc. I assure you, he is a trusted source," Elric said.

"A fae that allied himself with our enemy?" Lord Mavik asked.

"Bailoc can solve their situation, and we will work to solve ours." Lioran's voice roared above the murmurs. "We will aid our people with whatever resources remain. We will not stop searching for a solution." Lioran stepped in front of Elric.

"Lord Orion and I plan to review inventory from the surrounding villages to assess how to streamline our shipments." Fyn tilted his head to Lord Orion. "We will gather what information we can from other territories too."

"We needn't seek out support from Kybar yet," Lioran interjected.

"Your Highness... soon, we may not have a choice," Lord Orion protested.

Elric hesitated before his lips parted. "Prince Pyrran would want to help."

"When the time comes, I'm sure he will be glad to," Fyn spoke quickly, before Lioran could respond.

"We will exhaust every resource," Lioran said.

"Oh, I certainly hope you will, Your Highness." Elric's glare cut to me again, lingering too long.

CHAPTER 22

Fyn held the door to Lioran's study. "Lioran will be here soon."

"Fyn, I need a moment with Aelira...alone." Cora's words were sharp. Fyn turned toward me, his brow raised. "Fyn. Now."

I nodded and he left. The crisp chill of the leather met my skin as I sank into the sofa.

Cora sat in the armchair across from me. "I was worried about you last night and maybe I had no right to be, but seeing you today..." She let out a heavy sigh.

I tightened my grip on the onyx, consumed by thoughts of them together. Neither its warmth nor chill greeted me. It felt exactly as a stone should.

It shouldn't even matter, but it did. "You knew from experience..."

"We don't need to go there. I don't even know what I want to say. I'm just worried about you. As your friend."

I studied her. "You're worried he took things too far? That we both did?"

She hesitated. The firelight flickered across Lioran's dim study.

"I stopped things from escalating," I said.

Cora released a sigh that echoed through the study. "I'm sorry. It's none of my business."

"I appreciate you looking out for me." She eased at my words. The rest of my thoughts remained unsaid. She tried to shield me, but still I couldn't help feeling upset about what they used to be. Even if it no longer existed.

I nestled my hands under my thighs. They quaked as Lioran and Fyn entered the room.

The fire crackled in the hearth. I stiffened, the memory of last night echoing with it.

Lioran trailed my gaze, and his breathing slowed. "Aelira?"

"I'm fine." The words barely escaped my lips—I wanted to extinguish the fire, but for now I'd have to focus beyond the popping embers that tormented me.

"Perhaps you were right. Thalen had something to do with it all." Fyn rubbed his temples. "The king promised you to Thalen, didn't he? It's why his men came after us in the woods..."

"I am still promised to him." My words barely carried over the roaring fire.

Fyn shook his head. "Still? Lioran, you are awfully calm about this revelation."

Lioran's fingers trailed my back. "I knew."

Fyn's jaw tightened. "You knew...and you thought it would be no problem to be with his bride?" I had never seen Fyn truly snap.

"Fyn." Lioran slammed his hand against the arm of the sofa.

Cora leaned back further in her chair. "You could have told us."

"Please. This is my fault," I cried.

"You didn't choose him. Ardyn did. You didn't even know who he was," Lioran said.

Fyn's hand slid over his lips as he glared at Lioran.

Cora pressed the wrinkled fabric of her gown. "Elric's ties to Thalen are concerning. There's something more underneath it all." Her lips pursed as a short breath escaped her.

Lioran shifted. "You've seen something haven't you?"

Cora shifted in her chair. "Nothing about Elric, but he knows things he shouldn't—couldn't possibly. Maybe Thalen's magic is guiding him, but even still it doesn't make sense." She watched me carefully. "Aelira, does Thalen know about your magic?"

"I never told him. I didn't even know," I said.

"What are you implying, Cora?" Lioran asked.

I leaned into Lioran. "Does Elric have magic?"

"Odds are he does. He likes to point out that I don't have any," Fyn interjected. "He's always showing up, especially around Aelira. Maybe he's just watching her for Thalen."

My fingers gripped Lioran's. "He's been using everything he can figure out about me against me—against us."

Cora swallowed hard, her gulp echoing through the chambers.

"I know the High Court assigned him here, but he can do serious damage if he stays," Fyn said.

"It may do more if he goes. I want him here where we can keep an eye on him." Lioran shifted behind me on the sofa. "As if the blight spreading wasn't enough to deal with..."

"Speaking of the blight. I had a vision—one that may hold the answer you've been looking for. It's been in front of us for a while now, but you may not like it." Cora fidgeted with her pale green gown.

"Why will I not like it?" Lioran's fierce voice echoed in the quaint study.

"It's Aelira." Her emerald eyes widened.

"How?" I still struggled to control my magic at times, it still felt so new.

"I have only seen pieces, so there has to be more to it than I know. She restored the land by connecting her magic to the tree in the center of Myrwood Grove." Her words trembled along with her fingers.

"Absolutely not." Lioran shot to his feet. He paced the length of the study.

Guilt hovered over me. It lingered in the stillness that followed the council meeting. Threat of rebellion loomed over Bailoc. My choice only made things worse. If I had any way to fix the land, to ease the blight, I wanted to hear how.

"Connected how?" I asked.

Cora shifted, her nerves gripping her with each breath she took—even her eye twitched.

"That grove is full of dark magic that settled after the war. It has a way of undoing the most powerful of fae. It doesn't matter what she saw. You can't just go there and expect to return." Fyn shook his head.

"Or so we're told...we don't know anyone who has faced it before," Cora said.

No one they knew had faced it. None that remained to tell the tale, yet suddenly I found myself hanging on her every word.

"Tell me what I can do." I glanced past Lioran.

"I've been waiting, hoping more would be revealed to me." Cora's eyes stilled, her expression shifted as if her mind was somewhere else entirely.

"What did I do?" I squinted at her.

"You gave your magic to the land. You gave all of it...until the blight reversed."

"All of it?" I played with the loose fabric on my gown.

Cora blinked back tears that pooled in her eyes. "All of it."

Lioran's voice boomed. "Enough! I'm not letting her do that." He bolted upwards, stopping inches from Cora. "I'll do it instead."

Cora flinched. "Lioran, you weren't in my vision—it was Aelira."

If she saw it, maybe I could do it.

I couldn't blindly agree to it, but if it was an answer, I would hear whatever she had to say. "Tell me what I would need to do."

"No." He pointed at her. "You will not tell her anything else about it. Aelira, I will not let you do this."

"Let me?" I lifted my chin.

Fyn gripped the arm of the chair.

"I've heard enough. It is not happening." Lioran's voice boomed. "You should have come to me with this sooner."

"And then what? You would have made a choice for me?" I gripped the leather beneath me.

"Cora, maybe we should give them a moment," Fyn said.

She was inches from the door when my words broke the silence. "This is what you saw? What our relationship started?"

"Yes. I only saw a glimpse of it originally, but it keeps replaying...and slowly building." Her head hung low—she looked only at her feet.

"How did us being together have anything to do with this?" I asked.

"He's connected you to your fae side. He awakened part of your magic. It was the start of it all." She slipped out the door and didn't look back.

Fyn left with her, without saying another word.

"You knew she had a vision about us, and you didn't tell me," Lioran scolded me.

"I didn't know why. She said if she told me, it would influence things. Maybe she meant influence us being together...But that's impossible. I chose you." I leaned back into the couch, my heart racing. "I need to decide. You can't choose for me."

He sat back beside me, his hands bracing my arms. "It's too dangerous." His hand extended, settling beside mine.

"If I can do this—I need to consider it. I left an entire kingdom behind—they're my responsibility. My sister is still there." I had barely spoken of Ashlyn to Lioran. Thinking of her left me in tears.

He pulled me in closer as I spoke. If anyone understood the duty to protect others, it was him. His hands settled on my back. "They're not your responsibility—you do not need to solve this on your own. Cora's visions sometimes shift. There will be another way." He kissed my forehead.

I closed my eyes, clinging to his with warmth, before Cora's words settled again.

Cora's palm trailed over the rose petals. I had searched everywhere for her.

"I want you to help me—so I can be prepared." I hadn't even decided if I would do it. "If I choose it."

"Just because I saw it doesn't mean you need to do it." Her hand took mine. Cora's eyes were red, as if she had been crying. "I believe visions are one version of the future, a fate we may choose. Nothing is binding you to that fate."

"I didn't have any magic left?"

"It took it all." Cora's voice softened.

A single dew drop hovered on the edge of a petal. I poked it and it trickled down the petal. "All the decisions I've made… everything I've dragged Lioran into. I doomed my people when I crossed the divide." I folded my hands across my chest. My fingers stiffened as I felt the pain of it all settle.

"You care deeply. Not just for yourself, or for Lioran, but for our world. It's why the stars chose you." With her words, the weight lifted, a subtle shift that steadied me.

I reached out and hugged her. Her hands squeezed around my back.

"Thank you," I whispered to her.

"For what?"

"Believing in me." I smiled.

"Only you can decide what is right for you. Don't let others define your choice." A glimmer of hope reflected in her emerald eyes.

CHAPTER 23

Lioran rode to Othryl with a supply shipment, and I avoided saying goodbye. I needed time that only space would allow.

Fyn tried to assure me Lioran wasn't angry, but I wasn't sure I believed it.

Cora and I spent endless hours working with plants, trees, and the dirt itself until I felt the magic run deeper in my veins. I could call on it with little thought, but even with my newfound ease, it took from me still. My daily pain was a constant reminder of what I would give every time I used my magic.

The corridors of the castle echoed with each aching step. My heart throbbed in beat with the sound.

Lioran caught me deep in thought. He waited for me outside my door.

I wanted to embrace him but resisted. "You're home."

"I know you don't want to see me right now." His body stiffened.

"No, I do." My arm settled on the door to my chambers, pushing it open.

"We need to discuss Myrwood Grove."

"You need to let me make this decision on my own."

"I can't..." He exhaled. "The Grove is far too dangerous. The cost is too great. Cora may be wrong."

"My existence...started a war. A war that resulted in a blight—and if I'm the solution, I must consider if I can pay the price."

"I don't know of any fae that have had their magic severed from them. What if it takes more than your magic?"

He wouldn't stop until I backed down—until I told him I wouldn't go. I didn't want to discuss it any longer.

Sunlight danced across the high ceiling, casting leafy shadows over my bed. My head lowered—this room was a constant reminder of who I would never be. As much as I hoped to keep the thoughts at bay, they crept back in like the tide—unpredictable and unrelenting.

"Maybe we shouldn't be doing this. Maybe it's time to stop."

His breathing intensified. "What are you talking about?"

"I mean this..." I gestured my hand around the room. "It's meant for someone who isn't me."

"It is yours. Please. We just don't agree on Cora's vision." His words were desperate. A stinging chill slid down my back.

The color slowly drained from his cheeks, and his eyes dimmed.

"You will be the king your people deserve." My lips grazed his—if I could keep this moment—this feeling for all eternity, I would. "I will be your loyal subject always."

He cupped my face in his palm. "You will never bow to me."

My heart unclenched with his touch, but my jaw tightened with his words.

"The stars have other plans for us. Maybe it's time for us to accept that."

"I will never." He leaned closer, his lips hovering over mine —as if he were asking permission to kiss me again.

My lips greeted his and I sank down inside of myself.

"Maybe there's another way..." I hesitated to say it, unsure if I even believed it. "A way for us to still love each other, even when you...marry someone else." I could never promise it, but I said it like I could.

"What life would that be for you? Keeping secrets..." His hands wrapped around me, holding me in front of him. "You'd stand there and watch me with my wife...with my children... while we exist in stolen moments?"

It was never what I wanted for myself.

Someday he would marry her, his queen. She would love him maybe even how I had. It wouldn't just break my heart to steal away in secret, it would break hers.

I couldn't do that to either of us.

"Could you?" He wouldn't stop until I answered him.

I could see it all.

His wife. His children. His life without me.

A bitter taste settled on my tongue.

"When the time comes for you to marry, you will do what you must." I would disappear somewhere else—far from the high court, maybe even far from Lythira.

He wouldn't hear from me again, because even with glimmers of his love, it would never be enough.

I knew our time would be limited, but I chose to live in this fantasy.

"You deserve a home—a place where you're safe and happy."

"Don't." I pulled from his grasp.

"Be honest with me, because I can't stop wondering how you really feel—what you truly want." Lioran stepped closer, his hand reaching for mine. "I need to hear it for myself. That you don't desire any of the things that being with me in secret would take from you—that you never wanted to be a wife, or have children of your own..." He inched closer. "You'd be hidden, living a life that you could never make your own."

"Just stop." I could barely speak, barely breathe.

I had never told him how much I wanted those things. Never shared the future I always envisioned.

"Tell me. I need to hear you say that you're okay with that life. That you could exist only as my—" He flinched.

"I want all of that. I've always wanted all of that. Now I'm supposed to go watch you live that life with someone else. She will give you everything you truly want in a way I will never be permitted to."

"No one else ever could." The lines around his eyes hardened with my words.

"When you must marry, I will find someplace else to go." He wrapped his arms around me as I collapsed into him.

"Where will you go?"

"I don't know. I will figure something out."

He saw Cora's vision as a threat against me, but I held onto it still. It brought me hope that maybe my future would carry meaning that was bigger than the heart break.

He would never understand. As much as I feared the fate she described, I couldn't stop thinking about it.

"My heart would never recover." His truth filled the void between us, gripping my heart harder.

"One day this will be nothing more than a beautiful memory."

"I'll live in it every day for the rest of my life," he whispered in my ear. "If it's too painful for you to stay...I understand."

"If my heart has to break, I will let it break." My voice cracked.

His finger slid over my lip—his head shook.

"I will be with you until I can't any longer."

I would live in our love for the days, months, or years that remained.

The musty scent of paper wafted in the air. Shelves as tall as the ceiling were lined with books bound in dozens of hues.

I found Fyn hovering over papers in the library. "Cora said I might find you here. I need to do something, and she doesn't have time for training today. Is there anything I can help with?"

"Are you alright?" He asked.

"No." My lips quivered.

He patted the bench beside him. "Want to talk about it?"

"We can never truly be together."

A hint of sympathy glimmered behind Fyn's eyes. "You've had his heart the entire time. I think you're the only one to ever truly hold it." Fyn dropped his quill on the parchment, his hands motioned me closer. "This struggle isn't just yours. He was here a moment ago. You two are more alike than you think." He cleared his throat.

"Fyn?"

"I know what it feels like..." His words crept between us. "It is a wonderful thing to love deeply, but unbearable to know it'll be taken from you." He choked on his words, as his eyes hazed over.

"Who is she?"

A smile tugged at his lips, but he fought it back. "Her voice was..." He grabbed the quill again. "She is no one."

"No one... has you this emotional?"

"I am not emotional. Goodness—I try to relate to you, and you turn it around on me."

"Okay...so this relationship with no one has you feeling like you understand what I'm going through?"

"Fine. She lives in Eyrsea. Her magic was tied to the sea, but my duty to Lythira kept me here. It wasn't tragic or anything."

"Sure," I nodded. "I shouldn't have pried."

"You really shouldn't." He continued scanning his list. "The moment she said I couldn't give her what she wanted; I stopped trying. I should have done anything, but I never went after her." He rolled up the parchment and placed it aside.

"I'm sorry, Fyn" I said.

"Don't waste your time with him. Allow yourself to have whatever you wish with him, while you still can. So you don't live to regret it."

"That is exactly what I want, but sometimes it feels too painful."

"You will find your own way, in your own time." He chuckled, but despair entangled with the fading sound of his laughter. "You always do. Probably because you're so stubborn."

"Just when I think you're about to say something nice about me."

"I say nice things about you to others all the time."

"Sure you do, Fyn." I smirked at him. "Is there anything I can do to help with your work? I haven't been able to stop thinking about the conversation in the emergency council. I need to do something."

He pushed a scroll over towards me. "Lord Orion and I are organizing a group to pack supplies for Othryl. We'd love the help if you're willing to do the work."

"I'm willing to do whatever is needed." I unrolled the

paper. A detailed list of healing herbs was transcribed line by line.

"The others will be waiting outside—Lord Orion, Lady Aura, and whoever else he's gathered."

Their world had slowly become mine, but I remained an outsider. "They won't mind me helping?"

"No one turns down an offer to help around here." Fyn gathered his paperwork.

Voices carried through the castle halls as fae ladies and lords carried crates to the courtyard.

"You can help Rowena with the herbs," Fyn said as he gestured to the fae healer that helped Lioran during his time in the infirmary. "Rowena, Lady Aelira is here to assist you."

"I will gladly take your help, my lady." Rowena nodded to me.

"Please, just call me Aelira."

She nodded. Her hand extended to crates beside her. "We will take the supply list and make sure everything is prepared for the next shipment. The healers there are without many essentials."

"We stopped in Othryl, with Prince Lioran." My heart hardened with the thought of the healer, so frail she couldn't help him.

"You know how essential this work is then." I nodded, blinking back the tears.

Lady Aura eyed me from across the courtyard as she directed crates of produce into place. Lord Orion checked them each off his list.

I sat beside Rowena, reading names of herbs off the list. "We don't have oregano?" The glass bottles clanked in the crates as I sifted through the contents.

"No, it won't grow as fast as we use it. It's a shame, too, it has so many wonderful medicinal properties—to fight off infection."

I thought of the lavender fields, of the roses blooming beneath the willow. Maybe I could make it grow. Everything I grew I had touched before, but I wasn't sure if I had ever even seen oregano.

"Rowena?" I hesitated to ask, to admit what magic I had hidden from them all. "Do you have any oregano?"

"Yes, but we need it desperately here, too. I don't mean to be selfish, but I can't part with it."

"Can you bring some oregano to me? Even if you have just a sprig. I can give it back when I'm done."

"Done with what?" Her eyebrows rose.

"Are you almost done packing the herbs?" Lady Aura ran her fingers along her dress, trails of dirt fell on the fabric.

"Almost. Can we have a little more time? I wanted to try to prepare something for the shipment." I stood beside her.

Fyn watched from a distance as he crouched beside a crate.

"Whatever you and Rowena have will be welcomed," Fyn interjected. A hint of a warning glimmered through his gaze.

"If you bring me the oregano Rowena—I may be able to make more." I looked at the dirt beneath a nearby oak tree.

"Make more? How?" Lady Aura's gaze softened.

"With my magic." My voice was a low murmur.

"I'll get some." Rowena stood and darted back inside.

Fyn leaned over me until only I could hear his whisper. "Do not get me in trouble, please."

Rowena returned moments later, a sprig in her hand—my fingers trailed it, I closed my eyes as I caressed the soft fuzzy leaves, the pungent smell lifted to my nostrils. I handed it back to her and ran my fingers in the soil beside the castle wall.

Magic awoke within me, my skin still carried the scent of the sprig and tingled as if the fuzz from the leaf still lingered there. I felt the land call to me, a whisper that pulsed up through the ground. The ground felt firm beneath my fingers, as my energy drifted away from me. When I opened my eyes again, all those who came to help Othryl stood beside me.

They assessed the oregano as it came to life beneath my fingertips.

Fyn extended a hand to me. "Of course...You had to do that." He winked as he raised me to stand. "He's not going to love this," he murmured under his breath.

Rowena ripped a sprig free from the soil, and inhaled. "You made them grow? How?"

"My magic sometimes helps flowers grow, I thought maybe it would help the oregano, too."

Lady Aura placed her hand on my arm. "Thank you." Her gaze greeted mine—I thought I saw a hint of acceptance behind it.

Rowena wiped back tears from her eyes. "Thank you, Aelira."

"Your Highness," Lady Aura called to Lioran as he walked out of the castle. "You didn't tell us you had one with such interesting talents amongst us." She gestured to me.

The stone castle wall felt cool against my back, settling me as my body trembled from the weight of willing the oregano to grow. My muscles pulsed with a dull ache.

"Aura, not everything needs a grand explanation," Lord Orion interjected. "We're grateful for your help, my lady." He lowered his head to me.

"You did this?" Pride beamed in Lioran's eyes as he looked back at me.

"There wasn't enough to give the healer in Othryl."

"Thank you. They will be delighted to see the full shipment." Rowena's eyes met mine.

I stumbled. Lioran caught me by the arm, but released me quickly.

"Are you alright? I'm sure that was exhausting. Your Highness, maybe you can take her inside—get her out of the sun for a while?" Rowena asked.

I quickly nodded.

Fyn crept in between Rowena and me. "You did good." He placed a firm hand on my shoulder. "If he asks though, this was completely your idea. I am in no way responsible."

"It was my idea, Fyn." I laughed.

"Exactly." He nodded.

Lioran rolled his eyes at Fyn as Rowena stepped away to gather more bottles for the oregano.

CHAPTER 24

L ioran trailed behind me into the castle. "You..."

"It had to be done." I didn't look back at him.

"You gave them a gift none of us could, not even me." His fingers found mine for a stolen moment before he dropped them. "You gave freely, knowing they could all see the depths of your magic."

"Anyone could have seen hints of my magic at any time." My shoulders fell. "I don't need to hide who I am. The High Court will know, if they don't already. Othryl needed me. The village is desperate."

His head hung lower. "I wasn't trying to hide you. Only to keep you safe from those who would try to use your power for their own gain...or reveal you to my parents."

"I don't care the cost. I can help."

He rubbed his temples. "I can't get past the irony."

"How is me helping them ironic?"

He pushed an oak door open, revealing a room full of wooden crates. "That by our laws you can't be queen, yet I couldn't think of anyone better to wear the crown."

I didn't want to go back to that conversation, to that state. He closed the door behind us. The scent of oregano still clung to my fingertips.

It felt good to use my magic to help Othryl. I could still give my magic to restore everything that plagued them, but once it was gone, a part of who I was would vanish with it. I hadn't asked Cora any more about the vision, but I didn't have to. Every day it hovered over me.

"Can we just pretend that none of it matters? We can just exist here together. For now."

I thought of Fyn's pain. His words hung over me still.

He was mine, and I would love him until the stars divided us.

"I savor every moment," he said, tracing the curve of my jaw with his fingers. "My heart will only ever belong to you."

I pulled him closer, pressing a slow kiss on his lips.

"Aelira," he whispered my name. The heat of his breath was hot on my neck. "I..."

"Stay here with me," I whispered

A part of me would still pretend he could give me always. Visions of him poured into my mind as my eyes shut—sipping drinks by the fire in his chambers. Strolling through the courtyard together, with my hand in his. Riding with Gaia and Veylar openly, freely wherever we wished through the Heart. If fate had determined otherwise—it would have all been ours to keep.

It was the only future I could picture—the only one that gave my heart exactly what it wanted. I didn't need anything else. Only him.

He pulled his lips free from mine. "If I found a different way..."

My finger pressed to his lips.

"If I left it all behind..." The words trailed off almost as if they were never spoken.

The air grew thicker. My skin became hotter with his touch. I wanted his words. Wanted that truth, but I wouldn't let him make that choice. He would be the king his people deserved.

"You will make a wonderful king," I whispered the words I didn't want to speak.

His dark curls tumbled in his face as he shook his head. "Sometimes I think about leaving...taking you far away from here." His lips forcefully pressed into mine. "We could have the life we want without the crown. Without any of this."

A pleading gaze. Hands that slid over my head. Our kiss ached with desperation.

His leather tunic laces caught on my fingertips.

The door creaked. I stumbled out of his grasp.

Fyn didn't bother hiding the amusement in his eyes as he reaching for a crate. "You could have at least taken her somewhere more romantic."

I straightened my dress, pressing the emerald fabric down.

Lioran fumbled with the laces on his tunic. "Do you mind, Fyn?"

"No, I don't really..." He hoisted it off the shelf. "Lord Orion was looking for you. Good thing I found you first."

"Go," I said, nodding to him. "I'll find you later."

Lioran leaned in and kissed my forehead. My fingers gripped his as he stepped toward the door.

A slow smile spread across his face as he turned around to look back at me.

Desperation consumed me. His words left me aching.

The taste of his lips lingered on mine for a moment more.

I sank deep into the tub in my chambers. Rose petals bobbed at the surface. I traced each one.

If he meant what he said—if there was a way we could be free, I would gladly take it.

I held my breath and plunged under water.

We couldn't rearrange fate's design.

I twisted my drenched hair until the water dripped from it, trickling back into the tub. A woolen blanket hung off the edge of the tub. Its scratchy fabric shifted over me.

I watched the clouds drift from a haze of white to a perfectly painted sky as the bed cradled me.

Chirping crickets awoke me with their moonlight song. Their music startled me.

Lioran. I never went to find him.

Moonlight illuminated my reflection in my dressing mirror. I slipped into a robe of golden silk. As I tied it closed, my shoulders fell back—my chin lifted. I knew what I wanted. It had only ever been him.

As I closed my eyes, I felt him lingering nearby. His energy pulsed with mine. Like he was calling to me.

My feet carried me down the hall. Before I could even knock, the door opened. Lioran gripped my waist. He pulled me into his chambers.

"I haven't been able to stop thinking about you," he said.

Candlelight flickered from every shelf and window ledge. He kissed my neck. Heat simmered from deep within me.

His lips danced with mine, slowly, deeply. When he released me, his chrome eyes glimmered with moonlight.

My fingers nestled in the fabric of his robe. They slid over his chest as it rose with every ragged breath. I studied the angles of his jaw, his eyes, the lines in his skin.

This dance between us was dangerous.

It was reckless.

It was his. It was mine.

The smell of him wasn't enough. The taste of him wasn't enough.

I needed all of him.

He exhaled sharply. "You're shaking." His eyes narrowed on mine. "We should stop."

"No." I led his hands down my curves. "Don't stop."

My back arched as he traced his fingers along my spine. "I am yours," I said as I leaned into him.

"I'll never understand the stars, but just for this moment. I won't question them. They led me to you." Lioran gripped my waist, bringing me closer until I felt his body settle against mine.

I lifted his hand in mine, backing toward the bed.

"Aelira..." He waited. I guided his hands to my robe. He gently unwrapped the fabric. It fell to the floor.

I watched him remove his.

His fingers ran through my hair, his lips leaned desperately into mine. Heat engulfed me as he leaned into me. I let myself drown in him—each sensation pulsing through me.

I ached for him.

I watched each measured breath he took. My heart was a shell of what it once was. He would always hold the rest. I nestled my head against his chest—his heartbeat lulled me back to sleep.

When my eyes opened again, he sat in his armchair, watching me. The sunlight highlighted his loose curls. It danced on the silver flecks that shone in his eyes.

He smiled—slow and deliberate.

"You didn't wake me."

"You looked so peaceful. I wanted to keep this moment." He rose from the chair and laid down on the bed beside me. His hand ran down my back, he pressed his lips to mine—a shiver ran through me.

My muscles ached—a quiet reminder of what I freely gave him.

Of everything we risked.

I gripped the covers tightly.

"Lioran." My jaw clenched.

"What's wrong?"

"I wasn't thinking..." I exhaled a rigid breath. "About what we just risked...about what could happen."

Nothing had prepared me for this moment. In Bailoc no one made this choice. If they did it was never spoken of.

"Aelira," he whispered, fully understanding my spiral. "You'll be fine. I have something to prevent life from taking hold. After the Verdant Alignment, I retrieved a vial from Rowena's supplies. In case you chose this."

The cabinet creaked as he pried open the door. A vial of glowing violet liquid sat on the shelf. He carefully lifted it and brought it to me.

I pried the stopper from the vial. The purple liquid rolled slowly. One little vial to protect us both.

His gaze rested heavily on me. "I wish you didn't have to take it."

"If only you could really leave it all behind." I tilted my head back and drank every drop.

My eyes only watered.

The sweet liquid sat on my tongue—lavender, rose, chamomile, with hints of something I had never tasted. As I inhaled, I felt it settle within me—warm and calm.

He embraced me as I still clutched the vial. "I meant what I said."

"I love that you did." I blinked back the tears. "Council will be waiting for you."

"I can be late." He held me tighter.

"Go," I whispered.

He took the bottle from my hands, and with a loud thud set it on a table in the corner. The sound echoed in the silence between us.

When he left, I slipped from his chambers back into mine.

I would never regret the choice we made.

My hand trailed the window ledge. Sparkling light shifted through my fingertips. It trailed the vines that still clung to my chambers. Blooms sprouted—roses woven into the vines. Brighter and faster than before.

My arrow sailed through the clearing. It lodged itself in the center of the target.

The last month passed in a blur—stolen moments, making love under the moon's glow. Together we were whole, but the land wasn't.

The blight crept slowly into the Heart. More trees became infected. Outer edges of the Heart began to decay. Lioran and I could not ease the land's pain. Even as the shadows crept further inward, I tended to the castle garden. My favorite flowers filled every open space. Each one just as I remembered them in Bailoc, until one bloom outshone the rest.

Deep within me something altered—a swift heat that traveled through me, it left me breathless. My magic simmered with it. With a wave of my glimmering magic, a single dahlia bloomed. The stem was a midnight hue. The fuchsia petals unfurled in waves of color, fading from pink to a blazing coral. I had never seen anything like it before.

Lioran marveled at the dahlia, but he didn't speak a word about it. His tender smile flashed in my memory whenever I gazed at the flower, but his hesitation lingered beneath it. I still didn't know if he approved, or if it worried him. It held a dangerous kind of beauty. Still, I cherished it.

Dark circles etched further beneath his eyes. The land's destruction took a toll on him, but it wasn't long until I discovered something else was weighing on him, too.

An emissary arrived from the High Court, bearing a command from the king and queen: there would be no more time granted. Their patience was withering.

At any moment he could be called to take the throne. A fae king didn't need to die for power to shift—the fae lived far too long to always rule. The crown would pass to Lioran when the stars decided it was his time. He was the chosen one, marked as the heir to the throne at fate's command. When he came of age each tattoo appeared for his three chosen roles—prince, guardian, and future king.

A decision on his marriage would be made with or without him. I heard it all when I went to find Lioran in his study. My heart was breaking, but he didn't know it. He didn't tell me at all.

I lived in fading moments.

"The High Court will not wait any longer." Lioran pulled the bow back from hands, peering into my eyes. "A summons has arrived."

"When do you leave?" I lowered the bow.

"*We* leave tomorrow. They've requested your presence, too." He held a rolled-up parchment scroll.

"I'm not going." The air caught sharp in my lungs. I wasn't ready to face it.

"It is not in our power to refuse them."

"What if they make me go with Thalen?" My muscles clenched, trembling beyond my control.

"I will do whatever I can to keep you in Lythira." He placed the bow at my feet and wrapped his hands around mine. The circles set even darker beneath his eyes.

"Without you...while they prepare you to take the throne?" I didn't want to have to say it.

He should have been the one to tell me, but it didn't seem he intended to at all. Lioran looked at the blades of grass beneath his feet.

"Have you already chosen your bride?" The tears wouldn't stop the moment they started.

"No." His voice grew unsteady.

"When were you going to tell me?"

"When I exhausted every possible solution. When hope was gone entirely. Until then I thought it was better if only I was breaking...but you knew."

"I heard it all," I finally admitted.

He looked back up at me. "I'm so sorry." His shoulders rounded. "I couldn't break your heart, especially if I didn't have to."

"In what world do you think you don't have to?" I scolded him.

He cupped his hands around my face. "I need you. Only you." I slipped back out of his grasp. Too many could stumble upon us and see.

"I'm not yours to keep." I lifted the bow. It quaked in my grip. Anger boiled within me, but it wasn't all his to claim.

Fate would destroy me.

It had always intended to.

I had no control of what the future held, but for now, I would keep him just a little longer. "I love you," I whispered. "I will always love you. The stars gave me something beautiful, and I will never stop thanking them for every single moment."

"I love you," he said, but his voice carried as if he didn't care who heard. "And I will never let you go."

"Tonight, you don't have to," I said.

CHAPTER 25

The road to the High Court was long, winding through forests and quaint villages. It would take days to reach the palace.

Birdsong woke me. I stared up through the canopy of leaves overhead. As I gently lifted Lioran's arm off me, he shifted. A soft groan escaped his lips.

I studied him, memorizing the freckle by his eye, so soft and faint it was barely visible.

We had only one day left until we reached the High Court.

My few important possessions lay packed beside me. I would not go back to Lythira. Juniper emptied my room before we left. She prepared the chambers for his wife while I bathed. Everything was brought in fresh.

I asked her to.

They didn't wait for me to leave—I told her not to.

The preparations were done in silence. Lioran wasn't told. He would never let it happen if he knew.

I needed to watch. I needed for it to break me.

So I'd remember—he wasn't mine to keep.

Blades of grass crackled beneath my boots with each careful step I took toward Gaia. I was desperate to feel her warmth—for her to ground me. She settled in my touch as my fingers slid down the bridge of her nose. I loosened the rope that held her still.

In my mind I told her to go to the pond, she trotted ahead without another command.

Veylar's breath blew, its stark cadence startling me. He pawed the dirt. As I released him from the long lead, a chill gushed through me—it wasn't mine, it wasn't Gaia's. This was new.

His nostrils flared and then I knew who I sensed—it was Veylar. He paced, watching me. Maybe he was wishing Lioran was by his side instead.

"Let's get you some water," I whispered. Veylar stepped back. The feeling lingered, it wrapped around me. "Everything will be okay," I crooned as our foreheads met, my tears releasing onto the stallion.

Lioran shifted on his mat, turning toward me. Even though I didn't utter a single word, Veylar followed me to the pond. When we reached the water's edge, he lowered his head to drink. Lioran's eyes met mine and he nodded back at me.

The sea of green parted until the golden tips of the palace towers glinted in the distance. It towered higher than my home in Bailoc. Sunlight painted the silver walls, like starlight through crystal.

This was his home—it was the very last place I'd ever see him again.

My grip on Gaia's reins tightened, but she did not falter. Even as we slowed to a steady trot.

Golden gates drew back at the sight of the future king. Each metal rod was topped with a golden arrow that pointed up to the sky.

Lioran's chin angled upward as he climbed from the saddle. Dozens of guards lined the path, bowing to the heir to the throne.

My twitching fingers slid into a guard's cold, clammy palm. I longed to feel Lioran's hands around my waist, wishing he would be the one to lift me from the saddle.

But he proceeded without a glance in my direction. A sharp chill trailed my spine.

Each guard held his head high as we walked past.

"Your Highness," a fae knight greeted Lioran.

"It is good to see you, Sir Roman." Lioran extended an arm out to the lord, who greeted him the same.

"You must be Princess Aelira." Sir Roman towered over both Lioran and I, but his smile was tender and bright. "Welcome to the High Court, Your Highness."

"Thank you, Sir Roman." I bowed my head to him.

"No, Your Highness...a Princess does not bow," Sir Roman said.

My title felt foreign. Everything had changed since I crossed the divide—Aelira was the only part of me that remained.

I looked to Lioran; afraid I would falter again. His eyes softened, but he quickly dropped his gaze.

"Prince Lioran, Prince Calyth would like to speak with you. He says it's a matter of urgent importance."

"Send him to my chambers," Lioran commanded, his tone formal and cold.

"You haven't much time. You'll be expected in the throne room within the hour," Sir Roman said.

Lioran warned they would waste little time when we arrived. Even still, I hadn't expected to stand before them immediately.

"I would like to change." The grime of the road had settled on my skin. I was desperate to wash it way.

"Certainly. We will have a lady's maid show you and Lady Cora to your chambers," Sir Roman said.

Our chambers. A place for Cora and I to remain, but Lioran wouldn't enter. The air released from my lungs and threatened to live outside of me only.

I forced an inhale so that I could speak again. "Thank you, Sir Roman."

"Your Highness, my lady. I will show you both to your room. Your things will be brought up shortly. You must prepare to meet the king and queen," an older fae woman greeted us, silver streaks peeked through her jet-black hair. She smoothed a plain, gray gown. I glanced over my shoulder at Lioran as we stepped forward into the palace.

One last look at my heart as it left my body.

Crystal doors walled off the palace from the outside world, but the outside glow trailed inside. Cora offered her arm to me. I was grateful for her steady presence.

The winding halls of the palace were etched with golden filagree. Paintings full of muted hues spanned the length of the walls. Chill air held stagnant as if the entire wing of the palace were rarely ever used.

Cora walked beside me, her focus set on our guide. She had known Lioran since she was a child. Maybe she had walked these halls before.

An arched ceiling hung overhead framing the center of our room. A large bed lay in the middle, ivory fabric hanging from its wooden frame. A quaint smaller bed lay along the side wall.

Cora and I had never existed in such a formal space—in Lythira we were friends, we were equal. She showed no resistance to the space, but bowed her head politely as I stilled mine.

"You will have staff at your service whenever you need it, Your Highness. Shall we draw up a bath for you and your lady?" the lady's maid asked.

"Our journey was long. I would very much like to freshen up." The words slipped from my lips as if I had never left Bailoc.

Lady's maids stripped me of my dirt drenched gown. Warm rose bathwater greeted my skin. I reached for the soap and the lady's maid gripped it before I had the chance.

"Your Highness, it is our job to assist you."

"Thank you," I said.

Cora was left on her own to bathe and dress.

"I have my own gowns," I said as they began to open a wardrobe.

"I've seen them Your Highness," the lady's maid replied. "We've been instructed to fit you with gowns that suit your station. Nothing you've brought with you is suitable for your audience with their majesties."

I wasn't sure they'd find me suitable either.

Layers of tulle, an underskirt, and a corset were fastened in place. Inky-black fabric layered with delicate gold floral embroidery draped from a fitted bodice.

I rubbed the onyx between my fingers, but only the chill of the chain could be felt around my neck. The boning pressed into an under corset, my lungs compressing beneath it all.

Lioran's touch still lingered, even though it had been hours since I last felt it.

I savored the feeling, knowing that someday I would forget the way he felt.

"You look beautiful, Your Highness." Cora bowed to me. Her dress was a dazzling cascade of pink fabric that flowed freely over her hips.

"As do you." I clutched my corset. "I would like a moment alone with Lady Cora." My stark voice filled the space.

"There isn't much time before your audience with the king and queen, so please make it brief." The head lady's maid bowed her head before they all took their leave.

"Cora..." I gasped as the weight of the dress constricted around me.

"You will find your way."

"What makes you so sure?"

"All we ever have is the faith we give ourselves. You must believe you will rise above this."

"And what if I have no faith? No strength left to give myself?" I asked.

"You do—you are just afraid."

"He will never be mine again. Never." My voice cracked. "None of this is my choice."

I had resigned myself to the fate that lay ahead. Lioran was to marry. I was to be dealt with. None of it was new—none of it was a surprise.

But as I stood there, looking at myself in the mirror, the ache took hold. There was no turning back. His wife's room had been reset. The plans had been made for his future—maybe a bride had already been chosen.

I thought I was ready to give him up, but now that we were here, I knew I never would be.

She gripped my shaking hands in hers. "You are the Princess of Bailoc. They will never admit it, but your words have weight here. Choose them carefully."

"I value his future. Everything he must be."

"You can value his future, but you must also value yours. One is not more important than the other." She hesitated for a second, her eyes fixated on the window as if it somehow revealed how much time remained. "Don't get so caught up in what can't be that you can't see what already is."

"I can't go on without him." I knew I never would.

Cora lay my dark waves over my gown. "One day, you will look back on all of this. When you do, you need to know you did everything you could to honor yourself. This is your life... your future." Her voice trailed off as her weight shifted.

"Even if it breaks me..." I whispered.

"You will only get one chance."

Choice was not something I had been granted in Bailoc, and if they ruled like King Ardyn did, I wouldn't have the ability to choose here, either.

Footsteps echoed, and the door creaked back open.

It was time to meet the king and queen.

CHAPTER 26

Fragments of rainbow light glimmered behind King Thalorys and Queen Rhaevin, reflecting off their mirrored thrones. The king and queen held their stoic stances as they looked upon their son. My slippers echoed as I stepped across the ivory floor.

Rich hues graced the room, from hair to dress—each were different and beautiful.

The court was a masterpiece—just like in Lythira.

The half-human, half-fae princess that crossed the divide without permission or warning was on display for the High Court to judge.

It was the first time Lioran laid eyes on me as the Princess of Bailoc. His silver eyes flickered as they caught mine.

"We meet at last, Princess Aelira of Bailoc." King Thalorys settled into his throne.

Lioran's dark curls, enchanting eyes, and sharp jawline were all his father's.

"It is my honor to stand before you, your majesties." I

lowered into a curtsey, but my chin held high. Tradition would be held here, but I would not be silent.

A flash of a smile danced on the king's face. "You were called here to settle a debate." The king's voice boomed over the court.

"I hear a pact was broken in the human realm and you sought sanctuary in mine."

Only one person could make that claim—Thalen.

Elric watched me from across the room. He didn't travel with us, and yet he was here. Watching and waiting for whatever the king commanded.

Boots echoed across the floor. I hadn't forgotten their eerie cadence.

Thalen stepped beside me, towering over me. His presence made me shudder.

"What is the nature of the claim?" Lioran broke the silence.

"Lord Thalen, you may make your claim known," King Thalorys commanded.

"Your majesties, it seems Prince Lioran has been holding onto something that is mine." Lord Thalen stepped into the center of the throne room.

He said it like it was a sword, or a horse—but it was me. I was the something he traded for.

"What would that be?" Lioran held his calm.

Thalen examined me. "The Princess of Bailoc."

With a sharp inhale my knees locked.

King Thalorys shifted to the edge of his throne. A wry grin settled on his face. "Explain the nature of your claim."

"She is my wife," Thalen said, moving closer.

My lips parted, desperate to correct his words, but I couldn't speak.

"Well, my wife to be...our wedding was unfortunately interrupted." Thalen lifted his chin higher. He carefully studied

Lioran and me, as if he was assessing who would break first. "She is promised to me."

Lioran's nostrils flared. "Human pacts have nothing to do with the fae High Court."

"A pact is a bargain, is it not? A bargain with a fae can't be broken," Thalen retorted.

"You made a pact with the King of Bailoc. Not me." I couldn't let him stand uncorrected any longer.

"There is truth in his claim?" the king asked.

"King Ardyn of Bailoc and Lord Thalen made a marriage pact—a trade for supplies. I never agreed to it." King Thalorys and Queen Rhaevin exchanged knowing glances.

"Oh, didn't you?" Thalen crept closer, his breath grazing my cheek.

Lioran's expression was stoic—unreadable.

"I still remember our kiss, Princess Aelira. After the pact was announced, we shared a rather passionate moment. It didn't seem like you disagreed at all." A thinly veiled smile spread across Thalen's face.

I never admitted to kissing Thalen, because I didn't do it willingly.

Lioran's gaze fell to the floor.

"Princess Aelira is this true?" the king asked.

With a shaking exhale, I was ready to tell them all the truth —to reveal Thalen's lies, but I knew I couldn't. Challenging Thalen further was too dangerous. It was a game I couldn't win.

"He kissed me." The half-truth left my lips.

Thalen waited for me to say more, but the murmurs of the court were the only other words spoken.

"That's enough." Lioran rolled his fingers into his palms.

"The tension still exists between the human and fae

realms. News of the Princess's whereabouts spread to Bailoc. The king is outraged." Thalen assessed the king and queen.

A magic barrier divided our worlds, but when Thalen spoke, it was as if all memory of it had faded.

The queen angled her head at the king, their lips moved, but their voices didn't rise above the crowd.

"Out of respect for the crown, I seek a private audience with you both," Thalen said.

King Thalorys waved his hand. "The court is dismissed." Trailed whispers followed the ladies and lords of the court. Cora looked back, offering a subtle nod before she left.

Calyth stood beside Pyrran—both brothers carefully studied me.

"Proceed," King Thalorys commanded.

"A rather large grievance was made against me, but I may be able to look past it." Thalen stroked his jaw. I swallowed hard. "And it shall be handled with absolute discretion."

"It's in your best interest to stop talking," Lioran interjected.

Calyth flinched as Lioran's voice boomed.

I held an inhale waiting for him to speak, dreading the words that would follow.

Thalen faced the king and queen. "Prince Lioran knows my bride intimately. Which poses as quite a problem for all of us." Thalen exhaled.

Heat radiated through me, rising into my cheeks. Lioran drew in a sharp breath, each inhale quicker than the last.

"A lesser fae would discard her for even the accusation of it." Thalen took a step closer to the king and queen, before he looked back at me. I felt the cruel power his stare carried.

"What evidence do you have to support your claim?" Lioran asked.

My heart drummed harder in my chest. The lines around

the king's eyes thickened as he squinted. The queen sat in silence, her skin growing paler.

"I back his claim." Pyrran commanded the attention of the entire royal family. "I saw the two together in a rather heated moment in the Heart of Lythira. I tried to stop him, but from what I hear things have only since progressed."

My cheeks reddened with every word.

I had given myself to Lioran. It was intimate and private. They would take it all from me—even the beauty of the memories that lingered—to humiliate me.

Lioran gritted his teeth. He could have torn Pyrran apart with his glare.

"My son, what do you say to his claim?" the king asked.

"Why would you seek to destroy her reputation before this court? What do you have to gain from it?" Lioran clenched his jaw.

"Interesting. He avoids addressing the accusation entirely." Thalen folded his arms over his chest as he inched closer to me. His voice was a soft whisper only I could hear. "You gave yourself to him and he won't even stand up for you, but I will." Thalen's hand grazed my shoulder, my stomach clenched with his touch.

"Prince Lioran, are you going to dispute the accusation, or stay silent?" Thalen pressed further.

Please. I begged him with my glare.

I was desperate for him to end it.

But Lioran's gaze dropped from mine. It landed directly on the throne.

It broke me.

"You could at least claim her here, Your Highness. In a way you already have," Thalen spoke before I could.

He would ruin me—Lioran would let him.

"I am not yours to claim, nor am I his," I snapped.

King Thalorys tilted his head. The queen studied me as she raised her chin higher.

"We have a joint problem we can easily solve." His shoulders set back as he strode closer to me. "If you honor my accord, I will keep the ever-growing threat of Bailoc at bay. The lingering consequences of her transgressions will be handled."

I shuddered; the onyx sent a chill spiraling into my chest.

Thalen knew how to bend me, to break me.

"You tread on dangerous ground, Lord Thalen. Coming to the High Court...making accusations that involve your future king." King Thalorys's voice left the room trembling. "Handle her discreetly. My court is not a place for you to air your failings. You lack control over your bride—take her from my sight and reclaim it."

I clutched at the gown, silently gasping. Thalen's hand settled on my back, with a gentle nudge, he tried to guide me to turn, but I still held the king's gaze. My eyes narrowed, threatening his. It wasn't wise. It wasn't even intentional—just a silent promise that I would never forgive his lack of grace.

I was not Thalen's—I would never belong to him. Not even if I chose it.

They could demand I leave with him. Force me to marry him and I would.

But it would never make me love him.

Lioran's chest shuddered. His gaze caught mine—there was a glimpse of terror laced with pain. He stood there still. There was no protest—no claim. He would just let me walk away as if I meant nothing at all. Nothing in my life had ever stung so deep—not the wound from the sylkren, not when King Ardyn called me worthless, or traded me for supplies.

Thalen nudged me again and pushed me closer to the

throne room doors. I don't even remember leaving, but suddenly we were standing out in the courtyard.

The doors slammed behind us.

Thalen's shoulders stiffened. "This isn't what I wanted."

I pried his fingers off my back. "That is all you have to say? I thought you were here to reclaim me."

The vile words settled on my tongue. Thalen's gaze sharpened, and then I knew I shouldn't have said them.

Fyn and Cora waited near a single tree that lay in the center of the courtyard. It twisted up through an arched opening. The sun shone down on Fyn—it highlighted the glare in his eyes. Cora watched the others as they passed through the space, only once did her eyes lift to look back at me.

"He stole you from me. Tried to steal a future from you," Thalen said.

"You humiliated me...you treated me like I was nothing but a—"

"You were humiliated?" he snapped. "It was *your* choice."

The glare in his eyes cut through me. I bit my tongue to keep from saying more.

"What did Lioran have to say? Did he say anything at all on your behalf?" Each word was more pointed than the last. "Everything you risked...and he just stood there."

Thalen inhaled slowly—his exhale was even more controlled.

His hand slid down my waist slowly—his gaze trailed me. As his thumbs grazed my stomach, it revolted. "You don't have to face this alone; I will be there with you...every step of the way." He spoke with complete certainty. "I want a life with you —as my wife."

How could he want that? He still barely knew who he stood in front of.

"Face what?" I asked him as I pulled away.

"What you've created. You'll need me."

"Lord Thalen, an urgent correspondence arrived for you." Lord Elric walked up behind me. He didn't address me at all —only held out a slender piece of parchment. Thalen's fingers wrapped around it, but his eyes didn't lower from mine.

"Your Highness, please consider my offer—before it's too late for you to decide otherwise." Thalen spoke the words like he hadn't just threatened me—like he wouldn't force me to marry him, but I didn't believe it.

Without even glancing back, Thalen left with Elric. The moment he disappeared from view, Fyn and Cora headed toward me.

"Well that just confirmed what we were all suspecting..." Fyn growled. "If Thalen touches you again—"

"What happened?" Cora asked.

"Thalen accused Lioran of knowing me..." Nausea rolled through my body reliving the accusation—heat returned to my cheeks. I struggled to say the word. "Intimately."

"What did Lioran do?" Cora asked.

"He avoided the accusation." My eyes squinted in the sun's glare.

"What could he have done?" Fyn's eyes surveyed mine.

"Anything," I whispered, blinking back the tears that finally formed.

"What does Thalen want now?" Fyn asked.

"He says he wants a life with me." I heard the words as they escaped my lips and almost didn't believe them.

"I can think of many ways to propose to someone, but that isn't one of them," Fyn scoffed as he gritted his teeth.

"Lioran will figure something out. I'm sure he has a plan." Hesitancy laced every word Cora spoke.

I scoffed. "There's nothing to figure out."

Fyn's hand rested on my shoulder. "Don't just resign your-self to—"

"A life without Lioran?" I leaned into Fyn as everything spiraled around me. His hands steadied me. "It's too late."

I didn't mention the king's words. The command Thalen was given. None of it mattered anymore.

All I could do was hope that there was a way I could choose a future without him still.

The sun kissed the sky and slid from view. I waited in my chambers for word from Lioran, but as night crept in—I simmered in the dark.

He wasn't coming.

"Thalen knows..." I said. "He knows how Lioran and I were together."

Cora sat in a chair near the window. "How could he?"

"I don't know, but there was something about the way Thalen spoke. He was so confident about what he knew."

"It's a part of his game—strengthened by his magic. He strategizes, he manipulates—he leans on what makes you weakest. So that you'll fall."

"It wasn't just strategy. He knew," I murmured.

"Maybe he does. If he does—what more can he do with it?" Cora lifted a plate toward me. "Eat something...please?"

"I can't." I took the plate and placed it back on the table. "He will make me marry him—then, he can do whatever he wants.

"He hasn't though. You are standing here still." She eyed my untouched plate.

"What does it matter? Lioran hasn't come to see me."

"I'm sure he will come find you soon." Cora's voice wavered.

A sinking feeling gripped me, tormented me, and wouldn't let me go.

Our time was over.

"He's not coming." My voice grew meek.

Cora blurred through my tear-tinged vision. "You don't know that."

"I'm exhausted. I think it's best I retire for the evening."

"We will be summoned to dinner shortly," she said.

"With the king and queen?" I shuddered.

"There's been no mention of a formal gathering, but something will be set up for visiting guests. Lioran may be there."

"Then send him my regards." I slipped into the bed, still in my gown—too exhausted to shed the weight of it.

"How can you be so upset with him? What could he have done, Aelira?" Her words hung over me—anger crawled through me. "What did he do?" She asked again when I didn't respond.

"He did nothing," I said.

CHAPTER 27

M y chest ached under the strain of the pale blue corset—another gown provided by the High Court.

Cora bit into a plump strawberry. "Maybe we should go for a walk. The gardens here have the most beautiful blooms."

I forced a bite of eggs onto my tongue, but my stomach churned. "Fresh air sounds nice."

"I'm glad you're finally eating something. You had me worried last night."

Cora's life would always be free. She would never understand the pressure of a pact, made on her behalf.

I tugged at my braid as I caught my reflection in the mirror. A princess stared back at me, but I didn't recognize her anymore.

Ladies, lords, servants, and guards filled the courtyard— each one staring at me as I passed. Fyn shadowed us. He came as soon as Cora called for him.

A winding path led us to a garden enclosed by stone walls,

slender chambers with methodical arrangements of flowers on display.

My fingers lingered on a sunflower's petals—it wiggled in response. Light whirled at my fingertips, kissing the tops of closed rosebuds until new blooms unfurled.

The onyx chilled at my chest as Thalen watched me from across the enclosed space. He leaned into the stone wall, entranced by the blooms beneath my fingertips. Thalen shifted his weight, and then slowly sauntered in our direction.

Fyn placed his hand on my back. "We should go."

"Your Highness." Thalen stopped before me. "I was hoping I could get a moment with you—to explain." Hesitancy lingered in his words.

"We were just leaving." Cora's body angled between us.

Only Thalen stood before me, but still I clung to my dwindling hope that Lioran would intervene.

"Fyn, Cora, you can go ahead. I'll be with you shortly."

Fyn's hand gripped mine, his eyes pleaded with me, but I slipped my fingers from his.

"You don't have to do this." Cora's fingers trailed my sleeve.

"I will call for you the moment I need you," I whispered to Fyn.

"I'll be right over there." Fyn pointed to the wall where Thalen once stood. "If you do anything to harm her, I will not hesitate to intervene," he growled.

Fyn hovered for another second, his eyes threatening Thalen, before Cora wrapped her fingers around his arm and pulled him away.

Thalen extended his hand to me, but I did not move. "You are never without a crowd."

"Why didn't you come for me sooner?" I don't know why it mattered, but his words hung over me still.

Thalen stepped closer until his arm brushed mine. "You left

me on our wedding day." He swallowed hard. His jaw tightened. "If I had just gone to you, you wouldn't have given me the chance to explain."

"You accused me, embarrassed me in front of everyone. Did you think I'd go with you then?" I seethed.

"I was desperate. He will ruin you." He was unraveling with each word he spoke, as if it pained him to even think about us together.

I glared at him. "And you came to save me?"

His head held high as he scanned me. "I came to free you from him, Aelira." He said my name like they did in Bailoc—shorter and less melodic.

"And the men you sent after me in the woods? You risked my life."

"I instructed them to find you and bring you back safe—unharmed."

"One of your men tried to use me as a shield to ward off a sylkren...and another almost killed your future king."

Thalen swallowed hard.

"What would the king and queen have thought if I spoke that truth in the court?"

"I didn't know. I swear it." He clenched his fingers into a fist. "You didn't tell the king and queen...Why didn't you?"

Saying it then would have only made me look desperate, proof that I was guilty of Thalen's accusation.

"To spare you." I lied. "You're lucky Lioran didn't either. Do you think I'm so foolish I can't make choices for myself?"

"No. You are capable and resilient." His breath was hot on my cheek. "I fell for you, deeply from the minute we sat under the stars together. I hadn't planned it. I wanted the political strength our marriage provided, but I didn't expect to fall in love with you." His voice softened.

He couldn't have—he barely knew me.

My chest tightened under the weight of the corset.

"I have been sitting in agony since I heard the news that you were his. Knowing what you had done with him."

"How would you know anything? You weren't there and yet you accuse me of something, you don't even know to be true...in front of the king and queen." I slid my quaking hands behind my back.

"I know you let him have you." His hand trailed down my arm, the heat of his body lingered on mine with his touch. "The way you're looking at me right now. I know it is true." He spoke with such certainty. "You were supposed to be mine. That moment was supposed to be for me...and you just gave it to him." His nostrils flared.

"I am not yours," I snapped. "You know nothing."

"You're mistaken. I know way more than you think. Maybe even more than you know yourself." He hovered over me. Waiting. Watching. Wondering when I would crack. "The consequences of your actions have already...manifested."

I stepped back.

He glanced me over. "I've come to give you the future he can't."

"Why would you want a future with me at all?" My breathing quickened.

"Despite what you've done with him, I want you still." Pain flickered in his eyes. "I can keep you safe as my wife—the mother of my children."

Water pooled in my eyes, but I blinked it away.

"I love him, Thalen." I spoke the truth in a way he couldn't protest. Thalen was too boastful to accept that I love someone he loathed.

"You will learn to love your husband, Aelira."

I would never get over my heart being shattered.

Thalen slid his arm around my waist as I stumbled,

catching me. My trembling body was pressed against his—my eyes locked onto his, searching for the truth.

Fyn cleared his throat in the distance, but Thalen didn't release me, nor did I fight it.

"We will get married. Just as we planned. Together we can build a beautiful life—one you've always dreamed of."

Thalen released me from his hold, but his hand lingered on mine, before he disappeared beyond the stone walls.

"Tell me you're not even thinking about it." Cora stepped beside me, but I couldn't look at her. They may have heard every word we spoke. "You can't be seriously considering his offer."

"Really Aelira?" Fyn shook his head at me before he walked off.

I slid my hands over my hips. My stomach tossed as I considered Thalen's words. "Lioran is already done with me."

"None of us have seen him," Cora said.

I swallowed hard, wanting to believe there was a reason, but I couldn't. "I'm going back to our chambers to lie down."

"Let's go for a walk. We can figure something out, together." Cora reached for my hand.

"I can't. I'm exhausted, Cora." I slipped away from her and traced my steps back, desperate for a moment of solitude.

Lavender tea settled on my tongue. Its scent unraveled my nerves. Life continued in the courtyard below, a complete contrast to the serenity of the Heart of Lythira. I longed to be back at his castle, to feel his embrace—the moments I craved were taken from me.

My heart was hardening. Each hour that passed, the

distance between Lioran and I only grew. I sank further into the sofa as Thalen's offer settled on me.

He said he wasn't hunting me; he was trying to save me from the High Court, from this heartache. I entangled myself with Lioran, but he still came for me. I would never understand his actions, but I understood just how far I'd go for love.

Still, every warning Lioran gave about him hung over me. I knew who he was—what he was capable of, but the choice wasn't really mine to make.

The deal was made—Thalen had every right to claim me.

It would be easier to go without protest. If I married Thalen, I could still have a life of my own making. There would be no secrecy, no threat of watching the man I love be bonded to someone else—I could leave it all behind and build something new.

Darkness swept through the chambers. The endless flicker of candlelight held my gaze. Cora had come by, but our conversation only spiraled. She hadn't returned since.

The door creaked, severing the stillness.

"Leave me alone." I growled before Cora could enter.

Cora didn't respond as she entered, but as I spun to face her, Lioran stood before me. His rage-filled glare glowed in the darkness. I hadn't even felt him enter. Maybe whatever tethered us together was severed, too.

"Fyn pulled me out of a very important meeting, with news from the palace garden." His biceps bulged beneath his midnight tunic.

I sat in silence as he came closer.

"I need you to tell me he was wrong about what he saw. Tell me—you weren't in Thalen's arms." His eyes narrowed.

"I wasn't aware Fyn was reporting on my whereabouts." I clenched my jaw. "Or that you cared where I was at all."

"So, you did…you let him hold you? Like I would hold you… after everything he did to you…to us."

"Us?" I seethed. The storm inside me whirled, a pit settled in my stomach. I rose before him. "You know Fyn wouldn't lie to you. Why are you even here?"

His chest trembled with each unsteady breath.

"You're really considering what he's offering?" Desperation leached between his words.

I didn't dare raise my gaze to meet his. My hands ran over all the layers of fabric that encompassed me.

"You *are* considering his offer." He slapped his hand over his chest as if I struck him. "You hated him, were so worried he'd come to Lythira. His men almost killed me," he growled.

"It wasn't his instruction."

"You know what he is—what he is capable of. I didn't think you'd fall for his manipulation. You let him use his magic on you and then you pretend he didn't." He reached for my hand, but I slipped from his grasp. "Thalen defiled your reputation in the High Court."

"My reputation was gone the moment I made the choices I did with you. You didn't even hesitate to discard me when you were done with me."

"He made you believe you're worthless, too."

"No. I am fighting for my future, because no one else will."

He stepped backwards. "So, you're choosing him, because—"

"You'll never give me what I want."

"And he will?" His hand reached for mine, but his fingers rolled inward. I held on to hope for too long, but seeing him here in front of me, I knew our time was done.

"That is not your concern anymore."

He flinched. "I came here to—"

"Make decisions for me? Soon you'll have someone who you can make decisions for—it was never me."

He shook his head wildly, and his mouth gaped open. I didn't know who I was looking at anymore, but it wasn't who I fell in love with.

"Then go be his wife, Aelira. Bear his children. Live out your time in his precious Vale. I have other matters to attend to." He slammed the door behind him.

I clutched my knees to my chest, a sobbing puddle on the floor.

A thud came at the other side of the door along with a low growl. I waited for the handle to turn, for Lioran to tell me anything at all, but his boots only echoed down the hallway.

A lady's maid slipped into my chamber. I longed for someone to talk to, wishing Milana or Juniper were here instead.

This world wasn't mine. No one here cared who I was.

"Your Highness, a letter arrived for you." She held out a tray in front of me with a pressed parchment. A dagger draped in thorns ingrained in vermillion wax illuminated in the firelight—the seal of the King of Bailoc. The door closed swiftly behind her.

I was alone with his concealed words.

The letter shook beneath my fingertips as I held it above the blazing flames. Each ember threatening to destroy King Ardyn's commands. The fireplace crackled. I pulled it out of the hearth. Whatever it said was only a threat if I allowed it to be —he was on the other side of the divide.

I unfolded the parchment and familiar handwriting greeted me.

It wasn't Ardyn's, the forced letters belonged to Agan.

Aelira,

You are in grave danger—the King and Queen of Nythrel will stop at nothing to strike against Bailoc, especially in our desperate state. A rebellion has risen. When father couldn't appease the rebellion leaders, they took his life. The state of unrest continues, and I am desperate to resolve it.

Your union with Lord Thalen will be our salvation. You both can help rebuild Bailoc and protect our people from a desperate future. Thalen has ensured me he can keep you safe from the fae—that your marriage to him will grant you protection. Please, I beg you to go with him not just for me, or for our kingdom, but for your safety.

Ashlyn and I are so worried about you.

- King Agan of Bailoc

My trembling fingers clutched the letter, indents forming on the perfectly pressed paper. The rebellion had surfaced—the king was murdered. I reread Agan's words, determined to find what lay hidden beneath them.

Marrying Thalen would ensure a future for Ashlyn—one I couldn't give her on this side of the divide. It wouldn't erase the blight, but maybe she would be safe with me in the Vale.

The letter sat on the table beside me. It was a glaring reminder of what I must do. A trace of warmth radiated from the onyx to my fingertips.

Choosing Thalen would never give me what I wanted, but maybe it was never about that—maybe it was always about finding my own peace, my own way.

CHAPTER 28

I rose early the next morning, dressed in silence, and slipped out before Cora woke. My feet traced the steps through the hall, down to the garden. I needed to find Thalen—to discuss Agan's letter.

"I thought I might find you here." Fyn stepped in front of me as I entered the walled garden. "Don't do this." His eyes pleaded as his fingers wrapped around my shoulder.

I struggled to get free of his grasp. "Why? So, you won't have to report back to him again?"

"He deserved to know. You were in Thalen's arms." His voice was a low roar.

"It doesn't concern you, Fyn. It doesn't concern Lioran, either."

"He loves you." Fyn grimaced. "I thought I knew you—knew what you stood for. Maybe I don't."

"I deserve a future. I'm not going to sit and wallow while Lioran does whatever is best for him."

Fyn shifted his weight, his hand resting on the hilt of his sword. "How easy was it for you to forgive him for what he ordered his men to do? I still picture Lioran's blood on my hands, but you...you've forgotten entirely."

Flashes of crimson crossed my vision as I held an inhale. "I will *never* forget, or forgive him for it." Tears pooled in my eyes as my heart thundered.

"But you'll choose to marry him anyway?"

"There is no way out of this," I snapped.

"You can tell yourself that all you want..." Fyn's tone went flat. "But it still doesn't explain why you just let him hold you. You weren't being forced—you let him."

"Lioran didn't stand up for me in the throne room. When I was broken from it all—he didn't come for me afterwards. He abandoned me."

"He hasn't." He leaned in closer to me. "The king and queen have been keeping him busy with endless meetings and introductions."

"Introductions?" My blood went cold. "To find his bride?"

Fyn winced—it gave me all the answers I needed.

Whatever we were was over.

"He will do as he must, and I will do the same." I pushed past Fyn, but he circled in front of me again.

"Lioran's been trying to find a way out of your arrangement with Thalen. Trying to pave a future for you."

"He said nothing of the sort when he came into my chambers and berated me. If Lioran cared to do anything for my future, he'd tell me himself. I don't see him anywhere. Do you?"

For a moment I thought I felt Lioran's warmth again, but I knew better than to turn around and find an empty space.

Fyn's eyes darted well above my head.

Lioran's voice cracked behind me, "My heart is still yours. It never stopped being yours. But as long as it is, you're in danger. If I care too much—too deeply—they'll force you to marry Thalen. You won't have a choice, Aelira. I won't be able to stop it."

I pivoted to face him.

He braced his arms across his chest. "It turned out none of it mattered. No amount of fighting will reverse your decision. Do you need help finding your betrothed?"

"The rebellion—King Ardyn—they killed him." The parchment shook in my hands as I shoved it into his chest. "Agan is on the throne." My breath caught, and for a moment I couldn't speak. "Ashlyn is in danger."

The corner of Lioran's lips slipped as he carefully read each word. "You would give your freedom to help them? Agan did nothing to help you. He tried to—" He seethed.

"I'm not going for him." I tore the letter from his grasp. "I have to protect my sister."

"Thalen can't help Bailoc."

"You would hate to think he could," I said.

Fyn's boots scraped the dirt. "Lioran."

"Leave, Fyn," he scolded.

"Don't you dare go anywhere," I commanded.

"Enough," Fyn's voice sharpened. "Figure this out—both of you. I will stand here so you two are not seen alone together, but I have nothing more to say." He became a silent wall beside me.

"Thalen's supplies come from Pyrran. Pyrran gets shipments from Lythira that he disperses to every territory under our protection—shipments I can't keep up with because of the blight," Lioran explained. "Without those shipments he will barely have enough food to feed Kybar, let alone the Vale."

"Thalen knows this?" I asked.

"I'm not sure how much he knows yet. There is a process that Pyrran maintains as Guardian of Kybar—his merchants prepare everything in advance. Our territories are now just starting to see the impact."

"He lied to me." I knew he would, but I was desperate to believe him.

"If you go with him, you may be able to protect Ashlyn. I will send whatever I can to the Vale, I can't promise the same for Bailoc." His gaze hardened and I felt my heart sever.

Tears streaked my vision. "You must have found your perfect match."

"I have." Lioran glanced the other way. "But I can't keep you."

Lioran left as quickly as he arrived.

Rough bark greeted my fingertips, as I braced a tree in the walled garden. I felt it hum just as I had in Lythira, but it was different here—a steady marching beat, that echoed my heart.

Ladies and lords walked throughout the walled gardens; their voices elevated above the winds.

My fingernails settled into the grooves of the tree and the onyx warmed against my skin as my eyes shut. Humming vibrations resounded in my chest, poured into the tree from my fingertips. The murmurs faded—rustling leaves and bird-song echoed above it all.

Footsteps struck the dirt, not one set of feet, but two—their cadence stilled before me.

The queen's cold gaze greeted mine as my eyes opened, followed by Calyth's. Dozens of newly formed white blooms danced around the tree. The queen's lips pursed.

The silky petals slid beneath my quaking fingers. My

fingernails pinched the stem, freeing the foreign bloom. I presented it to the queen.

She let the bloom fall between us. "Moonflowers? What an unusual choice. I hope you can remove them as easily as you make them grow."

Calyth held his mother's arm as he assessed the fresh blooms. He looked so much like Lioran—the same silver eyes and dark locks.

"Perhaps you can convince your brother to pick a bride. He can't reject them all." The queen's tone was flat. "I've finally found a proper lady who will entice him. He was never going to choose you, Aelira. My son will always prioritize the crown."

Lioran's future was sealed. Soon, mine would be, too.

"I need a word with Princess Aelira." Calyth bowed his head toward his mother.

"You will be expected in the throne room shortly, for the remaining introductions. We can't keep Lioran's future wife waiting." The queen left us without another word.

"Will you walk with me?" Calyth extended his arm, but my grip tightened around the tree. "I fear Pyrran has given you the worst impression of us."

"Pyrran is...unforgettable."

Calyth chuckled. We passed the rows of neatly arranged tulips, they swayed in time with the breeze—I breathed in their scent, savoring their sweetness.

"My mother sees you as a threat—one she must control."

"I'm well aware." My eyes met his only for a moment.

"They will not entertain his wish."

"They haven't sent me off to marry Thalen." The words escaped my lips without thought. I had no idea what Calyth was capable of, or if I could even trust him.

"They haven't. Which works in *our* favor. Your magic is too powerful to be silenced in the Vale."

"Our favor?"

"I would like for you to return to Eyrsea with me." He tilted his head toward me.

I didn't know why he would offer it. "Why would you want that?"

"My parents may be blind to what you have to offer... but I am not." He shielded his eyes from the blinding sun. "The sea is mine to command—the land is yours. Together, we would be powerful. Eyrsea would thrive and you would be protected."

My hand fell from his. "Protected how?"

"As my wife, Aelira."

A pit formed in my stomach with his words. Lioran couldn't know about this—he would never accept it. I couldn't accept it.

"And Lioran...does he know what you propose?"

"He has enlisted my help in giving you a future you deserve."

This was his plan. This was how he would alter my fate?

Nausea ripped through me. I almost reached for Calyth to brace me, but my body instinctively recoiled.

"Think it over. I leave to return to my territory in a couple of days—I think you'd love Eyrsea as much as I do." He bowed his head to me.

I would be passed around and traded for the sake of Nythrel—Lioran approved of it.

"Your offer is generous...I will think it over." I could barely say the words.

Calyth could free me from a life with Thalen, but every day I would look at him and I would only ever see Lioran.

I was resigned to accept my fate with Thalen, but Lioran never would. He would rather I bond with his brother.

If I went with Thalen and shipments stopped coming from Pyrran, I wouldn't have power to change Ashlyn's fate. Going with him wouldn't reverse the blight. I thought of Thalen's hands around my waist—the way his eyes searched mine as if he was uncovering every truth hidden behind them.

Thalen wouldn't leave without me, not unless I made a choice that made it impossible for him to take me from Nythrel.

I gripped the bodice, unlacing the ties that crushed my chest and waist—the pain was unbearable.

Calyth promised me a future. A life with him may grant me peace and freedom, but I would be his wife—bound to him for the rest of my days.

It wouldn't protect Ashlyn—the divide wouldn't allow her to pass through.

The velvet curtain curled beneath my fingertips as the wind rapped on the window. Each day since we arrived, I watched people come and go through the garden—all admired a perfectly arranged display of flowers contained within stone walls. Every bit monotonous and organized, except the tree that bore my flowers—a complete outlier.

I crossed the divide, defied all logic, broke every rule—held magic that only the heir to the throne should have possessed.

Footsteps echoed beyond my chamber walls. Life would continue here without me—but my life, my choice still mattered.

The cold metal latch released beneath my fingers. A whisper of wind caressed my cheek, carrying a familiar melody. The song of the land simmered inside me; my magic responded to it. It settled within me, pulsing and beating in time with it all.

It had to be what certainty felt like.

There was only one place I ever felt I belonged, only one home I longed for even still—Lythira. It needed me, called to me even here. Cora had a vision that I could restore the land and bring it back to life. If her vision was right—if I was capable—I wouldn't need Thalen or Calyth to determine my fate.

I could create my own.

It was time to seal it in a way they couldn't reverse.

I would make a bargain with the king to reverse the destruction my legacy created.

To heal the lands—I would give a part of myself that I loved most.

Myrwood Grove would take my magic, I would give it freely—until only pieces of me remained.

The door handle turned. Lioran peered around the door.

"You spoke with Calyth..." His words were hesitant.

I had hoped he didn't know what Calyth had planned, but he did.

My hands settled on my waist. "I tried to make sense of your absence—of your plans. But I can't."

His eyes widened. "Please. Let me explain."

"There is nothing you could say that would justify it. Telling Calyth...to take me to Eyrsea—to bond with me."

"He offered what?"

"To bring me to Eyrsea as his wife. He said you came to him—"

"We discussed him offering you a place in Eyrsea—a life that could give you a future without Thalen." His nostrils flared. "I didn't know he expected to bond with you."

They were all making plans for me, without me. Lioran didn't even know what he was asking—he was just desperate to find a solution.

"Did you agree to it?"

I stumbled gripping the back of the sofa. "I thought..." He braced me as I slipped again. I collided with his chest, but I pulled myself from him the moment I felt his warmth again.

"Whatever future you decided—is yours, even if you choose to be with him." He cleared his throat. "At least you would be safe."

"Lioran..." He slid a finger over my lip, silencing me.

"I should have come here sooner, to be with you while I still could." He kissed me. This time I didn't pull away. The warmth of his lips lingered on mine.

"You weren't here at all." I swallowed hard.

"I was trying to secure a future for you—trying to show my parents that you weren't a threat."

I backed away from him. "This whole time I thought you were done with me."

"No, I never will be. You are the only one I could ever love. I've refused every match. I will not bond with anyone else." His breath lingered on me. His words were exactly what I wanted to hear, but I couldn't allow myself to have hope.

I lost him. It was already too painful.

"Be with me. At least for tonight, then tomorrow, the decision is yours," he said.

Part of me wanted to resist, but I let his lips sink into mine.

"I've been breaking in the silence..." I tried to finish my thought, but it was lost as he pulled me closer.

"I should have been there for you, and I wasn't." He lifted me up and placed me on the bed.

Footsteps trailed down the hall. He twisted the key in the lock, sealing us in for our stolen moment.

"What about..." My words escaped me as he pressed his lips into my neck and trailed down my shoulder.

"I don't want to know. Don't tell me anything at all. I want out last night together to be only about us."

I wanted to tell him I made my choice, but I didn't.

He would accept me marrying Calyth, or maybe even Thalen, before he'd accept me choosing this fate. Despite every warning sign my heart gave with its thundering beat, I would allow myself to have this final moment with him—knowing it would destroy me in the morning.

Pure desire shone in his gaze as he unlaced my gown, pulling the fabric from me. Heat filled my body as he leaned into me fully.

CHAPTER 29

L ioran slipped out before Cora returned. His scent lingered on the pillow beside me. I clutched it when sleep escaped me.

Cora and I had barely spoken since my conversation with Thalen in the garden.

As the morning light crept in, another summons arrived. It was my only chance to make the bargain they wouldn't refute.

"You can't go through with it," Cora warned, breaking the silence between us. "You can't convince me that you want to be with Thalen."

"I don't." My fingers slipped into the folds of my gown.

"Then why are you doing this?" She stepped forward and stopped. "Lioran is trying to help you. He will find another way."

"He did." The ache hadn't dissipated. "I could marry Calyth instead."

Cora gripped her throat, her fingers curled down toward her chest. "It would be better than marrying Thalen."

"It isn't what you think. I just need a moment to myself."

Cora's brow knitted. "Fine, but can you at least eat something? You've barely eaten in days."

Bile churned in my stomach. Even when the bitterness settled, I couldn't force myself to look at the food on the plate. "I'm not hungry."

"Your heart is broken, but someday it will mend." Her hand lingered on my shoulder. "Whatever you choose. I'll stand beside you."

"Cora." I called as she stood at the door. "I'm not choosing Thalen."

Cora rushed to me. "Will you go with Calyth then?"

The words lodged in my throat. "No. I will go to Myrwood Grove."

"He…thinks you will marry."

It was my secret to keep. "He will know my decision soon."

"You don't know what you're risking. My vision was only a glimpse of the future."

"A glimpse of hope." I pressed my hands together. "It's all that matters."

As she exhaled her eyes lifted to mine. Not another word was said between us. She nodded with a grim smile on her face.

A cascade of colors sparkled onto the throne room floor. I stood alone in the center, waiting in silence for the king and queen. Footsteps echoed behind me—and his energy shifted over me. I heard his breathing—uneven with ache. He stepped in front of me.

King Thalorys strolled in with the Queen Rhaevin on his arm.

"It is not in your power to deny Lord Thalen." King Thalorys's head angled as he evaluated me. "Tell me. Now. Why do you deny his claim still?"

I couldn't move. The silence thickened around me. Air drew from my lungs. Lioran caught me as I stumbled. His hand lingered on my back.

"Your future king requests that your fate be treated with kindness. We have obliged, but now my patience wears thin." The king gripped Lioran's arm and pulled him in front of me. "Tell her your command."

Panic rippled through the silver flecks in his eyes. The pink in his cheeks slowly faded.

Lioran's eyes pleaded with mine. "You must make a *choice*, for your future."

The king sneered at his son.

"Bow to him," the queen demanded. Her voice shook me. I froze before him. "You will bow to your future king," she commanded again.

I lowered my body into a deep curtsy, my gaze lay at his feet.

"That's enough." Lioran's voice stammered, his fingers twitched as he extended them toward me.

The queen shot a withering stare at her son.

I stood in silence, unable to utter the words I knew I must.

King Thalorys wrapped his arms across his chest. "You will answer him."

I studied Lioran—desperate to remember every silver fleck the sun illuminated in his eyes.

The king raised his hand in front of me. The onyx felt like ice on my chest. Lioran's jaw clenched.

"Thalen can't claim me. I was never his." The words flowed from my mouth without thought. I shouldn't have uttered them at all.

The room spun. Each breath caught in my throat. The corset pressed into my chest—it seized my lungs.

"You can't decide my future." My arms shook. I shouldn't have utter anything else. I didn't want to, but my mouth parted again. Every thought spilled from my throat—without control. "You can't demand anything of me."

I recoiled with my own words. An inky darkness tugged at the corners of the room.

Lioran's nostrils flared.

"Thalorys..." The queen rose to her feet. Her mouth formed a half grin that felt threatening, not to him, but to me. She turned over her shoulder to look back at the king. "Let her speak of her own free will," the queen said.

A sharp pang rang out in my lungs.

"You promised you wouldn't harm her." Lioran examined me as his hand steadied my back again.

"She appears unscathed to me." He waved his hand, releasing me fully. Air rushed into my lungs at a forceful rate. "If you answer what I ask, I will have no reason to compel you to answer me again."

"Yes, your majesty." My chest pounded with each breath. The king pulled at the bottom of his tunic.

This wasn't Bailoc. I had no say there, but here, I had even less.

The queen's icy glare settled on me.

"Tell her what has been decided about your future bride, Lioran," the queen commanded.

I couldn't bear to hear about her. "Please..." Each word I spoke threatened to take more than I could give.

"It hasn't been decided." Lioran hadn't moved.

"Enough," King Thalorys interjected. "Your future king commanded your decision. You will look him in the eyes and give it. Tell him you will marry Lord Thalen of the Vale. Now."

They could have commanded it, could have sent me away, but instead they wanted me to say it—they wanted me to crush him with my words.

I wouldn't.

My chin tilted upwards, until my eyes locked with Lioran's. "I will not bond with Lord Thalen," I said.

Lioran exhaled. I watched his shoulders fall.

It was a dangerous game. There was little hope I would win.

My lungs drew a deep breath, free and steady. I looked out the massive windows at a tree that arched over it. Its abundant leaves shone in the sunlight.

Nausea claimed me, the bile singed the back of my throat.

Lioran would never be mine again, but I would stand on my own.

My eyes settled on his. In my mind, I told him how much I loved him, how much I always would. He wouldn't hear my thoughts, but from the look on his face—he knew.

My breathing hitched. "I propose a bargain. I will use my magic to ease the blight. A visionary has seen my fate—I can mend what is broken at Myrwood Grove."

The onyx warmed again at my chest. Certainty settled.

"No." Lioran trembled, his head shook. "I do not accept her claim. She doesn't know what she's speaks of."

"A fae bargain can't be broken. Magic of that kind may break you," the queen warned, her pale blue eyes softened. A moment of silence hung in the air between us. "It is not too late to accept Thalen's offer."

One day I may regret this choice, knowing that I'd live on with part of me missing—without the one person who mattered more than anything. The life I desired would exist only in daydreams.

"My magic can heal the lands. It is meant to be my fate." A

sharp pain settled in the middle of my chest with my next inhale. If there was a glimmer of hope that the blight would be reversed, they would accept my bargain.

Lioran gripped me. "Aelira, don't...say another word."

"I will use my magic to restore Lythira—no matter the cost." The queen winced as I spoke.

"I accept your pact," King Thalorys said.

"Reverse it!" Lioran wailed.

"It will not be done." King Thalorys didn't look at Lioran when he spoke. His eyes only settled on me.

My magic stirred within me, heavier than before. It pulsed and thickened as it coursed in my veins. I waited for something to surface, but it only settled deeper.

Lioran couldn't save me from what I promised.

I would offer my future king a solution he so desperately needed.

It was how I would love him, even when he was married to another.

Color drained from Lioran's face when we left the throne room. "You should have told me. When I came to your chambers, you could have..." He gripped my shoulders.

"You said you didn't want to know." I knew he would, but it was better to lean into his words rather than risk him stopping me.

"We could have..." His words trailed off.

"Could have what, Lioran?" I leaned my back into the wall of the palace, sliding down to the ground. "They will never give you the power to choose. Not for me. Not for yourself."

"Why did you leave letting me believe you were marrying someone else?"

"I needed to stand on my own. Without a protector to do it for me." My words settled between us. "You would have stopped me."

"Aelira." He slid his arm around me, pulling me to stand.

"Where can we go to talk?"

"Go to your chambers. I will meet you there." His voice was a low desperate hum.

I decided my fate, a fate I barely understood. The queen gave me a moment to alter it, but I didn't take it. It was the only path forward—a life that I wouldn't be at anyone's mercy, but my own.

The gemstone pulsated against me. Neither hot, nor cold. It only pulsed with each beat of my magic inside of me.

I rounded the corner the winding halls curved in ways I didn't remember—my mind was still in the throne room, still with him.

"Did you agree to go to the Grove?" Cora walked toward me.

"I can't find the way back..." I couldn't breathe—couldn't think. "I need to meet Lioran in our chambers."

She slid her arm under mine. With one step at a time, I brought my breath back. Cora steadied me as I trembled.

"I didn't just agree to it—I made a bargain." The tears caught in my eyes, pooling there until they fell on their own accord.

Her eyebrows lifted as she slowly turned her head toward me. "Why would you do that?" We rounded the last corner, and a familiar painting of a flower field caught my eye. A display of color splotched throughout a grassy field.

"So no one could take my future from me." Irony laced each word. The tree would take my magic and hopefully nothing more.

Cora pried the door open to our now busy chambers.

"The princess requires a moment of solitude. Please leave us." Cora's voice was bold. The lady's maids left the room.

Color drained from her face. Then I knew it.

I hadn't just determined my fate—I had sealed it.

Lioran darted toward me as soon as he opened the door.

"I'll be back to check on you later." Cora's voice cracked as her hand lingered on the door before she finally slipped through it.

He wrapped his hands around me, pulling me closer. For the first time since I stepped into the throne room, I could fully breathe. I laid my head on his chest. Tears pooled deeply in my eyes until I couldn't hold them back any longer.

"I could have found another way." His voice cracked as he slid his hand over his mouth. The other arm held me tightly, like he may never let me go.

"Would you have rather me married Thalen or Calyth?" I don't know why I asked it, because I already knew.

He slammed his fist into the wall behind us. My tears fell faster.

"Yes, I wish you'd marry either of them." His breath fell heavily on me. "It would have killed me inside to think of you with someone else, but I would deliver you to Thalen myself if it would save you from that fate." Pain leached into every word.

"You wouldn't," I protested.

"Your magic will be gone..." The rest he left unsaid.

"I can live on without it."

The weight of the corset dress pushed on me as I fumbled with the ribbons, pulling it free, gasping for air. Lioran loosened them for me. His hand brushed mine.

"You didn't just make a bargain with my father—you made one with Lythira, too. Both will take from you slowly until you travel to the Grove. There is no way for me to undo it."

"The cost will be worth it. I will restore it so everyone I love can thrive—including you."

I kissed his lips, gently, softly savoring their sweetness for what may be the last time.

"You were the only future I ever wanted," he said.

"I always thought you wanted this life—to be king." The weight of my body collapsed into his. He wrapped his arms around me tighter. Waves of nausea ran through me.

"All I ever wanted was our life in Lythira." His hands cupped my face. "I want to hold you every night and every morning, to grow old with you, to have a family with you."

Everything we couldn't have seemed heavier than before. I closed my eyes, trying to imagine it in my mind. The way our mornings in Lythira would look—the way our babies would look, whether they'd have his dark curls or my golden eyes. I blinked it all away. Too afraid to hold on to moments I couldn't keep.

"I was just picturing them."

"Picturing who, my love?"

"Our children... what they would look like." The words caught in my throat and hung there for longer than I'd liked.

"Aelira..." He gripped me tighter.

Silence fell in the dimly lit room. He held me as if he'd never let me go. I needed more time with him, away from here. Time to love him, to be with him freely before it was too late.

"Can we go home?"

"Home?" His voice cracked.

"Yes, to Lythira—can you take me home before I go to the Grove? Before you marry? I want one last night with you away from here."

"I can't endure you talking like this."

"I need to be home with you for however long we can be together. Even if it's only one more night." I lay my head on his chest again.

His chest rose and fell.

"I would love nothing more than to go home with you." He

pulled me into him, holding me against him. "I will see if I can arrange it. Someone needs to escort you back."

After what they did to him in throne room, I knew they would never let him leave.

My future wouldn't be what I envisioned, but it would be my own. I couldn't be claimed, controlled, or forced to live a life not of my choosing.

Time would reveal a path illuminated by the stars.

With a chilling breath, I released my expectations, allowing light to wash over me.

CHAPTER 30

The sun had slowly shifted in the sky and dipped down toward the horizon when Lioran slid back into the room.

He leaned in toward me, his lips lingering on my forehead. I sank into the bed, resigning myself to the journey without him.

"I will take you home," he said.

"How?"

Lioran folded his hands together. "It doesn't matter. We will have our time together."

My heart stalled in my chest as I sat up. The moment the lines etched further in the creases around his brow—I knew. There was something he wasn't telling me. "How, Lioran?"

"I promised I will marry."

Hearing his words, I felt something shatter within me. I wept. My fingers wrapped around the posts of the bed, pressing tightly into the wood. Lioran wiped the tears from my cheeks.

"Aelira?" Cora peeked her head around the massive door.

Fyn was beside her, but he looked as shaken as he had when Lioran was unconscious on his horse.

"Fyn..." I lifted my head toward them.

"What's wrong?" Lioran asked. Cora's fingers trembled—her whole body trembled.

She choked on her tears. "I...had...another vision."

"What was it?" Lioran's tone was sharp.

Cora stumbled back—Fyn's arm embraced her. "You..."

"Tell them, Cora." Fyn's voice unraveled.

"It was about the Myrwood Grove. I know exactly what you must do." Cora sobbed.

I gripped Lioran, waiting for her to finish. "The tree in the center of the Grove—you must connect with it and bind your magic to it. Once you do, you will give to it until it can restore."

"And then my magic is gone?" My voice cracked.

She stumbled again, and Fyn held her steady. "It won't just take your magic."

Lioran gripped my arms, bracing me as we heard the news together.

"Don't say it." Lioran's words fell flat even in anger.

The weight of the onyx bore down on me, its chill running into my veins.

"I'm sorry, had I known—I would never have said anything at all."

Even without her words, I knew. Fyn's eyes watered. Lioran's grip on me tightened.

Cora reached for me. "It's all my fault. I thought it would just take your magic, but you..."

"I won't survive it," I said.

Cora held a desperate silence.

The onyx ran ice cold on my chest; I attempted to warm it with my fingers—wanted to feel its lull, but it wasn't there. The air pulled from my lungs. They constricted with what little remained. My choice didn't give me a future of my own—I had bargained my life, so that everyone I loved would live.

"There has to be a way around this." Lioran stiffened behind me, his arms wrapped around me, holding me upright.

"Lioran." Fyn's hand set on Lioran's arm.

"I will find a way..." He rocked me in his arms. "I can't lose you."

I gasped for air, until my eyelids fell heavy—life slowly being drained from me.

"Aelira, you need to breathe." Cora's words pierced through her muffled sobs. I couldn't...I pulled at Lioran, desperate.

"Leave us." Lioran's tears soaked my hair. "Leave!" he yelled.

"She needs..." Cora reached for him, but pulled back.

He lowered me to the floor. "Aelira, I've got you...breathe. Breathe with me." Lioran inhaled and exhaled loudly. I mirrored each breath until the room stopped spinning around us.

"Just breathe." I was desperate for the hope he offered.

Lioran remained with me. I stopped shaking in his arms. Our time here was stolen, but soon, we would be together in a way the High Court could not control.

The glaring truth haunted me. I gripped the leather book, trailed the familiar embossed flowers. I hadn't stopped to speak with my father since we arrived.

My mind was too cluttered with the decision to be made. It was one that only I could make. I didn't want him, or anyone else to tell me what to do. But since I made the bargain, everything had shifted. I needed him.

"I am here at the High Court. I need to find you."

I am not at the High Court.

Someday we will be together again, but the time is not now.

The words fell heavy on me. "I made a bargain...to heal the land." The words barely escaped my lips. "Cora had a vision. I didn't survive it."

Your magic is strong, stronger than you imagine.

No one can know what will happen.

"I'm scared." I said it out loud for the first time.

It is normal to fear what you do not know.

When you came through the divide you knew nothing of this world.

You crossed with only your hope that it would be worth it.

Was it?

I thought of Lioran, Fyn, and Cora...my family. The family I always wanted, they were there for me always.

"Yes, it was."

Go into Myrwood Grove with the same hope.

Embrace your days with those you love while you have them.

We never know when our days may be our last.

You will never regret the moments you take with those you love.

"I just wanted..." I couldn't bring myself to say the rest. My eyes closed as I pictured the life with Lioran all over again—all the things we would not have.

What you want is beautiful.

Allow yourself to have those thoughts, those dreams—stopping them does nothing, but deprive you of joy.

"Do you think I will die?"

I think you live a beautiful life...

revel in it as long as you can.

Live, Aelira.

He was right; it wasn't over yet. I would choose to live until I couldn't any longer.

I barely slept that night, nor did Cora. Our tears filled the void of the foreign room, echoing and cracking in the stillness of the night. I longed for Lioran, wishing he was there to hold me. We would return home to Lythira—there, I would love him until the very end.

I dressed in my riding tunic as Cora silently tidied our things. The few possessions we brought were carted out of the space. As we quietly escaped the palace halls for the last time, I noticed how somber the paintings were. The flowers lacked their natural hue—as if stifled—molded to what they should have been.

Lioran and Fyn greeted us at the end of the hall. Lioran's bloodshot eyes met mine before the four of us walked in silence together.

Wind poured in through the open palace doors, lulling me out into the open. The instant I stepped beyond the grand entrance, the onyx's warmth returned. A melody danced on the wind, distant and faint—Lythira was calling me.

It was time to go home.

As we descended the grand silver steps, I heard a frantic, but familiar voice call. "Lioran." The queen trailed the steps behind him, she was a blur of silver in my tear-streaked view. "You will take them back and return to us quickly. Your future bride will be waiting." She reached out to touch him, but Lioran pulled away.

He wouldn't look at her. The queen's smile vanished.

"Thank you for inviting me to your court." My voice held steady, even though I had nothing to thank her for at all.

"Don't forget your promise, Lioran." Her words softened.

"Rest assured, Mother—I will not forget anything we discussed." He glared at her.

"Your sacrifice for our kingdom has not gone unnoticed. Your father would have been very proud of the woman you've become." Her hand grazed my arm. I stilled under her touch.

I gripped Lioran as the words settled.

He *would* have been proud...*would.*

CHAPTER 31

The journey back was solemn. No words could ease the pain.

But the moment Gaia crossed into Lythira, something in me shifted.

It felt so good to be home.

Sunlight slipped into Lioran's chambers as I nestled into his chair—watching him, waiting for him to wake. I refused to enter my old chambers once we returned.

The weight of the bargain consumed me.

Each moment was fading faster. We returned to enjoy our last moments together, but as I watch him in his quiet slumber, I knew there would never be enough moments to keep. The bargain would claim me. His future would be tied.

The queen's final words hadn't left me. On our journey home, I couldn't bring myself to ask the book if what I assumed was correct. My fingers met the leather book's embroidery.

"You aren't here anymore, are you?" I whispered.

I am with you through these pages only.

The book was meant to be a guide for you when I knew we'd never find each other again.

He would never be with me. "How did you know?"

I was a visionary.

I saw my end, before it came.

Even if I hadn't, I knew he wouldn't let me live with what I had created.

I would never know the father that loved me. He was stolen by the one who raised me. I would never get to sit with him, or see how I resembled him. The dull ache sat, before I could say the words. "I love you," I whispered. He was gone. He couldn't feel it, but if there was a chance he could hear my words still, I needed him to know.

My daughter—I love you still.

"It's not fair."

Our fate isn't fair.

I knew it never would be.

Before our worlds were divided, your mother brought you to me.

I lived in that moment every day.

"I wish I remembered it; I wish I remembered you."

Someday we will meet again, Aelira.

"That day may be soon."

Don't speak that way.

Only the stars know your future.

Even visionaries can be wrong.

"I don't think Cora is wrong."

I saw it all unfolding, maybe even the way Cora sees it now.

We are not always correct in what we see.

The smallest shift can alter everything.

"What did you see?"

I saw the woman you would become.

I saw you mend the dying land.

There may still be a way.

Tears collected on my sleeve.

"Thank you for everything," I whispered as I pressed the book closed. If there was a way, perhaps we would find it, but even if we didn't—I had everything I wanted beside me.

Lioran rubbed his eyes "Please come back to bed." His curls lay across the pillow. I climbed in beside him, still gripping the book.

"My father is not alive anymore." The leather cover shifted between my unsteady fingertips.

"My love...I know you were hoping to find him." He brushed tears off my cheek. "He must have loved you very much."

"Your mother knew." It wasn't enough for her to take everything I desired from me—she wanted her words to plunge deeper.

"Why do you think that?"

"After she reminded you of your promise. She said he *would* have been proud of me."

Silence fell between us. His fingers curled inward, and his gaze narrowed.

"King Ardyn killed him..." I whispered the truth until my throat ached from each word. He killed him and let my mother live. Yet looking back I'm not sure if she was really living at all.

Tears often clung to her cheeks when no one was watching. She spoke with such softness that I never understood. Until now. Now I knew her heart was broken. He made her continue with life as if it never happened at all.

"Aelira. I'm so sorry. I can't imagine what it is like to find out after all this time. After everything you've been through."

For a moment I just looked at him. He drew me in to his side and held me closer.

"He doesn't think I will die." The words settled on me as I said them.

His eyes widened. "What did he say?" I placed the book into his hands. My father's words were still there, as if he wasn't ready to leave me yet.

"We will keep our hope." He moved closer behind me, his arms sliding around me, and I leaned back into him.

"What if it's false hope?" My voice trailed off.

"It's still hope...and I will keep hanging on to it."

The lingering chill sent shivers down my spine, but Lioran only gripped me closer.

"When you go back...I want you to find happiness—to fall in love again." My stomach clenched as my view became a cloudy haze.

"I'm not going back."

"You have to arrange your marriage."

He placed the book down beside us and released me from his hold.

I prepared myself for the words I didn't want to hear.

"I am staying with you. There is nowhere else I need to be. We are going to Myrwood together." His lips found mine again.

For a moment, I almost protested, but instead, I let myself settle in his words—in the promise of another tomorrow.

"I love you." I ran my hand down his chest, his silver eyes caught mine.

"You have my love always."

I examined a perfect, pale purple rose in the garden as I waited for Lioran to be done with his council meeting. Their scent lingered heavier than before. I heard every blade of grass sway, the call of doves in the distance.

Lythira's melody hummed through my veins. Each day since the bargain, something shifted and settled deeper within me. Today, I was weaker than the day before, but the sun's glow radiated over me—its warmth a sweet embrace.

"I thought I might find you here." Lioran's voice brushed over me, his hand resting on my shoulder. "I have a surprise for you, but you need to get ready for it. Juniper is in your chambers waiting for you." A sweet grin spread across his face. "Go ahead. I'll see you later." He raised my hand to his lips and brushed my skin with a gentle kiss.

I turned to look back at him before I stepped back inside the castle. His curls blew free in the wind, his eyes softened as they caught mine. He was lighter and almost joyful. I held the arch door frame, taking him in before heading inside.

He planned something just for us, my heart thundered as my mind raced wondering what it could be.

An opulent emerald gown lay on the bed. The silk was more magnificent than any fabric I had ever worn. Pink roses and leaves were embroidered into the fabric.

"The prince had it made for you. He sent word to our best seamstress before you returned from Nythrel. Do you like it?"

"Yes, I love it. It's beautiful." It was fit for fae royalty. She removed my simple gown and tugged the other over me. The sleeves hung low past my fingertips. I braced myself for the pull of ribbons. The dress was already tight.

"You look radiant in it," she softly mused.

"But the corset..."

Juniper giggled. "The prince had specific instructions for the design—no corset." I breathed freely, feeling the lightweight gown sway with my body as I moved.

He had thought of everything.

"Do you know what the surprise is?" I asked as my hands gripped the sleeves, playing with the flowing fabric.

She nodded. "I do, but I promised I wouldn't ruin it, only prepare you for it."

My smile flowed freely. Tonight, we would just exist, together. The bargain, his promise to his parents—it would all wait another day. Juniper twisted half of my hair back, leaving a cascade of loose, chocolate waves trickling down the open back of the dress. She placed a circlet of golden leaves on my head.

"He will be waiting for you in the garden."

"Thank you, Juniper."

Joy flooded me. The gown flowed freely behind me as I took in the ivy that cascaded over the castle halls—each step I took led me closer to him.

The sun dipped near the horizon, hues of pinks dancing with blue in the sky. Lioran stood in the center of the courtyard, dressed in a matching, satin emerald tunic. His back to me.

"Will you tell me what you've planned now?" He turned around with my words. His silver eyes sparkled, catching fragments of light.

His chest trembled with his exhale and tears pooled in his eyes. "You look stunning."

"I hear you are to thank for that." I reached out to touch him, but I pulled back in case others were watching. He pulled me in toward him, his hands wrapped confidently around me as his lips brushed over mine.

"What if someone sees us?"

His shoulders settled back, his chin raised high. "Let them," he said.

For a moment, he was himself again, and I was still me—

despite the bargain. The weight of it still pinned me down, but my heart was free.

He paused and inhaled deeply. My hands settled in his palms. "I'm grateful you crossed the divide." He stumbled over his words for a moment, his eyes filled with tears.

"You don't need to say anything. Tonight, we get to be together."

"I've spent too much time not saying what I need to," he said. "I was living half in the darkness, the decay of these lands consuming me, until the stars led me straight to you. Every flower you've brought to life, every tree you've embraced, not only revived these lands, but it restored me. My love for you runs deeper than the roots of the trees. It vibrates through Lythira's core and mine." His fingers trailed my cheek, until he pulled me in toward him, his lips heavy on mine. "We belong here, together—in our home. I choose you, Aelira, for all the days we can be together. I want to bond with you forever—live the life we imagined."

"Lioran..." My voice quaked through the tears.

His shoulders went rigid, as if he was bracing himself for me to say no. "Will you marry me tonight beneath the stars?"

My lips parted, ready to say yes, but I couldn't. "What of your promise to your parents, to the High Court?"

"I promised I will marry—I am delivering on my promise, binding myself to the only fae I could spend my life with. The stars insisted our paths cross, tested us, left us to fall apart, but we will rise above it and stand together."

"If they find out..." I shuddered.

"I will be the one to tell them. It is my choice—I choose you." He exhaled. "Will you bond with me, Aelira?" he asked again.

"I thought you'd never ask," I whispered with a smile. "Yes, Lioran—I am yours always."

I pulled him closer, kissing him deeply.

Joy glimmered in his eyes, bolder and brighter than before. His smile spread.

He removed a wooden box from his tunic, engraved with leaves. "You are my future." He pried open the box, revealing a dazzling emerald hugged by silver leaves.

Lioran slid the ring on my finger.

A quiet warmth flooded me.

CHAPTER 32

S tarlight trickled in through the open ballroom. Lush
vines danced up the columns framing the sky. My hand
settled into Lioran's as he led me down a rose-lined
walkway. Candlelight glimmered in the distance, rivaling the
stars' glow.

Strewn rose petals encircled the center of the room—Cora
and Fyn stood at the perimeter. The celestial rays illuminated
his unwavering gaze as we settled in the middle.

"Prince Lioran and Princess Aelira's union will be recognized by Lythira and the stars tonight. Bonded in this life until
one takes their last breath." Lord Orion read from a small black
leather book.

My head lowered. Lioran slid his fingers under my chin.

"They have chosen to love and honor each other always—
to serve each other as equal partners and to jointly serve
Lythira."

"Jointly?" My breathing hitched as I whispered to him.

"As long as I remain Guardian, as my wife, you are a

protector of these lands, too." My hands pressed into his, our bodies drew breath in unison. I nodded.

"If anyone believes these two should not be bonded, please speak your peace now," Lord Orion spoke.

The song of crickets filled the night. A soft breeze blew over us, without any sound, as if Lythira agreed to our bond.

"Prince Lioran, do you bind yourself to Princess Aelira, to take her as your wife?"

"I, Prince Lioran, bond myself to you...in every lifetime." He twisted the ring on my finger until the emerald illuminated in the moonlight.

I blinked back the tears, but they refused to hold. He added the words for me—in case I didn't survive.

"Princess Aelira, will you bond yourself with Lioran, to take him as your husband?" Lord Orion turned toward me and bowed his head.

"I, Princess Aelira, bond myself to you..." The words caught in my throat, even though I knew I meant them. "In every lifetime."

Lioran kissed me as if he was claiming me all over again.

"We will now proceed with the handfasting. Lady Cora, Lord Fyn, are you ready?" Lord Orion gestured for them to join us. Lioran lifted my hands into his so that our palms pressed together. Fyn and Cora took both sides of a silver ribbon, and each wrapped theirs around our hands. My hands stilled against his.

"All promises that are made here shall be protected by the stars," Lord Orion announced.

Cora's eyes caught on mine as she settled the ends of the ribbon around our hands. She smiled at me and then at Lioran. His breathing quickened—his hands trembled against mine.

"Lioran?" I whispered to him, desperate to ease whatever worried him.

"I not only bind myself to my wife, but to her bargain..." His words boomed through the great hall, lifting into the air. "I promise to stand beside you, to restore the land."

"No—you can't risk yourself for me," I cried.

"You can't just take on her bargain," Cora protested.

He didn't retort but only continued his promise. "Wherever we go—we go together. I choose this life above all else. The crown may pass to another if she can't rule at my side."

The air whirled around, the rose petals lifted and settled. Heat surged from my onyx through my hands and into his.

Lord Orion waited, he watched Lioran carefully, but my husband only nodded.

"With my magic I seal these promises." Golden light shimmered from Lord Orion's hands, through the ribbon—it wound around our hands until the ribbon disintegrated. "Your fate is tied. May you love each other for all your days—for as long as the stars allow." He choked on his words.

Fyn's audible sigh echoed, but when I looked back at him, a somber smile spread across his face.

Lioran wrapped his arms around me. He pressed his lips into mine.

I couldn't alter his fate, couldn't alter mine.

We would go into Myrwood Grove together, to face whatever lay ahead, bonded as husband and wife.

Lioran scooped me in his arms and carried me up the main stairs, where anyone could see—we didn't have to hide anymore. My hands wrapped around his neck. The train of my gown flowed behind us. He walked with such urgency, as if he couldn't lose a single moment with me.

"Lioran...how could you?" I still hadn't caught my breath when we made it into my chambers—the chambers of his bonded wife.

"I gave us a future." He kissed me as he put me down. "We can do this together."

"We don't know that."

He leaned backward into the bed, pulling me closer to him.

"The Grove won't just take magic from you—I will bear the weight of it beside you." I felt relief at his words, but the guilt rivaled it.

The moment I spoke in Nythrel—I doomed us both.

My head hung, my heart grew heavier.

"It was my choice to make."

"I thought you were doing it for the time we had remaining until I wasn't..." I couldn't bring myself to say the words.

He slid the cuffs off his wrist. "I did this for us—to create the life we deserve. Please, let us have our first night together as husband and wife...our first of many." He worked at his tunic buttons, sliding them free.

"How do I live with what I've done to you? What I've caused you to risk?"

"You just live. You've given me..." His hands drifted down my torso, settling at my waist. "Everything." Pain flickered behind his eyes as his hands lingered. My breath caught in my chest as he froze. "I ever wanted...everything I hoped for."

His hand fell over his mouth, and his eyes watered.

"Lioran?" He pulled me in, gripping me tightly against his body.

"The stars had bigger plans for us." He whispered in my ear before he released me.

Lioran pulled his jacket free. His arms looked different in the moonlight. The three bands on his arm were altered—only two remained. Something new replaced the third—two woven vines.

"Your claim to the throne..."

"I said I wouldn't rule without you by my side." He grinned as if he was content with the change.

"But...why do you have a new one?" As I held his arm up in mine to inspect the band, my sleeve slid back—revealing a matching tattoo on me—smaller than his. I twisted my wrist, taking in the beautiful vines that I loved from Lythira entwined.

"What do they mean?" I asked. "Is it from us bonding?"

He grabbed my wrist, inspecting the tattoo—his breathing quickened. "No. Bonding isn't marked with a tattoo."

"Could it be from the bargain? You committed to do it with me." But even then, I hadn't received one when I made the bargain.

"Maybe." The lines deepened around his eyes. "When I was made Guardian, I received one of the tattoo bands marking my role. Maybe this symbolizes us protecting Lythira together."

"Whatever it means...It's perfect."

It didn't matter what caused it. He was here, beside me.

Our lips met again. "You are perfect." His hands slid around to the laces. He pulled them free. The gown fell from my shoulders. "We will have to do something about this two-chamber thing... it won't do." A wicked grin danced across his face.

I stepped out of my gown in front of my husband.

He ripped the cords of his pants free until they dropped.

Lioran growled in my ear, his lips trailed down my collarbone. My body sank into each touch, each kiss. I laid back on the bed, reaching for him to come with me. As his body met mine, I pulled him in closer. His lips found mine and I gave into his fire.

"Good morning, my beautiful wife," Lioran whispered in my ears. My body curved with his, feeling the weight of him there beside me.

"How many more days do we have like this?" I wanted as many as I could get, but soon we would leave here, and I may not return.

"All of them. We're coming home."

A vial lay near the edge of the bed, waiting for me. As I reached for it, he intertwined his fingers with mine, pulling my hand back toward his chest.

"Don't." He looked different as he spoke. "You don't need to take it anymore." Fear encompassed him. "You are my wife now—we are allowed this. If the stars choose."

"You can't be serious. We can't go into Myrwood Grove risking—"

"When the stars choose to bless us with a child, we will embrace it." His lips skimmed mine.

Lioran always had a vial for me. I took it every time. No longer trying to stop it from happening felt like a dangerous game. But the thought that there could be a future for us— made me happier than I wanted to admit.

I pulled my hand back from his, gripped the vial in my palm, watched the purple liquid slide.

"Please. Let us have our hope." He spoke quickly, his eyes pleaded with mine. "I need us to have it."

"When the stars choose." I turned away from the vial and reached for him, felt the warmth of his body next to mine.

"Make love to me again." My voice was ragged at the thought of feeling every inch of him again.

I didn't know what tomorrow held, but these final moments, no one could take from me.

"Gladly." He grinned.

His kiss was deeper and more desperate than before.

CHAPTER 33

We sat around the table in the private dining room with plates stuffed to the brim with meat—every leafy green was pale and lifeless. Each meal we ate held less color than before.

The space could easily hold more fae, more food, but it was usually only the three of us—Fyn, Lioran, and I. Cora sometimes stopped by. Being back at that table made me feel like I was home.

I only picked at my food. Fyn ate every bite from his plate.

"You both look well...rested." Fyn offered a tilted grin as he raised his water glass toward us.

"Fyn," Cora grumbled at him.

I let out a laugh—the first in a while.

Lioran's mouth curved into a warm grin. "You made her laugh."

"You say it like I'm no fun anymore." I exhaled, but my chest held tight.

"Oh, I definitely didn't say that." Lioran's grin spread wide, his gaze devouring me.

"Okay...well, lunch was pleasant. We should probably leave these two so they can get back to whatever they had planned for this afternoon."

"Have you sent word to Nythrel?" Cora flipped her red hair over her shoulder. On the surface, she seemed calm, but something was off about her.

"Word was sent. They will know soon enough," Lioran responded.

"What will they do?" I asked.

"It doesn't matter. Time is on our side for now." Lioran's gaze remained on his leftover lunch.

Horror struck me with my next thought. I hadn't even considered what would happen when he relinquished his claim to the throne. "I sincerely hope it is not Pyrran."

Fyn snorted as he gulped his water. It sprayed everywhere. "The stars would never—he wasn't gifted with magic."

Lioran drummed his fingers on the table. "The only choice is Calyth."

Cora's emerald eyes dulled, only for a moment. "You really think it's that simple? The stars chose you."

"It's done. My tattoo, the mark of fate's choice, vanished," Lioran retorted as he dug his fork into a sliver of venison. The smell soured as it hit me, and I pushed my plate aside. Once we returned from the Grove, *if we returned,* I would be able to eat again.

Cora slid down in her chair. Her gaze turned to me. She didn't utter another word, but I knew she wanted me to intervene.

"The stars must have changed their mind," I said.

"Are you going to eat that?" Fyn eyed my plate.

"I'm not hungry." I pushed it closer to him.

Cora spoke up again, but the edge was gone from her words. "I had another vision."

I gripped the arms of the chair, my fingernails digging into the wood.

Cora played with the hem of her sleeves. "The bargain will take from you, until you complete it. You are on borrowed time —both of you." Her fork shook in her unsteady grip. "You must go to Myrwood, tomorrow." My stomach clenched. There was no avoiding it—our time, our moment, couldn't continue to exist like this.

"Tomorrow?" I echoed.

"Lythira's patience will dwindle. The bargain will not wait much longer." Her words ran cold.

"What did you learn?" Lioran ran his quaking hands through his hair, pushing his curls further from his eyes.

"Myrwood Grove is alive with dark magic—it will attempt to break you in ways you can't imagine. Not just anyone can pass through the Grove."

"Break us how?" Lioran asked.

Cora looked away from Lioran. "That I can't answer. It is all we know. Only fragments of tales remain of those who travel there."

"And if it doesn't think we are worthy?" I hesitated to ask.

"I don't know what happens." She gripped the table.

"Did you see the end?" My voice creaked. Every muscle in my body stiffened as she exhaled, staring out the window.

"I can't determine if what I saw was the end." It wasn't like Cora to hold back—she was hiding something.

"Don't tell us then," Lioran interjected.

"Lioran," I snapped. "It's my fate. I need to know."

"And if you hear you don't survive? Then what? You won't have the will to hold on—I *need* you to hold on." Each word was more desperate than the last—the light in his eyes dimmed.

"It will deplete you entirely—"

"Don't say another word." His hands slapped the table. The flatware bounced, and I jolted upright.

"She deserves to know," Cora insisted.

Lioran braced himself against the back of his chair. "How can I protect her? She needs to be the one to walk out of the Grove."

Fyn bit his lip at Lioran's words.

"Why does it have to be me?" I asked. His chest rose, his lips parted, but he said nothing.

"I don't know that you can," Cora said.

"We will bear the weight of this together and the stars will decide." I wanted to believe each word I spoke. He had risked everything—given me everything.

Sunlight caught on the emerald on my finger, casting a green glow on the walls. Heat sifted through my body as the room spun. I clutched onto Lioran's arm, hoping he could steady me.

"What's wrong?" he asked.

"My nerves are getting the best of me." Nausea spiraled within me.

Lioran's jaw clenched, his arms stiffened against the chair.

"Try to eat something." Cora moved the plate closer to me.

"I can't." My stomach would never settle to handle it.

Fyn shifted nervously in his seat.

"We will need to arrange everything we can for the journey. Fyn, I'll need your help." Lioran's fingers trailed down my arm. He squeezed my hand. "Cora, please keep an eye on her."

Cora followed them both to the door. When Fyn slipped through, she pulled Lioran back. "She's barely eaten anything since our visit to the High Court."

"She will eat when she's ready." Lioran's words were firm, but there was something behind his eyes. Maybe his fear was just as crippling as mine.

"I think she needs to see a healer. Maybe Rowena has something that can help with her nerves." Cora stepped in front of him, blocking the door.

"All of this is to be expected, considering the situation." Gently, he guided her aside and left.

"I'm worried about you. Please consider seeing Rowena before we go," Cora said.

"There's nothing anyone can do. I'm just...afraid." My gaze remained at the door.

"My visions evolve...what I see one day, may alter the next. It may not be as I see it." Her voice quaked with each word.

"Have you seen what happens when we go there together? Have you seen Lioran there at all?" I wasn't sure if I even wanted the answer.

Tears welled in her eyes. "He hasn't been in any of my visions...only you. The Grove wants you..."

"It doesn't matter...does it? If he goes or not?" I pulled back my chair, ready to stand, but the room spun again. "I don't make it..."

She couldn't blink the tears back anymore. I couldn't watch them fall.

"I don't know if it matters. I can only tell you what the stars have chosen to show me. Hope is not lost. More may still be revealed."

"As long as it doesn't reveal an end where he doesn't return." Our home could thrive without me—Lioran could move on too. Without him, I would crumble—Lythira would soon follow.

We spent our last night together falling further in love under the moon's glow. I wanted to stay forever in our home, but the Grove wouldn't wait.

Ever since the bargain, something new stirred in me, my body felt weaker—like it was no longer mine to command. If his felt the same, I wouldn't know it. Lioran would never complain.

My skin was hot as I freed myself from the covers. I undid the clasp of the onyx pendant, unable to bear its heat along with my own.

My hands shook as I reached for the leather book. Its delicate floral pattern was illuminated in dawn's light. I gently opened the cover and waited in silence. He stirred in the bed beside me.

"Lioran and I are bonded. We will go to the Grove together. He has taken on the bargain," I whispered.

I know how much you love him.

And now I see how much he loves you.

He will risk everything for you.

"I want him to be safe. I want us both to be safe."

Look to the stars to guide you.

You are the thread that ties humanity and the fae together.

Lythira has been waiting for you.

"I don't even know how..."

Your instincts will not lead you astray.

"My heart is breaking—it feels hollow."

Only because you fear, but fear will not guide you here.

It's time.

Go into the darkness and turn it into light.

"Thank you...I love you."

I love you, Aelira.

Your mother sends her love, too.

"Is she with you?" He hadn't mentioned it, maybe because he didn't want me to know he was gone. I knew she was, but seeing it on the page, knowing they were together let my heart settle.

Peace had been granted in six little words, etched in parchment.

Yes, she is here with me.

She is so proud of who you've become.

Do not be afraid.

You are our princess of the flowers.

She knew—just as he had—who I truly was. "Tell her I love her. I have never stopped thinking of her, never stopped wanting her here with me. She gave me a beautiful future—at the cost of her own, and I will continue to fight for it."

She's felt your love this entire time.

We will wait to hear about your journey.

And all the stories that are to come after.

As long as you have this book—I will be with you.

I pressed the pages shut. A single tear trickled down my face—it wasn't from fear, but feeling their love after all this time. Whatever the future held, I was grateful for all that the stars gave me.

Lythira greeted me as I stared out the window—its haunting call echoed off the wind.

"We must get ready. We will hold council before we leave." He exhaled. "Do you want me to get Juniper for you?"

"No, can you help me?" I slid off my robe.

"Aelira..." His eyes widened as I slid on my riding tunic and pants. The color drained from his face as he fastened the ties loosely around my waist.

"You can say what you need to."

"I..." His eyes filled with water that threatened to release.

His hands were stiff in mine as I waited to hear his words. "My love, there are no words I could say—your sacrifice pains me still."

"Our sacrifice..."

He looked away, his arm rubbed at his eyes. His chest rapidly pulsed.

"I will give everything I can so that our future here is secure. Anything the stars ask of me—to protect you—to protect our future."

"I know," I said as my lips collided with his. "But I pray to the stars that they leave you exactly as you are. This sacrifice is mine to give."

He shook his head as I ran my hands through his curls.

The council settled as we walked into the room. Ladies and lords bowed as Lioran entered, and then held the position as I followed behind him. He held his hand out to me to stand beside him.

"I've called you all here, because we are about to embark on a quest to Myrwood Grove—some of you have generously offered to aid in our travels. I will always be grateful as this path will not be without its dangers. If we succeed, the fate of Lythira will turn. If we fail..." He held his breath for a moment before releasing it. "The fate of Lythira will hang by a desperate thread."

If we fail...we could fail.

The room was still. I trembled, but Lioran wrapped his hand around mine.

"If I do not return, I must name a successor to guide Lythira." Murmurs cracked through the silence. Fyn nodded from the back of the room. Maybe Lioran would name him. He knew the land just as well.

"Your Highness, you do not yet have an heir to name successor." Lord Orion spoke. Lioran's uneasy gaze settled on me.

"Princess Aelira, my bonded wife, will be sworn in as Guardian of Lythira in my stead if the need arises." Murmurs shifted through the space, eyes all angling at me.

"A bonded wife can't assume the title of Guardian—she can serve beside you, but not replace you in the position." Lord Mavik crossed his arms.

"By law of the territory, only someone who can truly connect with the land can act as Guardian." He leaned forward in his seat, his hand bridging the gap between us. "My wife has grounding magic, like me—as many of you have witnessed—she is fit to act as Guardian in my stead."

Lady Aura's eyes settled on me, a quiet understanding.

"I..." I wanted to stop him—to protest, but I couldn't. Maybe it was because I couldn't bear the thought of what he was saying.

My heart caught in my chest. The world froze beside it. I tried to steady myself, blinking away any signs of the revelation as it finally hit.

"If she returns to Lythira without me, you must support her in her role as you've supported me in mine." He struggled with his words.

"I am not coming home without you," I whispered.

"Your Highness, while she is your wife...she is not fully fae." A lord I didn't recognize moved forward.

They knew—either Lioran prepped them, or we hadn't hidden it well enough.

"The king will never allow it," Lord Mavik said.

"He will have no choice. The stars chose her to connect with the land," Lioran said.

"She made the greatest sacrifice, is risking everything to aid our people. I've seen her magic, the way she cares for the people and the land." Fyn slid in between two ladies to stand before the rest of the council. "You have my support always, Princess Aelira." I saw it then, how much he saw me for exactly who I was—how he always had.

"Thank you, Lord Fyn." The words caught deep within my throat.

"She grew herbs for Othryl when there wasn't enough—packed the shipping crates beside us. And now she has promised to save our lands even when the land means to take from her...and you wonder if she's worthy. How many of you would do the same?" Lady Aura asked. "You have my support, Your Highness."

"And mine as well," Lord Orion spoke. I nodded to them both. Their support—their words—meant everything.

"Princess Aelira is more than capable. Her magic is as powerful as his," Cora spoke—something unsettling lingered behind each word. She knew the truth, but it wouldn't stop her from protecting Lioran's fragile state—or mine. "If the need should ever arise, I will guide her."

The room stood still—divided between certainty and question. Not all would stand beside me, but some did. It was more than I could have ever dreamed of.

"To those who still oppose her. Who will be left to protect us?" A fae woman with silver hair stepped into view. I had seen her before, but never heard her speak. "Lord Mavik, will you assume the role? Shall we wait for Prince Pyrran to assume it? He has been nothing but demanding of our land. Only one in touch with Lythira can guide it. If she is as capable as you all say, we are in excellent hands."

Lord Mavik bowed his head in response to her words. "We'll need all the protection we can get," he agreed. "Princess Aelira, if you promise to protect our land and our people, I will stand behind you."

This wasn't a life I ever imagined for myself.

My lip quivered as I spoke. "My heart is one with Lythira. I do not have the experience Prince Lioran does, nor can I guide you as effortlessly as he does, but if you work alongside me, advise me, I will stand beside you."

Lioran exhaled at my words, his hand squeezed mine.

"Do you all agree to it?" Lioran surveyed the crowd—silence settled, every head nodding in the group—even Lord Mavik.

"With my magic, I bind this pact. Princess Aelira will be Guardian if the need shall arise." Lord Orion unrolled the scroll. His hand waved over the parchment and the ink rose to the surface. Each word recording a version of my future I hoped I'd never see.

"May the stars protect you so that you both come home to us." Lady Aura bowed to Lioran and to me.

His hand stilled mine as the room emptied.

"Why did you do it?" I asked.

"It's what Lythira needs."

"If I come back at all—I won't even have my magic. How could you possibly promise them that?"

"The Grove can take from both of us. Maybe it won't take all of yours."

"The High Court won't agree to any of this," I said.

His plan wasn't concrete. It didn't make any sense, but still he spoke as if it did—as if he wanted it to.

Lioran kissed me on the head. "They won't have a choice but to agree to it."

He had resigned himself to this fate. I couldn't allow it. It didn't matter what I had to say—he was insistent.

"The stars willed it, and not even a king can undo their plans." He studied me as if he was looking at me for the very last time.

CHAPTER 34

Gaia's ears flicked as she made her way over the rocky terrain into Myrwood Grove.

We arrived too soon—the Grove was too close to the Heart.

An eerie hum rang through the desolate space—deep and frantic. My skin crawled with the sound. With each crescendo, nausea rolled through me until bitterness settled on my tongue. Threatening to linger.

Lioran said nothing, yet he flinched with the cascading sound. His breathing faltered

I gripped my bow, trembling as the wind thrashed against me. The quiver bounced at my back. It should have made me feel safe, protected, but it only made me feel desperate.

Gaia's hooves crunched over debris—the land crumbling beneath us. The trees arched, their inky barren branches reached into the path.

Fyn's blade caught a single ray of light that sparkled from the sun, before it faded again. His hand gripped the hilt. He rode beside me, without a single command from Lioran.

The Grove wailed.

Death had claimed it, but still it was alive.

"Lioran, do you hear that?" I called to him.

"Yes, try not to think on it." His voice was flat, his words flawless—but I heard the fear through each carefully spoken word.

"What is it?"

Fyn leaned in toward me. "Some say it's haunted by the souls that were lost here."

"How...reassuring."

"Yeah, it's just a totally relaxing ride through the woods." Fyn raised an eyebrow at me.

"Fyn. Quiet," Lioran warned.

"I don't hear you getting onto your wife," Fyn called to him a little quieter. I smirked at Fyn's words, but Lioran didn't respond. His silence left me empty.

The air stilled unnaturally.

A loud rumble thundered once. Then twice.

The Grove roared—the sound pierced my ears. A black branched veered overhead—swiping over us.

The tree moved. On its own. Without my magic or Lioran's.

The branches swung in a chaotic dance. Fyn's hand jolted my back, pushing me into Gaia.

We wouldn't make it through this—we wouldn't leave. The Grove would claim us—one way or another. Air held in my lungs—sharp and painful as I clutched onto the saddle.

"Stay down," Fyn warned. "I've got her," he called to Lioran.

Lioran couldn't stop the Grove—he couldn't save us from this.

We had to find a way to survive it.

Low lying branches grazed at Gaia's leg. She quaked

beneath me. Her fear pulsed through me, in time with my own. I gasped, unable to breathe through it.

A tree cracked as if an axe had been taken to it. Heavy limbs crashed between the horses—parting our group until only a handful of us remained together. Cora's cries echoed behind me, I let the sound drown out my own.

Branches beat the land—deep and insistent.

With an echoing crash, a branch swung toward Lord Mavik, severing him from the saddle. He was gone. The Grove had taken him.

"Fyn!" I cried, reaching for him. He held my hand as we steadied our horses. There was nowhere to go. I held my free hand steady and reached for the Grove. I called my magic, willed the Grove to listen to my pleas, but nothing answered. As if that part of me was already gone.

I pleaded with it, tugged at it deep within me. It fizzled before it even left my fingertips.

"I can't stop it." Each breath caught, more rapid than the next.

"We're going to make it out of here," Fyn said as he squeezed my hand in his. I closed my eyes—I couldn't handle the sight of it any longer.

One by one the branches beat the land like a war cry. The ground quaked in time with each crash. Suddenly, it fell silent. Fyn tugged my hand.

I opened my eyes and watched the branches snap back into position—as if it never happened at all. When I looked for Mavik—he was gone.

His horse stood without a rider in the middle of the Grove. Debris surrounded us.

"We need to look for him!" Lioran cried, dismounting from his horse in time with Lord Orion. He glanced back at me. His chest swelled as his hand covered his mouth, before he took off running.

There wasn't time to demand he stopped. He wouldn't have listened even if I had.

Before they even entered deep into the brush, Lord Mavik walked out of the woods. His hands desperately gripped his sword still at his waist.

"I'm alright." Lord Mavik shook his head. "I'm not even sure what happened."

None of us were.

Memories of his blond braid whipping through the wind would never leave me, but there he was—unharmed.

He climbed back on his horse as if it never happened.

"How?" My voice quaked.

Lioran's gaze caught mine as he raced back to Veylar. I had never seen terror run so deep beneath it. "I don't know," he said as he mounted his stallion. "We need to keep going."

"Some of the lords wish to leave." Lord Orion called to us. His eyes avoided Lioran's.

"Then let them." Lioran looked back at me. I swallowed hard. "If you wish to head back, then go!" He yelled to the party ahead. No one moved. "I can't guarantee you'll make it through here. Go, if you must."

They turned back. Three of them left.

Their names had been uttered, but I wouldn't remember them.

Maybe I'd never even see them again.

"They're leaving?" I didn't know why I questioned it. I would have left if I could.

"Let them," Lioran seethed. He wouldn't hold it against them. He knew their fear as well as he knew his.

There weren't enough of us to weather whatever came next.

The Grove wouldn't stop here. It wouldn't let us proceed untested.

Mavik and Orion stayed beside Lioran. "We will deliver you safely," Mavik said. "You have my sword, Prince Lioran and Princess Aelira."

"Thank you." My lips quivered as I spoke.

He was taken from his horse. He could have lost his life, and yet he remained.

They would abandon us, but he would not.

My eyes met his and his head lowered.

The Grove's cries became unrelenting screeches. We marched the horses onward. Gaia's ears pinned back. The branches rotated in a nearby tree, as if they were watching. Waiting to strike again.

A howl reverberated through the haunted space. The heavy mist that clung to the air thickened. A low hiss crept over the ground. Black smoke rose from ash. My insides twisted.

A beast formed. Steady, black legs gave way to iron claws. Its muscles taut. The smoke faded until I saw its head. The creature assembled piece by piece as if it was sculpted. Every hair on my arms raised as it stalked closer. Each threatening breath it took released puffs of steam.

Its inky fur glittered under fragments of sunlight that cast through the canopy of barren branches overhead. A bone-rattling roar released from its mouth—its canines glimmered, dripping with crimson.

With each step, it stalked slowly toward us.

Fyn drew his sword, followed by Mavik and Orion. My fingers wrapped around the shaft of my arrow as I set it in place. I pulled back the strings with vibrating force.

Lioran didn't move.

He didn't even reach for his sword.

The creature's black bulging eyes shifted toward him.

I needed him to move, to do something. He couldn't just sit there unarmed.

"Lower your weapons," Lioran warned, his voice steady.

"I can take it," I said.

With a swift pull of the strings, I could save us all.

"Put it away, Aelira." Lioran's hushed words hit me like screams in the darkness. "Now."

Lioran's hand raised—a golden glow that whirled at his fingertips. I felt his magic like it was mine. Until it vanished.

The beast paced in front of Veylar, unfazed by Lioran's wordless commands.

Its eyes locked onto mine—it called to me, threatening me. It sneered, its fangs still dripping with its latest kill. The stench carried between us.

My magic pulsed violently, loosening my grip on the bow, but still I would not lower it. The trees around me whirled as my view distorted, darkness crept in at the corner of my vision.

Lioran's hand lifted—he tried to call his magic again. The string of the bow rubbed my cheek raw as it hovered against my skin.

The creature darted for Lioran. I froze. Inky smoke engulfed him—I couldn't see him anymore.

I wailed, crumpling in the saddle—my sobs echoing in the Grove.

"I'm fine!" he yelled. Dust settled back into fallen ash.

"I don't... understand." Cora pulled her horse up behind Gaia. "What does it want from us?"

"You don't know?" Fyn settled back in his saddle.

My chest convulsed. The air was too heavy to breathe.

"It's thriving off fear, uncertainty...We need to keep calm," Cora warned.

"What if that's what it wants?" I asked.

My breath stilled—what if it only wants us to question

what's real and what isn't? If we grew confident that each threat would resolve without harm, then it could break us with something unexpected—something we wouldn't defend ourselves from.

"We need to keep going." Lioran's voice quaked.

"We have to trust what we know to be true—trust ourselves. Nothing else matters." Cora's voice shook with each word she spoke.

Veylar fell back beside Gaia. Lioran's eyes met mine. His hand gripped mine, bringing them to his lip. "We will make it through this. We're going home."

After all I had seen, I didn't know if I could believe it. Each of the Grove's threats were cruel—they made my fear run deeper. It wouldn't have to try much harder to break me.

I was already cracking.

I mirrored Lioran's breath, trying to keep steady on Gaia—so I wouldn't faint. I couldn't speak. Couldn't find the words for the threat looming over me. His hand tightened on mine.

"I've got you, my love." He knew. My words weren't needed, Lioran sensed whenever I was fading—when I couldn't control each breath.

"Breathe, Aelira. Just breathe."

My chest rose slowly. I quaked as I exhaled.

"What if we don't even make it to the tree?" I asked.

"Aelira, look at me," he commanded. "Remember when you told me you were picturing our future?" He struggled to say the words. "Keep picturing it. That is what we are fighting for. Someday we will have it...all of it, but I need you to hold on. No matter what happens. So you can live it with me."

I nodded, as the tears fell. He leaned in his saddle toward me, wiping them away.

"I'm here with you. Until the end. And even then, I will find you again." He spun the ring on my finger until the emerald faced me.

It took everything in me to will each breath. To not choke. To not let the tears drown me.

His promise gave my heart strength in the darkness—it was everything I needed. The Grove had taken my strength, almost taken my will to continue, but in this moment my heart felt free. Sadness tugged at his lips, but I was desperate to see him smile.

"Our children better not all look like you..." I muttered.

His eyes watered and a weary grin formed. "You'd like it if they did."

He was right, I would.

I needed to hold that joy, even if only for a moment longer.

"I think I remember this from my vision. We should scout ahead." Cora pointed to a twisted black tree marking a fork in the path.

"Which way?" he asked.

"I don't know." Cora tightened her grip on her reins.

"We will go to the left and you and Lady Cora can go to the right," Lord Mavik said. Lord Orion and Lord Mavik proceeded without us.

"Fyn, stay with Aelira. Do not leave her," Lioran pleaded.

Fyn nodded.

Lioran and Cora rode their horses further in the fog until only darkness loomed. My eyes scanned leafless brush as I led Gaia forward. No signs of them remained.

"Lioran!" I screamed. "Cora!"

My voice came thundering back at me through the dense fog.

"Fyn?" I pivoted in my saddle. Fyn nervously shifted in his. "Thank the stars you're still here. How do we find them?"

"They have to still be there—the fog has only separated

us." Fyn's hands trembled on the reins. "You're here with me. I'm not going anywhere."

A lump lodged in my throat. The mist was too thick to inhale.

I jumped down from Gaia, clinging to her side as we inched forward—hoping I would have a better vantage point closer to the ground, but still I saw nothing.

Fyn climbed down off his horse. "Should we be walking through here?"

The ground came alive, pulsing and trembling beneath my feet. White haze engulfed me, until even Fyn faded from view.

"Fyn?" I waited for his response, but it never came.

Something shifted.

The haze wouldn't fade.

I tried to take another step forward, but my feet wouldn't obey. Each breath I drew was shallow. My heart drummed in my ears.

Something was wrong—terribly wrong.

My hands gripped for anything around me, any indication of what was real and what wasn't. Something that told me I was still alive.

I felt the ashy soil in my fingers as I crouched down.

A shadowy figure approached from behind a tree.

"I'm crushed, Aelira." Pyrran pushed his crimson tunic sleeves up over his elbows. "You didn't even invite me to the bonding ceremony."

He wouldn't come all this way. Pyrran would never willingly enter the Grove.

It had to be an illusion.

He stood inches from me, glaring at me. "I bet it was lovely."

"You're not real," I murmured, my voice so low I didn't know if he could hear me.

Pyrran cackled. "Do I not look real to you?" His eyes were wild. His hand clenched around my wrist, pressing deep into my skin.

My free hand trailed the embroidered sleeve of his tunic, feeling the raised threads, the buttons on the cinched-up fabric. It was all real. I felt it all.

I trembled, reaching for the quiver. It was still on my back.

"Don't be a fool," he said as he seized my free hand in his— he pressed firmly on my fingers until I feared they would break. His breath was hot on my cheeks. The onyx chilled against my skin, pulsating with each word he spoke.

"You don't belong with my brother—you don't belong here at all. You are nothing...not human, not fae. Neither realm wants you."

His words couldn't undo me.

I belonged in Lythira, I would guard it beside my husband.

"Lythira is my home," I said.

"Then why is no one here to protect you? Look around. You are entirely alone."

"You will release me."

"I will do nothing of the sort. He has lied to you—left you delusional. Every promise he made is fleeting."

"You're lying."

"Tell me...how did you get to be so naïve?" He released his grip on me. Pyrran pulled the arrows from my quiver and flung them into the thicket. "Don't try me again. You'll regret it."

I darted. The minute I did, he tackled me to the ground.

"I can't let you go just yet." Pyrran hissed. "Your bond must be reversed."

Lioran said it was irreversible, only death dissolved a bond. A bitter bile burned in my stomach.

He meant to kill me. I would die. Lioran wasn't here to save me.

"This is not real," I said, hoping there was truth to my words. The Grove wanted me confident so it could break me.

What if this was real and I played along like it wasn't?

"You can keep telling yourself that." Pyrran shook his head as he stood, his hands released from me. "Run again, and I will kill you myself." A dagger hung at his waist.

I couldn't outrun him, couldn't fight him.

"Why haven't you already?" I bit my lip.

If he wanted me dead, he could have taken my life in an instant.

"If you're dead, you don't get to watch it all unfold," he scoffed.

I swallowed hard. My stomach clenched tighter. Footsteps sounded behind me.

"Aelira." Lioran's voice cracked. My gaze set on his—panic gripped him.

"Don't," King Thalorys warned, his hands held the hilt of Lioran's sword. "This mess will be discretely handled. And you will not defy me again."

"If you harm her, I will never do what you want," Lioran pleaded. "We are bonded. If you wish for me to rule, she rules beside me."

"You will sit on the throne, Lioran, but not with her. The bond will be reversed."

"No, I will not allow it," Lioran protested reaching for me, but he froze in his spot, gripping at his chest. King Thalorys held his hand on his son, compelling him. Lioran's chest heaved under the strain.

As I stepped toward him, Pyrran's hand pressed firmly against my chest. The leather armor chafed my skin under his grip. I had made the bargain. Told them where we would be.

Lioran shared the news of our marriage and now they would do anything to stop us.

The visions of our future were fading faster than I could grip them. I closed my eyes, trying to recall everything I once saw, but it was lost.

Pyrran pulled the dagger out his sheath. The blade scraped at my flesh—it pricked my skin, until drops of blood ran down with it. "Would you rather we kill her, brother? It can be arranged."

"Release her, Pyrran. Now!" Lioran screamed.

"Enough! You will bond with another, or I will kill her myself," Thalorys warned. Beads of sweat collected at my brow. Tears streamed down my face.

"I will—if you let her go. Take her back to the divide if you must."

My death. Cora, saw it.

No matter what he agreed to, I wouldn't walk free.

My body trembled as my knees sank further into ash. Shades of black and grey spun around me.

"The bond will be undone, by magic—and you will bond with another, here today. Aelira, will leave unharmed if you agree." King Thalorys waved his hand, releasing Lioran.

"Who?" Lioran gasped for air.

"Turns out there's was a suitable match already amongst you. She came with you," Thalen said as he dragged Cora into view. Her hands bound behind her back.

No. She wouldn't. He couldn't.

"She's fully fae, with magic too. I believe you two used to have feelings for each other. It shouldn't be hard to rekindle the spark." Pyrran crouched beside me.

My sobs rang through the Grove.

"I won't bond with him," Cora pushed at Thalen, ripping her bound hands from his.

"Your king commands it." King Thalorys held his hand up in warning.

She flinched with his words as her shoulders drooped.

A golden glow trailed out of the king's hands. It gripped us both. The light ran through my veins, tearing away what little remained of my heart. Something popped and twisted inside me.

Memories sped through my mind. Each one was being ripped from me, until my heart was severed. Crushed until only lifeless shards remained. Pain ricocheted through me.

Crumpled and lifeless I lay on the ground. Nausea surged through my core. I tried to rise, but tumbled to the ground again.

We were broken.

"I would have given you everything." Thalen wrapped his arms behind me and pulled me to stand. My back collided with his chest—he felt unnaturally warm, he felt wrong.

I needed Lioran's arms around me for one last time.

Thalen pinned my arms behind my back. The weight of him dug into me. My shoulder popped. A wave of pain over-took me. "Watch." He freed his hand and lifting my chin. "I have given you what you asked, your majesty. Honor our agreement—make her mine," Thalen sneered.

"I will never bond with you," I cried.

"Aelira will live out her days in my castle walls. She will no longer be your burden to bear." Thalen tightened his grip on me, ignoring my claim.

"It will be done," the king said.

It no longer mattered what I wanted, what I chose—my life was no longer my own. My words would never matter.

Lioran couldn't protect me any longer.

The King released Cora. Her hands pressed against my

husband's, just as we had during our bonding ceremony. A ribbon tied tightly around their hands.

Lioran's gaze never parted from mine, even as I screamed.

I sucked in air, quicker than it would come, collapsing back into Thalen.

Darkness loomed over me—I let it take me.

There was nothing left.

A firm grip tugged at my shoulder, its force repeated—steady and urgent.

Fyn's face came into view, hovering over mine. "You're safe. I've got you." He stilled my body with his—his weight grounding me as I convulsed. "Aelira, please," Fyn cried. "Stay with me."

I didn't know if the choice was even mine to make.

CHAPTER 35

I couldn't survive a world without Lioran. They broke him. They broke me. I gasped, desperate for air that wouldn't come. Stabbing pain filled my lungs. Sweat drenched my body. It vibrated uncontrollably. Muscles constricted against bone, as I screamed in agony.

A flash of someone, or something, beat across my blurry view.

"Aelira!" Lioran yelled. "She's alive?" He crumbled beside us.

Fyn's hands trembled around me.

"Is it done?" Tears pooled on my leather armor. "Where is Thalen?" I leaned into Fyn, desperate still to draw more air. My view was tinged with darkness. It waited for me.

"Stay with me, my love." Lioran crashed to his knees beside us. Horror set in his gaze as he reached for me—his hand hung in the space between us. My head settled on Fyn's chest and my eyes closed.

"Don't take her from me! Please!" Lioran screamed into the void. The winds thrashed in response.

The world slipped from view.

Darkness came for me. I slipped into it.

The wind brushed my skin. It sang to me.

Aelira...

Make a choice.

Stay and fight, or leave this world behind.

Agony filled me. The onyx no longer warmed on my chest. Nothing else existed.

Still, something fluttered deep within me, different from my magic. It was my only tether. I wanted to stay. To wake up from this nightmare.

My eyes opened as Fyn's tears collided with my forehead. He clutched me firmly to his chest. "Thank the stars." He exhaled as my eyes opened. I sobbed in his arms.

I turned my head to look for Lioran, but the world tilted around me, and I recoiled back into Fyn's chest.

"Lioran's here." Fyn knew who I was searching for.

Why was he still here? Cora and Lioran crouched near me.

"Where is Thalen?"

"Thalen isn't here," Cora said. "It's just us."

"You let them break our bond," I cried. "You let him bond you to Cora. I would have rather Pyrran killed me."

He had no choice. Lioran would never let them harm me. I glanced around for Pyrran, but he wasn't there, either.

"Where did they go?"

"They're not here. Whatever you saw—it wasn't real. The Grove taunted me, too. I thought I held you while you died, but you're alive. You're still here." His hands shook as he reached for me, but I pushed him away with what little strength I had remaining—too afraid to feel his touch when it wasn't mine to keep.

348

I didn't know what to feel, didn't know what to trust—what version was true and what was a lie. Sweat drenched Lioran's brow, his curls clung to his face. As he came further into focus, I saw his bloodshot eyes.

"Is this real?" My voice cracked.

"Yes, my love. Whatever you saw—wasn't." Lioran placed his hand on mine—I felt it.

"You were screaming in agony. I tried to wake you, to bring you back, but I couldn't." Fyn choked on his words.

"Tell me something real, Fyn. Something only you and I know." Each word I spoke grated at my throat.

Fyn held my gaze—he exhaled a ragged breath. "You never visited Lioran because you were bored. I would peek in on you both and saw the way you held his hand, watched over him even as he slept." He choked on his tears. "That's when I knew you loved him...and the way he looked back at you, I knew he loved you, too."

The corner of my lips tugged upward.

"Lioran and Cora...are they bonded?" My breathing slowed with each word. My muscles released, but a throbbing pain spiraled through me.

"No—You are bonded with Lioran. No one can break that—not even the king," Fyn said.

"I'm here. I'm still yours. Please Aelira, can I hold you?" Lioran reached for me again.

My sobs echoed in the Grove as I nodded. Lioran pulled me into his arms. His heart raced, but I counted each beat and let its rhythm pull me back.

"I almost gave up." I cried into him.

"But you didn't—you're here with me." Lioran cradled me.

"I chose to stay," I said.

"You chose?" Lioran gasped, crying, pulling me into him.

"I heard a voice. It gave me choice. I wanted to come back." I may never know what sang to me in the darkness.

"She needs to rest," Fyn said.

Lioran gently lifted me so I could sit upright.

The Grove's cries surged through me, my body quaking in their wake. "It won't let me." My voice was only a whisper.

Lioran adjusted his grip on me. "She won't make it through this if we keep going. There must be another way. Cora, tell me there's another way. I won't do this to her."

"Lioran...I wish I could tell you there was. I wish it for both of you." Cora's voice trembled.

"It's okay." I bit my lip, blinking away tears. "I will do what is needed, but something is wrong—I am so weak. My body can't handle much more." I was given a second chance, but I felt as if I was barely hanging on—the little energy I had when we entered the Grove was fleeting. I looked up at him. "Promise me something?"

Lioran pressed his forehead into mine. "You can do this."

"Promise me you will find my sister and protect her if this doesn't work. The bargain only meant to claim me—it still wants to." I shuddered feeling the lands vibrations rolling through me.

"No. I will not make promises for when you're not here. Don't ask me to do it." His head dropped, and a single tear trailed his cheek. "You don't understand what you're giving up —why you can't give up," Lioran exhaled. "You fought to stay. We need you to keep doing that."

"I will keep fighting until I can't anymore, but if that time comes, I need to know she will be safe."

"We will find her. Together." He held me tighter. "I promise to keep her safe." I relaxed in his arms. My sister would live— even if I didn't. He would protect her, when I couldn't.

I settled against his chest.

"I am yours," he whispered.

"In every lifetime," I replied.

His words cradled me just as he had. I couldn't control my fate. But this moment was still ours—for now, I was still here.

Cora sat beside me, lifting my hand in hers. "You have to hold on—for all of us. Our world needs you—I need you." My eyes locked on hers, a silent understanding settled between us.

I tried to sit, but my vision spun. Nausea rolled through me.

"You're..." The lines set around Lioran's eyes as he exhaled. "You're not alone in this. I'm right here, beside you."

I leaned over and vomited—a shiver traveled down my spine. Lioran tucked my hair behind my ears. Cora handed me her flask. I took it to my lips, hoping to settle my rolling stomach. Lioran lowered me onto the ground, propping me against Cora.

He leaned over to Fyn and whispered. I couldn't hear his words, but the light vanished from Fyn's gaze. He nodded in reply.

CHAPTER 36

Gaia carried me further through the Grove, the rhythm of her steps lulled my limp body. The haunting cries echoed until we reached the middle. A massive tree stood in the clearing—its trunk engulfed the only opening in the Grove. Every inch of it was covered in black ash and decay.

Lioran lifted me off Gaia. The ground reverberated under us, rolling and pulsing as if it were trying to pull me in.

"You feel it, too?" I asked.

Lioran didn't respond. With so little strength left in me, my muscles seized. He still held me in his arms. "Aelira, I love you." He whispered it like a goodbye. "You are my light. My hope. I'll carry it with me always."

"I love you, Lioran."

He kissed me—deeper than he ever had before. "We will be together again. Until then, promise me you'll create the future you always dreamed of."

"No," I clung to him. "Don't you dare say goodbye to me."

Lioran's eyes glistened in the dim light of the Grove. He bit his lip as Fyn stepped beside him.

"Keep her safe." He placed me in Fyn's arms, but his gaze was still locked on mine.

"Lioran, no—whatever you're planning...whatever you think you should do. It doesn't have to be like this. Please," I cried.

Lioran kissed my forehead. "Protect her for me, Fyn."

Fyn nodded as his grip tightened around me—too tight—too desperate.

"Fyn?" I cried through a ragged breath. "Please. Let me go." I thrashed against Fyn until I couldn't anymore. He only held me tighter.

"Lioran! Don't do this!" I screamed, but Lioran didn't glance back at me. He only continued walking to the tree.

Cora ran after him.

"I will never forgive you, Fyn." My body weakened with each word—until I could barely move anymore. "Let me go. Now."

"I know you won't." Fyn's words trembled. "I made a promise—no matter how hard you fight me, I will not break it."

"The Grove wants me. It doesn't want him." I crashed into Fyn.

My sobs echoed. The Grove roared in response.

Lioran placed his hand on the massive tree. His golden light spread from his fingertips. Cora remained beside him. I couldn't make out her words, but I watched the color drain from her face.

Lioran would not stop. His mind was made up.

"Fyn...please." I couldn't fight him anymore.

There was no sign of his cheerful demeanor. I waited for his smirk to settle, but Fyn only stared back at me.

My magic thrashed within me—wild and unrelenting. The golden glow coursed from my fingertips, racing toward the tree.

The Grove didn't care where I was—it would take from me. Lioran thought he could take my place, but fate never wanted him to.

It wanted my magic—it wanted me.

I would give it—I didn't even try to stop it. The onyx's warmth radiated through me.

"You can let me go," I told Fyn. He struggled to hold me, to bear my weight at all. He fell to his knees, clutching me still.

"No. I won't leave you." Fyn's sharp exhale crashed into me. "Lioran!" Fyn screamed.

Lioran turned to look, but it was too late.

The Grove's roar stopped.

He bellowed my name—it thundered through the Grove. His magic fizzled, but mine strengthened. The Grove released him from the tree, without question, but it tightened its hold on me.

Lioran ran to me. Cora darted behind him.

Aelira—you promised. The bargain was made.

A melody whispered through the trees. It danced on the wind—it called to me.

"I came to restore Lythira and Bailoc. Take my magic if you must," I whispered in reply.

It would be the end, but at least I made a choice.

"Aelira...no! Stay with me." Lioran slid in the dirt beside me. He lifted me from Fyn's arms.

Each pulse of my magic slammed harder through my veins. I wept as I looked up at my love, knowing I couldn't keep him.

The Grove claimed me.

Lioran gripped me tighter.

Pain hammered every muscle—I trembled, too weak to

move. My body convulsed. I needed it to stop—needed to break free.

"Take me instead! I'll give my life for hers!" Lioran roared.

Nothing responded.

My eyelids slipped closed. Each breath became slower than the last. Deep within me peace settled, grounding me through the lingering pain as it simmered.

"Please don't leave me." His words were a distant hum. "You can't leave me."

Darkness had taken hold, the light had vanished.

Then I saw it—the Grove glimmering with brilliance, its verdant display fresh and new. Fae traveled down the paths just as we had. They hummed and laughed as if nothing had happened at all. A flash of white light cascaded over everything and then everything turned red.

King Ardyn darted through the border, commanding his army to take down every fae. Blood spilled. Screams echoed. No mercy was granted. Amber flames engulfed the trees. I smelled the smoke, my skin seared with the heat of the fire. Death washed over the land.

My mother screamed as Ardyn tore her from a fae's arms— I saw his features how they matched mine. How he fought to the end to defend her.

The stars had no mercy. I pleaded with them to make it all stop. I didn't want to see the rest.

You feel the pain that was felt.

So you may learn the truth.

Only then will you rise.

"Stay here—with me, beside me. Don't let go." I heard each

painful word Lioran spoke as he gripped my hands in his. I wanted to tell him I was still here, but my voice wouldn't respond. I couldn't call out to him at all—I couldn't even squeeze his hand.

Remnants of my magic seeped from my veins. Deep within me something desperate pulsed. It felt whole.

My pain ceased.

Lioran wailed—it was a war cry to the heavens. It echoed throughout the grove, through me. He gripped me, he shook me.

And then I heard nothing—no wind or traces of his breath. I no longer felt him cradling me—I felt nothing at all.

My final moments weren't with him. They were taken. I screamed inside—desperate to come back to him—to come back to the life we never got to live.

Light seeped into the darkness.

Warmth ran over me, cradling me.

The land's cries have been answered.
   A sacrifice made.
   Fear did not break you.
   Weakness did not topple you.
   Still, humanity failed you.
   You must transform.
   The stars have chosen.
   You both will reign.
   Starwoven and bound.
   Hope carried within.

Blood pumped through my veins, magic coursing beside it. Trembling beneath a force I couldn't describe—my body renewed and strengthened. A steady inhale filled my lungs. The scent of something familiar greeted me—like leather and oak—like Lioran. The sound of leaves rustling in the trees— the sound of his sobbing.

I blinked as golden rays of light shone through the leaves of the trees overhead. Lioran hovered over me. His body convulsed as he roared in agony. I tried to reach for him, but my fingers stiffened.

"Lioran..." My voice sounded more melodic than before. He shook his head in disbelief. He scanned me. Horror etched into every line in his face.

He went rigid, his breath barely escaping his lips. "How?" Tears spilled down his cheeks.

I heard another murmur—a low voice I knew. I turned to see Fyn holding Cora—they were both watching me.

Cora gasped.

Lioran held his hand out toward them as he choked on tears.

Cora nodded, not another word was spoken between the three of them. Fyn guided Cora to a nearby tree, where they watched and waited.

Lioran set his hands on my abdomen and his lips parted. His chest heaved as he cried.

"What did it do to me? I don't feel like me anymore..."

All color faded from his cheeks.

I tried to sit, but the sky whirled over me. My body felt different, like something had been taken from me—like I was no longer whole. Panic gripped me as his fingers trailed my ears. My hands pressed to my ears. They were altered, completely pointed like his.

"You're fae..."

I didn't want this, didn't ask for it.

"The stars did this...to save me." I remembered their words.

"Humanity failed you. You must transform. The stars have chosen. You both will reign..."

"Both...will reign..." He barely uttered the words. Lioran's hand slid over his lips, and his bloodshot eyes widened.

Terror lingered in his gaze.

It undid me—my tears tumbled freely.

He pulled me into him, his fingers settling on my tattoo.

Black lines formed beside the vines—wildflowers bloomed into a point. I reached for Lioran's arm. New ink settled on his skin—thorns angled upward from the vines.

"Does that look like—" I started to ask.

"A crown." His throat bobbed as his voice cracked. "You will both reign..."

"Maybe I misunderstood." I hope I did—I didn't want that life.

He kissed my hand. "If the stars ask it of us—we will serve them, but right now—you're alive. It is the only thing that matters. We're going home."

"Can we go now?"

As he lifted me, green greeted me from every corner of the Grove. My body felt heavy again, and I crashed into him. "I'm so weak."

CHAPTER 37

I clung to Lioran. My body settled against his as we raced back to the Heart on Veylar. The world was spinning with tinges of emerald.

"Lioran..." I groaned. Each beat over the rocky path jolted me.

Fyn and Cora raced silently behind us with Gaia.

"We're almost there." Lioran adjusted his grip on me, pulling me closer into him. Nausea gripped me harder.

Veylar slowed cautiously as we approached the castle. Fyn darted toward us and lifted me from the saddle. Once Lioran dismounted he placed me back in his arms—his gaze softened as he looked at me and nodded to Lioran.

"We need the healer," Lioran desperately cried. A tear trickled down his cheek and fell onto mine. He carried me through the halls and into the infirmary.

I gripped him tighter as he lowered me into the slender bed.

"Rowena, thank goodness you're here." Lioran knelt beside me.

"Your Highness? What happened?" Rowena asked, her eyes scanning me. "The princess...she's..."

He had barely caught his breath. "She nearly died, Rowena." He tried to steady his voice. "I need you to check her out—to make sure she's okay. To check on..." His jaw tightened.

"What is your concern, Prince Lioran?" An uneasy silence settled between them and Lioran turned from us both. "I will make sure she is okay...I will check *everything*," she promised him.

I didn't know what he saw—what he was so afraid of.

"Your Highness, may I examine you?" Rowena asked.

She studied my eyes as I nodded.

Her hands shifted over me, down to my abdomen. My lungs tightened—my body dripped with sweat. I was no longer me.

"She's panicking, Your Highness, you need to try to calm her. Princess Aelira, you need to breathe...I need you to focus on your husband. Breathe with him." Rowena's voice was steady.

Lioran braced me as every part of me quaked. He took my hand in his and settled it on his chest. Each breath he took was my anchor—I mirrored it. "You're safe—you're home. We came home." He smiled softly, but the ache still lingered in his words.

"Your body needs lots of rest. Things are new—very new."

I continued to force each breath, until my muscles unclenched.

"I'm fae now?" I asked.

"Yes, Your Highness. Completely fae."

"My humanity was erased? It's just gone?" Tears gathered until they fell. My heart thundered in my chest. I didn't just cross the divide—I lost everything that tied me to Bailoc, to my family. They would never recognize me.

Lioran wiped away my tears.

"How can it be gone?" I cried.

His hand caressed my cheek. "We will figure this out together. Just breathe."

I clutched the pillow as the tears continued to fall. I was grateful to be alive, to be here, but I mourned the part of me that didn't exist anymore.

"Your strength will return. Perhaps you can take her to her chambers, Prince Lioran. I think she would be more comfortable in her own bed." Her hand rested on mine. "I will check in on you later and you may send for me whenever you need me."

Lioran scooped me up into his arms.

Rowena grasped my hand. "You are perfectly healthy, Your Highness. The stars have blessed you with a miracle." She bowed to us as we slipped through the infirmary door.

I clung to Lioran as he carried me through our home.

Days flashed by as I slept—each time my eyes blinked open I took in my chambers. I was still here, whole and fae in a way I never thought I would be. The reflection that greeted me forever altered, but my mother's golden eyes still glowed.

My strength renewed.

My magic still stirred.

I encouraged Lioran to return to the work that was piling up in his study. He had barely left my side, hovering even as I slept.

We didn't speak about our tattoos again, or the words the stars uttered. Our moments grew quieter. His words more tender. But every day he looked as if he was grieving. I wondered if he still saw me beneath all the changes—or if he was mourning the version of me he lost.

Scouts surveyed the land and brought back news—the Grove had been fully restored. Even Othryl saw a slow trickle of new growth. Signs of life were sprouting through the decay.

Juniper brought lunch to my chambers. She helped me slip into a gown for the first time since we returned. The fabric pulled at my chest. It squeezed my waist. She struggled to even lace it.

I traced my waist, fuller than I remembered it.

"If I may speak freely..." Juniper said.

"Of course," I replied.

"It may be time to consider some new gowns." Her voice was a soft whisper as her eyes avoided mine. "Your shape has... altered."

My stomach churned with the scent of the coffee as it wafted over to me. I pushed it away, completely overwhelmed. Juniper arched an eyebrow as she tidied up the room.

"Your appetite...has changed too. Is there anything else you'd prefer?" She removed the coffee from the table.

My strength returned, but my appetite hadn't. Nausea rushed through me as I gripped the table.

It hadn't stopped. We came back from the Grove—but every feeling lingered.

"Can you send for Rowena?"

"Certainly, Your Highness. I will get her for you immediately." Juniper's words trailed behind her as she left my chambers.

I was so consumed with losing Lioran, and later afraid of losing everything.

It had been weeks. No, it was even longer. I steadied myself, still glancing in the mirror as I counted the time that passed.

I hadn't bled.

It couldn't be—it wasn't possible.

We had been careful, but maybe the dream we wished for, the one I thought would never be, existed inside of me.

"Your Highness, Juniper said you needed me." Rowena peered in the doorway.

I looked out the window, still reeling in my discovery, too afraid to hope it was true. "I need you to confirm something for me." My melodic voice faltered.

"What can I help you with?" Rowena asked.

"I think...I'm pregnant." I finally exhaled. "I've been feeling so sick. I'm not sure if it's from how I changed...or if there's... life growing inside of me."

She walked over to me. Her hand drifted over my abdomen. "Your child is *still* perfectly healthy." Her voice was a quiet hum that interrupted my rapid heartbeat.

"Still?"

"I sensed it with my magic when Prince Lioran brought you to me. You were so panicked, so exhausted. He was shaken too. You both needed time to accept the change that had already settled, before I could deliver the news." Her head angled slightly. "I hope you understand. I would have come to you had I thought you needed to know sooner."

"I understand." I wouldn't hold it against her. We weren't ready to hear the truth then—couldn't have truly embraced the news. "How far along do you think I am?"

Her eyes scanned mine. "At least a month, if not a little longer."

"It's not possible. We were careful." I released an exhale. "I drank the vials. Lioran got them from your supplies."

Rowena sat with what I said. "It should have worked. I don't know of a single fae that's had it fail." She parted her locks from her face. "The main ingredient is a diluted toxin, that prevents life from taking hold."

"It's toxic? Did I hurt the baby?" I gasped.

"From everything I sense, the baby is very strong and healthy." She took her hands in mine. "The main ingredient could have caused harm, but maybe something was wrong with the potion. Did it taste bitter?"

"It tasted sweet. I sensed flowers I knew, but one that was different, too."

"Moonflower is bitter. You'd know it the instant it settled on your tongue." Her eyebrows raised. "Maybe the herbalist didn't mix it properly." Her cheeks grew red. "I'm so sorry, Your Highness."

"Did you say moonflower?" I recalled the white bloom I had never seen before I grew it in the palace garden. The one I tried to give to the queen, but she refused.

"Yes, it's highly toxic if not properly diluted. We use gentle flowers sprinkled with healing magic to make it suitable for ingestion. You are familiar with it?" Her eyes narrowed on me.

"I made it grow, but I had never seen it before."

"When you used your magic to create more oregano, you asked me to get you some first..."

"Yes, I have to experience it somehow to make it grow." My hand rested on my stomach. "I've been drinking it the entire time."

"And you never had cramping or discomfort after taking a vial?" she asked.

"No. I felt... completely fine." I tried to make sense of it. Our child was healthy and strong when it shouldn't have existed at all. "Rowena, could my magic have interfered with it?"

"It's possible. I don't think we could ever really know."

I took in the news—let it sit—until I couldn't hold back the tears anymore.

We thought we were doing everything we could to control the future, but the stars had other plans.

She placed her hand on my shoulder. "It's okay to grieve if this is not what you wanted."

"It's exactly what I wanted. I just didn't expect it to happen like this." Silent flutters rippled through me. "I feel something stirring in me, like my magic, but different. I felt it in the Grove."

"It's your child's magic." A warm smile crept across her lips.

I couldn't help but wonder how our child would fit into this world or what would happen when the High Court discovered the news. Would they accept our child? I wasn't sure I wanted them to.

"Can you tell if the baby is human at all? Or is it only fae?" I held my stomach.

"It is too soon to know." She spoke softly. "I will give Juniper some herbs for tea that may settle whatever sickness you're experiencing. She can be discreet until you're ready to tell your husband."

I nodded. They may not work, either. "I plan to tell him soon. I just need a moment."

"Take the time you need. He will be overjoyed to hear the news when you're ready to share it."

The whirl kept spinning inside me—tiny flutters of hope for the future—our future.

Lioran's study door was propped open. The familiar scent greeted me. It was my favorite. He hovered over his desk, sifting through paperwork.

The firelight cast a glow that illuminated the stars in the ceiling.

"Lioran?" My voice was a hum in between the crackling fire.

He dropped everything and came straight to me. "I wanted you to take it easy. You need to rest." His fingers intertwined with mine. "You could have sent for me."

"I wanted to come find you myself. Are you in the middle of something?" I almost said I could wait, but I knew I couldn't.

His eyes softened. "I would stop the entire world for a moment with you." He leaned in and kissed me.

I held him for a moment, afraid to break the calm between us. "The stars gave us everything we wanted."

His head tilted, taking me in, but his muscles clenched. "They certainly have. You are still here with me."

"It's not just me." I grabbed his hand and slid it over my stomach. "You're going to be a father."

His eyes widened. "You're sure?"

"Yes, Rowena confirmed it."

His free hand cupped his mouth as if he was holding the rest back. "When did she confirm it?"

"Moments ago." My voice cracked. I watched a single tear trail down his cheek. "You don't look happy."

"I thought..." His shoulder rounded forward. "We lost the baby."

"Lost it? You knew?"

He nodded. "The night after we bonded, I sensed you stronger than before. Then I felt something new—different from your magic, different from you. It was pulsing inside of you. I felt the life we created."

I hadn't even known, hadn't even recognized it, but Lioran had. Sorrow settled on his face.

"I deserved to know."

"I was grateful you didn't. You had sealed your fate with

the bargain. It took everything for me not to tell you. But I couldn't let you worry about what we'd lose."

"You never told me...even when I survived," I said.

"I thought I lost you—and then you awoke completely new. When I tried to feel for the baby, I felt nothing."

"It's why you went to the tree without me. You planned to sacrifice yourself for us?" I braced myself against him.

"It broke my heart to walk away from you both. Knowing I would never get to meet our child...never hold you again."

My throat constricted as I tried to swallow.

The moment Fyn held me, I hadn't gotten over it still—that Lioran even asked him to.

"Did Fyn know?"

"No." He flinched. "I had no other choice."

"You could have told me," I said quietly.

"I was desperate." He shook his head. "We tried to take on the bargain together. I thought it would be enough to save you, but then you shattered." He inhaled sharply. "I had to watch Fyn rock my pregnant wife in his arms while we all wondered if you would come out of it. While I wondered if I would ever be able to hold you again. It broke me."

"You took the choice from me. You both did." I had been silent about it since we returned, but I couldn't hold it in any longer.

"Fyn fought me over it. If you need to be mad, be mad at me. No one could have talked me out of it. Everything I cared about was being taken from me."

For a moment, he just held me. Neither of us said anything at all. Not because there wasn't more to say, but because we had both been through enough. We were desperately trying to fuse the fragments back together.

I slid his hand over my stomach when the flutters began

again. "Can you feel it now?" I asked, finally breaking the silence.

"A pulse...of magic?" His eyes welled. "For someone so small, it's so strong..."

I nodded, blinking back the tears, but they fell again anyway.

It was a glimmer of hope. A glimpse of light.

We sat with the baby's movement until it faded.

"Does Rowena know how far along you are?" He held my stomach still.

"She guessed over a month."

"This entire time..." Lioran swallowed hard. His jaw tensed. "Is she concerned you were taking the vials?"

"They're made from flowers. My magic...may have caused it not to work." I leaned into him. "The toxic flower that helps it take effect...I made one at the High Court and I may have handed one to your mother."

"You what?" His shoulders stiffened.

"I didn't know what it was. I had never seen it before."

"But you drank it," he said. "And it didn't affect you at all—didn't stop our miracle."

A glimmer lingered in his gaze. "Hopefully Rowena can make a different vial...not made from flowers." He smirked. "Otherwise, we'll have a lot of little ones in our future."

I laughed as my fingers trailed my stomach.

Standing beside him, my heart lightened.

CHAPTER 38

The news came days after we found out about the baby, days where we lived with love and hope for the future. The divide was crumbling—all that separated our two worlds fading. Unrest lay on the other side. A rebellion, Bailoc, my brother, the Vale—all those would not accept my choice.

"Can it be reconstructed?" The teacup rattled in my hands.

"I don't know." Lioran ran his hands over a map on his desk. "It should have only fallen when my parents removed it."

"The king and queen are coming to see it for themselves." Fyn's voice cracked into the silence. He assessed me cautiously as he spoke—tension lingered between us ever since the Grove.

I knew why he had done what he had. But something quiet shifted between us. He didn't push. He didn't pry. Fyn knew it, too.

Cora sat across from him, assessing me as I sipped my tea.

"They're coming here?" I knew it wouldn't last, the peace —the stillness.

"When they see her transformed..." Her voice trailed off.

Lioran stared at the fire—the flicker illuminated the outline of his clenched jaw. "I will handle it. Before they get here, I will need to see the divide."

"I'm coming with you," Fyn interjected.

"So am I." I stood, setting my teacup beside me.

Lioran gripped my hand in his. "It's too dangerous. We don't know what we will encounter." His eyes pleaded with mine. I wouldn't be silent. I wouldn't stay behind.

"Our numbers are strong. She will be safe." Fyn's hand shifted under his chin. "I will stand at her side."

"I can handle it. The tea works well." I smirked at him.

"Care to fill the rest of us in? Why does Aelira need tea?" Fyn chuckled.

Cora sat in silence, watching me—waiting. *She knew.*

"We've been waiting to tell you." Lioran wrapped his arms around me. "Aelira is pregnant."

A smile spread across my lips. I lowered Lioran's hand over my stomach—letting him feel the whirl. It quickly became our favorite sensation.

"That is why you asked..." Fyn went still, his smirk fell flat. "You wanted to save them both. You could have told me... You..." He stopped.

"He didn't even tell me," I said, looking at Fyn for the first time since the Grove. I felt his pain. I felt mine. It wouldn't fix everything, but for now it had to be enough.

"Then how did you know, Lioran?" Cora asked.

"I felt the baby's magic the night we bonded." Lioran swallowed hard.

Fyn shook his head as a smirk danced across his face. "You two waste no time..."

"It is wonderful news," Cora said, but still, something lingered unsaid.

"You knew?" I whispered as she hugged me.

"I just figured it out," she said. "All of my visions had been of the Grove. Until just yesterday...when I saw something new."

"Aelira, I need you to stay here," Lioran interjected.

"Lythira is my home. These are my people. I am going," I insisted. "I refuse to live my life in fear."

I felt his muscles bulge under my fingertips. "Our united front is more important now than ever. I will be there beside you, protecting you every step of the way," Lioran said.

"Princess Aelira, you have my sword now and always." Fyn bowed his head. "If someone so much as looks at you the wrong way..."

I laughed—it felt so good to laugh.

"The sentiment is nice, Fyn, but keep the sword sheathed," I said.

"The two of you..." Lioran chuckled.

Cora smirked. "Who will keep an eye on Fyn?"

The energetic hum of the divide rolled toward us. The sound was unmistakable. The grand tree in Myrwood Grove seemed as if it stood taller than before.

A chill darted down my spine. The Grove was green, it was lush, and fragrant with the sweet smell that graced me in the Heart. Still the memories haunted me. It hung over me still with every beat of Gaia's hooves.

The stars meant for me to break. So that I could rebuild, but I still didn't know if I had. My humanity was gone, never to return, and the rest felt changed beyond recognition.

Tiny flutters.

A steady beat sounded within me.

I smiled even as my eyes watered.

Our horses carried us closer to the divide. The beat of nearly a hundred horses sounded around us.

"We will dismount and approach on foot." Lioran commanded Lythira's warriors. He lifted me down from Gaia. For a moment, only the two of us stood in the Grove. A wave of nausea overcame me. It caught in my throat. I clutched his biceps.

"I will wait with you," he whispered. "It will be over soon." He held me close to his chest.

My eyes shut. I breathed through it, until only the flutters greeted me again.

"My love, do not push yourself. Fyn can take you back."

"I'm going to see it with you." I opened my eyes. He offered his arm to me, his free hand rested on the hilt of his sword. Fyn fell in place beside us.

"They say it only continues to crumble." Cora's voice trailed up to us.

The divide bellowed—a desperate warning leached through the air. Through the wave of glittering gold, I saw it— it wasn't just a crack. A hole had formed. A sea of knights lined the divide. They wouldn't all be able to pass through, the hole wasn't big enough, but we could see them. As I studied their armor, I knew what army we were facing.

"It's Bailoc," I said.

"I don't like the look of this," Fyn warned, but my husband needed no warning. He nudged me back, and with a single gesture, the entire band of warriors closed in tight formation around us.

"If anything happens, take her back," Lioran commanded to Fyn. He only nodded. Lioran squeezed my hand in his.

Barren, rotten trees and dried out soil spread as far as I

could see. The stench of rot wafted toward me on the wind. I gripped Lioran's arm harder.

On our side of the wall, everything was lush and on theirs, everything was dead.

"My magic didn't reverse it," I whispered.

"Assess the damage," a voice commanded. I was no stranger to that voice. I knew it as well as I knew my own.

The knights parted and Agan stepped to the forefront of the crowd. A gem studded crown nestled into his golden braid. He wore King Ardyn's cloak, with a golden clasp. His hand held his sword outward. The engraved blade shone brightly. King Ardyn's sword.

"Agan," I murmured. It wasn't loud enough for him to hear, but I was desperate for him to sheath his sword, for him to look at me.

Lioran gripped the hilt of his sword.

Agan studied me, his eyes flickered with something new as he looked at my ears. His lips pursed in disgust.

"King Agan of Bailoc," I called.

He mouthed my name as horror darkened his gaze.

"I've come with my husband, Prince Lioran of Lythira."

"We are here to assess the damage at the divide and restoration beyond." Lioran's voice carried majestically on the wind. He was calm and sure. "We mean you no harm."

Agan's glare pelted him. "Aelira..." He ran his fingers across his jaw.

I knew that glare—knew the tone he had taken. Diplomatic negotiations wouldn't happen.

"She is Princess Aelira of Lythira. We address you with your given title, and you will address her with hers," Lioran roared.

"The Princess of Lythira? How curious." Thalen's voice echoed and the bile burned in my chest. He walked through the crowd of knights until he stood beside my brother. They exchanged a knowing glance. "There will be unrest, your majesty. A most fortuitous situation for our realm has been foreseen. The divide won't be the only thing to crumble—the crown will, too."

My breath caught. A hunter doesn't just pounce on its prey —Thalen was only ever waiting for an opportune moment to strike.

"You stole the Princess of Bailoc. Claimed her as your wife —whatever that means to the fae..." Agan's words hissed through gritted teeth.

Ice seeped from the gemstone straight into my veins.

He couldn't imply such a thing. Lioran and I were husband and wife, in every realm. Our bond transcended his threat.

"He didn't just steal her from Bailoc, Your Majesty." Thalen crossed his arms over his chest. "She's been carrying his child for some time. Even before—" Thalen's voice held steady.

"That's enough!" Lioran hollered. His color drained.

Thalen knew.

His words at the High Court. The way his hands lingered over my waist. Had he known the entire time?

My vision blurred as my fury took hold—my magic thrashed with it. Blades of grass rose around my boots, too subtle for most to see, but Lioran watched it. He extended his hand out to me. I placed my hand in his and my magic surged through him. It collided with his. A muffled groan escaped his lips.

Calm washed over me, as if Lioran pulled away part of my fear. His warmth pulsated through me and suddenly I could breathe again.

For a moment, we only looked at each other—it was new.

Agan's lip grated over his teeth. "I hope the fae magic is strong enough to protect her and your child."

"She is your sister. A princess of both realms. And yet you

speak as if you intend to harm her." Lioran's arm held stiff in front of me.

Fyn shifted toward me. My throat dried.

"You've ruined her," Agan said to Lioran, his eyes avoided mine.

He discarded me in front of everyone. Heat seared under my skin.

Lioran's nostrils flared. He steadied his breath. Restraint was held, but his fury was rising.

The fae stood beside us still—none dropped their formation. Fyn hovered beside me still. "His words mean nothing," Fyn whispered to me. "We all stand with you."

They threaten my child. My husband. My kind.

Agan was hungry for war.

We would be ready for it.

I would fight for my home.

"You will no longer address my wife at all," Lioran commanded. "Thalen, I hope you've no business left in Nythrel." He waited for Thalen to simmer in his words.

Even as the wind thrashed against him, Thalen only raised a brow.

"You are hereby banned from entering Lythira again," Lioran commanded.

Thalen watched me. There was a glimmer in his eye and then he smirked.

"The war only ended when you hid behind the divide!" Agan yelled. "But now it crumbles beyond your control. Bailoc will show no mercy to Nythrel."

Lioran's magic flickered. With its pulse, he dropped my hand.

A roar descended. I had heard it before. An inky flash raced in front of us—the creature from the Grove. It stalked the border. The knights held their armed stance.

I clung to Lioran, but his calm didn't falter even as the creature turned toward us.

"Do not fear it, my love." Lioran's low voice spoke only to me as it stalked closer. "The land only seeks to protect us."

The creature settled beside him. Its black, bulging eyes held my gaze. As Lioran drew his sword the mighty beast roared. Its dripping fangs were illuminated by the sun's rays.

I stood proudly behind my husband's blade.

THE STORY CONCLUDES IN...

AVAILABLE NOW

PRONUNCIATION GUIDE

NAMES
Aelira (ay-LEER-uh)
Agan (AY-gan)
Ardyn (AR-den)
Ashlyn (ASH-lin)
Cael (KALE)
Calyth (CAL-ith)
Cora (KOR-uh)
Elric (EL-rik)
Fyn (FIN)
Juniper (JUNE-ih-per)
Lioran (LYE-or-an) *like lion
Milana (MIL-an-uh)
Pyrran (PIE-ran)
Reina (RAY-nuh)
Rhaevin (RAY-ven)
Rowena (ROH-wen-uh)
Selene (SELL-cen)
Thalen (THAL-en) *rhymes with Allen
Thalorys (THAL-or-us)

PLACES
Bailoc (BAY-lock)
Estlen (EST-len)
Eyrsea (EER-sea)
Kybar (KYE-bar)
Lythira (LYE-thir-uh)
Nythrel (NITH-rel)
Vale (VAIL)

ACKNOWLEDGMENTS

In loving memory of my bonus dad, Phil—you inspired the words from Aelira's father in her little leather book. Thank you for always believing in me. I wish we had more time together, and that I could share this with you.

Ever since I was a little girl, I loved retreating to secret worlds I created in my daydreams. This book is the first of many stories I've yet to tell. Every moment in my journey has somehow sculpted this story. Yet writing this book wouldn't have been possible without my family, friends, and professional team.

To my loving husband, Forrest—without your unwavering support, none of this would have been possible. You encouraged me to chase after this dream and never let it go. I love you always. Thank you for reading so many versions of this story (even though you don't love to read) and letting me keep you up until late at night while I shared every detail hidden beneath the surface.

To my daughter—thank you for cheering me on throughout this entire process. All the art you made, inspired by characters and the story (or at least the kid appropriate version I told you) kept me going. I'm so proud to be your mom and love seeing your passion for storytelling.

To my mother, who has always believed in me and guided me—thank you for all the ways you've shown your love. I'm so grateful for everything you've done. And thank you for reading your first-ever romantasy novel with such enthusiasm and dedication.

To my Nana, who kept everything I ever wrote or created. Thank you for always encouraging and supporting my creativity. I miss you every day and wish you could have read this too.

To my favorite professor, Cathy Sweitzer, thank you for believing in me all those years ago and even still today. I've carried your support—and enthusiasm—for the craft with me always. Now, it's ingrained in every one of these pages.

To my editors and beta readers, thank you for every moment you spent on my story. Your insights helped me to shape it into the version it was always meant to be. Special thanks to Maia Morgan, Micheala Stahl (Stahl Literary Lodge), Emilee Ploegstra, and Annie Adams for your encouragement and living in the story beside me.

ABOUT THE AUTHOR

britbryndell.com

Brit studied fiction writing in college. She draws inspiration from her hands-on historical experiences, including archery, falconry, and exploring ancient ruins. When she's not creating fantasy worlds, she loves to read, travel, and spend time with her family in Florida.

Want updates on upcoming releases, exclusive extras, and behind-the-scenes glimpses?

Join Brit's newsletter at **britbryndell.substack.com**

instagram.com/britbryndell
tiktok.com/@Britbryndell

www.ingramcontent.com/pod-product-compliance
Lightning Source LLC
Chambersburg PA
CBHW020016120726
47903CB00004B/1304